BONE FROG BROTHERHOOD

Books 1–5

SHARON HAMILTON

SHARON HAMILTON'S BOOK LIST

SEAL BROTHERHOOD BOOKS

SEAL BROTHERHOOD SERIES
Accidental SEAL Book 1

Fallen SEAL Legacy Book 2

SEAL Under Covers Book 3

SEAL The Deal Book 4

Cruisin' For A SEAL Book 5

SEAL My Destiny Book 6

SEAL of My Heart Book 7

Fredo's Dream Book 8

SEAL My Love Book 9

SEAL Encounter Prequel to Book 1

SEAL Endeavor Prequel to Book 2

Ultimate SEAL Collection Vol. 1 Books 1-4 /2 Prequels

Ultimate SEAL Collection Vol. 2 Books 5-7

SEAL BROTHERHOOD LEGACY SERIES
Watery Grave Book 1

Honor The Fallen Book 2

Grave Injustice Book 3

Deal With The Devil Book 4

BAD BOYS OF SEAL TEAM 3 SERIES
SEAL's Promise Book 1

SEAL My Home Book 2

SEAL's Code Book 3

Big Bad Boys Bundle Books 1-3

BAND OF BACHELORS SERIES
Lucas Book 1

Alex Book 2

Jake Book 3

Jake 2 Book 4

Big Band of Bachelors Bundle

BONE FROG BROTHERHOOD SERIES

New Year's SEAL Dream Book 1

SEALed At The Altar Book 2

SEALed Forever Book 3

SEAL's Rescue Book 4

SEALed Protection Book 5

Bone Frog Brotherhood Superbundle

BONE FROG BACHELOR SERIES

Bone Frog Bachelor Book 0.5

Unleashed Book 1

Restored Book 2

Revenge Book 3

SUNSET SEALS SERIES

SEALed at Sunset Book 1

Second Chance SEAL Book 2

Treasure Island SEAL Book 3

Escape to Sunset Book 4

The House at Sunset Beach Book 5

Second Chance Reunion Book 6

Love's Treasure Book 7

Finding Home Book 8 (releasing summer 2022)

Sunset SEALs Duet #1

Sunset SEALs Duet #2

LOVE VIXEN

Bone Frog Love

SHADOW SEALS
Shadow of the Heart

SILVER SEALS SERIES
SEAL Love's Legacy

SLEEPER SEALS SERIES
Bachelor SEAL

STAND ALONE BOOKS & SERIES
SEAL's Goal: The Beautiful Game
Nashville SEAL: Jameson
True Blue SEALS Zak
Paradise: In Search of Love
Love Me Tender, Love You Hard

NOVELLAS
SEAL You In My Dreams Magnolias and Moonshine

PARANORMALS

GOLDEN VAMPIRES OF TUSCANY SERIES
Honeymoon Bite Book 1
Mortal Bite Book 2
Christmas Bite Book 3
Midnight Bite Book 4

THE GUARDIANS
Heavenly Lover Book 1
Underworld Lover Book 2
Underworld Queen Book 3
Redemption Book 4

FALL FROM GRACE SERIES
Gideon: Heavenly Fall

NOVELLAS
SEAL Of Time Trident Legacy

All of Sharon's books are available on Audible, narrated by the talented J.D. Hart.

ABOUT THE BOOK

New Years SEAL Dream

Tucker Hudson has been off SEAL Team 3 for nearly ten years. He reluctantly attends his former Teammate's wedding on New Years Eve, vowing to keep his hands to himself and his mouth shut. Suffering nightmares from a tragic deployment, he barely left the Teams with an honorable discharge. Romance is one complication he does not need. And no one needs him either: not the Teams, not his family.

Brandy Cook knows she isn't as attractive as the skinny blondes who usually attend SEAL weddings. Although she's dieted for three months straight, she's only managed to fit into a size 16 dress, and only then with the help of a monstrous undergarment that nearly prevents her from breathing. So when the big grey-haired former SEAL with a body built like Shrek takes a passing interest in her, she figures he's been forced by a wager or some kind of trick.

But as the clock strikes midnight, the improbable happens and suppressed passions take over, ending in a steamy night neither will forget, but both will admit later was a huge mistake. When Brandy finds herself in trouble, Tucker turns out to be the only one who can keep her safe from the fury building around her world.

SEALed At The Altar

Despite his thirty-nine years, Tucker Hudson is in peak physical condition and is considering rejoining the SEAL Teams after a ten-year hiatus. What he hadn't counted on is a steady relationship with Brandy. Is this thing between them something he can count on or is it just a distraction? Now he's torn between his heart and career. Can he balance them both?

A plus-size girl, Brandy never fails to be there for her friends' and their happiness. But for her, relationships are little more than one-night stands, and she's made her peace with who she is. At least until Tucker shows up at a SEAL wedding on New Year's Eve. The intensity between them makes her wonder if marriage is a wise choice or just another misstep.

The evil forces surrounding them will test their relationship. Will their love be strong enough to last a lifetime, or will it become just a pleasant memory of what could have been?

SEALed Forever

At forty years of age, Special Operator Tucker Hudson re-qualifies and joins SEAL Team 3 but must leave behind his young bride. He steps into a dangerous deployment in Central Africa to hunt down a drug and child sex trafficking warlord. But the hazardous duty is made even more perilous by the knowledge that his best friend and team buddy, Brawley Hanks, suffers from effects of his previous deployments.

Brandy Hudson knows her big man with his huge heart must do what he's called to do to protect his team both in the arena and at home. She hopes that his sacrifice will not prove too precious. But she also knows this comes with being the wife of an elite warrior. He's the man she's searched for her whole life.

Their relationship will be tested while they stay connected during his deployment and afterwards. Brandy knows she must brace herself for whatever happens when he comes home.

But life is not always fair as tragedy strikes their SEAL family, and rocks the foundations of their love to the core. Will they be the couple to survive, or will one of them be left behind?

SEAL's Rescue

Navy SEAL Tucker Hudson has barely recovered from his last difficult deployment in Africa, a near-failed operation, when he learns the American hostage they were unable to free that last time, has been found. His team is tasked with going in a second time to complete what was left undone.

Brandy Hudson's world is changing every day as she devotes herself to their new pregnancy and the purchase of their new home.

But danger from the hostage rescue across the oceans comes home to affect Brandy and Tucker's family in a desperate plot uncovered in California. Will it be in time to save the happily ever after they both desire?

SEALed Protection

Navy SEAL Tucker Hudson has made all the right choices the second time around: a retread, re-joining SEAL Team 3 after ten years of wandering, he has a new wife, and now a new baby on the way. He struggles to hold on to his precious hard-won happiness, living a life he barely thought possible beside a woman who is in many ways stronger than he is.

Brandy has proven she has what it takes to be married to an elite warrior, including being left alone during his dangerous deployments. But as she welcomes their new addition, a dark cloud descends upon her family as evil shows up closer to home, making them all rethink their life plans.

Is it going to take more than their strong love for each other to protect everything they hold dear?

TABLE OF CONTENTS

AUTHOR'S NOTE

I always dedicate my SEAL Brotherhood books to the brave men and women who defend our shores and keep us safe. Without their sacrifice, and that of their families—because a warrior's fight always includes his or her family—I wouldn't have the freedom and opportunity to make a living writing these stories. They sometimes pay the ultimate price so we can debate, argue, go have coffee with friends, raise our children and see them have children of their own.

One of my favorite tributes to warriors resides on many memorials, including one I saw honoring the fallen of WWII on an island in the Pacific:

> "When you go home
> Tell them of us, and say
> For your tomorrow,
> We gave our today."

These are my stories created out of my own imagination. Anything that is inaccurately portrayed is either my mistake, or done intentionally to disguise something I might have overheard over a beer or in the corner of one of the hangouts along the Coronado Strand.

I support two main charities. Navy SEAL/UDT Museum operates in Ft. Pierce, Florida. Please learn about this wonderful museum, all run by active and former SEALs and their friends and families, and who rely on public support, not that of the U.S. Government. www.navysealmuseum.org

IF YOU GOT ANY CLOSER, YOU WOULD HAVE TO ENLIST

I also support Wounded Warriors, who tirelessly bring together the warrior as well as the family members who are just learning to deal with their soldier's condition and have nowhere to turn. It is a long path to becoming well, but I've seen first-hand what this organization does for its warriors and the families who love them. Please give what your heart tells you is right. If you cannot give, volunteer at one of the many service centers all over the United States. Get involved. Do something meaningful for someone who gave so much of themselves, to families who have paid the price for your freedom. You'll find a family there unlike any other on the planet.

www.woundedwarriorproject.org

NEW YEARS SEAL DREAM

Bone Frog Brotherhood Book 1

SHARON HAMILTON

CHAPTER 1

"**N**O THANKS NEEDED, Tucker. I didn't ask you to be part of the wedding party because I didn't think you'd fit into a 5X tux on top with your XL waist. You're an action figure, Tuck. Besides, you drool."

Tucker growled as he turned his back on the groom, Brawley Hanks. The dressing room full of handsome penguins grunted and politely guffawed, since they were all dressed up and on good behavior.

"And there's no room for even a Barbie on his arm. Damn those church aisles," barked Riley Branson.

Another former Teammate, T.J. Talbot, grabbed Tucker's arm and drew him out of the Room of Doom, as the single SEALs called it. "Pay no attention to them. They're assholes. Also, who wants to walk down the aisle with a Barbie Doll?" He winked at Tucker.

He felt at ease immediately. Tucker's huge hands and fingers knotted themselves to oblivion, having no place to hide and looking like a bushel of antlers he was carrying. "Thanks, T.J. I hate these things," he said, pulling on his lapel. "But I've been out of commission so long, thought it would be nice to see some of the guys."

"And now you've seen that nothing has changed." T.J. was nearly as tall as Tucker, perhaps an inch shorter. He bumped foreheads. "But the girls will be younger because of Dorie, and that's probably a good thing," T.J. whispered.

"You having regrets, you old married fart?" Tucker murmured back.

Brawley's dad appeared in the church hallway before T.J. could answer and slapped both the former Teammates on the back simultaneously. "Glorious day, isn't it?"

Tucker knew old man Hanks was relieved his son had finally settled down and picked somebody. Brawley had more breakups than a pre-teen homeroom class.

"Yessir. Just took the right woman." T.J.'s face was shriveled up, like his last comment had soured his tongue. Tucker knew he was lying through his teeth. Privately, he thought, it took more alcohol than could fill a battleship to convince Brawley it was time to man-up.

"Dorie's a real nice gal," Tucker offered up. "You're gonna be a lucky father-in-law. She should fit in well with the rest of the family," he added, trying to keep a straight face. He knew it would be painful for T.J.

Both gentlemen looked back at him, T.J. not showing an ounce of expression. Mrs. Hanks was raised in the local Mennonite community. She was as plain as a saltine cracker, without any makeup or hair curling or adornments. Her two daughters were younger, even paler copies of her. Whereas Dorie looked like she could handle a Las Vegas pole and entertain a whole room of men. Those were going to be some interesting family dinners during the holidays, Tucker figured.

When he had the courage to look back into Mr. Hanks' eyes, he realized old man Hanks married her probably because little Brawley was on his way, and for no other reason. He felt the man's pain.

"You believe in miracles, son?" Hanks said, his eyes folded into thin slits.

"Yes, sir, I do. I surely do. That and redemption, too."

T.J. cleared his throat. "Well, congrats, sir. Must be a load off to have Brawley settled. I think those two will be happy together."

The far away look Mr. Hanks gave them back was difficult to read. Tucker had been feeling a little lonesome and sorry for himself until he encountered Hanks Sr. today. Now he was damned pleased he'd never hooked up with anyone.

Sure, they're pretty, but they're dangerous. Unpredictable. Who needs them? Certainly not me!

At last, Hanks pushed through the two younger men, heading for greener pastures, having exhausted any thought process he was following. He turned his head back to them and whispered, "Happiness' got nothing to do with it. All a state of mind, gentlemen." His fingers pointed to his temple, oddly positioned to look like a gun. "All a state of mind." He sauntered off, straightening his jacket and making room for his crotch as he walked, swinging his feet at the ankles to shake off wrinkles.

"Close your mouth, Tucker. You're gawking," T.J. reminded him.

"That's a complicated man right there," murmured Tucker. "I can see how he gutted out twenty years on the Teams. Thank God Brawley made it. Would hate to be a son of his and not make a Team."

"You know the family better, but I'm guessing being on the Teams was summer camp compared to growing up in the Hanks household."

Tucker knew T.J. was right. They'd grown up together in Oregon, and the two boys got acquainted by competing for spots in high school sports teams. They joined their BUD/S class together, but Tucker disengaged after ten years. Brawley re-upped for a short tour and was going to leave as well. Then he met Dorie, so he extended and used the bonus to buy a house. Dorie had a lot to do with that decision.

The rest of the wedding party began to spill out onto the walkway leading to the sanctuary. Blossoming orange trees gave off a gentle and pleasant aroma. Tucker punched Brawley hard in the bicep, nearly knocking him over before he gave the groom and his groomsmen a fat-fingered wave. He was going to find a seat toward the front, but not too close, give himself enough room to spread out in case he fell asleep during the wedding. His goal was to keep his big mouth shut and his eyes glazed over so he could just swim a little with his former Teammates without getting into trouble. That meant he'd keep his hands to himself and wouldn't ask anyone to dance. He'd also pretend not to look for cleavage or evidence of a proud bony mound or ample ass beneath layers of swirling chiffon and taffeta.

Piece of cake, he thought as he entered the sanctuary. Organ music played, accompanied by a violin and flute combination.

Hospital music.

The two Hanks sisters were dressed in identical maroon dresses with white lace collars, revealing their beanpole stature. Both girls had their long brown hair parted in the middle, tied in a bun at the back of their neck. No curls, ribbons, or sparkles to adorn them. Each had a deep pink lily wrist corsage on their right hands, folded identically next to each other.

The moms were ushered in next. Mrs. Hanks wore a darker shade of maroon, but her brownish grey hair was pulled back similar to her daughters'. Mr. Hanks looked around the room, catching eyes of friends and landing briefly on Tucker's face. He sat down hard, making the pew squeak.

Dorie's mom was lead in by Riley Branson. The lady was the same kind of bombshell for the older crowd, and Brawley had told

Tucker stories of her younger years growing up in San Diego. Though she was close to sixty, her hair was as blonde as her daughter's gorgeous locks. She wore a tailored light pink suit with a flared waist jacket covered in glistening crystals that flashed all over the interior of the narthex and the aisle going down. The skirt below her tiny waist didn't leave much to the imagination. She wasn't as tall as her daughter, so the high heels were giving her some trouble on the cushy rug.

Dorie's mother sat next to her already seated boyfriend, an obvious sign that he might not be a permanent fixture in the family, but he gave her a peck on the cheek anyway.

The organ music crescendo rose, and a majestic non-wedding style march was on, signaling that the audience should rise for the bride and her father. Everyone came to their feet, Tucker one of the last to stand. He turned to the narthex and saw beautiful Dorie all decked out in bright white. Ahead of her were several bridesmaids, all Barbies, except for one, who was a big girl with about the largest chest Tucker had ever seen. He found himself praying for a clothing malfunction as she paraded down the aisle with Riley. Her tight bustier looked like it was going to explode any second, which might even knock Riley off his feet. He found himself chuckling under his breath at the image in his head until someone in the row ahead of him turned around with a frown.

But Tucker's daydream was shattered by the presence of Dorie, looking every bit the virginal angel. She was probably the prettiest bride he'd ever seen. Her veil was loaded with little crystals, like her mother's suit. By candlelight at the evening service, it created the effect of a thousand little faeries dancing down the aisle all around her. Mr. Carlson looked tanned and about as proud as a father could be, since his daughter was marrying a war hero.

Brawley was gaping and looked pale as the creamy skin on his bride's beautiful face. His best man whispered something to him, which caused a quick glance to his crotch, followed by an annoyed sigh as he realized his best man was messing with him. He presented his elbow to Dorie as her father kissed her good-bye. Dorie grabbed Brawley's hand instead.

Tucker prepped himself so that he wouldn't fall asleep, but found he needed very little help. The girls were ten point fives, even the heavy one. He told himself to stop it several times, but he was used to ranking women in front of him. Dorie would be number one, of course. Then there was that red-head, but the dark-haired heavy one kept catching his eye. He matched them all up to her, and, to his surprise, his dick preferred her.

The Hanks sisters began a duet that was about as bloodless as the middle-aged female lab tech at the VA who actually sported a five o'clock shadow. It was about as pleasant, too. The slightly off-key rendition of a country song he couldn't remember had people in the audience coughing to clear the pain in their ears. Tucker was going to burst out laughing if he wasn't careful. He opened a package of gum, made too much noise, and found people frowning at him.

Who cares? He chomped his gum silently and appeared not to notice.

With that out of the way, he tried to concentrate on the words of the reverend's message to the audience, and that's when he fell asleep. He startled from a very pleasant dream to find several in the crowd reminding him they still didn't approve. An older bony fist leaned over his shoulder to hand him a tissue because he had drooled on himself.

Can I help it? Sermons put me to sleep.

Then he noticed the dark-haired plus sized girl staring right at him with daggers. Okay, so he messed that one up. But he wasn't there to take home a date anyhow, so he shrugged, stopped looking at the girls, and started staring back at the people in the audience who had caught the snoring or grunting or drooling—maybe all three.

I need some spiked punch.

He knew that someone was going to do it. Mrs. Hanks had forbidden alcohol, but she was about to learn a lesson. It was no SEAL wedding if there wasn't a heavy dose of alcohol.

Come on. Come on. Let's get the party going.

The rings were exchanged. The kiss was pornographic, as a good SEAL should behave, and included a gentle squeeze of the bride's ass, which made her giggle when they both got tangled up in her veil. Tucker noticed the big girl didn't like that, either.

Mercifully, the wedding was over. Brawley and his young nymph floated down the aisle, followed by the bevy of lovelies, Tucker was suddenly jealous that T.J. had accompanied the brunette. The shit-eating grin he gave Tucker in exchange meant he knew full well what he was doing as his elbow leaned a little deeper into the lady's chest, which extended her left boob and created about eight inches of mouth-watering cleavage.

I got assholes for friends.

But since T.J. was happily married to the lovely Shannon, Tucker didn't have to worry about anything.

Except to keep from drooling, get drunk with dignity, and pretend this was a good idea.

Because it wasn't. He knew he'd made one of the biggest mistakes of his life.

CHAPTER 2

B RANDY WAS GLAD the party was beginning. Her plan was to get considerably sauced, dousing and putting out the fires of a disastrous year. She'd been let go earlier in the year for speaking a little too plainly to a customer of the advertising firm. A competing agency hired her the next week—until she found out they were moving their operation to Silicon Valley from San Diego. Her father still owned and operated the local organic grocery store, and so Brandy came back to work for him until something else came on the horizon.

When Dorie asked her to be part of the wedding party, her decision to stay in Southern California was set in stone.

Thinking it would be helpful to meet her diet goals for the wedding she took up a part-time job as a weight loss counselor. The free meal plans and extra income were at first a double bonus. She had some early success, but then her diet stalled and crashed. The food started tasting like cardboard, and she was secretly supplementing with things from her dad's store. Her lack of progress and her MIA at weigh-ins caused another termination.

But that was last year. This was New Years Eve, and she was going to have a great year. She'd land that dream job after all, get down to a size eight or ten—one she'd never achieved before—and who knows what else could happen? Perhaps Prince Charming would notice her new svelte physique. She'd start lifting weights and perhaps learn to run so she could enter a 5k with Dorie.

She watched the bride and groom glide over the dance floor. The weather was spectacular and clear, surprisingly warm. By candlelight, they swayed and swooned, and there wasn't a woman in the crowd who didn't want to trade places with Dorie and her handsome new husband. The hush that fell over the group made her begin to cry. The glittery twinkle lights and silky drapes at the sides of the tent blew in the gentle breeze coming right off the bay.

She approached the group of her fellow bridesmaids and noticed their chatter stopped the instant she was upon them. Several brittle smiles greeted her.

"Having a good time, Brandy?" asked one of them.

"Isn't it the most gorgeous wedding you've ever seen?" she answered, aware she was gushing like a schoolgirl.

"I'm looking at all the eye candy," one of the other girls remarked, nodding to the group of nearly twenty young men, all fit and handsome, dressed in black tuxes and suits.

"Your Randy is deployed, Sheila. You can look, but better not touch."

"I hear that the guys on SEAL Team 5 don't have much to do with these boys. They're all Team 3."

Brandy was disgusted with her attitude, but the rest of the crowd tittered, and closed ranks. Soon she was left alone as they wafted off to grab some punch. On the way, two girls were asked to join the dance floor, as other couples from the partygoers began to pour into the revelry. In a matter of minutes, the bride and groom were hidden by other dancers. When the tune turned lively, the dance floor got even more crowded.

Earlier, she'd watched one of the SEALs on Brawley's team add some rum to the punch, along with something else, so she was fairly sure it would be strong. But just in case, she had a flask of brandy, her namesake and always a good companion in case the evening turned lonely.

She checked her watch as she headed to the punch and saw it was forty-five to midnight, the beginning of the New Year. Soon all those bad dreams of this year would be wiped away forever.

As she reached for a glass, another hand crossed hers. In the collision, several drinks fell to the floor, and several more fell over on themselves on the pretty lace tablecloth, making a light pink stain. The hand she'd collided with could easily palm a basketball or clean off a windshield with one swipe. Enormous beefy fingers, dripping in the sweet mixture, shook, sending droplets of punch all over her face and upper chest. The surprising spritzer caught her off guard.

A deep voice made an apology to the plain woman behind the punchbowl who looked like she'd faint from fear. Then the voice came her way.

"So sorry. I didn't mean to make a mess."

It was the beast from the sanctuary, the one who reminded her of Shrek. And now he even sounded like Shrek. She stared up at massive shoulders and a puffed out chest so large he could have trouble getting through a doorway without going sideways. He wasn't young, like the other men, with a healthy dose of salt and pepper in his hair and a solid white full beard. It was a lot to take in, but she finally found his eyes, and that settled her nerves just a bit.

"Are you okay?" he whispered. His warm eyes twinkled and were kind.

"Y-Y-Yes." Then she felt the coolness of the punch covering her. "Napkin."

It was quickly delivered to her flailing hand.

"Another one. I need another one," she said since the small napkin began to fall apart as she dabbed her face.

He handed her a fistful nearly an inch thick.

"Oh! That's too many," she mumbled, but took the wad anyway.

"You got a lot on your-your-your chest there. I hope it doesn't stain." He pulled her aside to make way for one of the caterers to mop up the floor.

The slip made her angry. He gave her a fistful of napkins because of the *size* of her chest. She turned her back to him and continued to dab off the droplets dripping down between her breasts. Out of the corner of her eye she saw one of the other bridesmaids whisper to her neighbor.

She abruptly turned again so she could address the monster, but the area was vacant. She caught sight of his back and head as he ducked under the tent cover and walked out into the night.

The young catering staff member brought her a filled cup of punch. "Here you go. Don't be concerned about this. That guy looks like an accident waiting to happen. Not your fault."

"Thanks." It was all she could think of to say.

The punch was indeed strong, and Brandy discovered upon finishing it that, although she was relaxed, her breathing was still just as difficult. She tried not to think about the help she'd needed getting the big undergarment on before the bustier could go on. It took two of the bridesmaids to work alternating to get the large zipper to close. At one point, she thought her breasts would reach her chin, but she was able to position herself until she was somewhat comfortable. The bustier was easier, since it closed with a row of large hooks and eyes.

She wobbled her way to the women's restroom and reapplied lipstick, really laying it on heavy. She loved the bright red shade of her new purchase. Adding a little blush, removing two dried droplets of punch, and rinsing her dress with a little water, she felt put together and ready to take on the world. It was only twenty minutes to midnight. All this would go into the folder of old news in just a little while.

Brawley was standing at the edge of the dance floor, watching his friends taking turns dancing with his bride.

"She's lovely, Brawley. I'm surprised you share her," she said and smiled.

The handsome SEAL had always been nice to her. Her crush on him was hard to hide. He leaned over and whispered in her ear, "Well then, let's make her jealous. You game?"

When he leaned back to check her expression, she gave him the biggest smile she could muster.

"Game on, mister."

They danced a modified swing to a lively Motown classic. She knew Brawley had benefitted from the instructions he had taken with Dorie. Brandy had taken lessons with her father after her mother passed. The two of them moved around the floor like a choreographed routine, causing a clapping circle to be formed around them. Brawley's bow tie was undone, as were the top two buttons on his shirt. Brandy wished she could remove or discon- nect something, too, but in the end, she stopped just long enough to take off her shoes and throw them into the corner. Brawley swung her around with his powerful arms. She felt lighter than air.

This is a good way to usher in the new year.

Finally the music ended and the crowd cheered them. Brawley gave her a big bear hug that nearly toppled them both. She re- gained her balance, and, breathing heavy, she accepted his polite kiss to her cheek—a cheek she would hate to wash off.

Dorie was smiling as she re-attached herself to her beau, using his handkerchief to wipe the sweat from his forehead. All Brandy could do was watch them.

The room seemed to rumble behind her, but it was only the sound of the beast's voice.

"Tell you what. I'll go kidnap Dorie, and then you can have him."

Even the hair at the back of her neck stood straight out. Her shoulders felt the tiny beads of moist breath against her flesh. It set up a vibration that traveled briefly down her spine. It was a curious reaction, especially for someone so beast-like.

Upon turning, she faced his warm brown eyes again. They were still twinkling little laugh lines evident at the sides. Somewhere the bevy of bridesmaids and their friends were laughing, and she didn't care.

"That would never work. Brawley would be too heartbroken. He'd probably throw himself off the Coronado Bridge." Her tongue nearly stuck to the roof of her mouth. "I need something to drink."

"I think we should try this punch thing again, don't you?" His voice was gentle, almost melodic, but very, very deep. She felt the words vibrate in her chest.

"Yes, let's try to do it better this time. I think they're out of napkins," she answered.

Was that a growl she heard? She wasn't sure. But it was a wicked growl that could fend off anything.

They walked together side by side.

"I'm Tucker," he said flatly.

"And I'm Brandy."

At the table, he chose the larger clear plastic cups, handing her one and taking the other for himself.

"To a new year. No accidents," he said.

She met his cup with a dull click. "No accidents. To a perfect year."

The cool drink was refreshing, and she finished the whole glass faster than he did. His face was full of surprise.

"All that dancing," she said between deep breaths, "I needed that. Probably should have had water—"

All of a sudden, she felt light-headed. The air constriction had finally caught up with the alcohol floating around her stomach and brain. As she began to see black spots in front of her eyes, she felt his arm underneath her back, holding her, keeping her from falling. Just before she blacked out, she heard the words,

"I've got you. No worries."

CHAPTER 3

TUCKER CARRIED HER to a row of chairs setting just outside the tent. He hurried to get her out before they attracted much attention. Instinctively, he knew she'd be embarrassed if she caused another incident.

She was beginning to moan as he did a light jog towards the chairs. He laid her down, then removed his coat and placed it over her, pulling it up all the way to under her chin.

"Brandy, stay right here and stay warm. I'm going to get some water and a clean washcloth for your forehead. But stay here, okay?"

He saw her nod. Her face was pale, and she'd attempted to open her eyes, but closed them again with another moan. He suspected she'd be sick next.

He ran to the curtains where the catering equipment and staff were housed and got a clean dishcloth and a bottle of sparkling water. When he returned to Brandy, she had already rolled over on her side and was starting to vomit.

"It's okay. You eat anything today?"

She shook her head and then retched nothing but a pink liquid. All she had on her stomach was alcohol.

"You need to eat something. That will soak up some of the alcohol."

She ignored him and retched again. He held her hair back from her face before wiping her forehead, cheeks, and then finally cleaned her lips. He helped her roll back.

"Not too far back. Stay on your side. It might help."

She sighed and snuggled under his jacket. "I hope I didn't get your tux."

"Nope. All's safe. You were actually quite dainty about it. You should see it when I get sick. Not a pretty sight."

"I can only imagine," she mumbled. Then her hand searched and grabbed his as she opened her eyes. "Sorry. Sorry. I'm so sorry. I didn't mean that."

"Yes, you did." He held her hand, and then his thumb began to rub over her knuckles. He stopped himself. "You didn't eat anything before you drank. It happens to the best of us. I'm going to get you something."

"No. I'm on a diet."

"Hogwash," he said as he got up and headed for the food tables. Glancing back, he saw that her gaze followed him. He loosened his tie and unbuttoned his collar. Brawley was on him with concern written all over his face.

"Is she okay?"

"She's gonna be fine. Liquor on an empty stomach. She just needed some fresh air, and I'm getting her something to eat." He searched the small finger sandwiches and bypassed the frittata and vegetables.

"You let me know, promise?" Brawley answered. "We're cutting the cake at midnight. Just a couple of minutes now."

"I'm on medic duty, but I can only imagine what that kiss is gonna look like. You gonna mess up her face with it?"

"Nah. I wanna get laid tonight, Tucker. It's my wedding night."

"Smart move. Don't worry about Brandy."

"She's in good hands." Brawley winked and left to join the

crowd gathered around the cake.

Tucker piled the dish with the sandwiches and returned to Brandy. She was attempting to sit up. He knelt in front of her. "I've got some bread here, which should be good for your stomach. Some kind of mystery meat in the middle, so go easy."

She had pulled his jacket around her shoulders. She smiled. Her beautiful chest and cleavage was hard not to stare at, so he focused on the plate offered to her. She popped the little sandwich into her mouth and closed her eyes.

"Hits the spot."

"Good." He took one. "They're not bad. You should have another."

Brandy did as she was instructed.

"Feeling any better?"

She nodded. Her hair was hanging down over her shoulders as she put her elbows and forearms on her thighs. The gap in her bustier was enormous.

"I wish I could take this damned thing off and go topless."

"A dangerous thought," he said, slightly embarrassed she'd caught him looking.

She smiled. "So tell me something, Tucker. Did someone put you up to this? Be nice to the fat girl?"

The thought had never occurred to him. He was surprised.

"No. No one put me up to anything. Why, you think there's something unattractive about you? Are you an axe murderer or serial killer or something I should be afraid of?"

She shrugged and gave a small laugh. "You know the expression. Age old tale. '*Always a bridesmaid, never a bride.*' That sort of thing."

"Whoa!" Tucker handed her the plate and stood up. "Who said anything about being a bride. If you're thinking—"

"Happy New Year," came the shout from the tent.

He looked down at her. She'd set the sandwiches to the side, took a deep breath, and said, "Shut up and kiss me, you idiot."

With the room erupting in horn and popper noises, Tucker came back to his knees, reached for her face, and melted his lips into hers. It wasn't the wedding cake kiss Brawley would have, and tasted like a ham sandwich, but it definitely got the sparks going deep inside him. Almost painfully, his libido lumbered into full action mode. He felt like a battleship heading out to sea on its final mission. His heart pounded, almost hurting from inattention and need. The subtle scent from her perfume and the way her hair felt on his cheek nearly made him dizzy.

He pulled back and looked into her eyes.

"You okay?" he asked.

"I'd be better if you kissed me again. I needed that."

Her fingers sifted through his hair. Their deep kiss left them both breathless. As his cheek set against hers, he whispered, "What was that?"

"You okay?" she asked, twisting the conversation and letting her eyes flirt. Her forefinger traced over his lips as she focused on them. He squeezed her shoulders but kept his hands in place. He desperately wanted to explore what was being so cruelly smashed underneath all that fabric.

He'd promised himself he wouldn't be looking tonight and would keep his hands to himself. But his promise was going down in flames. He just wasn't sure what he should do. He knew what he desired, but he didn't want to take advantage of her, since he was fairly sure she was still pretty drunk.

"I don't do this," he finally said.

"I don't, either."

"I mean—what I meant was, you're drunk, and I don't think it's right to—"

"If you've changed your mind, just say so. Don't blame it on honor or some other BS, Tucker. I'm a big girl. I can smell a turn down when it's coming. I'm used to it."

His heart was breaking for whatever her experiences had been in the past. It was clear there was some damage there. But it just didn't add up. He could not see any reason she should feel that way.

She'd started to stand, began to remove his jacket.

"Wait, Brandy. You got it all wrong."

"It's okay. Don't patronize me."

"Damnit. I'm not patronizing you. Would you get that god-damned chip off your fuckin' shoulder, Brandy? What I'm telling you is I'm attracted to you. And I don't want to take advantage. I'm not that kind of guy."

He stood with her, putting the jacket back around her shoulders.

"Cake?" A silver tray with slices of wedding cake was presented to them by one of the wait staff.

Brandy eyed the tray, and Tucker could tell she wanted a piece. He took two plates. She was weaving slightly, so he guided her to sit back down. Then he got on his knees again, setting one plate aside. He cut a piece without frosting and held it in front of her. "Probably not the best thing for you to eat, but it might not be that bad."

She watched him while she opened her mouth. He placed the cake on her tongue.

"Perfect. Delicious. More. With frosting," she said.

"Brandy, you sure?" He could see some of the earlier dreaminess return to her eyes.

"What if I put some frosting here," she said as she touched the top of her cleavage with her forefinger. "Or what if it got smeared lower. Would you lick it off?"

Tucker's knees were shaking as his groin refused to behave. He inhaled her scent and the way her eyes were half-lidded while she dipped her finger in the frosting and slowly slid it down between her breasts. She leaned back on the chair, spread her knees, and dared him with her eyes.

His mouth watered as his tongue tasted her flesh beneath the sweet fluffy frosting. He sucked, pulling the top of her right breast into his mouth just short of creating a mark. But he wanted to. He wanted to see her naked, her nipples dripping with frosting, her sex wet with her desire for him. He needed to lose himself in those breasts as he took her deep.

Her fingertips touched his temples. She kissed his forehead, holding his head to her chest. Then one hand slid down the outside of his shirt to his waistband.

"Can I take you home with me?" she breathed into his ear.

"Darlin', I'll go with you anywhere. You just name it."

"I should go get my shoes."

"I'll get them. But I don't think you'll need them."

"Why?"

"Because, sweetheart, I'm going to carry you."

"Really? Why?"

"Because it's just what's done on New Years. You stay right here, and I'll go get them. You think about having that perfect year. You think about what a perfect night would be like, and then let's go do it. Okay?"

He could feel her eyes on his back as he made his return to the party. One of the bridesmaids tried to drag him to the dance floor. She got his shirttails untucked from his waistband before he got away. In the corner were Brandy's heels. He dipped to pick them up and sauntered right through the center of the dance floor, carrying his trophy in his right hand.

He saw the looks. He saw the surprise. He saw Mr. Hanks nod and smile some secret appreciation. Dorie winked at him. Brawley gave him a thumbs up.

He was back. Tucker was back in the real world. The night had turned from the biggest mistake of his life to something else quite extraordinary.

It was going to be the best night of his life. And this was only the start of a new year.

CHAPTER 4

B RANDY SAT BACK in Tucker's bright red truck that set so high she doubted she'd be able to mount it without help. But Tucker had placed her delicately on the seat, strapping her in securely, and then pressing a warm-up kiss to her willing lips. In his own way, he was gentle, but it took effort to not break or hurt things, she noted. The engine revved, and then the truck lurched, headed to Brandy's cottage. She decided not to tell him her father lived in the house in front.

The inside of the cab smelled like him. He fiddled and adjusted the heater, asking if she was comfortable. It was only a ten-minute ride, but in that short time, she noted how he and the huge truck were one giant machine, like a Transformer. The dash and black leather seats were immaculately polished. The floor mats washed like a brand new vehicle. She noted a little decal on the driver's side of the windshield, shaped like an anchor.

When they arrived at her cottage, she was grateful all the lights were out at her father's house. Tucker insisted on carrying her to the front door and then let her slide down the front of him. There were bulging body parts she rubbed against, which would be impossible to miss.

She fumbled for her keys and then led him inside.

Tucker made her small living room feel even smaller. The cottage was a converted outbuilding. Therefore, the ceilings were a few inches lower than normal. He ducked and followed her to the single bedroom. Along the way, she asked, "You want anything to drink?"

His eyes were fixated on her. The slow shake of his head was sexy and deliberate. "No ma'am."

"I'm going to need some help getting out of this."

"Just show me what to do."

"There are these hooks at the back," she said as she turned to show him. "You have to undo them one at a time."

Tucker fumbled with the fabric and the closures. She could tell he was getting frustrated. "Holy cow, Brandy. How in the devil would you get yourself out of this thing by yourself?"

"I can pull it over my head, but it would be easier if—"

At last several of the hooks were released, and she was grateful for the extra breathing space.

"You got it."

The bustier fell to the ground. Brandy unzipped her skirt and laid it over a chair. The ugly diaphragm-squeezing undergarment was the only thing between them. She removed her stockings and panties, and once again presented her back to him.

"This is going to be hard. You have to unzip me here."

Tucker was on it, his huge fingers slipping beneath the off-white fabric, while his other hand grabbed the zipper and had it undone in just a couple of seconds.

"Piece of cake."

The rush of air to her lungs was so sudden she nearly fainted again. He braced her before she could fall over. He pulled her to his chest while his hands took hold of her ass and squeezed until it hurt.

She began to unbutton his shirt, then lifted the cotton tee shirt up, and kissed him, placing her palms over his pecs. She reached below, fingers creeping into his pants when he quickly undid his belt and stepped out of them.

She was going to step to press herself against him, but he abruptly picked her up and brought her over to the bed, where he gently placed her down.

"You have some protection?" he whispered as he kissed her neck. One callused hand squeezed her left breast and then slid down lower.

She started to sit up to grab the condoms from the bedside table, but he pressed her back, rising to his knees and staring down at her.

His hands massaged both boobs now. "You're incredible. I think I've died and gone to Heaven," he said as he nuzzled her cleavage, sucking and pinching her nipples. His scratchy beard tickled as his kissing moved lower until he was at her core. His thumbs pressed her open, rubbing her nub as she shuddered with anticipation.

She watched him pleasure her, his giant shoulders rising and falling as he dipped lower. He kept one hand massaging her breast. He was nearly delicate the way he explored with his fingers and tongue. It filled her with electricity as she heard him moan between her legs. She pulled his hair, massaged his temples, and then writhed to the feel of his fingers inside her, calling her to ride his hand and lose herself for him. She came up to her knees, reaching for his cock while she pressed herself into his giant palm.

She gripped him, moving up and down, squeezing his balls and covering his tip with precum. After some minutes of play, she raised herself up and reached for the drawer, bringing out the condom, then tearing it open with her teeth. As she looked up to him in the moonlight, their mouths closed on each other, tongues exploring, becoming more and more intense. Her fingers slid the thin condom down his shaft and massaged him while they finished their slow, sensuous kiss.

Tucker leaned back and brought her up on top of him. With her knees hugging his hips, he gripped her body, snagging her sex on his cock and then pressing her down so he was deep inside her.

He was urgent to move against her, raising and lowering her on him, drawing the rhythm faster and faster until he quickly picked her up, threw her back against the mattress, and mounted her. Plunging deep, he buried his head in her chest.

They moved together like old dance partners, reveling in the miracle that was their bodies. Beneath him, she felt delicate. She melted under his kiss, rising again into multiple orgasms as he plundered and then softened his penetration.

He was an innovative lover, consumed with desire for her, yet very attentive to her needs, begging her to come and then thanking her as she shattered beneath him over and over again. She knew that as the minutes turned into the early pre-dawn hours of the morning, she had never before felt so loved, so coveted and consumed. As the first rays of early dawn shone through the window, he held her close as he came hard and deep inside her, then folded her into his arms, and fell asleep.

She worried her beating heart would wake him as she luxuriated in the heat between them. Every cell in her body screamed for him. Her ear was pressed against his chest, and she listened as air filled his lungs and then expelled. Her skin was bathed in the sweet sweat between their bodies, the way her legs wrapped around his enormous thighs, and how his arms squeezed her so tight it rivaled the bustier just before she fell asleep.

But in the shelter of his arms, there was room to breathe, and finally to dream about a perfect evening, and the beginning of a perfect year.

CHAPTER 5

A SLIVER OF bright sunlight traveled slowly across Tucker's face like a laser. At first, he startled, since his own apartment was heavily draped in blackout shades. Even on workdays, he was able to sleep in until at least eight. This seemed just minutes from when he'd last closed his eyes.

And then he felt her moist flesh melting all over him. He carefully opened one eye to peer at the lovely brunette resting on his chest. Her lips were still puckered and red, her cheek bulging against her nose. *And she drooled!*

He tilted his head back to avoid giving a belly laugh that would surely wake her. He didn't want to be robbed of these delicious moments. How could he have met a girl who drooled in her sleep?

He scanned the walls of her bedroom. She had tacked several tissue paper sketches of what looked like produce labels and several other ones of large flowers done in chalk or pencil. There was a sketch of a light pink sandy beach cradling white surf coming from a bright turquoise ocean. He noticed a poster made from a picture of Brandy dressed in a large purple grape costume. She was holding a bottle of wine and standing next to Dorie, in an identical costume. Their legs were bright purple from the knees down as they stood in a large stainless steel vat, stomping grapes.

She had a calendar with pictures of beaches from around the

world and a photo of her as a young girl sitting beside an older gentleman driving a tractor at a pumpkin farm. Her burgundy bustier and bridesmaid skirt were draped over an easy chair, mixed with his black pants, white shirt, and red white and blue cotton boxers. He was a little embarrassed at the rah rah in his underwear, but he couldn't help it. It was the way he was.

Her bookshelf burst with paperbacks, spilling over onto the floor in several stacks. It appeared every one of them had a picture of a naked man on the cover. The bedside table still gaped with the open drawer containing a box of condoms. He noticed she owned a bright pink vibrator, and that nearly ruined his composure.

But it was all good. All normal. These were the trappings of a woman he'd been trained to protect. Her precious way of life was valuable, something worth saving. This was evidence that what he'd done as an elite warrior was all worth it. He hoped to God she never had to endure some of the things he'd seen out there on the other side of the planet, where children inhaled a steady diet of uncertainty, misery, and smoke from the ashes of their crumbling civilization that knew nothing but war. His job was to make sure that war stayed there and didn't come home.

Brandy was moving against him, stroking him like she'd done so delicately last night. Her pubic bone pressed into his thigh. He raised his knee to help intensify the feeling.

At last, she placed her chin on his sternum and fed from his eyes. What did she see? He hoped she wasn't disappointed. He wasn't. He remembered every kiss, every stroke, every shudder, and every time he pinned her to the bed with her arms outstretched, as if he could will himself to climb inside her and shelter in place.

She was twirling his frosty chest hairs, biting her lip, and waiting to say something, or waiting for him to speak first. But he didn't feel under any pressure to talk so he just watched this dark angel with the red lips he was ravenous for. He wanted to see her enormous breasts bounce in the morning sun as she writhed above him. He wanted to see her face as he filled her, made her come.

She opened her mouth to say something when the door to her living room opened and a man's voice called out, "Brinny?"

Brandy scrambled to sit up, taking the sheet with her, which left Tucker completely exposed. If the man in the next room came to the doorway, he'd also notice the enormous hard-on Tucker had developed.

She smirked, whispering, "My father."

He sprung to action and quickly slipped on his patriotic boxers, but remained seated on the bed.

"Just a minute dad. I've got someone here," she shouted to the next room. Twisting the sheet around her, she stepped to the doorway. Tucker got a nice view of her shapely rear, her long mahogany hair falling everywhere about her shoulders and upper back. He'd kissed every vertebra last night, kneaded the cheeks of her ass until she squealed. She could take everything he could give out, and then some. He hated having to be careful in his sex play. Brandy played at the same intensity.

"Oh, fine. Look, I'm headed off to the store. You coming in today?"

"Maybe later this afternoon. Would that work?"

"Sure. Sorry I didn't let you know yesterday, but I'm going to be one short today. If you can, that would really help me out."

"No problem, Dad. How about one or two o'clock?"

"Great. Hey, how was the wedding?"

She adjusted her sheet again, briefly shooting him a gaze as Tucker lay back on the pillow, his hands clasped behind his head. "Dorie was gorgeous. You should have come. They had a great band, lots of people you knew were there."

"A friend of Brawley's?" her dad whispered, but Tucker could hear it clearly.

Brandy nodded. "Dad, I've gotta go."

"No problem. See you later on this afternoon."

The door closed behind him.

Tucker watched her face recovering from the blush that also sent pink blotches to her upper chest. "That was awkward," she mumbled, fiddling with her fingers and refusing to look back at him.

He was charmed with the blush, but even more interested in getting the sheet off her. "Come here," he whispered.

Her face pinked up again, and he chuckled.

"After all the things we did last night, you expect me to believe you're really shy?"

She began twirling her hair around her forefinger, still avoiding eye contact.

"Come here, Brandy. Just for a little bit. Then I'd like to take you out to breakfast. I'm thinking pancakes."

Her large brown eyes snapped to attention. She crawled on all fours toward him. By the time she reached him, the sheet had been left behind. Her breasts overflowed in his hands as her young body undulated over his groin, pressing against the ridge of his hardness. Her fingers deftly slid his boxers down over his thighs while she guided him to her core. He held the sides of her hips, raised her up, and then plunged her back down on him.

Then he remembered. They'd forgotten the condom. Again. With his fingers digging into her flesh, he stopped her movements completely, knowing he had to ask the question and leave it up to her.

"Is it okay?"

"It's perfect," she blew back at his face, and then she kissed him.

THE SAMOAN PANCAKE House was always a Team favorite on

weekends. But today was a holiday so the place was packed. He nodded to several former Teammates, a couple of whom were at the wedding last night.

She chose a corner at the back of the restaurant, and ordered.

"So you used to serve with Brawley, right?"

"About ten years ago. We grew up together in Oregon."

"You're from Oregon?"

He noticed she had a dimple to the right of her mouth, which was cuter than all heck.

"*What?*"

"You have a very sexy dimple right there." He touched the spot and loved her blush, as she held his hand.

"I love it up there. My parents had plans to retire near McMin-ville, but my mom passed before they could sell everything and go do it. Now Dad's stuck with the store."

"That's close to where Brawley and I grew up."

"That's what I thought. So your family was farmers, then?"

"Still are. My sister and her husband and kids live with them and they all work in the family business."

"Sounds nice. What do they grow?"

Tucker was hesitant to explain the details of his parent's venture, so he deflected the question by giving a half-answer. "They do hydroponics, greenhouse stuff. They used to grow wheat, but over the years, they've sold off parcels so now they only have a few acres left. It's all they can handle."

"You miss Oregon?" Brandy asked as their breakfast was served.

Tucker poured syrup all over his pancakes and even his eggs and the extra biscuit he ordered. "I worked up a regular appetite, Miss Brandy." He winked at her, amused by the way her jaw dropped as she watched him take his first bite. Then she blushed again.

"I don't miss Oregon at all. I like it here. More sun, less rain. More to do outside, and I don't have to prepare for monsoons to do them, either. San Diego suits me just fine."

"Yup," she agreed.

"You grew up here, then?" He knew she had, but wanted to keep the conversation going.

"Right here. I'm not sure if I stay because of Dad or he stays because of me. I work for him, help him out a bit, since I'm between jobs at the moment."

"I thought you worked with Dorie at the ad agency."

"*Used* to. I guess I pissed off a customer. I don't think the advertising business is for me."

"Brawley said your dad's store is quite upscale? Can he make it with Amazon and all those other players fighting for the retail dollar?"

"I think he makes just enough to live on. Dad's not someone who could ever work for anyone else. He owns the market outright, and the half-acre lot behind. He has some fantasy of doing a little truck farming, perhaps grow his own organic produce."

"Farming, even on a half-acre, is a lot of work."

"I think that's the point, Tucker. When he gets tired of it, then he'll sell. This gives him something to do. Keeps him from missing my mother. She was everything to him." Then she added, "I don't think our family does well with retirement. It's kind of a dirty word."

Tucker nodded and completely agreed. "Smart man. Men have to do things. They can't just sit around and watch the world go by. They have to get into action, or at least the men I hang with do."

"So now that you're off the Teams, what do you do?"

"I run some trainings for guys, mostly high school age, who are interested in joining the SEALs. I try to get them in good physical shape to help them pass BUD/S. I'm kind of the guy who tells them the truth, dispels the garbage the recruiters fill them with. I make sure they know what they're signing up for."

"They're lucky to have you."

"It's only part-time, but it gives me a chance to give a little back to the community. I also do some personal training and I work at the glider port, instructing for the skydiving school."

"Skydiving? Wow."

"You should try it sometime. You'd have a ball."

He was surprised to see she appeared resistant.

"No, thanks. I'll stick to the ground, thank you. If God had wanted me to fly through the air, he would have given me wings."

"Or an expert tandem buddy. It will change your life, Brandy."

"Or end it."

"No. These guys are safe. They train all the SEALs down here. Some of the most experienced skydivers and stuntmen in the country. It's all completely safe." He drew her hand to his mouth and kissed it. "All about trust, Brandy. And finding out about your limits."

They finished breakfast, and Tucker reluctantly took her back to her car. She turned towards him before she got out of the truck.

"I had a great time, Tucker. I had a goal to have one perfect evening, and it was all that and more. Sorry I got sick on you."

He leaned over and cradled her jaw with his palm before kissing her. "I did, too. I don't want to tell you my goal because you dashed it all to hell. This is the part where I ask you if I can see you again. I'm hoping the answer is yes."

She held his hand between both of hers. When she looked up, he thought at first she might say no.

"I was just looking for one perfect night. I guess I could handle two."

CHAPTER 6

B RANDY CHANGED HER clothes and put on her comfortable cross trainers since she'd be standing the entire afternoon. She drove down the strand past the SEAL Qualification course and thought about what it had been like for Tucker and Brawley going through the training together. Many times, she'd watched the boat crews of new recruits working their way over the rocks or running down the beach carrying telephone poles over their heads. She mused that Tucker could actually make a telephone pole look small.

She turned off the highway and into the tree-lined streets of an older suburban neighborhood then headed away from the bay where things were a little more spread out. Small ranchettes dotted the landscape. She came upon the boutique strip mall containing a cluster of specialty stores with her father's organic grocery and deli at one end. She could see his silver pickup truck parked at the side, as well as Kip's beat-up VW. The five time college freshman had worked for her dad ever since he'd mastered the art of riding a bike. He was practically family. There were only a couple of other cars in the lot, indicating they were having a very slow day.

She loved the smell of the produce and the bright colors of the vegetables and fruit every time she arrived. It was like the smell of flowers at a florist. Her dad was famous for carrying unusual fruits from all over the world, but he specialized in California and Florida citrus and always did a huge business every Christmas sending fruit baskets to customer's relatives all over the globe.

She ducked under the portable canvas awnings shading the lovely displays, piled up in pine boxes. Two shoppers wandered down aisles inside the building itself. One was headed in the direction of the checkout, having spotted Brandy arrive.

"I'll be right back," she told the woman. "Just got to grab my apron and punch in."

Inside the store's tiny office was her father's desk, covered in catalogs, papers, and envelopes—most of them unopened. It was obvious he needed help with his bookkeeping and office organization. She intended to have a discussion with him about that very thing, and soon.

Brandy placed her purse inside the top file cabinet drawer, noticing it had been pushed aside and was slightly crooked. With a couple of shoves she righted it to stand snug against the desk, where it belonged. Her dad's chair was pulled out, and his glasses were folded on top of the closed laptop that was so old the Apple store refused to work on it any longer.

Slipping the kelly-green apron over her head, she deposited her cell phone in the large center pocket, tied the straps behind her waist, and began to look for her father.

"Dad?"

There was no answer so she figured he might be in the large cooler room at the rear.

That's where she found him. He was sprawled on the floor, his face turned to one side. A trickle of blood had seeped into the floorboards coming from under his upper body somewhere. His face was pale, lips slightly purple. She was immediately worried he might be dead.

"Oh my God. Dad! What's happened?"

She fell to her knees and tried to revive him, but his body remained limp. Then she checked for a pulse and was relieved to have found one. And he appeared to be breathing, but when she tried to arouse him again, he didn't respond. His face was cold and clammy.

With her own pulse racing, she dialed 911 and gave instructions to the paramedics who promised they'd be there within minutes.

She called out for Kip, but again received no answer.

"Hang in there, dad."

But her father didn't register any response, which sent a spear of panic down her spine. She wasn't sure if she should roll him over on his back and decided it would be safer to just leave him on his side. Beneath his head she felt the sticky dark red blood. Finding a clean hand towel, she applied slight pressure, hoping to stop the bleeding. In mere seconds, the towel was bright red and soaked. Her hands were dripping in her father's blood. She carefully rested his head against the soaked cotton and staggered out front to see if she could find Kip. It was hard to concentrate, but she managed to calm her nerves.

The customer was waiting not-so-patiently by the checkout, but when she spied Brandy's bloody hands, she began to scream. Brandy jumped as if she'd been slapped.

"Hold on. My father has taken a spill, and the paramedics are on their way. Give me a minute to get myself gathered. Have you seen Kip?"

The woman closed her mouth and merely shook her head briskly. "Who's Kip?"

"He's the other clerk here."

"I didn't see anyone."

Brandy looked at the woman's basket, then at the counter and discovered the cash register drawer had been pried open and was completely empty. A check was crumpled at her feet. It began to dawn on her that perhaps this had been a robbery attempt gone badly.

"Ma'am, it looks like we've been robbed, too. You sure you didn't see anyone?"

"No. No one was here. These folks," she said, pointing to a couple behind her, "arrived after me. Is your dad okay?"

"No. I'm worried. He's unconscious, but help is on the way."

Just then, she heard the familiar sound of Kip parking the company van. He entered the store, tossing and catching his keys. Upon seeing Brandy, he gave her a big grin. "Hey there."

"Kip, Dad's fallen. He's in the back. I've called the paramedics and they're on their way. This woman wants to check out, but I need to stand guard with Dad until the paramedics come. Can you get the backup working? If not, can we just close down the store?"

"Sure thing." Kip was already on his knees, extracting another register from under the counter, connecting the telephone feeds, and adjusting the paper. "I've got this. You go be with your dad."

She jogged to the back of the storeroom. Her father still hadn't moved.

She was relieved to hear the sirens getting closer until she saw just flashing red lights. Someone must have directed them to the rear because two paramedics ran through the back door and bent over to attend to her father. Their fingers deftly poked and repositioned his head and neck, checking out his neck, arms, and legs.

"Did you see him fall?" the handsome dark-uniformed rescue worker asked her as he scanned her bloody hands. He turned his attention back to her father, focusing on the bleeding from his head.

"No. I got here like ten or fifteen minutes ago. I expected to find him in the store, so I went looking for him and found him here. Just like this. I put the towel under his head. But there was so much…blood." Her voice wavered.

The other paramedic was up on her feet, barking instructions into the com strapped to her shoulder.

"Are you a relative or co-worker?" the male paramedic asked.

"I'm his daughter."

"What's his name?"

"Steven Cook."

"He have any illnesses or things I need to know? Medications?"

"Geez." Brandy wracked her brain, trying to remember if he'd told her anything about his health, and came up blank. "I don't think he takes anything. As far as illnesses, not that he's told me."

"How old is he?"

"Sixty-two."

"No pacemakers, history of stroke or heart attack?"

"No. Not that I know of. I really don't know. He's been healthy."

"So you didn't see how this happened?"

"No."

"Anybody angry with him for some reason?"

"No, why?"

"Sorry to have to tell you, but this was no accidental fall. It appears he was hit at the back of the head, you see here?"

He showed her a dark mass of clotted blood, hair, and tissue at the back of his head, slightly underneath him.

"And then it appears he fell, because this other wound looks like it happened when his head hit the floor. So we got two head injuries to deal with."

"I see." Brandy tried to sound as calm as the paramedic was. But in spite of her efforts, her teeth began to chatter.

"You going to be okay?" he asked.

"I don't like blood," she whispered. Black dots began obscuring her vision, and she could tell she was close to passing out.

The paramedic's quick thinking had him grabbing her upper arms with his bloody gloved hands and positioning her on a nearby chair. "Put your head between your knees if you need to. I'll get you some water in a minute. Better?"

She was starting to get confused and could feel her breathing becoming labored. So much was happening.

"Breathe. Take deep breaths," he commanded.

Her father still wasn't moving. His dark lips were getting darker by the minute. She abruptly threw off his hands. "Dad. He looks terrible! He's worse!"

"We got it. Just don't want you to die on me, okay?"

The woman paramedic returned with a gurney, which she lowered and positioned next to her father. She cut his long-sleeved shirt with scissors and then started an IV before helping her partner lift him onto the bed. They raised the legs on the cart, clicked it into position, and ran toward the back of the van. The woman stayed behind while the male worker came back to check on Brandy.

"Where can I get you some water? This *is* a store, right?" he asked.

"There's a case on the other side of this wall. Take a couple for yourselves, too."

He was back in seconds, snapping open the plastic cap and holding the bottle up to her mouth.

Brandy guzzled the cool liquid, trying to keep up, but wound up spilling much of it down her front. She didn't care.

"That help some?"

"I'll be fine."

"You have someone you can call?"

"Kip's here. I want to go be with my dad at the hospital."

"No, not in your condition. But we're taking him to Scripps. You can meet us there. No way I want you driving by yourself."

"Gene?" his partner inserted herself in the exit. "We gotta go now."

"Okay, we're outta here. The police will be arriving soon, so you'll have to give them a statement. Then get someone to bring you down. Right now, we gotta focus on Mr. Cook. So, you take care."

"Thank you so much." She started to stand, but he pushed her shoulders down.

"Don't be stubborn. Be smart."

She didn't like the comment, but she didn't have the energy to fight him back with some quick witty thing. If he only knew.

Stubborn is my middle name.

THE POLICE INTERVIEWED them both, promising to be brief so she could get to the hospital to see her father.

Kip answered another question. "He asked me to do the home deliveries because he knew you were coming in." He spoke directly to her.

"How long were you gone?" the officer persisted.

"Hour? Maybe an hour and a half. Normally, I'd go later, but I asked to get off early." He turned to Brandy again. "I got a date."

That's when she realized so did she. She'd promised to meet Tucker at the Rusty Scupper after work. He was working at the skydiving school all afternoon.

"You know of anyone who would want to hurt Mr. Cook?" the officer asked.

Brandy shook her head from side to side. "He doesn't have any fights or enemies of any kind. Everyone loves him."

"Well," Kip interrupted, "there is this one thing. He had a guy he let go last week. Several customers complained about him. Too friendly with the younger girls. I'm talking thirteen, fourteen-year-olds."

"When did this happen?" the officer asked.

"Thursday, I think. Jorge Mendoza. I never liked him. Steve got him from some church group recommendation. He'd been staying at a halfway house. I told your dad he was stealing beer and drinking on his breaks, but he didn't care until he started getting the complaints. Tats, even on his face. He stared at people. Cold eyes. Not a good dude at all. I was glad Steve let him go."

"I didn't know about any of that." Brandy admitted it was just like her dad to give someone a chance.

Several customers came asking questions, after hearing the sirens and seeing the police activity. Brandy told them they were closing for the day, and that her father was in the hospital. The police reminded her afterwards not to give out many details.

"Your father keep records here? Any way we could get this guy's address?"

"Um, yes. He keeps his records in the office, but I'll have to dig a bit. He's not the most organized owner out there. Some of it, he keeps in the safe," Brandy answered. One of the officers followed her, and she was able to get the employee folder from the second file drawer. She lifted a heavy canvas seed sack to access her father's safe and found it gaping open. "Holy crap."

Kip was at the doorway in a flash. "Ah shit. I was afraid of that." He put his hand over his mouth. "Sorry, Brandy."

"Did everyone who worked here know about the safe?" one officer asked.

"I wouldn't think so, but then, Dad was pretty trusting." shrugged Brandy.

Kip added, "We were really busy over the weekend with New Years coming up. Everyone was shopping for last minute things. I think he closed early last night. I'm sure he didn't make it to the bank. It's a shame, but I'm guessing he had a lot of cash in that vault."

"Which points to Mendoza again," said one of the officers.

Brandy took another long gulp of her water, finishing it off. Her eyes filled with tears. Her day had gone from spectacular to tragic. She needed to go be at her father's side. And what if he didn't survive? What would she do? She just couldn't bear to think about it.

The officers agreed to let her go if they could question her further at the hospital. Kip was in charge of closing the store. Brandy agreed to keep the place closed until the police had finished their work, and Kip agreed to open it for them in the morning.

Alone and headed back down the freeway, she left a message for Tucker, and then she burst out in tears, flushing out all the pain and pent up worry all the way to the hospital. By the time she arrived, her eyes felt like her lids were made of cardboard.

This was not the way she'd expected this day to go. As she entered the Emergency Room doors, she began to find some of her courage. She hoped it would be enough for whatever news they'd give her. She said a little prayer before she approached the admitting desk and strained to keep her lower lip from wobbling, Taking a deep breath, she told the admitting clerk, "I'm here to see Steven Cook. Can you tell me what room he's in?"

CHAPTER 7

TUCKER HAD REMOVED his flight overalls, stowed his equipment, and repacked his chute and the tandem chute, double checking each fold twice. He felt the vibration from his cell and noticed he'd gotten a message from Brandy.

"It's me, Brandy. I'm on my way to the hospital. Scripps ER. Dad's been hurt, and they rushed him by ambulance. I'm meeting the police there. I have no idea how long I'll be, but I don't want to leave him until I know he's going to be okay. So I'm afraid I'll have to take a rain check on that burger and beer. Call me when you get a chance."

He dialed her back, sorry that he'd missed her call earlier. It had been nearly an hour. She picked up on the first ring.

"Brandy, what happened? Is he okay?"

"I don't know yet, Tucker. He was unconscious when they took him away. I'm waiting to find out if they'll let me see him. He's alive, and that's a good thing, but I don't know anything else. I wasn't able to talk to him. I don't know if he's still unconscious."

"But how did he get hurt? Why are the police involved?"

"It was a robbery at the store. They got the cash in the till, the contents of his safe, everything. The police are following up on a lead Kip gave them."

"Kip?"

"I'm sorry. He's dad's helper."

"So how did he get hurt?"

"Apparently, he was hit at the back of the head, and then fell. I found him on the floor near the cooler. He didn't look good at all, Tucker. Lots of blood. I'm worried."

"Of course you are. Listen, can I meet you there? I'm about a half-hour away."

"I'd like that," she murmured.

Tucker could tell she was trying to stay collected but was having difficulty holding herself together. Her breathing was forced and ragged.

"He's at Scripps you say?"

"Yes. I can call you if they take him somewhere else. But their ER and critical care is one of the best in the country."

"You got that right. Okay, I'll be there as fast as I can. You need me to bring anything?"

"Honestly, I'm not focusing on me at all. I think I'm still in shock. Just come. That would help."

Tucker stopped by his apartment, wanting to take a shower, but knew he didn't have time. He changed his clothes, picked up a pillow and blanket, threw a couple of waters in a bag, and headed up the freeway.

The sunset was a rosy pink, which sent a glow throughout the waiting room at the ER. His arms overflowing with the blanket and queen pillow, he scanned the seats and didn't see Brandy, so asked the desk clerk. He peered over the top of his bundle, since the woman was taller than he was.

"Are you family?" she asked, examining his armful.

"Yes," he lied.

"Well, hon, the daughter is waiting outside the treatment room. They're getting ready to take him up to ICU."

"How's he doing? Can I come in and wait with her?"

"Sorry, can't give you his status, but let me ask her if she'd like some company. I'm betting she would," she said, scanning the pillow again, squinting her eyes and smiling. "Can I have your name, please?"

"Tucker Hudson."

"I'll be right back." The heavyset nurse winked at him and then moved with the speed of a linebacker, disappearing around the corner. It wasn't every day Tucker spoke eyeball to eyeball with a woman who towered above him. In a few seconds, the side door opened, and the clerk called out, "Mr. Hudson, this way, please."

Brandy was in the hallway, speaking to a uniformed female officer. She abandoned the conversation temporarily and ran to his arms. An instant before she collided with him, he dropped his load and pulled her to him.

"You holding up?" he whispered to the top of her head.

"Better now." She snuggled to press herself hard against his chest, wrapping her arms around him beneath his jacket.

"How's you dad?"

Brandy pulled away, biting her lower lip. "Haven't talked to the doctor yet, really. Dad's had a brain scan and some bloodwork and some other tests. They told me his vitals were strong, but I don't know anything else. Hoping someone will talk to me before they take him upstairs."

The female officer appeared behind Brandy. "If you give me just a couple more minutes, we can get my questions answered, and I'll get out of your hair. That sound okay with you?"

"I'm sorry." Brandy walked back to the row of chairs they'd been sitting at, remained standing, her arms still about Tucker's waist. Good as her word, the police officer finished her questions and then was gone within a handful of minutes. Brandy leaned against him as they sat down together. A male nurse had picked up the blanket and pillow and placed them nearby, neatly folded.

"So how did this robbery occur? They hold him up at gunpoint? In the middle of the day?" Tucker asked.

"We still don't know that. Don't even know how many of them there were."

"Your dad have cameras in the store?"

"Only for looks. They don't record."

"All this is appearing like it was someone who knows your dad. Knows his way around the store. Knows the routines."

"I think that's what the police are going on. But, honestly, I don't care about the money. I just want to be sure he's okay, without any major—"

"Ms. Cook?"

Dr. Harrelson shook her hand and motioned for her to remain seated. He extended his hand to Tucker. "I'm Dr. Harrelson. You the husband? Boyfriend?"

Tucker found himself stumbling for his words, a bit put on the spot. "Family friend," he answered grasping the doctor's paw.

"Now *that's* a handshake!" Dr. Harrelson barked, feigning injured fingers.

Tucker thought he'd been rather careful and wasn't in the mood for jokes. "Sorry, sir."

"Okay, well we have good news and bad news, Ms. Cook. We're not seeing much brain damage on the scan, and the wave patterns are normal. He's got a little swelling, especially in the back here." The doctor demonstrated on his own head, palming an area behind his right ear at the base of his skull. "There's probably some pressure, which also could be from blood pooling, but we will monitor that, and it doesn't seem to be increasing, thank God."

"That's good. So what's the bad news?" she asked.

"He's lost a considerable amount of blood, and he definitely has a minor skull fracture, probably a concussion as well. The next twelve to twenty-four hours will be the most telling, but we should know more once we see how he weathers this."

"Is he awake yet?"

"No, and right now, I'm not anxious for him to be. I think we need to watch him, let his body heal and stabilize itself. There's a chance we'll have to go in there to relieve the pressure, but the bleeding has been stopped. We're thinking the bones in his skull will heal on their own."

"That's good news." Tucker was feeling encouraged and hoped Brandy felt the same.

"I was able to contact his primary care physician. Your dad's in remarkable shape for sixty-two. His doctor gave me his medical history. That's going to help us out a lot."

"So what's the plan?" Brandy asked.

To their side, they all watched as her father was wheeled out of the treatment room and down the hallway by two male attendants.

"His color is much better," she remarked.

"Yeah. We were a little worried when he first came in, but he's responding quickly. We hope that continues," Dr. Harrelson added. They followed Mr. Cook's gurney as it entered the elevator.

Tucker noted the strong jawline and the shape of her father's nose, indicating a strong family resemblance. His face looked relaxed. A large white bandage was wrapped around his skull down to the level of his eyebrows and ears. Tufts of graying hair stuck out the top where it had been left open, some of it still caked in dark red blood.

"So we're taking him upstairs, now," the doctor started. "He'll be in ICU, on the fourth floor, tonight. Once we get him situated, if you want to briefly come in and say goodnight, that would be fine, but no more than five minutes. He probably won't hear you, and he definitely won't respond. Just preparing you for this."

"Thanks, doctor."

"I have rooms upstairs, if you need a place to crash, but honestly, it would probably be best if you just went home and got some rest. Nothing like sleeping in your own bed."

Brandy searched Tucker's face. "What do you think?"

"I think he's right." He knew his apartment was not more than five minutes away, but he was hesitant to suggest he take her there. He hadn't entertained a woman at his place in several months and was in the habit of trying to avoid it at all costs. He was trying to recall how bad the place was, since it would be Brandy's first impression of how he lived. Though a tiny niggling voice whispered caution, he found himself overruling it.

"I don't live too far. But if you want to stay here, I'm willing to sleep in a chair by your side. I've learned to sleep just about anywhere."

"You a Team Guy?" Dr. Harrelson asked.

"Former."

"That explains the handshake. So, you two talk about it and then let me know. Give us about ten minutes to get him all situated, okay?"

Brandy nodded as the doctor left.

"I think he's doing really great, Brandy." Tucker had never seen the man before, but in light of what he'd been through, he thought Mr. Cook was looking good. "If he's stabilized, no reason for you to get worn out trying to sleep here. Hospitals make me nervous. Just too much going on."

Tucker had an aversion to hospitals. Even when he'd broken his legs twice in combat, he demanded he be able to walk out on his own, whether in cast or crutches or both. The first time it was nearly impossible to navigate. He got good at asking people to get out of the way by swinging his crutch high above his head like a hammer throw. He even resumed his skydiving, until his LPO found out and put a stop to it.

"You sure it's no trouble?" she asked. "Do you have a roommate?"

"No roommate. It's sparsely decorated and probably not to your taste, but I guarantee the bed's great."

She smiled, slowly swinging her head from side to side. "Why am I not surprised?"

"There. That's what I've been looking for." He angled her chin up and kissed her lightly. "I wanted to see that pretty smile. Ready to go?"

"I want to see him first."

An ICU nurse accompanied Brandy to the expansive room housing several beds, most of them filled. Tucker waited against the wall, sneaking a peek through the wide open doorway. He was able to see Brandy sit in the chair provided, reach over, and take her father's hand. She spoke to him, but too softly for him to make out. A few minutes later, with a gentle pat on her shoulder, she was ushered out.

"How's he look?" he asked her.

"He actually looks comfortable, but the nurse told me they'd be on high alert all night in case something happened. It's amazing he didn't break his arm or one of his legs, the way he must have fallen."

"Someone definitely looking out for him," Tucker answered back. "Let's go."

He drove in complete silence the short ten blocks before he arrived at the gates to his complex. He was grateful he didn't have to ruminate any longer than five minutes over his choice to bring her to his place. He'd have been a nervous wreck. Putting it all out of his mind, he helped her climb down from his truck, tucked the blanket and pillow under one arm, and took her hand with the other.

The first thing that hit him when he opened his front door was that he'd never before noticed that his room smelled of man sweat.

Her room smelled of lavender and other floral fragrances. Before he turned on any lights, he stumbled in the dark, picked up the clothes he'd worn skydiving today under the jumpsuit, and tossed them behind the closet doors. Before he could choose the right lighting, Brandy turned on the bright kitchen lights, exposing the sink full of dishes. It was over three day's worth, even though he ate mostly frozen dinners on a regular basis.

Why hadn't he thought about this?

He hung his head sheepishly, hoping it didn't leave too much of a negative impression. "Between housekeepers," he mumbled, rolling his neck and left shoulder.

"You already warned me, so no worries. You also mentioned you don't have a decorator." She smiled, seemingly to enjoy his squirming. "I wasn't expecting an extreme makeover," she said, batting her eyes at him.

Tucker was definitely not feeling the least bit romantic. He was scared out of his gourd. He was on uncharted territory and regretted not paying attention to that little voice that usually gave him pretty good advice.

She wandered around his living room, examining the walls and bare corners. He had one couch, and it conformed perfectly to the contours of his large frame, even if it was ugly as sin. The table in front was a wooden shipping crate. She leaned over it and studied his choice of reading material. Several nudie magazines with specialty titles like *I Love Titties* and *Booty Call* were stacked five or six issues deep. All he could do was close his eyes and wait for her reaction. It was too late to whisk them away out of sight.

She picked up one cover and showed him the enormous boobs on the unfortunate girl. "Do mine look anywhere like these?" she asked, her face showing no expression.

"Holy cow, Brandy. No. *Fuck* no! Yours are…well, they're just right. A nice, full," he began to hold out his palms, fingers splayed and pointing up, "handful, just overflowing."

She had her hands on her waist. It was one of those attitude things women frequently gave him. He knew he was in some trouble, but wasn't sure how much. With his lack of sleep last night, his radar was not working, and his blood was inconveniently pooling elsewhere. He hoped she didn't notice. He wished she'd say something.

"But completely inadequate, compared to these." She held the magazine up, covering her chest.

"God, Brandy, those are unnatural. I mean if I wanted to play with a couple of deflated basketballs, I'd go take a drive to Sports City."

She flipped the magazine over to examine it again. "They do sort of look like basketballs."

Since she wasn't smiling, he carefully waited for the whole scene to pass. He tried to reassure her he liked her just the way she was built.

"And you have lovely curves, sweetheart. She's like a human tuck and roll. I like nice, curvy hips. I mean look at me. I want a woman I don't have to worry about breaking her pelvis when I make love. I hate skinny women."

He wasn't sure it was enough, so he waited, squinting as if bracing for a blow. She tossed the magazine back onto the table, and picked up one of the big butt issues. "Big Book of Booty. Nice."

Her darting glance at him was painful, but his dick was having great fun at his expense. Luckily, Brandy didn't look there. Instead, she smiled and asked him, "Does my ass look like this?"

Tucker was stumped. Brandy's ass did indeed look like the cover model's. She was round in all the right places. He decided he'd have to live or die, but he'd be honest with her.

"Yes, your butt looks sort of like that, only better. Smooth as silk. I love the way it looks and feels, sweetheart." He was hoping she didn't catch on that this was his favorite magazine.

"So why'd you buy this other one if you don't like basketballs with nipples? Or are you lying to me?"

"Look, Brandy, we're going places we don't have to go. But the truth is, there are some nice pictures on the inside. They aren't all like this. This is shock value, to make men buy the magazine. That's all. This is like a cartoon, a comic book, something men do to pass the time, like playing a video game or something. It's all fantasy."

He carefully maneuvered himself behind her, removing the magazine from her hands and turning her around.

"I don't need those things anymore. I got the real thing right here. You were created perfect for me. I mean that, Brandy." He massaged the top of her spine. With the other hand, he slipped it around her waist and slowly pulled her to him. "Perfect, in every way," he whispered. He let his hands massage her ass, squeezing and pressing her against his hardness.

"Why can't I be your fantasy, Tucker?"

"You are. You totally are. Men look. That's what we do. You do it, I'm sure. I mean, I saw all those romance novels overflowing your bookshelf. Some of those guys were *naked*. I'm sure it's done to sell those books to women, right?"

He suddenly felt like a louse. Here her father was in ICU, and he was having this discussion about boobs and booty. His lust was driving the conversation, clouding his better judgment. It wasn't fair to her. It wasn't even fair to himself. He wasn't acting like a real man. He was acting like a wolf—and everything he didn't respect. He was disgusted with himself.

He stepped away.

"I'm sorry, Brandy. This isn't right. I brought you here so you could get a good night's sleep, to help you rest." He chanced stepping back to her until he could feel the heat of her body again. "Let's just keep things simple and do that, okay? Let's forget about all this crap. I'm beat, and I'll bet you are, too. Can we call a truce and just sleep? I'll even keep my clothes on if you like."

He could feel her soften as she bridged the gap between them, all those lovely curves fitting so nicely, making him come alive. She placed her palms on his chest.

"It was my fault, Tucker. But I think you have a good idea there. Why don't we just go to bed?"

"You're on. No objections here," he lied. He tried to keep his grin from looking too lecherous. He took her hand and gently pulled her to the bedroom. He pretended he didn't notice the posters of well-oiled ladies on motorcycles, stark naked, or how she was staring at them with interest. She approached the poster with the row of ten perfect asses. He heard her inhale and hoped she wasn't going to object. If she did, he was going to rip all of them off the wall and toss everything from his balcony to the pool level below.

But what she did next surprised him. She removed her clothes, giving him one of those looks that made him nervous. It was the thing that scared him most about women. He had no way of knowing what was really going on inside her mind. While she stood in her bra and panties, she undid the center clasp and allowed the magnificence of her breasts to shine in the moonlight, beckoning to him. He was holding his breath, mesmerized.

"I like your idea. Let's just sleep." She pulled back the sheets and slid her naked body under them, invading his man bed, defiling his private sanctuary that would forever after smell like her and bring back memories of what it was like to have her there lying next to him.

He hurried to discard his pants and shirt and then his red, white and blue boxers, turning to sit on the edge so she wouldn't see the enormous hard-on he had for her. She snuggled close, wrapping her arms around his upper torso and squeezing her lovely upper chest against him. She moved her head just enough so her lips touched his ear when she said, "And then maybe tomorrow morning you can fuck my brains out."

Tucker knew he was hopelessly flawed. But he also knew he was utterly hooked on this woman. And he'd only known her for less than twenty-four hours. This had never happened to him before. If he wasn't careful, he'd be taking her to dress fittings and window shopping jewelry shops.

It would be the end of his life as he knew it.

And he'd love every minute of it.

CHAPTER 8

A S THE DAYS and weeks flew by, Brandy's father recovered with only a slight amount of memory loss. He still had headaches that drove him to bed from time to time. He was able to identify his attacker as Jorge, his former employee. Although both the Sheriff and the San Diego PD searched, when they couldn't find him and he stopped reporting for meetings he was required to attend, it was assumed he had fled to Mexico. With his prior record, when he was apprehended, he'd be going away for a long time, since the assault caused injury that necessitated a hospital stay, and drew blood.

Brandy and Tucker spent time with Dorie and Brawley when they returned from their honeymoon in Hawaii. She also worked longer hours at the grocery, and assisted her father in hiring two more experienced clerks. She hired a professional organizer to work with her dad to get the office looking more like an office than a storage unit.

But Brandy knew she'd have to get another good job like she had with the ad agency. The rents in San Diego weren't cheap, and with Tucker staying over at her cottage so much of the time, she wanted to get someplace more private and not under her father's watchful eye. But she was in no hurry. She allowed her relationship with Tucker to take it's own path. The longer she was around him, the less of a difference their fifteen-year age spread made.

But today was going to be an important test of their relationship. Tucker had worked on her non-stop until she finally relented. She was going to allow him to take her tandem skydiving. Although she'd visited the glider port and watched him jump and land safely a dozen times, it did nothing to remove her fear.

"You just have to ignore it. Just like you did when you learned to ride your first bike," he'd told her.

"But I wasn't going to fall thirteen thousand feet if I had a mishap on the bike." She couldn't imagine she would enjoy falling through the sky, even with Tucker securely strapped to her back.

"Trust me, it doesn't feel like you're falling. It feels like there's a blast of wind coming straight from the earth, holding you up so you can fly. It really does feel that way, Brandy. You'll see."

The old converted bomber with the door removed loaded everyone and their buddies up after some ground instruction. Brandy and Tucker were to be in the middle of the jump, since it was her first one. Several SEALs and former Teammates of Tucker's jumped solo, doing cartwheels and in-air formations. At last it was their turn. She stood at the edge of the door, barely able to see cars moving below. Houses looked no bigger than her pinkie fingernail. The air that blew back through the jump door was freezing cold.

She wasn't sure when she was supposed to jump, and worried she'd catch her foot or shoelace on the flange at the opening.

"When do we—" she began to shout, until she felt Tucker's weight behind her and effortlessly they were out of the plane and freefalling. As her heart rate began to return to normal, she realized he was right. It didn't feel like she was falling at all. It felt like the earth was slowly moving to reach out and touch her, but very, very slowly. He tapped her arms, signaling her to make a human "W" as she extended them out to the sides and spread her feet.

He kissed the top of her head and shouted, "Close your mouth.

I'm getting slimed."

Her wonderment and awe had caused her to forget that little part of the training. "Sorry," she shouted back at the top of her lungs.

Tucker handed her the cord to the chute and together they pulled it, which yanked her straight up several hundred feet, or so it seemed. As the glider extended, Tucker steered them around in circles, even driving them through wispy clouds, soaring up and then doing high-banked turns in mid air. As she came closer and closer to the earth, the air began to warm.

He pointed out the border. "That's Mexico right over there." He also pointed out several other landmarks. The San Diego Bay appeared like it was a shallow bowl of silver pebbles as it glistened in the morning sun. She took his hand and kissed his palm.

"Thank you," she said to him in the quiet. It felt like the ride went on for an hour, that they would be suspended all day, but finally the ground began to loom large. She threw her legs out in front of her as they landed on Tucker's, collapsed and rolled together in the long grass, entangled in the chute.

Looking up to the sky, it appeared twice as big as before, and twice as blue. A gentle breeze rearranged her hair when her cap fell to the side. Tucker's face and beard was pressed to her cheek. "I knew you could do it," he whispered. But even that whisper had the deep raspy tones that made her whole body vibrate.

"Amazing," was all she could think to say in return, as she continued searching the blue spans above her. "It wasn't anything at all what I imagined."

"It's like a lot of things. Scarier to think about than to do. We do thousands of these jumps on the Teams. Twice as high. At midnight when you only have your night vision specs on. You see oceans of glittering lights and hope that they're harmless animals, not the eyeballs of the enemy."

"I could never do that," she answered. "But I can see you doing it. Must have been fun."

Tucker hesitated before he said anything at all, and then she couldn't make out the words. She left him to his private thoughts. She knew he missed the life, and would ask him sometime how he replaced the adrenaline he used to have coursing through his veins. She wondered if being a farmer, or a father or husband would ever be really enough.

"Come on, we gotta get up before we get overrun with the newbies." He pulled her up by the straps, unhooked her from him and from the chute and began gathering the colorful fabric, shaking out the blades of grass and small rocks. She noted how happy he looked, with the sun shining behind him, greying hair blowing in the breeze.

She touched his cheek, making him stop, his hand wrapped around her wrist.

"I mean it. Thank you, Tucker." She stood on tiptoes and kissed him until he swept her up and carried her off the field, the lightweight nylon chute tucked under his arm.

Afterwards, they went for a seafood lunch down by the marina. She scanned the million dollar vessels and the people out walking their dogs or jogging on this sunny Sunday. Every day was sunny here.

"See, you wouldn't have this in Oregon," she chided him.

"That's very true. This suits me."

"Me too."

Over their soup he asked her, "Where do you want to go for Valentine's Day?"

That sent a zinger up the back of her legs. She recovered quickly, but couldn't make a decision. "Anywhere. You just name it."

"How about we go up north? Several of the guys and some of the wives are doing a road trip to Sonoma. Can you get a couple of extra days off? It takes a day up and a day down. Gotta stay and do some wine tasting. And I understand you're proficient at grape stomping."

"In February? You know anyone who has grapes this time of year?" She wrinkled up her nose and then winked at him.

"I love that picture with you and Dorie."

"Ah, the good old days, when I thought I had a job." She allowed her voice to wander off.

"You want me to move in? I could help with the rent."

Brandy's pulse quickened as her stomach turned. "I was thinking I'd move someplace else." She drank her water and didn't look at him for a couple long seconds, not sure she understood how he'd take it. "And no, your apartment is completely out of the question."

"Why would you ever want to move? Your place is perfect."

"And it's right behind my father's house."

"So? You don't think he understands what we do all night long, Brandy? Come on. He knows his little girl is all grown up, with grown up appetites. Besides, I think he'd be relieved you had someone to watch over you when he wasn't there to protect you himself. Give him a break. Let him relax. I'll do the heavy lifting for awhile."

The "for awhile" stuck in her chest. But, she had it coming. The conversation had come to the edge of their limit on what was safe to discuss. They never talked about long-term futures. It was way too soon.

"I think dad likes having me around, but it's hard to make ends meet with what he pays me. It's like my life's on hold each week I stay there."

Tucker was quiet, and then he spoke down to the tabletop. "Why not look at it like you don't have to decide right now. If you stay there you'll probably make him happy. He gets to see more of you than most fathers get. You're not pressured to go knock yourself out trying to swim upstream with all the other people clamoring for a fat paycheck."

She knew there was more he wanted to say, but was finding the choice of words difficult. She reached out and took one of his hands. "And I'm hoping you wouldn't mind, right?"

His brown eyes saw everything about her. He saw her insides, how her heart was beating, saw all her uncertainty. Saw how grateful she was that they'd met.

"That would be an understatement." His thumb caressed her knuckles and she thought she saw traces of a blush. "Can I ask you a question?" he asked.

"Shoot." She inhaled deeply and braced for something momentous.

"If we did decide to move in together, could I keep just one of my posters?"

CHAPTER 9

T UCKER HAD SCHEDULED a fishing trip to Baja for early March, but that wasn't going to change his plans to take the road trip to Sonoma County. As they were preparing, he received an enormous rent increase, so Brandy presented him with a key to her cottage.

"You sure?" He was thrilled, but surprised.

"Nope. But I think it's time and I did ask Dad. You were right, he said he was relieved."

"Just human nature."

"So have you decided which poster will come with you?" He loved the way she teased him.

"I'm leaving them *all* behind. Why have an imitation when I've got the real thing?"

He'd been doing extra workouts with several new boys graduating in June, looking to enlist after the summer. His back and knees were bothering him somewhat, so he decided he'd take his time moving his stuff, do it gradually so he didn't send himself over the edge. For the first time in his life, he was feeling his age. He could still bulk up, and work all the machines at Gunny's even better than when he was on the Teams, but his agility and speed was lacking. He was stiff in the mornings and sometimes woke up with leg cramps.

But when Team 3 got orders to do a temporary deployment back to Baja, everything changed. The Team Guys were to work on the sex trafficking ring they had slowed, but now had flared up again. The fishing trip was still on, but Tucker was going as the real civilian, and it would be no picnic for the active duty SEALs. He'd gotten special permission after initially having his participation rejected. He was excited to be of service, even if it was logistics support, to the men he'd previously served with.

Brandy wasn't pleased.

"I think the Navy is using you as bait, Tucker. I mean, you have to pay for your part of the trip, but you don't really get to do whatever you want to. You have to hang with them. They should at least pay for your way down and back and the cost of the rental when you're there."

"I'm actually happy about spending more time with them than I would if it was a real vacation. We usually can only get two or three days, like our Sonoma trip."

But she didn't understand Tucker would have paid anything he could afford just to be embedded deeper within the community. He knew it was a hard thing to explain, so he didn't try.

He was nearly settled with the move, just ahead of their road trip. He had so little furniture, only the closet revealed the secret of his residency. Brandy got rid of her bed. He got rid of the old couch. Everything else he left behind for a young recruit who was beginning his first workup in BUD/S—someone who also appreciated his stash of magazines and posters.

He offered to rototill the back lot for Mr. Cook as a thank you for letting him share the cottage with Brandy. He even offered to pay a little more in rent, but Cook wouldn't have any of that.

Tucker fixed the clutch wires on the "mangler", as he called the tiller, switched out the gasoline after installing a new gas tank and filter. The machine purred like a kitten. Afterwards, the sandy light brown soil looked like chocolate sugar. He imagined Cook would have a field day while they were gone, planting all his early spring seeds.

At last, they took off for Northern California, driving in one long caravan of ten vehicles. Their destination was Frog Haven Vineyards, where several of the SEALs had invested some of their re-up bonuses. Brawley told him it was run by the infamous *Pirate*, who had also been a member of Kyle's squad. Tucker had never met the man.

But he'd also been on earlier road trips when he was active and knew all about Nick Dunn's winery in Santa Rosa, which was on the way. His sister had left the property to Nick. He and Devon converted the nearly bankrupt nursery site into a world-class wedding center, lavender farm and winery. Tucker had been part of several work parties in past years, but had never seen the final result, and knew Brandy would love it.

After only two stops along the way and nearly ten hours later, they arrived in Sonoma County, not stopping until they got all the way up to Healdsburg and the famous Dry Creek Valley. Traveling the winding country two-lane freeway through the valley floor, they found it covered in blooming bright yellow mustard flowers between rows of blackened and gnarled old grapevines. Vineyard workers were cutting back last year's growth to make way for trellising new ones. The air was lightly scented by the smoldering piles of clippings and farm debris all along the way.

"I can't believe I've missed this area," Brandy remarked. "Never thought I'd find anything prettier than Coronado, but this comes pretty close."

"People come here from all over the world just to drive around, eat incredible food and taste great wines. Barrel tasting is really big in the early fall."

"Sounds like Heaven," she answered back.

"These guys have it good. Zak's nickname is the pirate. He got injured on his first deployment, shot in the eye and is real lucky to be alive."

"I'd say. But except for the eye, he was okay?"

"Yes ma'am."

"Were you close?"

"He came on board after I'd gone, so I never got to meet him. But after the injury, he wanted to come back. He worked like a dog and qualified Expert with his other eye, and went through most of the BUD/S training again. You don't find many guys who could do that."

"So he went back?"

"Well, Kyle wanted him back, I was told, but in the end, the Navy thought better of it and asked him to scratch. He met a local Realtor and they found this property and bought it, along with a whole bunch of Team Guys and their relatives. Now they're making beer, along with the wine. I hear it's real tasty."

"Zak sounds like one tough dude."

The caravan slowed down, the first car turning up a crushed granite drive, quickly disappearing from view. As Tucker began his approach up the driveway, he drove past a handful of mailboxes, and pointed out the winery sign.

"Frog Haven. That's it. Got the Bone Frog logo and everything, not that the average tourist would know. You won't see a Trident anywhere."

They drove past more vineyard workers doing pruning and cleanup. A herd of small goats was grazing between several rows, hedged in by portable fencing.

"Am I seeing this correctly? Goats?" asked Brandy.

"They keep the grass down, leaving behind nutrients. A lot of the wineries in the valley are doing the same. Pretty smart. Rent-A-Goat." Tucker could see she was amused.

"No way. Really?" she asked.

"I don't lie. This herd is special. They make artisan cheeses the owner sells for big bucks. Your dad might even carry some in his store."

Once they approached the top of the swale, the jockeying for parking space began, with a couple of the big trucks nearly colliding. One by one everyone poured out, stretching and adjusting themselves after the long ride. In front of them was a quaint farmhouse with a large covered porch surrounding three quarters of the sides. It had been restored to perfect condition. An attractive woman in a smock apron, with two children hugging her legs stood at the entrance. Leaning against one of the porch posts next to her was a handsome man dressed in black, sporting an eye patch over one side. It had to be Zak. Tucker was looking forward to meeting him, finally.

Brandy shuffled over to Brawley and Dorie, striking up a conversation. Kyle's wife, Christy, ran to the porch and gave Zak's lady a big hug. A couple of the other wives did the same. Zak and Amy's two kids scattered into the vineyard to go play with a group of workers kids.

Tucker took Brandy's hand and they joined the small crowd that had gathered in front of the house, just as if Zak was going to make a speech to all of them.

Instead of Zak giving the speech, it was his wife.

"Welcome to Frog Haven. I'm Amy and this is my husband, Zak. I guess the kids are around here somewhere, so be careful pulling in or backing out of the driveway, *please!*"

The group chuckled.

"We're so excited to have you with us for a couple or three nights. We can sort all that out later. I don't think Zak has been able to sleep for a week, he's been so looking forward to your visit."

"Thanks you two," directed Kyle, taking charge. "Let's give

them a big round of applause for making this one of the more frugal vacations we've been able to take."

The group clapped and several whistled or cheered.

Amy thanked them with a big smile. "Now, we have two unoccupied bedrooms here in the main house, but the bunkhouse sleeps twenty-four. No queen or king beds, so you'll have to put your singles together and negotiate the crack down the middle."

"Notice she said two beds together? No threesomes!" yelled Kyle.

After the laughter died down, Amy continued. "I'll let you sort all that out on your own. We eat in an hour, family style out back on the other side. I've got some heaters but there's no way I can feed you all in my little dining room, so wear your sweatshirts and jackets. If it's too cold for you, tomorrow we can arrange for supper to be served in the bunkhouse."

"Dinner attire?" T.J. Talbot asked her.

"Something you wouldn't mind getting stained with tomato sauce. We're going Italian all the way."

A cheer broke out, and as the crowd dispersed, Zak called them all back.

"Almost forgot. Short showers or only the first five of you will get one. My personal favorite is sharing, two-by-two. We have a nice hot tub you can take your time and soak in after dinner, if you like." Zak checked his cell phone. "On my mark….Go!"

The group took on the atmosphere of a church camp. The men were in sync because they were used to working together that way without anyone having to bark instructions. Tucker noticed several of the newer wives and girlfriends were completely confused, and Christy was a big help with some timely advice, discretely placed here and there.

Tucker and Brandy selected a dark corner in the bunkhouse. Wire cables worked like stringers, attached with hooks to the walls in both directions so old sheets could slide into place, giving each couple some privacy like in a hospital room. Tucker moved their two mattresses together and then re-made the bedspread to stretch over both sides. He'd been told to bring some comforters, so he retrieved them from the truck, and added them as well.

At the opposite wall, there was an old Franklin pot-bellied stove and a generous pile of wood stacked halfway to the ceiling. Several rocking chairs made a semicircle around the stove for evening chats. Against one wall was a tiny kitchen with a sink, a refrigerator, a picnic table that could seat eight and a microwave toaster oven.

But the highlight of the entire bunkhouse was the bathroom, containing a two-stall unisex toilet and one shower. Tucker was looking forward to the hot tub after dinner to work out the kinks in his neck and shoulder. He doubted he could even fit in the shower, let alone share it with Brandy.

They washed up quickly and then joined the whole group outside on Zak and Amy's patio. Zak placed both their kids at the head of the table on a loveseat with pillows so they could see everyone. They were bundled for the ski slopes, wearing matching bunny hats.

At this time of year, the vines were bare, so the trellis they sat under left gaping holes where Tucker could see the stars. Some of the magic rubbed off when it turned very cold, with a slight breeze. He excused himself and grabbed their comforter from the bunkhouse and wrapped the two of them together while they devoured their steaming hot lasagna, green salad and a little too much red wine. With the slight buzz relaxing him, soon even the nippy night air stopped bothering him. He'd forgotten how different Northern California was from San Diego, where no matter what time of year, the temperature never fluctuated more than ten degrees.

Brandy was laughing at Christy's story of how she met Kyle,

when she attempted to hold the wrong house open and found him naked and asleep—stretched out on the master bed.

Although the ladies were last to bond as a unit, as the wine continued to flow and the stories got louder and more daring, Tucker could tell they were already well on their way to coming together on their own team of sorts. It was important that the sisterhood of the wives and girlfriends stay strong and tight, since they would help hold each other up in case the unthinkable were to happen. Dr. Death stalked them all: men, women and children. And with the world exploding more and more every day, he was making house calls at home, in the good old US of A.

You son of a bitch.

Tucker had only had to hold one of his buddies as the young man's life passed from him. He never wanted to repeat the experience.

By candlelight, he studied the faces of those men he'd served with, and served under. He felt so lucky to have had that opportunity to be a grown up Boy Scout, doing crazy dangerous things, all the while making the world a safer place. He'd been able to push himself to his limits, the adrenaline nearly exploding from the veins in his neck, but as a force for good. Never evil. It was hard to explain to someone who hadn't experienced it for himself. It was probably the heavy wine, but right now he couldn't explain why he'd ever left. There just wasn't another job on the planet as good as being a Team Guy.

Amy put on some music and the ladies rushed to their feet to dance. It was fascinating to watch how women could just be so demonstrative, so ready to just throw their heads back, laugh and toss their cares over their shoulders.

Brawley scooted over next to him, and shared part of the blanket.

"You guys are getting along most excellently, my man. Brandy's a good influence on you."

"Nah. I still got the dirty thoughts, same as ever."

The two men chuckled. Brawley's eyes were sparkling in the candlelight as he watched his new bride dance with Brandy. Christy and several of the others became the girl group backup singers, line dancing in unison to the funky rhythm from an oldies satellite channel.

"We've missed you, Tuck."

"Missed you too," Tucker returned without looking at Brawley. "So you're staying in for another turn?"

"For now. Honestly, I don't know what I'd do if I didn't have this community or these things to do with my friends."

"I hear you." Tucker was trying not to dwell on it. He wanted Brawley to change the subject, but it was awkward sitting next to him, wrapped in the same blanket. He was sensitive about that sort of thing. As a youth, he'd probably spent more time with Brawley than he did his own parents.

"You'll have to hang around more when we get back to San Diego," Brawley said just before he finished his wine. Zak placed another opened bottle in front of the two men.

Tucker read the label out loud. "*Frog Haven Winery. A little piece of Heaven.* That's about how I'd describe it up here." He was hoping the change in focus would get the discussion off the Teams.

"First time I've seen it all built out. When they first bought it, I thought they were nuts." Brawley scanned the patio, smiling at the girls. "Now look at it. Piece of Heaven, indeed."

"Thought you invested like Kyle and Coop and everyone else," remarked Tucker.

"Nope. I bought a house with my re-enlistment bonus instead. Maybe the next time."

"So you're going career, like your dad?"

"I'm thinking PA school, or maybe med school, if I can get some tutoring."

"Geez, Brawley. You won't have any time if you do that. And you'll owe them another ten years at least."

"Well, it's a pipe dream." Brawley casually glanced at the ladies again. "They're getting smashed."

Tucker found this funny. "I think living here and doing this would be a whole lot easier. And no schooling or the cost of it."

"We'll see. First, I have to get in."

"By then, you'll have chipmunks running all over the place," Tucker reminded him. "Bills, gymnastics lessons and soccer practice. You ever spend any time with Kyle and his brood, or Coop? We can hardly get them to come out with us to the Scupper."

Tucker was convinced Brawley had forgotten his earlier remark, until his friend cruelly drove the point home again.

"Hell, Tuck. What's stopping you? I mean Kyle says you're paying for a vacation chaperoning the Team all over Baja next month. Some vacation. Why don't you just re-up? Come back to us."

"Because I'm thirty nine, Brawley."

"So am I, nearly."

"But I've been doing other things. I'm just not sure I could get through BUD/S again."

"They'd have to give you a pass on that," Brawley barked.

"Nope. I already checked."

The two of them sat in the few seconds of quiet while the ladies searched for another station. In San Diego, there would be crickets on a night like this, even in February. Tucker had heard an owl earlier, but no crickets.

Brawley turned, speaking to the side of his face. "Well, you just confirmed what I've been thinking for the better part of five years now. Don't deny it, Tucker. You want back in."

He wasn't going to make a big objection to Brawley's remarks because that would make him look guilty as charged. But his friend had nailed him fair and square. That little confidential talk with Collins about whether or not the Navy would consider a re-entry for him was kept under wraps. But he had to go open his big mouth tonight and tell Brawley he'd checked. He wondered if he'd done it on purpose.

Wouldn't that be something if I could do it?

Brawley stood up and positioned the entire blanket around Tucker's shoulders and gave him a gentle pat on the back. "I think I'm going to go out there and rescue Dorie before someone gets hurt."

Tucker nodded. "Think I'll do the same," and stood to join him.

Brawley grinned like he'd been told a dirty joke.

"What's so funny?" he asked the newlywed.

"I think everyone's gonna get laid tonight."

CHAPTER 10

"WE SHOULD HAVE taken a week off, Tucker. I had no idea there was so much I wanted to see." Brandy was folding her clothes when Tucker made his way into their sheeted cubicle. He'd been stacking wood and making sure the fire was fully stoked so they didn't have to wake up in the morning to a cold building.

"Next time. I promise." He pulled her to him, fingering the red lace bra she'd bought for the trip. "Where on earth did you get this dangerous device?"

"You like it?"

"Turn around. Let me think about that for a couple of minutes."

She loved taking direction from him. She peered over her shoulder. "Like this?"

"Keep going."

Brandy slowly kept moving until she was facing him again. "Should I take my bra and panties off now?"

"I can't make up my mind."

His smile was bringing on a wave of hot, wet lust she could smell.

"Is it my imagination, or are these lovely lace things even more sexy looking when they're so—so—ample?" He darted a worried look her way. "Did I just make a huge mistake?" he said as he winced. He bit his lower lip and, in spite of his enormous size and white beard, looked like a little boy about to be punished.

"I used to let things like that bother me." She slowly slid her panties down her thighs. "But—"

"Don't touch that!" he whispered.

Brandy had her hand on the front clasp of her bra, ready to peel it away and stand before him naked. Instead, she splayed her fingers over the satin and eyelet lace, squeezed her flesh and took two little steps until their bodies touched.

"How is it that I'm always the one who's naked first?" she asked, her lips just barely touching his. She could hear his heart pounding in tandem to hers and took a gentle moan from him as they kissed.

"I guess it's because I always like to watch, and I forget myself," he whispered.

"I think it's healthy to forget yourself now and then, don't you?" They kissed again, but deeper. "You want me to leave it on or take it off?"

"I think you should leave it on for now. I'll get to it in about an hour. I have other things I want you to do first. Is that okay with you, Brandy?"

She watched him remove his jeans and underwear, his erection bouncing with anticipation. She held him between her palms like she was praying.

"It's perfect."

IT WAS PAST midnight when she awoke, grateful Tucker held her tight because the room was freezing. Someone in one of the other spaces was snoring up a storm and would have rattled the windows if there were any.

Her heart was still racing from their urgent lovemaking. He'd played her body like an instrument, hard, and incredibly deep, expressed both in body language as well as their frantic whispers. It had been so intense, at one point she broke down in tears and Tucker thought he'd hurt her somehow.

But in a way he had. She was forever altered as if she was a willing participant in her own destruction.

It was hard not to notice a man as tall and strong as he was. But now that she knew him better, had kissed every inch of his body and answered his need with her own, she understood that everything he did he was the master of, except sometimes finding words. But he loved with abandon, never holding back, pushing her to the edge, and then just a little further, until she'd collapse in his arms. The coiled, cloud-of-butterflies-feeling in her belly were physical manifestations of what she knew to be true in her heart. She was falling in love, as she never had before. She also knew this came with risks, since there would be no getting over that kind of intense love. In fact, it was delicious and painful at the same time, even with the absence of a breakup on the horizon.

She tried not to think about where it all was going. She'd been included in the community of brothers, felt herself blend in with the ladies who were lucky enough to also be loved by one of these warriors who turned their worlds upside down. Brandy just took the waves of emotion and passion as they engulfed her and tried not to focus on what it all meant. She knew that was a rabbit hole.

It hardly seemed possible they'd known each other for such a short period of time. He'd been the missing piece she didn't even know she'd been missing. If she ever had to be without him, life would never be the same.

She thought about Amy and Zak, who was nearly killed on his first deployment. Shannon had lost her first husband, T.J.'s best friend. She'd also heard stories about the women who couldn't handle the lifestyle, the intensity of their play and their hearts. Still, it was a family, a community of brothers and the women they loved.

But one thing bothered her. Tucker had been talking with Kyle and Brawley, and she knew he missed being a SEAL. What would she do if he decided she wasn't the right one? What if he tried to re-join his team and failed? How could she ever make up for that incredible loss he would feel.

Or, what if she never could keep him happy enough to stay? Could she meet him halfway, match his energy, and carefully tend to him if he ever fell apart? She wasn't sure she was cut out for it, any of it.

Try to sleep. You have to rest. You'll drive yourself crazy with all these thoughts.

"Everything okay, Brandy?" His words startled her.

"I'm sorry, did I wake you?"

He sifted his fingers through her hair. "Yes."

"I can't sleep."

"That happens to me sometimes too when I drink too much. It's like I'm over-drunk."

She lay on her back and enjoyed the feel of his large callused hand caressing her breast. The plank beams on the ceiling were barely visible in the reflection of moonlight. Brandy waited, trying to notice some sign her eyelids were heavy and her mind was quieting, but that sign never came. She inhaled and tried to sigh very carefully so he wouldn't detect her worry. But even that was unsuccessful.

"Talk to me, Brandy."

"I don't want to do it here."

"Hot tub?"

They threw on some clothes and took their towels, discovering that they were able to be alone under the stars. The warm water helped Brandy put her thoughts into words.

She wrapped her legs around his waist and floated with her arms about his neck. The white in his hair and beard made him appear to glow in the dark.

"Is it that bad?" he teased.

"What?"

"Whatever it is you don't want to tell me."

"No, Tucker." She paused and thought carefully before she spoke. "Let me ask you a question. Does the speed of all this scare you just a little?"

"You mean does it fall somewhere between skydiving at midnight and getting my ass shot off by a sniper? That what you mean by scared?"

Now she felt ridiculous. "I got the impression you weren't the kind of guy who just jumped into relationships."

"Oh. Okay. So now we're talking *relationships*. Is that what this is?"

She would have been worried but saw the goofy grin on his face. "Watch it. Don't you make fun of me. I don't like that, as you know."

"Well, you're right about me. I don't do this. I've never done this."

She didn't want to look at him in the eyes, thinking he might begin to get uncomfortable. The last thing she wanted to do was put him on the spot. But she wanted to know where she stood. And maybe that was the right way to put it.

"Tucker."

"Yes ma'am."

"Would you be able to give me some indication of where all this is leading? Like, do I fit into your life anywhere other than in your bed?"

He tilted his head and stared back at her without smiling, and her heart fell to the bottom of the hot tub.

"First, if you'd have asked me that about ten years ago, I'd be gone by now. Maybe even five years ago. But, believe it or not, I've mellowed. When I went to the wedding on New Years Eve, *my* goal, and remember I told you I didn't want to tell you what it was?"

"I remember."

"My goal was to keep my hands to myself and to not rank or otherwise check out the ladies at the reception."

"Okay. And how did that work out for you?"

"I didn't even come close to achieving my goal. I sat there in the church, and I watched as you walked down the aisle, and into my life."

Brandy was stunned. It wasn't what she'd expected at all.

"I've been watching you when you were sleeping, talking to other people and didn't know I was looking. I watch you from across the room and out of the sides of my eyes when we go places. And I've come to the conclusion that I don't ever want to spend a day when you are not a part of my life."

She scrambled to her feet, separated herself from him and stood with her back pressed against the other side of the hot tub. Her heart felt like it was going to jump right out of her chest and go running down between the vines.

Tucker just waited. And then that grin overtook his face. "Oh my God. You're scared." He approached quietly, relentlessly, and without hesitation gently took her head in his hands and kissed her. "It's just like skydiving, sweetheart," he said between kisses. "You put your arms out to the sides, and fly. And I'll be strapped right there behind you. I will never let you fall. And I'll never stop loving you."

Thank you for reading this prequel novella New Years SEAL Dream. The full-length novel, **SEALed At The Altar** *is out now! You can order it by clicking* **here.**

But just for fun, here are some answers to some of your questions in advance.

Does Tucker decide to re-join SEAL Team 3? Yes.

Does he make it? I'm not telling! You're going to have to read it to find out.

Will they be together? The answer to that is a resounding yes.

He will never let her fall. And yes, they'll never stop loving each other.

I hope you will continue the journey of Tucker and Brandy. There's going to be a beautiful wedding in the story.

In wine country.

Happy New Year, dear reader!

Sharon Hamilton
Santa Rosa, California
January, 2018

SEALED AT THE ALTAR

Bone Frog Brotherhood Book 2

SHARON HAMILTON

CHAPTER 1

TUCKER THOUGHT ABOUT his hot tub lovemaking session with Brandy the night before. It sprang from the long kiss he'd given her after he told her to just lean back, put her arms out to the sides, and fly away with him to who knew where? He'd told her to just trust him, that he'd be right there behind her, just as they'd been the day before skydiving. He'd professed his love for her and promised to take care of her.

But he'd stopped short of asking her to marry him. That was what was giving him problems today as they drove to the winery picnic the whole group of SEALs and their wives and girlfriends were attending in Wine Country. Last night under the stars he'd taken her body as they'd floated in the hot tub, thrusting as if he rammed her hard enough, he'd stick there forever. He wanted to dig deep and never leave, and she accepted all of him, begging for more as he pleasured her every way he could think of. He kissed away all her tears as she released so beautifully in soft moans, shuddering and spurring him on, stroking her insides until his full release.

He'd even carried her wet nude body back through the patio and back into the barn where their cubicle was carved out with sheets hanging over stringer wires. He laid her back on the bed and worshiped her, nuzzling all the softness of her curvy hips and wonderful breasts. Her white flesh and droplets of water shone in the moonlight as his arms covered hers and clutched her fingers in his. Even as his kisses lowered to her belly he knew she was fast asleep, and he'd put her there in the land of Nod.

Was she dreaming of him?

He hadn't slept, even after trying to sync with her breathing, but it was no use. He was not going to be able to sleep until whatever was needling him worked its way out, like an old splinter.

Morning came softly and he watched her sleepy body awaken to the sounds of birds outside. Her eyes were full of wonder as she lay next to him and stared at the wooden ceiling, like he had done all during the night.

They'd spoken very little this morning. The two of them showered together and she teased him but didn't demand anything. Their fondling and tickling and kissing was always a pleasant start of the daily routine, most of the time leading to another sexual encounter. But today, it was enough that they couldn't keep their hands off each other, as if the words spoken so sparsely last night under the night sky was enough to last them a month.

Maybe that was it.

"You're so quiet this morning, Tucker. What has you so preoccupied?"

He smiled to cover up his surprise that he'd failed to mask his pensive mood. He glanced to his right and she wasn't having any of it. He could lie, of course. But he wasn't going to. He just wanted to remain silent until he figured out what was bothering him.

"I'm just happy, Brandy. Really happy." It was the truth. But would it work?

She reached into his lap and felt his semi-hardness, and stroked him, coaxing him to lose himself between her fingers. He wanted to unbutton his pants but was hoping she'd do it. He did need release.

She continued to stroke up and down as he spread his knees

further and he presented to her warm palm he could feel even through the fabric of his pants.

"This what you're thinking about?" She asked. "We could always take a detour…"

He had a flash of clarity. He saw her in a wedding dress, and then he saw her belly grow large with a child. He was definitely having dangerous thoughts. Sex had always been just that: sex. With Brandy, he'd wanted to fill her, make her have his baby.

This scared the pants off him. While that would solve one problem, it left another one glaring: the more they made love the more he wanted her. This had never happened before. Even Shayla, his first wife, when they were young and fresh and fucking like rabbits all the time, even then he didn't feel like this. He was burying himself to make roots, not to get himself off.

His hands were sweaty. His forehead too. His deep breathing was mistaken for arousal, causing Brandy to deftly slip her fingers inside his waistband and unfasten him. She seared him with a sultry smile just before she went down on him. He nearly went off the road, quickly checking his rear view mirror.

Her tongue curled around him. With one hand on the steering wheel, he placed his other palm at the back of her head buried in his lap, and pressed her onto him. She moaned as she sucked and kissed him to oblivion.

The sunshine was extremely bright outside as they continued down the winding two-lane country highway. It got brighter the more she worked on him—the closer he got to climax. And, bless her soul, just as he began to spill, she placed him between her enormous breasts and squeezed.

Brandy's tee shirts were always too small for her, and the look of the cotton shoved up under her chin, her double large chest all ripe and firm, was a sight he'd never tire of looking at. A few seconds later and that tee shirt was desperately needed.

He laced his fingers through her hair. "God, Brandy, I've died and gone straight to Heaven."

She rose to her knees, leaned over him, removed the wet shirt, and grabbed another one from her bag in the second seat. Pulling it tight over her breasts, her nipples puckered under the new pink fabric, bulging and knotted.

"You're going to distract everyone at the picnic, sweetheart. No bra?"

She leaned back on the seat and tickled her nipples outside the cotton shirt. "No bra," she said, with her eyes the size of a small child's. "Will that make you jealous?"

"No, honey. I'm a man of action. I don't dwell in those places of self-doubt and pity. I'll beg you to ride my cock hard until you behave."

She grinned, and then stared out the windshield. "I'm happy too, Tucker. Really happy. I wish I hadn't been so afraid of this."

He nodded, understanding he'd been her nearly first sexual partner, though he would have been easily fooled to think otherwise. She was preening, reapplying her lipstick that had been smeared all over his organ, which he now stowed back into his pants with one hand.

That word again came up: *this.* Just what *was* this? Should he tell her about the fantasies he'd been having? Or, should he not distract from her delicious mood, exploring the newfound feeling of love and lust all wrapped up in one velvet package? He'd experienced the cravings, but not these cravings that only lead to that stronger desire to have her again after every encounter.

Tucker knew he'd been intense as a SEAL, and perhaps that's why Shayla left him for the other Team Guy. He'd been so focused on his career, on the brotherhood of men he was absolutely digging serving with, the danger and excitement of being a man's man doing things most people couldn't even comprehend. Now that he was out, perhaps that's why he and Brandy had made the instant hook-up. He willingly let her be needy with him because he needed to give it all back. With Shayla, their carefree spirit gave way to routine and eventually boredom, where they were just going through the motions. They were pretending to be a couple long after she'd mentally and even physically moved on.

It was fucked up, and after the breakup it caused him to force a change of scenery, but he never felt he lost something he needed.

He *needed* Brandy.

That's what made all this talk between them last night and internal thought this afternoon so dangerous. Brandy was *very* dangerous. She was lethal. And still he allowed his wrists to be bound by those golden ropes, his chest bleeding from the pain in his heart. He needed her so much he might die over it.

He saw the three Hummers and trucks pull up to the large steep-roof buildings of the winery created from a hop-drying kiln. Kyle and Cooper directed traffic and that's when it hit him. He needed them too. He missed the contact he used to have with the Team Guys all weekend between deployments. Even when he knew Shayla was staying out late, making naked calls to the Team Guy who was on deployment, he still needed his buddies. It's where he wanted to be most of all.

He barely had time to think about it as he was directed to park. But, would the same thing happen to them if he got accepted back on a SEAL Team? Would Brandy, now erupting with womanly wiles and enough pheromones to sink a battleship, find someone else to satisfy her when he was no longer around? Four and six month deployments were common these days, Kyle had warned. Would she wait for him? *Could* she wait for him?

Or, was that too much to ask?

Because he was still deep in thought, Brandy made it out of the truck before he did, and sauntered over to Christy and Dorie. He hoped she didn't notice his lack of attention. Her voluptuous body swayed down the driveway in front of him, her long mahogany hair fluffed up by her fingers as she called out to her best friend. He could watch her all day, and had many nights.

But still, he felt like a heel. That talk show doctor would be wagging her finger at him. He was taking the cookies out of the cookie jar without paying for them. But had that doctor ever found two things she couldn't do without like he had? Was it really fair to judge him so harshly?

At the precipice of an epic change in his life, Tucker wasn't sure which pursuit he should concentrate on first. If he pursued joining a SEAL team, would marriage interfere with his training? And if he made the team, would he be able to be as devoted a husband as she required? Was it fair to Brandy to put her through all this?

He decided to wait on either event until he could see himself having both. Then he'd give the choice to Brandy and pray like hell somehow it all worked out.

Although he knew that was never the way to run a mission, it was going to have to just stay that way for a bit until he could figure things out. Because when he moved, he wanted to be balls to the wall. No excuses. No holding back. Going for it with every ounce of his being. He'd throw his heart out there in the ring too. Mix it up, and hope she'd agree to take him, wounded, more unsure of himself than he ever wanted to admit.

She could love out all the kinks and inconsistencies lodged like pieces of glass inside him, while he was planting roots inside her.

There was a chance this could work. But just a chance.

In either event, it would be worth it.

CHAPTER 2

B RANDY COOK HAD never been to Northern California Wine Country before and was stunned with the beauty surrounding her. Every direction she beheld world-class views of green hills dotted with acres of vineyard cornrows. Yellow mustard flowers and gnarled old growth vines lay before her on the famous Dry Creek Valley floor. She was so overwhelmed, she could hardly speak.

She drifted into a dreamy fantasy of growing vegetables and raising brightly colored flowers, as Amy had been doing at the Frog Haven Winery, where they were staying.

Dad would love this place!

An avid gardener himself, Steven Cook owned an organic fruit stand and general market, catering to health-conscious San Diego tourists out for an afternoon drive near the ocean. She and Tucker lived in a cottage behind Cook's farmhouse, some five miles down the road. Tucker had been helping Mr. Cook prepare the land behind for planting just before they'd left for vacation up north.

Her best friend, Dorie Hanks, slipped quietly next to her as they both approached the tasting room.

"You're upsetting the animals in the zoo, Brandy. I should have warned you." With her pert smile, the new bride showed perfectly aligned white teeth—the kind one needed shades to fully appreciate.

"Excuse me?"

"That tee shirt shows every curve and each little—" She was eyeing Brandy's chest, pointing and trying not to be too obvious.

Brandy noted that her replaced tee was even smaller than the one she'd shown up in. She blushed.

"I didn't even think," she whispered. "I *hate* wearing bras— those contraptions that feel more like some sort of Victorian torture device. I'd much rather have rounded hills than taillight rockets or peaks resembling the Himalayas."

"That's a visual. You're great with words, Brandy." Then she nodded in the direction of a bevy of young men not in their SEAL delegation, all of whom quickly turned away at exactly the same time.

Brandy sighed. "Point taken. Dammit."

"Where is your other shirt?"

"I got it dirty on the ride over." Brandy didn't want to look into Dorie's eyes. "I'll see if they have some sort of wrap I can buy inside the winery store."

"Come with me." Dorie grabbed her hand and led her to Brawley's Hummer. She brought out a multicolored oversized silk scarf. "You have to wear layers up here. This comes in handy." She wrapped it around Brandy's shoulders, tying the front in a knot. "There."

Brandy stared down at the ridiculous colors that didn't match anything she was wearing, including her personality, but she was thankful, just the same.

"Appreciate you looking out for me, Dorie. What would I do without you?"

"Get into trouble," her friend answered, scrunching her nose up. "Probably have more fun than I'm having."

Brandy was surprised at this. "Already? The newlywed glow has come off?"

Her best friend cocked her head from side to side and rolled her eyes. "You know these guys. The chase is better than the catch. They are relentless until they get you nailed." She winked and whispered in Brandy's ear. "I mean that in every sense of the word." She stood back, adjusted the scarf at the hem so it covered Brandy's upper arms evenly. "And then they're off chasing other things."

"No way. Not Brawley!"

Dorie was examining her fingers laced together waist high. When she looked up, Brandy could see the pain in her eyes. The sober realization between the two best friends was left unspoken, as if that would help stamp it out.

Brandy wanted to give Brawley a piece of her mind. She could put pepper in his coffee, laxatives in his morning milkshake. Maybe put itching powder in his jeans and underwear. Place some really stinky cheese in his favorite running shoes. There was so much she could do. He'd been like a brother ever since he'd met Dorie, always so respectful and fun. She'd harbored an enormous crush on him for the past eighteen months while they were dating, and then got engaged. She'd never picked up that he would be a wanderer. *That louse!*

This changed everything. This meant war.

Before she could say anything, Dorie speared her with her baby blue eyes. "Not. A. Word."

Brandy tried to look offended, frowning, but was having difficulty making eye contact.

"I mean it, Brandy. You don't do or say anything. And you never heard any of this from me, either. I'll completely deny it and call you a crazy. Don't say anything to Tucker, either."

"Is Tucker?—"

"Not a word. And no, Tucker's fine."

She was picking up the habit of fisting and unfisting her hands, along with the deep breathing exercises she'd learned from Tucker. It helped keep her calm until she could resign herself to the inevitable. She was going to have to act normal, and play with Brawley, like she didn't know. It was going to be a long day in close proximity with him. And she was dying to have the question and answer session with Tucker that she dared not have. So much to stuff down. It was totally unfair.

The two of them walked side-by-side and, as they often did, they bumped hips. It was the lazy familiarity she'd grown accustomed to being plucky relief to the gorgeous Dorie Hanks. They headed to the entrance to the tasting room, crisply crushing the pink granite rocks underfoot.

Dorie giggled.

"What?" Brandy asked.

"I can't believe how loose you've gotten. Tucker has that affect on women, I'd say."

Brandy considered her statement. Was Tucker a player? If he was Brawley's best friend, then perhaps they got into trouble together. She tried to recall if the two SEALs had been out in the evening alone since their return from Dorie's honeymoon, and she discovered that yes, they had. She didn't like not trusting Tucker, but she couldn't stop the doubt from creeping in. Her wine country bliss was fading.

"Come on, Brandy. Get over it. If I can, you can." Dorie nudged her, almost setting her off balance.

"Sorry." Brandy knew the only thing that would cheer her up would be to do something devious, hurt Brawley in some way. But not get caught—by anyone!

"It will all work out." Her friend sighed. "My father was the same way and I got a lot of practice watching my mother deal with it. After they finally split up, the first time she brought someone over to the family home, he was nearly twenty years younger and cute as a button." Dorie was giggling again. "I never laughed so hard in my life. My dad never quite got over it. Served him right for how he treated my mom all those years."

It wasn't the kind of family dynamic Brandy had any familiarity with. But then, her mother was gone and her father had been totally devoted to her and probably always would be. This type of behavior wasn't going to be what she wanted to get used to. And if that was a red line and ended things, so be it.

So she focused on getting revenge instead. An evil smile crept across her face. "I admire your mother for getting even. That was the only way to take care of it, in my opinion," she said to her beautiful blonde friend.

They slowly made their way into the cool tasting room smelling of fermented grapes. Gentle music echoed throughout the space, hushing the crowd who whispered their wine selections over the hammered copper bar to the two servers behind. The civilized explanation of all the features and characteristics of the wine was hard to hear, due to the echoes and the size of the late morning crowd. People listened. They nodded. They wrote notes on small chits of paper with little red pencils, consulted the luscious brochure laid before them, sipped their wine sample and savored the taste like it was a tiny orgasm.

As she studied the crowd, she found Tucker staring at her. He raised an eyebrow and tapped his collarbone with his fingers. She let him wait, considering what to do, and then allowed her sex-infused fantasy weekend to take charge again. Her right hand slipped under the silk and she pulled it aside, revealing her nipple pattern beneath the cotton shirt.

The effect on Tucker was immediate. He raised both eyebrows, tilted his head back, licked his lips, and then gave her a wink.

She covered her breast with the scarf again and turned to watch the tourists imbibe. Dorie pulled her toward the bar.

"Let's get something to taste. Like a mob scene in here today. Everyone's so polite, we'll never get a chance to drink anything."

Brandy chose to taste the Dry Creek Cabernet instead of starting with white wines the server recommended.

"I hate white wine," she said when the server asked Brandy about it. Dorie followed her lead. The wine was smooth and full-flavored, the aftertaste coating her tongue dangerously. She craved sharp cheese and crusty French bread, or a good steak.

"I like this," said Dorie.

"I do too," she answered. "But darned if it doesn't make me want to chow down a big steak. They say wine enhances your appetite, and for me, it certainly does."

"Makes me horny," added Dorie.

The server was holding another red selection, his eyes wide and his cheeks suddenly pink. Dorie flashed him a smile and the server nearly dropped the bottle.

"Some Pinot?" he asked with difficulty.

"Oh why not?" Dorie held her glass out and accepted the deep burgundy-colored elixir. Brandy followed suit.

Tucker followed behind Brawley as they sliced through the crowd to join the ladies.

"Find something you like?" he asked his bride.

"The Cabernet." She spoke to the server. "Can I have another taste?"

"Of course." The winery employee picked up another glass and poured Dorie a generous amount, then held out two more. "Gentlemen?"

While Brawley reached across the counter to accept his sample, Brandy turned to address Tucker, swilling the beautiful blend to coat the sides of her glass. A few drops spilled over the top and landed at the small of Brawley's back. He arched up quickly, felt the back of his shirt, and then examined his palm.

"You got me there, Brandy. A little less wrist action or we'll all be soaked." And then Brawley inhaled the contents of his glass in one gulp dismissively.

"Why Brawley Hanks. I didn't know you were afraid of a little action."

Dorie stared daggers at her while Tucker frowned. Brandy wished she'd gone with the itching powder or the stinky cheese. But for now, she was satisfied.

She'd have to reassure her best friend that the secret they shared would remain that way.

CHAPTER 3

TUCKER STOPPED TASTING at the third winery they came to, unwilling to sacrifice his clean driving record. But it humored him to see Brandy get smashed. She was going to need some food soon. The picnic had been postponed and finally, at two o'clock, they were ready to stop to eat.

The air was chilly so they decided to eat at the old Healdsburg General Store, an old Pony Express station and roadhouse that were a hundred and fifty years old. Horses in the front were replaced with Mercedes and Bentleys, and today, a herd of Hummers and four-door trucks.

The ladies lined up to use the restroom and Tucker ordered for the two of them and took his place at the long table that could easily seat twenty. The old wooden floors had a slight bounce to them. The noise of dragging chairs over the oak planks reminded him of one of his grammar schools in Oregon growing up.

His mood had lightened, but he still remained focused. Like several others, being the sober driver, he took his job seriously so as to protect the women who were mostly laughing and hanging off their men. He saw Coop grinning at him. The tall Nebraska farm boy didn't drink but that didn't diminish his enjoyment of the day. Libby, his wife, sat beside him, in a pink alcohol flush, fanning herself with a menu.

Kyle Lansdowne appeared on a chair to his left.

"So, I gotta ask you, are you in for the next BUD/S class?"

"I just haven't finished the paperwork. Collins said I can have a shot and he'd do what he could."

"You know you'll spend a few months at Great Lakes first. Same program all over again," the Team 3 LPO said.

"I'm prepared. This time I get to do it in the summer. Last time I froze my ass off," answered Tucker.

As the ladies started filtering back into the store, Kyle shot the important question Tucker knew was coming. "You told Brandy yet?"

"Not exactly."

"What does that mean?"

"I want to do that before I turn in my forms."

"So what you're telling me is that if she objects, you may not continue?"

He looked into the eyes of a Team leader he greatly respected, knowing he had Tucker's welfare at heart. It didn't make the answer any easier.

"No, Kyle. It means that if I turn it in without telling her first, I'll have my butt on the street." He took a gulp of ice water. "I already screwed up one marriage because I didn't handle that right. If she's the one, I got to do this careful."

"If she's the one, she'll stand by something you want to do," said Kyle.

"Roger that for sure." Something tickled his insides. "You know, old married Kyle, you're what, five years younger than I am? And here you're giving me advice?"

"No advice, man. Just asking."

"So let me ask you a question. Do you ever really know what a woman is thinking until you ask her? Even if you ask her, are you really one hundred percent sure you're getting the truth? Be honest with me, Kyle."

Kyle chuckled and nodded. "Got me there, Tucker. Nope, I love my wife with all my heart and I'd lay down mine anytime for her. But, damned if I know what she's thinking every day. I just hope and pray I live up to what she wants. It ain't up to me. The woman chooses. You know that, right? We just gotta hope that they have all the facts to make a good informed decision."

Tucker laughed. "That's what I keep telling myself every night in bed. Helping her make an informed decision."

They both chuckled again. "That's one way of putting it. But time's running out. I think you'd make a helluva Team Guy, and I want you with us when we next go over."

"Thanks, Kyle."

"And one other thing. If you're going to Great Lakes, you can't come with us to Mexico. That BUD/S class reports in two weeks, but I suppose you already know that."

"Indeed I do," Tucker said, finishing off his water. "Collins told me they've got one of my trainees going with you guys in my place. But I don't get a refund on the fishing trip I already paid for. That sucks. But I hear you, and I'm getting to it." He grabbed Brandy's water and crunched down some of her ice as he gazed at Brandy's lovely body headed right for him.

"Good." Kyle patted him on the back and slid down a couple of chairs to make way for some of the women, including Christy, to join the group.

IT WAS CHILLY back at Frog Haven. Tucker gave Brandy one of his heavier jackets, took her hand and asked her to come for a walk with him between the rows of vines just beginning to bud. At first her expression was one of surprise. But her nervous banter told him she was afraid of something. She was taking deep breaths, doing rhythmic breathing and even shivering slightly.

"You cold, Sweetheart?"

"A little, I guess. I'm hoping we can turn in early. Think I had a little too much today."

"Ah, but it was a thing of beauty to watch you and all the other ladies." He'd enjoyed saving her from falling or holding her close so she could walk steady. He also kept her separated from Dorie, because the newlyweds were having an argument, and a fairly serious one at that. He decided to let her bring up what was concerning her so he didn't appear to pry. And then he'd let her know about his plans.

In a few short minutes, she approached the subject of Dorie and Brawley. "I think they are arguing about his wandering eye. Do you know anything about that?"

Tucker was aware Brawley had strayed off the path during their engagement, and it was the one thing he was most disappointed with.

"I didn't know about the argument, or specifically what was the problem, but, well, Brawley has had lots of experience being single for many years. I didn't think he would ever get married, so I kind of suspected Dorie was pregnant, but he says no. Some men are just that way, Sweetheart."

He could tell that statement sent a jolt through her body.

"What about you?" She stopped walking and waited for him to turn around and face her.

"I've never cheated on anyone in my life. I never intend to. But, you remember that conversation we had over my magazines—the ones I *used* to have anyway. Men like to look. Women are beautiful creatures—all sizes and shapes and ages or coloring. Hard not to stare at God's handiwork."

She gave him back a weak smile that he could barely see by moonlight. The shadows made her look a bit sad.

"You and Brawley—"

"I'm not Brawley. I don't do what Brawley does. I would never do that to you. Is that your question?" He stooped down so they could make eye contact.

She melted into him, throwing her arms around his shoulders and neck. His huge hands scooped her rear up and held her against him while her knees wrapped around his hips.

"Thank you," she said before they kissed. "I want to trust you."

Tucker let her down slowly, feeling her mound travel over his member. "You *want* to trust me? Or, you *do* trust me?"

"Same thing."

"Oh no, Sweetheart. Vastly different. I need to know if you trust me."

"You've never done anything—"

"And that's not trusting. That's being okay for now. I'm talking about trust, especially when it's not convenient to do so."

"Yes, I think I do. I think some of this is new to me. Give me a chance, Tucker. I'm running as fast as I can to catch up."

He drew her back to him and held her head, raising her chin and planting a deep kiss on her hungry lips. "I like the way you run. I like the way you try to catch up. Sweetheart, I love the way you do everything."

They kissed again. He could taste the remnants of the wine from today, felt her body need him again, and his desire flamed. But before it grew to a bonfire, he needed to tell her.

There was a stack of wooden pallets left between the rows they were traversing. He moved three of them, making a seat for her. Then he sat next to her.

"I've made the decision to go back to the Teams. But I wanted your opinions about it first before I turn in the paperwork."

There. He'd said it.

She took a gulp of air. The hand he was holding clutched his and he felt her pulse quicken.

"I—I want you to do what's best for you. When would this be happening?"

"Soon."

"How soon?"

"I'd have to report in two weeks."

She dropped his hand. "And how long would you be gone?"

"About four months, maybe less. You could come visit."

"Where?"

"Michigan."

"Okay. And then when do you go overseas, or wherever you go?"

"The training will take over a year all totaled. But most of it takes place in San Diego. We do jungle training, desert training and some in the snow country—Alaska, Norway, all over. I have to qualify just like I did the first time. They won't make it easy on me, which is why this next question is important to me."

He could see water had formed in her eyes. She was experiencing already saying good-bye and it hurt him to see the pain written on her face.

"Go ahead." Her voice was timid, weak.

"When I get done with training, and before my first deployment, I'd like to marry you, if you'll have me. But only if you're sure."

She stared down, studying her fingers entwined with his, resting on her lap.

"So, no honeymoon in an exotic place like Dorie and Brawley. It's *I do* and then *Good-bye*."

"We don't do anything like Dorie and Brawley. We are Tucker and Brandy and our lives are in our hands. Like this." He drew her fingers up to his lips and kissed them. "We're a team, you and I. But, only if you support what I'm doing."

He had to wait for her answer and wasn't surprised her reaction didn't match the movies when the girl jumps for joy and hugs the guy to death. He hadn't even bought a ring to give her. But this didn't diminish the commitment he was making this evening under the stars—a commitment he hoped she'd share.

"Yes. But on one condition," she whispered.

He braced himself for something he worried he'd not want to hear.

"I get you body and soul for the next two weeks."

Her follow-up smile warmed his heart. "I'll be your slave."

Brandy cocked her head, still smiling. "You might want to think about that a little bit before you promise. I have appetites and demands and—"

He grabbed her close, interrupting her message with a deep penetrating kiss he hoped sent her spinning. "Nothing would make me happier," he said when they came up for air. "I can't wait for my instructions, because, honey, everything you want, I *need* to give you. Everything. But I'm going to go back to the Teams to help me be the strong man you'll be able to count on." He kissed her forehead. "You understand that, don't you?"

"I do." She nodded, meeting his eyes, unflinching.

He knew they had a real good shot at this. He was going to do everything in his power to make it happen. With her help, he could have both things he wanted more than anything else. He could be the man he knew he was created to be, and he could love the woman he was created to love.

He'd spend the rest of his life blowing her mind. All she had to do was trust him.

CHAPTER 4

T HEIR RETURN FROM the Wine Country began with as much excitement as the trip itself. Brandy was overjoyed Tucker didn't hesitate to discuss their future plans, although their wedding wasn't going to take place for at least another year. Tucker told her he wanted to complete his Corps School and requalify as a SEAL. That meant taking BUD/S all over again at the ripe old age of forty. He showed her his enlistment paperwork, ready to submit, naming her as next of kin and beneficiary of his insurance, should something happen while in the Navy.

Little things like this reassured her when the cobwebs of doubt crept into her frame of mind. Life was looking like it could have a real happily ever after—just like some of her friends. Lady Luck was finally smiling down on her. She realized her mother had been right.

"When the right man comes along, he's going to love you just the way you are. You'll be perfect together."

Thanks, mom.

On the fourth day back, she went with him to the Induction Center where he turned in more paperwork and submitted his lab work and physical evaluation. On the way home, he suggested they stop and go shopping for an engagement ring. She'd told herself she wasn't going to push him on it, since they had so little time together. But she was overjoyed he'd made the suggestion. She had never brought it up.

She picked out a very small diamond, insisting they could upgrade later on. Tucker argued with her a little, but in the end gave in and allowed her to get the modest token of his undying love. Brandy didn't care how their future finances went, this simple ring meant so much to her, it would forever be her most prized possession.

She'd lost count how many times she'd been in friends' weddings, but now she'd have one of her own. Every time she thought about it, her heart raced.

I'm actually getting married! Me!

The ring could have been made out of aluminum, for all she cared. It was that he wanted her to be marked as belonging to him. He even insisted on putting it on her finger and kissing her tenderly on the palm. This big behemoth of a man had a tender heart, with a great love growing stronger every day. She could see it, feel it. Brandy experienced that complete hero's devotion she had considered might never find her.

Her father was thrilled, and allowed her to take time off work, since his health had greatly improved. The new hires Brandy made were working out well for the little business. There would be time for throwing herself back into the stand once Tucker left for Great Lakes.

Until then, she didn't want to think about it—pretending they had years and years before she'd have to be separated from him. The little internal lie worked, too. His body gave her strength the more he kissed and massaged his way into her flesh. She relaxed further with her inhibitions, the more intense their lovemaking became. His need to completely wring her out and satisfy her in bed nearly left her in tears on a daily basis. She even asked him to take her to a local X-rated strip club some of the SEALs had frequented. He insisted it wasn't necessary, that he was no longer a single man, but Brandy needed to present to him the gift of her trust. No matter the environment, she loved him and everything he wanted to do, and needed to show it.

They spent little time with Dorie and Brawley. There was a rumor circulating in the community that the two of them were still fighting. One day she got a call from Dorie, which confirmed everything Brandy feared. With only five days left before Tucker was to leave, Brandy was called to the Hanks home with urgency.

"You have any idea what's going on?" he asked.

"No. Just said for me to come. Alone."

"Jeez. I don't like it. I should take you over there."

"I'll be fine. I'll text you if I see his Hummer, or he walks in. I promise."

He reluctantly agreed. They cancelled Tucker's plans to go to dinner at Kyle's house, though she had insisted he go alone.

"Oh sure. You expect me to sit there all evening and get pummeled with questions about where you are? No thanks. Just easier to reschedule it, saying something came up, or you're not feeling well. Something."

"Fine."

"And you let me know. No secrets, okay? Perhaps Kyle needs to be informed," he said.

"She made me promise not to tell you. I've broken that promise, obviously, but I won't break the other one."

"But they deploy a few days after I leave. Someone's got to keep an eye out for him. I wish I were still going as their civilian. I'd feel better if I could watch over him."

"Tucker, you can't save the world. Brawley's gotten himself into something dark, and he'll have to get himself out of it. I want you to focus on the training. Give yourself that chance and forget about the rest of the world." She angled her head and teased. "Seriously,

Tucker. If you are distracted, you'll regret it."

"On one condition, then."

"Fair enough."

"Something happens—either tonight when you go see her, or after I'm gone, you let me know. I can't leave a friend in need. That's not how it works."

Brandy could see why having relationships in this very intense environment of the Special Forces could be tricky. They couldn't have a bad day. She'd learned that the SEAL Motto: *Only Easy Day Was Yesterday,* was created to remind them that they could never let up and coast. They were always on call and it would always be tough, regardless of what else was going on at home.

"I promise," she said to him, giving him a swift kiss and then breaking their embrace to exit the cottage. "I'll text you when I'm on the way home."

She was getting used to driving Tucker's big truck. The San Diego dusk was very mysterious tonight, showing off hues of turquoise and salmon, the palm trees and profile of the coastline was dark the blacker the night sky became.

Brawley was one of the SEALs who had bought his first house with the re-enlistment bonus he obtained tax-free when he'd been on deployment a year ago. Since that time, she'd been told the house had nearly doubled in value.

But as she approached the front door, the woman who greeted her, her best friend of nearly ten years, looked disheveled and red-faced from crying. Her normally beautiful hair had been unwashed and she was dressed in her sweats and bare feet.

She reached out and Dorie fell into her arms. To the side and back of her head, she whispered, "Come on, just tell me about it. It's going to be all right, Dorie. Don't worry. This won't last for long."

Dorie released herself, pushing to arm's length and studied Brandy's face carefully. "You can't tell anyone."

"Tucker knows I'm here, but I didn't tell him anything." It was true, since Dorie didn't go into much detail, just indicated that she needed her shoulder to cry on. "So explain please what's happened."

Brandy took up a spot on the living room couch and prepared herself for bad news. Dorie sat next to her and they held hands. "He's been talking to old girlfriends again, or, rather, one old girlfriend. But I know there are others. He slept with someone before we got married."

"Again? You said again."

"Yes. Happened before we went up to Wine Country. He promised he'd hang up that life, but something snagged him." She pulled a tissue from the box on the coffee table and blew her nose. "Or should I say some*one* snagged him. And it might be more than one former girlfriend."

"Ah, Dorie. I'm so sorry. Are you sure?"

"He has this bimbo calling him all the time. Her profile picture was of her in her lace underwear—that is, until he erased it after I caught him.

"Could it just be innocent friendship?"

Dorie looked at her cross-eyed. "Brawley doesn't do innocent. You know that. He'll cut it right to the bone. He says he loves me, but I don't know what's going on. He can't stop chasing other women. It's getting to be that I don't even want to go out with him any longer, he's so preoccupied with women who cross our paths. He gives off the vibe or something and they come flocking to him."

It was part of her own curiosity that made her ask the next question.

"Does he take any of the Team Guys with him, by chance?"

"Well, since your guy is pretty tied up with you, he hangs at the

Scupper too long with some of the newbies. All his other regular guy friends seem not to want to have anything to do with him. I'm expecting a call from Kyle or Christy one of these days."

Brandy was sorry for her friend.

"Honestly, some of those new recruits look and act so young. Like teenagers—who've been trained to act with deadly force. But they're like a bunch of teenagers with guns. I worry sometimes they don't have the maturity to—and, well, now look at Brawley. You'd think he'd have sense to just quit being in high school. And he's so angry all the time. Little things set him off. That's new. It scares me."

Brandy touched her cheek. "It's a handicap, Dorie. It's a flaw, like someone who can't stop spending. He has to want to get better and work on it. If he loves you, Dorie, he will. But you'll probably have to call him on it, and demand it. You ready for all that?"

The beautiful blonde sighed. Brandy could not understand how Brawley could ever want anyone else. She was perfect in every way—the most flawless beauty she'd ever known. And she had a wonderful heart. Looks mattered little to her. She read people the right way. It was a shame.

"Dorie? You ready to take this on?"

Brandy's stomach dropped to the floor when Dorie didn't make eye contact. "You have to put a stop to it." She squeezed her hand. "You have to be honest with yourself. You're the one who gets hurt as a result if you just let it slide."

Her friend jumped to her feet, pacing back and forth. "Ahhh!" she shouted to the ceiling. "I wish I could just understand what's happened to him all of a sudden. I never remember his fuse being so short. It's like something is wrong, and he doesn't want to tell me."

"You need counseling, Dorie. Get some help, or get with some of the other wives—call me!"

"Don't be silly. Tucker is leaving very soon, right?"

"Um hum."

"I can't take up your precious time."

"But Dorie, consider this. What if you're in danger? Physical danger?"

"Oh, it's not that bad. He's just very prone to agitation. You know Brawley. He was never like that."

Brandy admitted she'd always seen him as fairly easy to be around. "Do you feel comfortable just asking him what's going on? Or, should you try this in front of a counselor?"

"I don't want to go pouring my heart out right before he's supposed to deploy. They get all keyed up and tight before they go. It's like Brawley on steroids. Finding the right counselor will be hard for us."

"Then *you* go. You get some assistance. Bounce everything off them and give yourself a break. I think you're blaming yourself too much."

Dorie nodded.

"And come stay with me, if you want. I'll be all alone. I could use the company."

That brought a smile to her friend's face. "You also have a lot to learn, my dear. When they're gone, especially if you fight right beforehand, it hurts so bad. I feel so guilty. He's putting his life out on the line, and I'm complaining about him not paying attention to me any longer when he's home. The last deployment they lost a guy. I know that haunts him."

CHAPTER 5

T UCKER WATCHED THE little bedroom brighten, light filtering through Brandy's sheer curtains. They did nothing to stop the oncoming morning. This was the day he'd be leaving. The day he was filled with both regret and excitement. He'd told himself he'd be prepared for this big event, but now discovered he was not. So he lay immobilized, allowing the early morning sun to work its magic.

Her window was open a crack allowing a soft breeze to wash over their bed. He was on his back, his right arm holding her sweaty body deliciously close while she slept. He'd miss seeing her wake up each morning. He'd be in a dorm room with five or six other men—most of them ten years or more his junior. And it would be just his luck to get a world-class snorer assigned to his group. He had all kinds of ways to get even with one of those.

He hadn't doubted his decision to serve again in the Navy. He didn't doubt he could pass the rigorous qualification course at BUD/S. He didn't mind that two of his recent trainees were now going to be in the same class as their former instructor. He didn't mind that another new recruit had taken his place as the lone civilian component to the next SEAL mission in Baja—an honor he was supposed to claim before they learned of his intention to re-join.

What he was concerned about was his thirty-nine year old body stressed and under pressure. The first time through, he was just a dumb kid who made it because he just wouldn't quit. It didn't mean anything to him back then. Now, it was different.

He knew guys in their late forties who still served. But most Team Guys served six or eight years on average, and less if you got injured. So, he wouldn't be the *oldest* SEAL on Team 3, or wherever they put him, but he'd be the oldest in his class, and that bothered him.

Brandy was mumbling in her sleep. It always gentled his whole demeanor when he got to trace down her spine with his palm, sliding it over her derriere and giving her a soft squeeze. This would be the last morning he could feel the ecstasy of making love to her under the soft glow of first dawn.

He inched down the sheets, opening her crossed arms and nuzzling between her breasts as she began to awaken. He watched her eyes open with lazy enjoyment as his fingers slipped over her belly to the magic juncture between her thighs. His forefinger encircled her bud until one of the little presses made her jump.

His mouth was on her opening, his tongue taking over the work from his finger. He gently bit her labia and let the delicate flesh feel just the tip of his canines. She moaned, bent her knees and arched her back, making her breasts heave and then fall as she exhaled, widened her knees and accepted two of his fingers inside her. Her hands flailed on top of his, pushing him deeper and massaging every knuckle and joint. Her arms forced her beautiful orbs with the knotted dark pink nipples to overflow. They called to him. He was hungry for her in so many ways, he vowed to try every one of them on her, until she could hardly move. It was that important that he leave her exhausted and begging him to stay. He needed to hear and feel that need in her.

Because it matched his own.

AT ELEVEN O'CLOCK sharp he kissed her good-bye just outside the gate that housed the busses to the airport. He smoothed the backs of his fingers over her wet cheek.

"No need to cry, Brandy. Nothing on this earth would keep me from coming back to you. Be good to your father and be a good friend to Dorie. I think she's going to need it."

She wouldn't take her eyes off his. "I will." Then came her sweet smile. "But I'm going to miss you so much, Tucker. Can we talk every day?"

"Not sure if the rules have changed, but if I'm off on a training, which will happen after I finish the Corps School, then no. There will be days, maybe even a week or two I'll not be in phone contact."

"When can I come visit?"

"Working on it. Good news is, Great Lakes will be pretty then. Early summer. Perfect time to come out. So, let me do a little research and I'll let you know. Have to scope it all out first."

"Roger that," she whispered.

"Hudson! Get your ass over here and quit fondling the wifey," one of the instructors barked.

Tucker winked at her. "Hear that?"

She sent him off with another quick kiss, and then watched him board the bus. He felt her eyes on his back, and then saw her face between the bars at the gate, her little ring glistening in the sunlight as she gripped the metal barrier.

Her form got smaller and smaller as the caravan of two busses traveled down the frontage road, then turned the corner around SEAL Team 3's building and hit the back road to the airport. Just like that, she was gone.

On the bus, he knew he was the object of discussion. He caught the sideways glances and the faint whispers. He was going to graduate as a forty-year-old man, trying out for a young man's job.

But Tucker had never been injured and had hardly ever missed a workout. The messy divorce with Shayla had truncated any dreams of finding love, so he'd thrown everything into his Teammates, by taking a job supporting the community—helping the would-be recruits get in the kind of physical and mental shape he knew they'd need to be able to qualify. It was the closest he could get to actually being on a team these past years.

The morning's activities were a blur. Everything moved at light speed. Their soft lovemaking, the quick double check on his packing list, something he'd gotten drilled into him from his past. In a full-on retro deja-vu, he harkened back to his childhood in Oregon, when he and Brawley sat side by side and compared lunches while they bounced down the country roads in the big yellow bus. The day was judged based on what kind of dessert his mother had packed. Watching the murky water and the Coronado Bridge come up, then the city of San Diego proper, he felt just as when he was in grammar school. He was waiting for the rest of his life to happen.

He had placed a call to his mother earlier as he drove Brandy to the base. He wanted the two most important women in his life to talk together for the first time.

"Mom, this lady is going to marry me. Can you believe that?" he'd told her.

His mom laughed. "Well, I guess there are miracles in this world after all. First Brawley and now your turn. She's probably very special if she is in love with you, not that I blame her one bit."

"She's right here, Mom." Tucker handed the phone to Brandy, who nearly dropped it before she took up a light-hearted conversation with the elder Mrs. Hudson. She promised a road trip North after Tucker's graduation from Corps School, and before he started his first phase of SEAL training back in Coronado.

A young, lanky black kid he'd been training who took the seat next to him interrupted his memories of the morning.

"Jamal. If this isn't old home week. Now I've seen four of you on this trip. Is there some kind of conspiracy?" he asked, following it up with a grin.

"Don't know that, but feel free to kick my butt if I forget anything you've taught me. Can't make you look bad now can we?" he said in his slow, Southern drawl.

"May I offer a piece of advice?"

Jamal enthusiastically nodded his head, yes.

"Not sure where we'll be housed, but if I don't get a chance to tell you, go ahead and volunteer to take *any* tests they give you. But if they tell you you're going to dental school, sub school or some other specialized career path, tell them to pound salt. You've been promised a berth in the next BUD/S class, and if they give you any guff, give Collins a call."

"I certainly do appreciate it, Tuck."

The kid sat back in the seat and then had an afterthought, "I hear they do a timed run as soon as we hit the tarmac in Chicago. It's going to be a pleasure to see you overtake the drill instructors—*all* of them!"

Tucker reveled in always being the fastest runner in any group of men. He could also bench press more than nearly anyone else as well. He was most worried about the swimming portion of the course, and for that, he would be looking out for an expert swim buddy.

Jamal chuckled right along side Tucker. He was glad that, even though his hair was prematurely gray, his run times had never been better. He was starting to believe he was the machine Brandy always told him he was.

HE WOKE UP with a jolt when the wheels touched down on the

runway. They'd been put on a commercial flight. One of the overhead bins popped open and began spilling things over his shoulder, into the aisle.

At the training facility, they were set up into quads, in sets of two rooms with a quasi-living room between them. Nice thing about it was that they had a small kitchen, equipped with a full-sized refrigerator and microwave.

Several of the men in their pod were from the east coast. One was from Montana. Tucker and two others hailed from California. One of those men, Conner Newsome, was also a SEAL candidate, and looked extremely fit, so Tucker made a point to arrange project workups and P.T. with him. He knew that sometimes it didn't take much to get a guy to quit, especially if he felt he was doing it all alone. Having a swim buddy, or someone to watch your back or help with some aspect of the course he didn't understand was a smart move. The bonding would give them both an edge they could draw on when they needed to.

As the days went by, he began to settle in to a routine, studied hard and tried to curry favor with his instructors. He knew this was a safe bet now, since when he began the first phase, he would seek anonymity. He didn't want to stand out or he would get picked on. But because he was re-qualifying as a medic, the math and science courses were more challenging. He'd been out of school longer than anyone else.

In the third week, several of the men had dropped out or been reassigned back to the fleet, leaving a vacancy in their pod of eight. It remained that way for nearly a month before they found a replacement.

The Navy allowed one recruit for roughly every ten thousand men, to try out for the Teams, and guarantees were not always given at enlistment any longer. Because Tucker was returning, he'd have his shot, unless he just blew his courses. That didn't mean they'd make it easy on him. They did want his experience, he'd been told. Having served for ten years, he walked into the field with skills and knowledge of the way the Teams operated that no amount of training could ever duplicate.

He talked with Brandy by phone nearly every day, and enjoyed hearing about life back in San Diego. It took his mind off dwelling on BUD/S, only a few weeks away now. Her dad was nearly up to his old speed and the police had some leads they were following, trying to locate the former employee who had stolen from them and nearly killed her father.

"And wait until you see Dad's garden. I've never seen him so happy," she told him.

It had been his gift to her father, rototilling the nearly half acre space. It had been part of elder Mr. Cook's dream to raise his own vegetables and then sell them through his store.

"Can't wait to be back in the San Diego climate. It's getting nicer up here, but damn, it's still cold, especially at night. And it doesn't just rain here. It monsoons, and the wind blows right in your face, coming off the lakes. Sometimes, even at this late date, the rain is laced with snow. It chills you to the bone."

"I've got some ideas how you can warm yourself up on those cold nights, Tucker. Just say the word, and I'll be up there tomorrow."

He was getting horny talking to her and couldn't wait to see her. "I think we get a weekend soon. We'll stay in Chicago. You'll love it."

"So—Kyle's group left yesterday. Not sure if you knew that."

"Figured it was coming up. How's Dorie doing?"

"Not so good. She's really struggling."

"Keep close, Brandy. It will be the best thing for Brawley, for everyone, when he comes back and she's got her head on straight. Maybe he'll squeeze those demons out of his system. He *could* come back a changed man."

"Hope so. You have any clue what's gotten into him though? I mean, was he like that at all when you two were growing up in Oregon?"

"Don't think so, but I honestly don't remember. I mean, I've known him so long, he's like a brother. What's he doing?"

"Well, remember I told you about the calls he was getting from some girl?"

"I do. That still going on?"

"Not sure. But he smashed up the Hummer. Pretty good scrape all along the passenger side, denting the rear door. The truck had to be towed since the frame was bent."

"Just a single car accident, then?" Tucker wanted to know.

"He said he was avoiding a deer. I believe him."

Tucker had noticed the increased drinking at Brawley's before he'd left. And Brawley had stopped coming by to visit him, using the excuse he didn't want to get in the way of his still new relationship with Brandy. It was one of his regrets, not being able to spend a little more time with Brawley before he left. It was unsettling. "When he gets back from deployment, I'll be just finishing up Phase I. I'll make sure to reach out, see if I can get together with him. I hope you won't mind."

"Not if you behave yourself. Because when you come home, your ass is mine, Tucker. I don't much like the idea you'd be his sidekick if he's looking for girls."

"I should be so lucky." He chuckled at Brandy's brazen attitude.

"I mean it, Tucker."

"Duly noted. I promise, sweetheart."

As the weeks progressed, Tucker still hadn't heard from anyone on the Team. He didn't expect a report on a classified mission, but he always stayed loosely connected even after disengaging from the Teams. He was hoping the new guy was being useful.

But Brandy told him Dorie had also been virtually left alone. The longer this went on, the more he worried about his friend.

As the two friends got older, Brawley attended a different high school, so most of the time their sports teams were competitors. Both athletic and gifted in multiple sports, the matchups between the two of them became the whole story of the game, and drew lots of fan interest.

But unlike Tucker, Brawley didn't have a sweetheart in high school. Instead, he played the field. Tucker wasn't aware of a reputation for being a womanizer. He'd often wondered if perhaps Brawley hadn't been the smarter one between them. There was just so much unfinished. So many holes creeping up on them, it felt like this childhood friendship might be in peril.

One day, he got the call he was dreading. Brandy was coming for her first visit in two days. Brawley's long, rambling message made no sense at all. He wished he could talk his friend down.

"Must be nice and warm in Baja now," Tucker said to Brawley.

"Fuckin sweatin' bullets. They got cockroaches the size of dogs. You should see them."

"Well, at least the local cat population is under control then." Tucker thought Brawley would find it as funny as he did, but silence hissed on the other end of the line.

The awkward gap between them made Tucker's hair stand on end. The back of his neck was hot. It felt like there was a hole in his rebreather, or tent. "Hey dude. What's up? You don't sound like your frisky asshole self." He wanted to break the frostiness between them.

"I've been seeing things. Scary shit."

"Not following you, Brawley."

"Well, we're deep into May, past Cinco de Mayo and everything. These people have those skull masks? You know the ones I'm talking about?"

"I believe they call them sugar skulls."

"Yea. They paint their faces to look like one of those bright skulls. Starting to depress me a bit. You know how that guy Randy what's-his-face said if you start to get scared, well you need to get out."

Randy had been their pre-enlistment fitness trainer, with over twenty years on the Teams.

"You're one of the bravest men I know, Brawley. You're careful. Don't go do dumb stuff. There's a little tension because of the immigrant population and border issues with the government. But we're cool. Just be glad you're not Trace. I heard Kyle and him owe their asses to some General down there who wants his daughter to marry a SEAL. I'm glad I didn't make that promise."

Brawley didn't answer.

"You there, asshole?"

"There. I just saw another one?"

"Another one what?" Tucker asked. Now Brawley was starting to scare him.

"One of those little senoritas of death. She wants a playmate."

"Horse shit. Don't go there, Brawley."

"Ask them to stop it, Mr. Tuck and Roll. That's all I see when I close my eyes."

Tucker knew a corner had been turned. It wasn't a good sign.

"Make sure you get lots of rest, Brawley. Get some meds and get a long, long rest."

Just before Brawley hung up, he whispered, "I'm being followed, Tuck."

CHAPTER 6

S TEVEN COOK, BRANDY'S father, had discovered items missing from his store. It started out small, but progressed until several days in a row he'd lost a whole case of fruit. But what bothered him was that the person stealing from him hadn't tried to cover their tracks. He immediately thought about his earlier assault.

Detective Clark Riverton was on semi-retirement duty from the San Diego P.D. He was skilled in homicide cases, and missed his former job, but investigating stolen fruit from a mom & pop grocery store was where his career was headed these days. He took it like everything he did: swore and complained to anyone who would listen, but did nothing about it. He'd been reminded it was an option to just quit. Being the kind of stubborn man he was, that wasn't anything he considered for more than a second.

Riverton's presence, waddling between the aisles, picking up oranges, apples and melons, sniffing them and then setting them back down, made Mr. Cook wonder if it was such a good idea to call him.

"You can't tell anything by smelling the fruit. At least, not those," he said as he nodded to Riverton's hands. Cook extended his hand. "Steven Cook."

"Clark Riverton." He retrieved a dog-eared card from the shirt pocket under his blazer.

"Thanks." Cook slipped the paper inside the front catchall pocket on his green grocer's apron.

"So what can I do yous for?" Riverton looked out of place. "You've got a fruit burglar I hear."

Cook winced at the obvious slight. "That's right. But it's more than that," he continued. "It's like I'm being left a message."

Despite his manners, Cook heard Riverton swear under his breath, and then clear his throat, standing tall. "And what makes you think that? The fruit talking to you these days, Mr. Cook?"

"Not the fruit—" Then he realized he'd been played. "The guy who assaulted me had been an employee of mine, Jorge Mendoza. Your colleagues are trying to find him as we speak."

Riverton's expression didn't change. "Okay, so we got a serial fruit burglar, then. Anything else you wanna tell me about? Like, when did this happen, and how often?"

"After hours, of course. He's getting in somehow. I don't keep the money here anymore."

"Smart. That's been stolen too, or did he just prefer fruit?"

Cook examined the lines on the Detective's face. He couldn't see any laughter beginning to break out but was fairly sure it was there, just under the surface. Riverton was a pro at masking his feelings, but Cook detected he was about to split a gut.

"No money missing. Not yet, anyway."

"This—" Riverton consulted his small spiral-bound note-book—"Mendoza fellow, you or any of your staff spot him hanging around?"

"Nope. No one has. The police told me he was a known gang member. Which reminds me, while I have your ear, why can't an employer like myself consult a database of known gang members before we make that hire? It sure would save us all a lot of hassle."

"It doesn't work that way. It's not like we can consult their corporate records. He doesn't carry a membership card."

Cook was annoyed with the teasing.

"Well, don't ask me how, but I know it's him and his friends."

Riverton asked other questions, making notes in his little book. He stuffed it in his shirt pocket again, and suggested he talk to every employee at the store, which Cook agreed with and gave permission to.

"My daughter comes this afternoon, should be here anytime now. Other than Kip, and Brandy, the others are part-time, going full time in the summer when their school is out."

"Seasonal. I got it."

Cook hesitated, and then asked the question he'd been dying to know the answer to. "Detective Riverton, do you believe me about all this, or do you think I've been getting high?"

Riverton took a deep breath and pulled his pants up by the belt, readjusting it. "Sometimes it takes awhile for me to get a feel of a crime. But trust me, if it's there, it will come to me. Right now, I'm not seeing why someone who is already in trouble for the first offense, try to mess with you a second time. I mean, a case of oranges? What's the point in that? What? Ten or twenty bucks of oranges?"

Cook was at the end of his rope. Riverton's attitude stunk. When Riverton didn't give him a straight answer, Cook added, "That's what I thought."

CHAPTER 7

B RANDY HEADED TO Dorie's to return the scarf she'd borrowed on the trip up north. That beautiful weekend seemed so long ago, but it was just three months. She was packed for the trip to Chicago, leaving early in the morning. She had a few hours to do at the store, then she was going to get to bed early.

Dorie's face was gaunt and appeared almost gray, not the beautiful tan and pink skin she normally had. From the appearance of the bluish circles under her eyes, it was obvious her friend had not been sleeping.

They embraced and Dorie allowed her in.

"First of all, thank you for letting me borrow this. I had it dry cleaned." She handed over the scarf, folded in tissue.

"Thank *you*. I'd totally forgotten about it."

Brandy examined her friend's body posture, her shoulders slightly slumping. She was wearing distressed blue jeans, partially unbuttoned, and a big white fleece sweatshirt and silver flip-flops. Her hair was wrapped up in a clip atop her head.

"Are you working today?"

Dorie smirked and examined her clothes. "No. I asked for a few days."

The two had met at an upscale advertising agency, until Brandy had been fired. "I have to be honest. I'm worried about you,

Dorie."

The new bride attempted a smile. "I'm pregnant, Brandy. I just don't know if the father of my baby wants to be my husband anymore."

She began to melt into sobs when Brandy held her, directing her to an overstuffed living room chair, where the two collapsed. Brandy was reassuring her it would all work out. She hoped she was telling the truth.

"Does Brawley know?"

"Nope. Haven't heard from him in a month. This early in the pregnancy, anything could happen, so I don't want to distract him."

"We can always ask Kyle to let him know, if you want."

"Not on your life. It's my story. Probably my fault too, or at least that's what Brawley will say."

"You don't think he'll be happy with the baby? Perhaps it's the perfect something that would cheer him up." Brandy wasn't sure if this would help.

"He's been a ghost. I'm not sure where he's at." She began another bout of tears and leaned against her for comfort.

Brandy was heart broken. She'd never considered Dorie's marriage with Brawley could be so loveless. And now with a baby coming, there was added pressure she didn't need.

"Whatever happens, Dorie, understand that the baby was not a mistake. One of God's little angels coming into your life at just the right time. Brawley might be acting like a jerk, but the baby is truly a gift, an angel, and messenger from up above. Just remember that."

"I'm scared. Never felt this way before, Brandy."

"Well, girlfriend, I'm certainly no expert, but I'd say you're developing some pretty powerful hormones. Mood swings are supposed to be one of the side effects early on."

"That could be part of it, but I also got another one of those calls from that girl, asking for Brawley again. I told her I was his wife, and she said she knew and hung up." She shook her head. "What a douchebag. What's he done now? Maybe I don't want to know."

"I agree. It's like he's become a completely different person. You think he's hurting about something? Something he doesn't want you to know about?"

"I have no clue. None whatsoever."

"Well, the main thing is the two of us should stick together. You lean on me until he gets home and you guys can go see a counselor. I'm sure, in time, you two will sort it all out."

Dorie separated from her and stood. "You want some wine or something?"

"I'd love a glass of ice water."

"Done! As a matter of fact, that's what I'll have as well."

She was in the kitchen in a flash. Brandy joined her. All her life she'd envied the beautiful girls, like Dorie. The ones who just walked into a room and all the guys would come to their knees. Brandy had begun to feel invisible. She told herself everything her mother had drummed into her about character and real love. But it was a fact that she felt unattractive, until she met Tucker.

Dorie had more men around her constantly, vying for her attention, cozying up to her, even though they knew she was married. It was just inconceivable that all this be happening to her. She watched her friend play with her blonde curls, sorting and sifting her long fingers through them. She allowed silent tears to flow.

Brandy wanted to be a good friend, but she always felt Dorie was out of her league. Tonight, her perspective had shifted.

Dorie gave her a weak smile, as if she'd read her thoughts. "You must think I'm a bit crazy."

"Not at all. It's just that you don't have enough information. The waiting must be hell on you."

Her best friend appeared to be thinking about that. Then she asked, "Have you eaten? You wanna go out somewhere to have a light lunch? Or, I can fix us something."

"I ate, but I'm also due at the store." Brandy answered. "I fly out to Chicago tomorrow morning, so I was going to go to bed early after that."

Dorie grabbed her. "Here I am, raining on your parade. I'm so sorry, Brandy." The tears began to form. She covered her face with her palm. "Oh, what am I going to do?"

"Why don't you call his LPO's wife, Christy? Perhaps she can give you some suggestions, and take my place for a week while I'm in Chicago. I hear she's a great confident."

"Except for the fact that I know something is going on with Brawley. That information will go straight to Kyle, then. Brawley wouldn't want me to jeopardize his career."

"But by shoving it under the rug, you could actually make it much worse. Whatever it is, you're far better nipping it in the bud. It *could* save his life."

The two said good-bye. As Brandy was walking out the door, she heard the phone ring.

"Hang on." Dorie coaxed her to stay long enough so she could answer the phone. She took the clip out of her hair, loosening it vigorously and grabbed her telephone.

Her expression changed after she heard the first few words coming from the other end of the line. Her forehead puckered. Her eyes squinted and she began to tremble. Brandy rushed back to her side.

"What is it?" she whispered.

"Yes. I'll be here," said Dorie, her voice trailing to oblivion. Thank you for calling."

Whatever she was going to say next, Brandy knew she wasn't going to like hearing.

"He's gone missing. Brawley has just disappeared. In Mexico. The Navy is sending someone over to discuss a possible hostage negotiation."

Her friend's normally sparkling bright blue eyes were filled with pain.

"I'm going to stay with you, Dorie."

"No. You go. You're leaving for Great Lakes and I don't want to interfere with that—"

"But I can't leave you alone. At least call Christy Lansdowne, okay?"

Dorie nodded her agreement. "I'm sure she's got some advice. I'll do that. Now go, and I'll update you when I have news."

As she drove to her father's store, Brandy knew her best friend's nightmare could soon consume them all.

CHAPTER 8

T UCKER WAS SWEATING profusely as he drove to the airport to pick up Brandy. His fingers dug into the leather steering wheel, leaving ridges.

Her plane was delayed, but force of habit still made him show up early to the original arrival time. He'd rented the bridal suite downtown at a small boutique hotel with a beautiful view of the sparkling towers of the city center that seemed to stretch for miles. It had nearly emptied his bank account, since he had to pay for the weekend in full before he could reserve it. And his check hadn't been deposited yet.

He was worrying about a lot of things these days. And money was one of them. Would Brandy be satisfied with how little he would make? Even as a SEAL, the pay was ridiculously low. And, he had to admit, he'd never been good at managing his money, so at almost forty years of age, he was still living from paycheck to paycheck. His truck was the only thing of value he owned, and it was mortgaged to the hilt. He knew a lot of Team Guys who kept re-enlisting so the bonuses they received could pay off all their debts. Lots of guys never got ahead.

He should know better. That's one thing he was going to have to fix. With Brandy's help, he knew he could.

He'd placed a call to Kyle as soon as Brawley had hung up on him two nights ago. And now, nearly forty-eight hours later, he didn't get a call back from him either.

It was strange feeling part of the team without really being on it. He wasn't allowed to know everything they were doing, but, God willing, he would be joining them in another year. So, here he was, sitting in classrooms, marching to cadences, having room inspections and having to listen to pre-pubescent conversations all around him with kids that barely shaved. He'd killed people with his bare hands. He'd married, loved with abandon, got totally dumped on while he was deployed, and probably made love to another forty women after his divorce. These guys didn't have a clue what was about to fuck with them. The medics in the class were still embarrassed to watch a woman give birth in the hospital.

He hoped Brandy had some answers for him, because he'd thought about everything so many times his brain was fried.

The world bloomed when he saw her running toward him in the airport lobby. Without caring, she'd dropped her carryon and slammed that big, beautiful body against him, he nearly fucked her right then and there. Just holding her vibrating form, smelling the sweet perfume of her womanhood and her desire for him made him drunk with all the right things. Blood flowed to body parts that had gone dormant. It could have been the dead of winter, but it was spring in his body. There were lights, music, birds chirping and all the other fuckin' things that guys feel when they're in love. It was so funny, he nearly cried from the irony. He'd signed up to kill people for his country and have to leave this woman alone while he did it. What kind of a decision was that?

"Tucker, I ache all over I'm so excited to see you."

"Baby, I haven't slept in a week. I've not thought of anything else." He *wanted* to feel that way. He just had to lie about the worries, because that wasn't how he was going to talk to her. That was going to have to be between him and his maker.

They were ushered to their room. He gave the bellman twenty dollars because her suitcase was the heaviest he'd ever seen. The guy studied Tucker, all buff and huge, easily a hundred pounds heavier than the skinny guy too small for the uniform. But he made great effort to place the enormous bag on the bed, as Brandy had requested. He loved that about her. She was oblivious to those little details, like the princess she certainly was.

So, the kid backed out the door, wiped his forehead and beamed when Tucker gave him the twenty and a wink.

"Thank you, sir."

"You earned it. Get some ice on that lower back, okay?"

Brandy had started unpacking.

"We're only here for three days."

"I don't care, I want to get all my things hung up and refolded so they don't wrinkle."

She didn't even look at him, as she picked up each article of clothing and shook it out and either added it to the closet or the drawers.

"So, you going to give me a fashion show, where you take your clothes off and put them back on every hour? That what we're doing?" He leaned against the wall, more relaxed than he'd felt in two months. And it had nothing to do with alcohol or the extremely good vape one of the boys in his dorm had brought from home. He just loved watching her do her thing. That's what he'd missed.

But his pantsbunny reminded him that he'd missed the sex, too. She'd worn a white stretchy blouse over a pair of black slacks. Lucky for him the dresser was directly across from him, and, after she'd filled up the top two drawers she had to bend over to get to the third one near the floor. Suddenly there was that vision before him that drove him to action.

He ran across the room and grabbed her so quickly she screamed. "What are you doing?"

"You can do this later. Right now, I'm here for the sole purpose of satisfying that ache you talked about in the airport. Can we talk about that now, please? I've been very patient." He said all this while he was pushing her suitcase off the bed. It crashed on the floor and spilled contents, some jars of something rolling down the carpet trying to escape through the front door.

But she didn't notice because she was laughing so hard. He hoisted her on the bed and dropped her and she continued to laugh.

"Now that, that's a heavy suitcase!" he said.

She propped herself up on her elbows, looking up at him. "Hey!"

"Oh shut up and help me get you naked please. I don't want to ruin anything, but honestly, honey, I really don't care."

He pulled her shirt over her head and viewed a spectacular pushup bra with flower stitching and pearls. The thing gave her easily an eight-inch cleavage.

"Perfect!" he said. "You're gonna leave that on."

"It opens in the front."

"Like I said, perfect. When I release, you can release that too, okay?"

She laughed again, unzipped her pants and shimmied them down her hips and thighs. "You'll want to take note of these," she said as she splayed her hands to the sides to show him the matching panties. "And just watch!" She scrambled to her knees and bent over. Just below the beautiful butt crack that was revealed, and above that perfect ass, was a little bow stitched in place.

"Hold that pose," Tucker said as he kicked off his shoes and removed his slacks, nearly losing his balance and falling on the floor. At last, fully naked, he demonstrated his treat for her eyes. "Ta-Da!" His hands splayed to the sides, revealing his enormous boner. It was nearly bright purple it was so throbbing and hard.

"Oh my."

"Indeed. Now, honey, you be careful now, because this might hurt."

"Oh dear. Really?" She whispered in return, still on her knees, looking at him with those sultry red lips and her mahogany hair mussed up all over her shoulders. "And here I can't even pleasure myself." She rolled her head back as she pressed her palms down the satin and cotton of the bra, lower to smooth over her belly and then down over her hips. She leaned onto her shoulders, placed her palms at her rear, spread her cheeks and slipped the panty elastic to the side to insert a finger in her core. "I'm so ready for you Tucker."

He shook his head. "Nope. Not going to fit, But I do admire you for trying. My dick is so hard your panties are going to chop it off. That might ruin our evening."

She nearly fell to the bed, laughing.

He crawled to spoon over her, his hands fondling her from behind.

She groaned and leaned into his touch, wherever he chose to place his hands.

"I like that. Very compliant. You want a little bit of me, baby?"

"I want it all."

"Even if it hurts?" He pulled the panties down over one hip and leg, and then removed the other side.

"You can kiss it and make it better."

"I can kiss it right now and make you come. I know I can. Shall I try?"

She didn't answer him, but nodded, viewing his face through her hair.

He slid beneath her on his back and drank from her sex looming above him. She undulated to the rhythm of his tongue, moaning and clutching her chest. He added his thumb and she started to vibrate.

"Told you so," he whispered.

"Don't stop now."

He climbed to his knees behind her, massaging her slit from her bud to her anal flower. "I've missed you. How you taste. How smooth your skin is, and how beautiful you look when you're pink and aroused, and when you come on my mouth."

He lifted her gently so he could position her over his rod, and then slowly pulled her down and back on top of him. She hissed and made little mewling sounds as he filled her with each tiny thrust up inside her. And when he could go no further, he pressed her hips down to go beyond.

Their breathing was in tandem, as he held her there on the bed. He kissed the back of her neck, slowly smoothed over her thighs and her round ass, returning to her bud where he gently pinched her, which brought another hiss.

"Love this, Tucker. No rush. I want this all night long."

"Absolutely, sweetheart. Anything you want. I'm here. Not going anywhere."

CHAPTER 9

BRANDY WOKE UP against Tucker's back. He had one arm twisted behind him, resting on her thigh. The scent of his neck was sweet, almost feminine. She inhaled deeply and let all that delicious, moist air refresh her lungs.

There wasn't any part of him she did not love. She hoped it would always be like this—each of them totally consumed in their passions, attentive, hard at work to create joy and get as close to each other's souls as possible. In bed with him was the only place on earth where she felt the true meaning of life. Where there were no barriers, only truth in gentle movements. They gave, and took. They rested and gave more. It was a cycle she doubted she could ever tire from. She felt cherished in his enormous arms. He'd do anything to protect her, and she felt the same for him.

He turned, kissed her tenderly and rubbed his thumbs over her cheekbones. Her face felt small, like a little child's in his hands. She'd forgotten that.

"I'm a big liar," she whispered.

"Oh really? What little lies are you telling me, then?" He followed this up with a kiss.

"I've been telling you over the phone I've been doing fine. I haven't. And now that I'm here, I don't want to go back to San Diego."

He started to say something and she placed her fingers over his mouth.

"I know, I have to." She kissed him.

"No, I was going to say stay. You could easily get a job out here. It's just that it's so expensive. I could try to get you a room—"

"And know that you're in a dorm with a bunch of Navy brats? Stay with a family I don't know?"

"We could find someone really nice. And then I could see you more often. Cheaper than getting a hotel on a short term. Than airfare."

"But there's my dad. I can't leave him without any notice."

"It will only be another month, Brandy. Then I get a few days off until Indoc. And they'll give me another few days before we start Phase I. But all that, Indoc, Hell Week and everything, will be done in San Diego."

A month seemed like an eternity, though she'd managed to wait three already. She pouted.

"Do that again," he whispered.

"What?"

"That thing you did when you sighed. That thing with your lips."

She sighed again, and pushed her lips out and immediately his mouth was on hers, his tongue making its way to play with hers. She pulled back and grinned. "You're so funny."

His eyes danced in the reflection of the night-lights outside. He pulled her into him again, his enormous paw on her left breast, squeezing and kneading it into submission. He kissed and sucked her nipple, getting more serious by the minute.

There was a vein in his forehead that pulsed when he was in deep concentration and right now her breasts were making him very, very focused.

He turned his head and examined her from different angles. He explored with his fingers and tongue, and then let his hand wander down her midline, stopping before touching her nub.

Tucker's were the only fingers that had ever touched her there. And every time he did it, he made her feel like it was the first time all over again.

"So sweet. So wonderful." His forefinger found her.

"All yours, Tucker."

"Yes."

He got to his knees, bringing a pillow underneath her hips, which was the perfect angle for him to go in deep. He pressed past her swollen lips and soothed her with his gentle back and forth movements, bringing his kisses between thrusts. His powerful hips ground into her, lifting her pelvis and slowly increasing speed.

She let him do everything this time. Let him open her, set her on fire so she could watch the process as well as be the lead actor in it. She waited for that little phase when she lost complete control. Ravenous for him, she bit his neck and clutched his back. Still, she could not get enough. Sweat rolled down her chest and from her forehead into her hairline. With her hunger building, she found it difficult to get air, so inhaled deeply at last and finally felt the delicious rush of her orgasm when she exhaled. Her long sensual journey lasted minutes as he continued to help her fly, kept her afloat, and gently set her back down, thoroughly exhausted.

He collapsed on top of her just as the sky was turning pink. She fought sleep, but the warmth of his body and the sweat of their lovemaking pulled her into a dream state where she fell on a cloud.

CHAPTER 10

T HEY WERE AWAKENED by Tucker's cell phone ringing. He'd tried to ignore it, but a few minutes later the ringing started again.

"I'll turn it off."

He got up, wandering naked, checked the screen and swore.

"What is it?"

"It's Kyle. I gotta call him. There's something wrong with Brawley."

"Tucker! Yes, there is. Oh my gosh! I should have told you."

"Told me what?"

"He's disappeared. Yesterday—" She hit her forehead. "Yesterday Dorie got a call and he was listed as missing in Mexico."

"What? When was this?"

"Yesterday, about noon? I think? No, earlier. Eleven. That's when I went over, just before I had to go to work. She said she'd call me when she had updates. I think she was going to call Christy."

"Who called her?"

"Someone from the Navy. Oh gosh, Tucker. Why didn't I contact you right away?"

"I got a call from Brawley night before last. Very strange. He's been talking to me off and on, but this was out of the blue. Said he was being followed. I rang Kyle immediately, but couldn't get through."

He redialed the number and Kyle picked it up on the first ring.

"Hey Tuck, sorry I didn't call you sooner. So you've heard about Brawley, then?"

"Yea. Brandy's here with me in Chicago for the weekend. Dorie got a call from the Navy yesterday about Brawley missing. Is that true?"

"I'm afraid it is. Our op here got real fucked up. And we were watching Brawley like a hawk. Something wasn't right."

"What do you figure happened, if you can talk about it?"

"Well, this is a need to know. Right now, time is of the essence. We don't exactly have good support here. Not quite sure if we should just focus on finding Brawley and forget the cover we've created. But I got the go-ahead to call you, at least."

"Glad you did."

"You start with your observations. Any clue, Tucker?"

"Well, he's pretty fixated on this Day of the Dead stuff. At least that's what the call was about. Seeing faces. Skulls and stuff."

"You think he's using something?"

"I don't think he takes anything. At least nothing I know of," answered Tucker.

"I checked and there's nothing on his record of any kind of mental illness. Did you notice anything growing up?"

"Not a thing, Kyle. He did mention that kid you guys lost last year on that quickie in Africa. He took it pretty hard. Felt responsible. He told me about it right after you guys came back, and then everything got all fucked planning the wedding. I barely saw him after that until after their honeymoon. If there was a sign something was wrong, I totally missed it."

"Okay, well I'll look into that."

"So is this missing of his own accord? Or, was he taken?"

"We don't know. That's the ugly truth. But he's been drinking. That we noticed big time."

"He told me he was scared."

"Yea. He mentioned it to Coop too. Coop thought it was a delayed PTSD."

"Sorry, can't help you there. I know nothing about that. What about the kid last deployment?"

"Brawley knew the family. Used to date his sister, of all things. This was a few years back. The kid idolized Brawley. But hell, wasn't his fault. The two of them made a wrong turn and wound up facing some bad guys. Carlos was in front and got hit. Brawley got three of the four of them, but it was too late to save Carlos."

"That's a shame. I never knew the story. Wish I had. Maybe something I could have done."

"So, if anyone contacts you, let me know immediately. We were working pretty deep, and I left my cell behind for a couple of days. Won't happen again."

"Okay. I'll keep my ears open."

Brandy touched his arm, and then took the cell from Tucker. She put the phone on speaker. "Kyle, this is Brandy. Have you called Dorie? She's been going out of her mind."

"Nope. I knew Collins and the boys back home were doing that. Was going to call her tomorrow. She should have called Christy."

"She was hesitant to say anything to either of you. She was concerned about him, and she's told me he's not tried to contact her once since you've been over there. That's not like him."

"No, it isn't. Okay, well we've got a couple of places we have to check out tonight. If either of you think of anything, call me."

"Definitely," answered Brandy.

"You guys have fun. Guess I don't have to say that, do I?"

Both he and Brandy answered in unison, "Nope."

Kyle managed to squeeze out a tiny chuckle. "Glad someone's

getting laid. Sorry Brandy, just how my brain works."

"No offense taken."

"Take care of my brothers," Tucker added.

"Always. Hey, when do you start Indoc?"

"About four weeks."

"Well, hurry it up and get your butt back down here. We need you back on this team. Your boy did real good. Strong kid. You trained him well."

"Thanks, Kyle. I'll be sure to tell him next time I see him."

"Okay. Better call Christy. You guys don't be too good."

"Not a chance," Tucker said, and hung up.

Brandy was sitting on the edge of the bed, still naked. He could tell she was nearly in shock.

"Poor Dorie," she whispered.

"You need to go back home?" He sat next to her and took her hand in his. He felt her begin to thaw. Then she returned his squeeze.

"No, what I need is some breakfast, and then I think I need a nap. And that, Tucker," she said as she punched his arm, "Is entirely your fault."

He grinned at the sight of the sun beginning to pierce the skyline and whiten the tall grey shadows of buildings.

"Yes, indeed, I am totally to blame. And I'd do it all over again in a heartbeat."

He decided he'd talk to her about all the things that could go wrong, but do it tomorrow. In the meantime, he noted she didn't panic. And she didn't run home to daddy.

Yup. I think this is going to work.

CHAPTER 11

THE WEEKEND WAS over way too soon. Tucker wasn't very familiar with Chicago, and neither was she, so after several times getting lost or waiting for a Taxi or Uber, they decided to just stay inside their room, ordering room service. Time was so precious, she didn't want to waste a minute of it.

Their parting and the long flight home were tearful. The heaviness in her heart reminded her that the love she felt for Tucker was real. This trip had cemented it. He'd even had that long discussion about all the terrible things that could happen, how dangerous it was being a SEAL.

He used the situation with Dorie and Brawley to demonstrate how she needed to stay plugged into the community. Alone and on their own, the wives never did well. The guys had it drummed into them, he said. But the ladies had to embrace that so everyone could be protected. He explained how people would be helping Dorie with meals. Someone would come and do housework or shopping for her. She didn't have to, and shouldn't have to feel alone.

So Brandy returned to San Diego with a new determination. She wanted to learn everything she could about being a wife of a SEAL. She called Christy Lansdowne and over the next week, got invited to a couple home parties and get-togethers. She found the women, as a whole, to be very resilient. They were used to juggling households without any help from their husbands, who were always gone. And when the men were home, they were allowed time to unplug and get back into the rhythm of life in California. Babies were born. Kids had lessons and recitals. Grandparents passed away. And yes, sometimes Team Guys didn't come home.

"When I was considering marrying Tyler, one of the wives told me I'd never feel as loved as I would married to him. She was completely right."

Others gave her pieces of advice. Everyone admired her for going into the job of marrying an elite warrior with her eyes wide open, and for doing her research up front. To be prepared. It still wasn't a guarantee, just like every brave or strong man didn't pass all the challenges of the BUD/S or SEAL Qualification Training. But it didn't take anything away from their bravery or honor.

Brandy's dad, Steven Cook, was back to full speed. He was already selling the squash, lettuce and peas he was raising in his new garden. He was growing cabbage and broccoli, as well as carrots and beets. His patrons delighted in occasionally being able to go out back and pick their own produce, and they paid well for the opportunity.

She took Dorie to her first doctor's visit and they both got to hear the baby's heartbeat. With Brandy's encouragement, Dorie went back to work and found it helped her get her mind off the possibility of having to raise a child without a father. Both of them hoped Brawley would be found eventually, since he had been seen on the outskirts of the village.

The girls talked about being able to accept whatever the eventual outcome was. Brandy also got offered her old job back, which she promptly turned down and felt great about it.

It had now been ten days since Brawley went missing. There still was no ransom demand so the search team Kyle left in place in Mexico was convinced he'd just abandoned his post, voluntarily because he'd been seen. He explained to Dorie that the team wanted to find him quickly, before the slow wheels of the Navy started in motion, stripping Brawley of his Trident and sending him home with a dishonorable discharge. Kyle explained that it still might happen that way. But he was confident Brawley was alive. His wallet had been found, emptied of cash. A convenience store clerk had seen him come in from the beach and ask for water on several occasions. He was also given food. The clerk said he looked homeless.

"I guess there are a lot of homeless vets out there," Dorie said. "I had no idea."

"Well, that gives us hope, then, if he was seen," remarked Brandy.

"At this point, I just want him safe. We'll sort everything else out later, if we can."

Brandy was proud of her best friend. She wasn't sure she could endure the same.

And then one day, the team found Brawley sleeping under a cardboard box at the shore. His skin was covered in insect bites, he had a distinctive red beard and his hair was full of twigs and debris. His bare feet were cut and beginning to show signs of serious infection. He'd also lost a lot of weight, using a rope to hold his pants up. The guys who found him said he didn't recognize them at first, but as he ingested some decent food, things began to come back to him.

Brawley was escorted home, along with the rest of the team. What his life was going to look like was still uncertain.

But Brawley was alive!

Tucker was pleased when Brandy gave him the news.

"So what happened to him?" he asked.

"No one knows yet. Dorie and I've been doing some reading. There are a lot of homeless vets who just disappear—walk away from families and houses. All sorts of mental issues made worse by some of the conditions—well, you know quite a bit about that."

"Indeed I do. We're all so young when we start out. It's hard on a guy, and he probably had some things he was covering up, too. He didn't want to get tossed from the Teams."

"And have to answer to his former SEAL father."

"Yup. Something like that. Wow. So glad he's safe, for now. Going to be a long road getting him all the way back."

"Dorie's looking for a place for him. Just started therapy at the VA hospital," she answered. "She sees him tomorrow for the first time."

"He's lucky. Life on the streets, even the beach, is very dangerous."

"Well, he's even luckier than that, Tucker. Dorie's pregnant."

Tucker chuckled. "Well, if anything can make a man jump to attention, that'll do it. Good for them. I'm pulling for them."

"Me too.

They made plans for another weekend when he finished his Corps School. But the Indoc, which sometimes was postponed by as much as a month or more, depending on the SEAL Team cycles, was all set to start the following week. If Tucker wanted to wait for the next class, he could do so, but it would postpone his eventual graduation. He explained that guys who got injured during training sometimes sat out a rotation and joined up with the next class. Tucker wasn't injured, and didn't want to wait.

Brandy's father continued to have cartons of goods raided, but began viewing it as an involuntary contribution to the local population, and not the former employee.

"The way I see it, if someone's that hungry, I say give it to them. No one should starve here. I've got plenty," he said.

"But you'll report it, right?" Brandy asked him.

"Oh yes. Riverton and I are now old friends. He logs everything in quite dutifully. He said if I was willing to spend the time to call him, he could do me the favor by keeping track."

She went home each night after work, walked around the cottage, touching things that Tucker loved, even slept on his side of the bed just to be a little closer to his familiar scent. She opened his drawers and smelled his tee shirts, even organized his socks. He'd be annoyed with that, she thought, but she didn't care. His absence left a huge hole in her world that daily phone calls could not patch up.

In just two more weeks he'd be home. He'd be here, preparing to do one of the hardest things he'd ever done in his life. Brandy was determined to help him do it.

CHAPTER 12

T UCKER WAS PREPARED for the P.T. the instructors at Indoc dished out, but he wasn't prepared mentally for all the insults he had to endure. Kyle and others had said he was a welcome commodity, being a former SEAL. That the Navy encouraged re-enlistment with his skillset.

Those lying sons of bitches.

It wouldn't have made any difference because he still would have gone through being the adult Boy Scout in Great Lakes. He was kind of looking forward to seeing some of the pimply-faced crowd getting a dose of reality, where every little infraction was noted, and the instructors didn't let anyone get away with not getting humiliated on a regular basis.

He knew what they were doing. They were trying to wash out the weak ones. Especially the officers who would not be able to lead a command on a SEAL Team. They could leave the program during this phase and not have a mark against them. But if they quit during one of the three phases, that was a whole different thing. They wouldn't likely have a very distinguished career.

Tucker's class was made up of about one-third officers. The instructors called them the "Gentlemen's Club." A lot was made of the enlisted men vs. officers, with choice comments. Tucker laughed at some of these, but didn't dare show it.

"You think you can carry that boat because you have a college education, boys? That you don't want to get your hands dirty, that it? Why, that just gives you an excuse to take it easy. In *this* class, we don't get over the finish line until we *all* get over the finish line. That means you officers are at a disadvantage. Life's about to get hard. Real fuckin' hard. I don't mean hard-*on*."

This usually caused one or two of the enlisted men to chuckle. That would send them scraping the bottom of boats with their own toothbrush, or running extra laps.

Every hometown was denigrated as breeding the lowest of the low, that they should consider themselves lucky to even be in their presence.

Tucker was called Grandpa and Pops more than he was called his name. One of the worst badmouths on the instructor team was a recruit he'd actually prepared. He was doing a rotation as an instructor while his leg injury healed.

"I remember you. You were that old guy who thought he was all buff and tried to scare the shit out of all us. Oh man. Payback's a bitch. Your ass is mine now!"

Tucker had to do extra pull-ups because he'd made so much fun of him during his own training.

"Show them how you fuckin' show off. We used to dream at night we'd find you in a dark alley."

These shouts and insults did get under his skin. But it made him wish he'd been tougher on the guys than he had been. If, God forbid, he should take a turn at being an instructor and one of them decided to go back in, he knew he'd dish it out even more. Because it was good for him. It was good for all of them. And it was meant to stress out the ones who were going to wash out anyway later on. Just like carrying boats over rocks in twelve-man crews, rubbing all the hair off their scalps, over and over again, there wasn't any way around this but to find the ones who could some-how get up and over those rocks without breaking their ankles.

After Hell Week, there were only about twenty per cent of the men left. The ones who dropped out had to chase the truck with the bell in the back of it. You couldn't just walk into the office and say you quit. You had to do a good quit, not a sissy quit. You had to be humiliated and catcalled so that you were clear this was not for you.

He called Brandy at the end of that week. He needed some TLC and he was going to take it.

She met him at the training facility parking lot, and had se-cured a nearby motel room, and not one of the expensive ones. Money was tight for them. He fell asleep in the car on the way over. He awoke to her trying to yank his enormous frame from the passenger seat. At first, he thought he was still at the beach inhaling saltwater, but as he regained his wits, he tried to help her lead him to the second floor room.

"Should have gotten a first floor."

"I can see that now."

"I told you to get the first floor," he whined, but he didn't care.

"Shut up and save it for the third time you qualify. I'll remem-ber then, okay?"

"Oh man, you got a mouth on you. I'll bet you do nasty things with that mouth."

"Sure I do, not that you'll ever find out, because you can't stop snoring. I'll bet you fall asleep in the middle of sex, too."

Brandy indeed had one of the most wicked mouths ever in-vented. He was trying to tell her so when she got him inside the door, and pushed him onto the bed.

"Ouch! I'm hurting all over."

"Really? That's what happens when you garden too much. You've just been lying on the beach, sunning yourself."

He tried to see that mouth that was making him mad, and horny at the same time.

"Come here."

"I don't do orders like that."

"Please."

"Okay, please."

"Please like *please pass the salsa* or please like *please stop talking and take off all your clothes?*" He was losing the battle and sleep was beginning to overtake him.

"Hey, lover-boy. You can talk a good talk, but I'll bet you don't even have the strength to get your clothes off."

She was smiling down on him, hands on those lovely hips. And she was wearing a nice scoop top with what had to be the strongest pushup bra invented because he could rest a basketball on her shelf with no problem. He was going to show her he could do anything he wanted. He could run five miles and still get it up with her. He could—

Tucker woke up the next morning with a smile, until he noticed he was still wearing the same clothes she'd picked him up in. She'd thrown a blanket over him, leaving him just the way he'd fallen. Even left his boots on. But, as his eyes focused and he beheld the warm fleshy glow of her body lying beautifully naked next to him, the urgency to join her was overwhelming. He suddenly had the power of a team of mules.

He sat up. He remembered why he'd been so happy. He'd made it through Hell Week. Brandy was here to help him celebrate, and heal. Yes, there was pain under his arms, and in his groin area. His feet hurt too, and soon he found out why. Every single toenail was bright green. The green algae extended to mid calf, where the socks and lace-up boots stopped. His shoes were so ripe, he tossed them against the room door. This woke her up, with a start.

"You didn't even take off my clothes!"

"What's that smell?" She held her nose and then followed his line of sight until she discovered his frog feet. "Oh dear. Your inner Shrek is sprouting. You didn't happen to cross paths with a witch somewhere in Coronado, did you?"

"That. Was. Unkind."

She rolled over on her back, giggling, one arm shading her forehead and gave him a very welcoming grin. The covers revealed just enough breast to make him hard instantly.

"Wouldn't have made any difference. You weren't going to do anything anyway. I just let you sleep." She followed it up with a sweet smile, but then she licked her lips and he forgot about his green feet, and climbed on top of her.

"Pew. You need a shower, sailor."

"Yes, I do. But you're coming with me." He kissed her, traveling down under her ear and then sucked that overzealous nipple that dared to pert up on her. He licked that thing to submission and it wasn't long before she was writhing, doing things with her hands he was supposed to do.

"Don't you get started without me, Brandy. I want to feel and taste all of it right there with you, honey."

She brought one of her hands up and saluted him. Her fingers were wet. It was so unfair!

He pulled her arm and got her to standing position, her long shiny hair covering her shoulders and those gorgeous mounds.

"Now you have to work," he said.

"What do you mean? You think it was easy getting you through that door and up the stairs? Ha!"

She crossed her arms, defiant. Oh, she was dangerous.

"Okay, so you worked a little bit. Now your job is to undress me."

Those lovely fingers slipped in and around his buttons, zippers, undoing his belt as she pulled the stiff saltwater-washed uniform off his body. When he was completely naked, she screamed and jumped back a foot.

He looked down to determine what she'd seen. Little rivulets of blood oozed from his underarms. A matching pair were in his groin area, caused by the friction of his wet suit which he had to wear or freeze to death during the midnight wet-n-sandys. But standing loud and proud, his dick was perfect. Smooth, and bright purple-red, veins bulging and ready to burst. He imagined she might think it was the cherry on top. He couldn't help it. She made everything perform like a rock star.

When his gaze returned to hers, he saw she was licking her lips again, and she began to kneel.

He wanted a shower, but, by God, if she'd just take him into her mouth, he'd take care of all the rest. He knew making love to her was going to get him healed and right with the world ten times faster than it normally would have done.

CHAPTER 13

IT HAD BEEN nearly twenty-four hours since she'd eaten and Brandy was starved. Tucker was snoring on his belly. The shower hadn't entirely gotten rid of the green.

"Lover boy," she whispered in his ear. One enormous paw grabbed her forearm.

"You're not getting away yet."

"I don't *want* to get away, but I'm hungry. Haven't I performed enough to deserve at least a cheese omelet?"

"How about room service?"

"Tucker, not sure if you remember, but this wasn't exactly the suite at the Hotel Del. The Lamplighter doesn't have a restaurant. They don't even have a coffee maker in the room. And I'm starving."

He let go of her arm, and then pulled himself up. "Oh, I suppose we could take a short break."

"*And* you did ask me to set up something so you could see Brawley, remember?"

His eyes were roaming all over her chest again. "I think that was your idea, not mine."

She hit him with a pillow. "You liar."

He laughed and feigned being hurt with the soft fluffy material. "Down, woman! Down! Remember, I have injuries."

"Not to the parts that count."

"I'm glad you noticed." His boyish grin made her melt. It would have been easy to just say the heck with it and just play in bed all day. She loved the play, but she was truly hungry. And arranging the visit with Brawley was tricky. In his delicate condition, she didn't think it was wise to keep him waiting.

"Tucker, we have to be at the clinic at ten. That gives us about an hour for breakfast. I. Need. Food."

"Yes, ma'am."

She handed him a change of clothes he'd asked for, and they set out in search of an omelet.

AT TEN, THEY were waiting for an audience with Brawley's doctor before seeing him.

Dr. Raj was from India. His handsome face beamed when he saw Tucker. "I heard all about you, Tucker. Going through all the qualifications again. Quite impressive!"

"Thanks, doc."

"What's it like doing it again? Harder or easier?"

"I really can't say. I mean, some parts are harder, some easier."

The doctor nodded.

"Actually, sir, I'm waiting for the easy part, come to think of it. I've got some pretty big chafing holes in my skin under my arms and right here." He demonstrated the spots at the top of his thighs on the inside.

Dr. Raj made a face. "I'll bet those wounds are huge, then. I can get you some good antibiotic cream. Best thing is to not move much, and keep it dry, clean and don't irritate it with clothing. But of course, you can't walk around naked."

Brandy could see the Indian doctor blushed.

"Oh we're doing fine on the last part. But not so much on the movement."

"I understand. Well, I'll see to it that you get some of that cream before you leave. Now, about Brawley."

"Yes, we'd like to see him," Tucker said.

"And I think that would be good. We're trying to introduce things back into his life that perhaps he forgot. For instance, he doesn't remember his wife at all."

"Oh dear," sobbed Brandy.

"I think he started to disengage before he actually left the team. It is a form of Post Traumatic Stress. Gradually, his brain will let him absorb other people, and then the memories will return. But, he could have a serious gap that won't return, I'm afraid. We won't know for some time. Every case is different."

"Does he know Tucker is going to see him today."

"He's been told, yes. Just don't react if he says or does things you don't understand. We want to include him in our lives. He can't do it the other way around."

As they walked down the softly lit hallway, Tucker whispered a question to Brandy.

"Is this the VA? Not at all the facility I remember."

She realized she'd forgotten to tell him about the clinic. "Libby Brownlee's dad arranged this for Brawley. And he's bankrolling it, too. He's getting the very best brain injury care in the country, part of Scripps. I'm afraid the VA has a ways to go before we see this kind of service for our Vets."

"Good for him. I met Dr. Brownlee many times before. He's our unofficial Team doctor, you know."

She took his hand, lowering her voice again, "Yes, I know. In fact, I know a whole lot more than I did just a couple of weeks ago. I haven't been sleep deprived and doing boat drills like you have. But I've been studying too."

Tucker squeezed her hand, then drew it to his lips and kissed her. "Thank you, sweetheart."

They were shown the doorway to a pleasant room decorated with pictures and live plants. Tucker saw that Brawley's family photos were displayed all over the wall, including his wedding pictures. On the space next to the window was a much younger Tucker photo. He was standing next to a younger version of his best friend, in front of some white mountains, their arms locked around one another, smiles as wide as Brandy had ever seen.

"From our first deployment in Afghanistan," Tucker whispered.

Behind a curtain, they heard the familiar voice. "Tucker, is that you?"

Doctor Raj gave them a thumb's up, and held ten fingers in the air. Tucker acknowledged with a nod. Brandy slipped into the corner and took a seat as her big hunk pulled back the curtain. Brawley's eyebrows rose.

"Fuckin' about time. They said you were on vacation or some shit. Get your ass over here, and break me outa this place, will you?"

Tucker embraced his buddy, tears streaming down his cheeks. Brawley also began to cry. "You're back, buddy. You came back."

"No shit, Sherlock. But hey, I didn't do the heavy lifting. They could have left me on the beach with all those senoritas, but no, they had to spoil the fun and drag my ass here." He wiped his face with the back of his hands, and then stopped as he noticed Brandy.

"Well, hello there little lady. When did they sneak you in here?"

"She's with me, you goofball," said Tucker, his lips still rubbery with emotion. "This is Brandy, and she's going to be my wife, so hands off."

"Sure. Just like you, Tucker. Tell me the prettiest girl is yours. You selfish bastard."

She approached the bed. "Hey Brawley, nice to see you again. So glad you made it back." She shook his hand and he grabbed her toward him and gave her a proper hug.

"I'll be damned. She said *again*, Tucker. So she's met me before too. Like the other pretty one." He glanced around as if looking for permission. "Can you believe it? She claims to be my wife!"

Brandy saw Dr. Raj cover his mouth just outside Brawley's line of sight.

"I know." Tucker drew his arm around Brandy's waist and claimed her back. "You could have done much worse. I'd just sit back and enjoy it. She could have been a horse-faced woman with a beard. It will be like falling in love all over again, my man. You lucky bastard."

"I intend to do lots of research."

"Yes, best to take your time and savor every moment."

Brawley blinked and appeared to lose continuity because his expression changed. "Hey, not sure how long you're staying, but could you ask that little Indian fellow if he could get us some pizza. I'm fuckin' starved."

Dr. Raj appeared on cue. "Brawley, I'll see to it right away. Unfortunately these two have to cut their time short today." He handed his patient a photograph from his own wedding. "But they brought this for you. See? This is them at your wedding just a few months ago. See? There's Tucker, and there's Brandy."

He stared down at the picture and then took it gently from Dr. Raj's fingers. "I remember that dance. That was you!" He pointed directly at Brandy.

"It was. We were showing off, remember?" Brandy said enthusiastically. She was delighted the old Brawley, or some form of him, had reappeared.

Dr. Raj winced and shook his head slightly at the word choice, but he left it to Brawley to react.

"You were sexy as hell. And you got sick. Now, I bet you don't remember that, do you?"

His grin was a joy to watch. And he was partially right. She'd been so drunk that New Year's Eve, lots of the reception was a blur.

"That's where we met, so I owe it all to you," whispered Tucker.

"How about that?"

Dr. Raj carefully extricated them after the good-byes were exchanged. In the hallway, all three of them breathed a sigh of relief.

"That was about as perfect as I'd hoped," he said.

"You gotta let the Team come in here. I think he can handle it."

"You might be right."

"And they'll needle the shit out of him, too. Just wait. He's gonna feel just like I do going through BUD/S. It's what he's used to. Been like that his whole life, even as a kid."

"Thank you." Now it was Dr. Raj's turn to develop tears. He was going to say something else, but Brawley's hoarse voice pierced the sound barrier.

"Hey, where's my pizza!"

CHAPTER 14

TUCKER FOUND THE next two phases of BUD/S easier. The instructors didn't yell at him so loud, which kind of pissed him off. He didn't want to be known as a weakling, or anything approaching being fragile. He wanted to be the one to show them how it was done. It was dangerous to have that attitude, so he worked to make sure it didn't show up in his team dynamics.

Because of his previous experience on the Teams, the instructors gave him hints about what might be sprung on the class the next day. "Don't bother to shower, you'll be wet all day," or, "Go light on the breakfast. A little choppy out there on the bay today." One suggestion he really appreciated was, "Pick the big guys today. The Smurfs are going to get wasted." Tucker had been nursing a cold and thoroughly enjoyed sitting on the sunny beach watching as every other boat crew had to go in and out all afternoon. Because they'd come in first, they earned the right to rest and restore. It wasn't much, but it was as good as doing wet-n-sandy in a heated bathtub.

But the instructors discovered he was an inspiration to those men who were struggling to push themselves to finish. Tucker's swim buddy, who could have been on one of the Olympic teams, dropped one day and didn't even say good-bye. He knew some day he'd run across the man and give him the chance to explain. But the loss of his strong swim partner made the "water features" as the instructors called it, more challenging. Another good swimmer who had also lost his partner started shadowing him, and they worked the channel like he had done with his former buddy.

He also knew word had spread what Brawley had been through. He was encouraged to share some of his private thoughts about P.T.S.D. and how it could creep up on even the strongest warrior.

In the last week before graduation a subtle shift had occurred. Tucker transitioned from student to teacher. He suspected this was the role he would play in the months and days coming up.

The graduation ceremony was held in the operations building, newly renovated since Tucker's first time out. Even the chairs were nicer and they had a screen for the hot sun that baked Coronado all twelve months of the year.

Brandy was wearing dark Navy blue, and not black, because she thought it would be bad luck. Her suit nearly matched Tucker's dark dress uniform of the enlisted rank. He noted all the ladies were taken with the dress whites the officers chose to wear.

It was a surprise when Kyle Lansdowne walked into the gathering and began his address to the new class five-two-six. They were a small group, only twelve of the original group, plus several who would go on to do further training from previous classes, having recovered from their injuries. Several had developed mono, which sometimes forced them to wait six months or a year to graduate.

Tucker was seated on the left. Brandy and his parents were seated on the right, along with other friends and family of the other men. He'd given an invitation to Dorie, but she respectfully declined, since she was due to deliver any day. She'd been touched by the gesture. They'd talked earlier.

"It's like Brawley's going through BUD/S all over again, Tucker. Just without the uniform and the speeches," she told him. "He already earned his Trident. Now he's proving to everyone why."

He'd been so overcome, he didn't have words to give her in return.

So he was waiting for his time to walk up front and get his pin to add to the other one he'd kept in a box in his underwear drawer. He chuckled, recalling when Brandy asked him if he got to wear both Tridents at the same time.

Kyle began his speech. Tucker had heard many of them before, but this one was special because he felt it had been written just for him. Unless that was his ego talking, and that was always a possibility.

He shook it off, clearing his head, ready to listen to the man he hoped to serve with and under, and risk his life with, *again.*

Kyle gave the welcome to the dignitaries, and told the families that he'd remembered this day, over twenty-two years ago now. He told them he never hesitated when asked to address a new class. He'd met some of his best friends here. And some of those he lost overseas.

"We aren't supposed to say we're the best, because any man who wears a uniform is a hero. There is no rank to the word hero. You don't get a medal every time you become one, or, in some cases, claw your way back to one." He nodded at Tucker. Tucker returned the short nod.

"We are trained not to brag, but let me tell you, and then I'll shut up about it, we are the best of the best. And so are the other Spec Ops guys, and the guys who deliver and pick them up. The ones who give support on the ground or arrange to get them home. The ladies who give birth to these fine men and then have to give them up to a country that doesn't always recognize her Vets as they should all the time. But we don't do it for that. In the old days no one knew what a SEAL was. A lot of us wish it was that way again."

He paused to take a drink of water.

"We are lucky enough to find something we so love doing, that we do it even though we may have to pay the ultimate sacrifice. We were created because it was determined our country needed a group of special guys who can gut it out and just get the job done, no matter what was asked, no matter what the risk. I guess history will eventually tell us if we were smart or just plain stupid."

The audience rumbled in amusement. Kyle gripped the podium and continued, scanning the whole crowd, both right and left. And then he motioned to someone at the back.

Tucker turned in his seat, winked at Brandy, who had been staring at him that way she did. His mother had her arm around her shoulders. He continued to scan the back of the room and saw a column of familiars walk up front in their dress uniforms, which was not required. There was Cooper, and Fredo, T.J., Lucas, Armando and Danny, and each one gave their wink or nod as they passed his chair.

"These are just a sampling of some of the guys we get to work with every day. Several of these men have saved my life. More than once. I've had a hand in rescuing some of them. We like to say that we never leave a man behind. That's true of all the branches of service. But we're a brotherhood and that never ends."

He winked again at Tucker. It was making it harder and harder to keep from releasing the tears that hurt his eyes. Hearing the sniffles from the family and friends who had gathered didn't help, either.

"Some of us come home in various stages of whatever has been our plight. We're ready to bring it on. Bring it *all* on. We may not like it, but we can take it."

He sighed and gripped the podium again. "I don't know when I'll retire. I can't imagine doing anything else with my life, and I say that with the full knowledge and love of my wife and kids, my extended family. There are some men who are made here. There are some men who leave here to go on and do other great things. And then there are some men who just belong here. I'm one of them. And I'm also proud that today, I'm witnessing the graduation of another of our ilk."

There was a smattering of clapping. As should be, Tucker wasn't named. Only the few that knew the story had that benefit and the rest had to take it on faith. But when the time came, and the men lined up to receive their Tridents, Kyle was the one to pin it on Tucker himself. His words, whispered in confidence, were ones Tucker would never forget.

"You inspire me, Tucker. You help show them the way. Keep it up, bud. We need men like you."

All he could say was, "Thank you."

CHAPTER 15

One Year Later

T HE SIGN OUTSIDE Frog Haven Winery indicated the winery was closed for a private function. Dozens of pink and deep red balloons marked the roadway in both directions. The gravel drive had been watered down the night before. Even the vines were celebrating, their shades of magenta and mahogany, golden yellows and faded greens standing fresh and proud in the fall sun. It was wine country and this time of year was always the most colorful. Harvest was just around the corner. Tourists were planning their new release tours and barrel tastings. Every weekend there was a festival honoring tomatoes, artichokes, artists and jazz. It was a feast for the eyes as well as the soul.

Brandy stood in the dress she'd picked out years ago and never told anyone. She'd gone with her mother to look at a party dress for a function she was attending, and they stopped by a bridal store. Brandy was still in grammar school. But when she saw the low-cut off-white satin gown, covered in beaded flowers and hand stitching, she was mesmerized.

"Very pretty, Brandy. You'd make the most beautiful bride of them all wearing that dress," her mother had whispered in her ear.

Brandy still remembered her mother's scent and it lingered around her today. This dress was just like that one she'd seen nearly fifteen years ago. The cut was perfect for her ample chest, showcasing it, as Tucker would soon appreciate. Even as a child, she must have had a sixth sense of what her adult size would be. She turned to see herself in profile and liked what she saw. Rose and burgundy roses were wired to the comb at the back of her head, blending with the mahogany shades of her own natural hair color. Facing the mirror straight on, she said those same words herself, but she heard her mother's voice.

"Very pretty, Brandy. You make the most beautiful bride of them all." She felt like her mother was holding her hand, fixing her hair and tending to the fullness of the big slip underneath. Brandy closed her eyes and saw it, felt it. He mother had come to be part of the celebration.

A gentle tap on the door announced Dorie's entry into the changing room, which was a converted case storage building, smelling of musty fermented and very patient wines.

"You need anything, Brandy?" Dorie's burgundy gown matched the accent flowers in her bouquet, deep pink and rose red.

"I'm good. Just enjoying the moment. All the planning, and everything, and it's all over so quickly."

"That's what weddings are. You're just walking through the doorway into your new life. It's what happens after you get there in those rooms that count. That's where you live. This is just where you mark the spot it begins."

"That's lovely." She hugged her best friend. "How's Jessica doing?"

The baby was trying to walk and was at a squirmy stage, needing constant supervision. She had Dorie's beautiful smile and blonde coloring, but she had Brawley's fearless personality.

"She's climbing all over her dad. She's already discovered his boutonniere and has thrown it to the ground."

"Serves him right. I guess he's getting a dose of what his mother probably went through."

The other bridesmaids entered, and they stood in a circle, locking arms behind them. The sound of rustling taffeta and giggles put a hush to the room.

"Thank you all. For years I never thought this day would come. And then, just like magic, Tucker appeared as my New Year's wish. It just goes to show that anything is possible, if your heart's all in."

"That's what love does. It makes the impossible possible, Brandy," Dorie began. "Or, I guess I could say, it makes possible what we told ourselves we could never have."

Dorie's mother brought them a glass of champagne and led the toast like the cheerleader she was. She and her daughter stood arm in arm while she raised her glass. "To a perfect marriage, complete with all the flaws in life that make it so perfect in the first place!"

The girls laughed, but everyone followed up by sipping the pink champagne until it was all consumed.

"Thank you all," Brandy said to her wedding party. You've made my day special and complete. And my father has enjoyed being father and mother to the bride, especially with all your help."

Everyone laughed again and began chatting nervously. Brandy glanced out the small tinted window in the corner, and caught a glimpse of Tucker in his tux, laughing and hugging well wishers. He looked stunning. But, he'd complained about it for days and the week before the wedding almost threatened to boycott the ceremony if forced to wear it. They found a tailor who fixed the fit, making the cut and style what he was comfortable with. His biggest fear was that he'd remind everyone of The Beast from the fairy tale. Or, worse yet, Shrek, which was how she'd described him that first night they met.

His SEAL buddies were lining up, so it was no surprise that just after they disappeared the wedding planner descended on them and asked them if they were ready. Brandy found herself nervous beyond what she'd experienced before. The dress had been made with a lace-up bodice that could be adjusted. She hoped she wasn't going to pass out. She grabbed the planner.

"Can you let it out a little more? I can't breathe."

"Sure, hon."

In a minute Brandy was much more comfortable, and thanked her. Maybe some day she'd decide to wear something that made her look like a skinny pencil, but for now, who she was fit her perfectly. And it was what Tucker liked.

The girls went ahead of her. Cooper's daughter and little Stephie, Kyle's daughter, were holding hands with Gretchen's youngest daughters. As flower girls they began walking down the carpeted aisle between the rows of vines. At a right angle, they turned and disappeared into the clearing where the ceremony was to begin. They threw their rose petals with abandon, and were done before they hit the tenth row. They took their place at the side with Christy Lansdowne herding them together.

They'd chosen a selection of Baroque music played by a local quartet as, one by one, the bridesmaids floated down in single file through the colorful leaves, to join the men in front.

Brandy's dad was close to having the meltdown she was worried she'd have. "What's wrong, Dad?"

His quivering lower lip gave the sentimental man away. "Your mother. She'd—"

"She's here. Honest. She came to me. She's all around us today, Dad. Everywhere. Can't you feel her?"

He nervously searched the area.

"Close your eyes. She'll come to you."

He obeyed her suggestion and soon had a smile on his face. "I think you're right," he said with his eyes still closed.

The wedding planner gently touched her dad's shoulder and encouraged him to start down the aisle. The beautiful lute music was Brandy's favorite tune. He guided her through the narrow aisle, the planner walking behind and unsnagging the dress as she made her way to the clearing. Standing erect and not looking anything like Shrek or The Beast, Tucker's chest pumped up as he inhaled big and looked startled. Her father gave her a kiss, and then retreated to the side.

Tucker's hands were shaking. He whispered something to her and she asked him to repeat it.

"I'm scared."

Though he'd tried to say it softly, everyone in the wedding party and the front two rows heard his declaration very easily.

"Dammit," he whispered.

"You're doing fine, Tucker. Just hang on. I'm right behind you. I'll never let you fall, and I'll never stop loving you."

His own words, spoken on the day they skydived together two years ago, echoed between them and he squeezed her hand.

The rest of the day whirled away like the magical ball in Cinderella's castle. The reception was held in the tasting room nearby. The mix of children chasing each other and the handsome SEAL Team members and their wives and girlfriends, plus extended family felt private and intimate, though the numbers were not small.

Tucker lured her out into the vineyard again. She had hooked her skirt up, but the long gown was catching along the way, making the trek more difficult. Tucker took care of the fabric, and stooped, carefully untangled where she was caught and did so with patience. The sight of his huge body attending her made her giggle inside.

He took her hands in his, and guided her to sit on a pile of wooden boxes.

"We were here before, weren't we?"

"Yes, sweetheart. This is where I asked you to marry me."

"That was a wonderful night."

"And it never has to end." He cleared his throat and began saying something she knew he'd rehearsed. "I was a real mess when I met you. I don't know what you saw in me. I still shudder when I think of bringing you that day to my apartment. I mean," he slapped his forehead, getting animated, "what was I thinking?"

"I had fun. I'd never met anyone like you."

"Well, that's probably true. There's only one big green monster on the planet, after all."

"No, you're wrong. What I meant was I'd never met anyone who was so much like *me*. I never had to adjust or be careful around you, because I could just be myself, without pretense. You make my life sane and you give me joy. You make me laugh."

"I never deserved this. But I promise, Brandy, nothing's going to change that. If I hadn't met you, I'd have never had the courage to try out for the Teams again. I'm always going to be here for you because you've always been there for me. No matter what."

"No matter what. That's a promise Tucker."

SEALED FOREVER

Bone Frog Brotherhood Book 3

SHARON HAMILTON

CHAPTER 1

NAVY SEAL TUCKER Hudson squinted across the beach bonfire that roared taller than any of the men on his SEAL Team 3. He was back—at least in all the ways he could be at forty years of age. A retread. He'd survived the landmines of past deployments and the vacancy of those years off the teams, as well as the grueling BUD/S training re-qualifying for his spot. He was ready for his first mission as a new *silver* SEAL, as the ladies called him. He was a Bone Frog, one of the old guys on SEAL Team 3.

He was ready for the do-over. Told himself he deserved it. But just to add a little gasoline to the fire in his soul, his childhood best friend, Brawley Hanks, was failing. And that's what ate at him.

Brawley had just spent six months in rehab while Tucker completed his SQT, SEAL Qualification Training. His chief, Kyle Lansdowne, had misgivings about allowing Brawley to go on the next mission to Africa, but since Tucker would be there, his LPO had overruled a suggestion from higher up to sit him out. This didn't help Tucker's nerves any. He knew it was his job to cover all that up and make those jitters disappear.

He watched the ladies dancing around the bonfire and looked for his wife of two months. Brandy cooed over Dorie and Brawley's little pink daughter while Dorie showed her off. The toddler was fast asleep. Several of the Team's kids jumped to get a look at the child until Dorie knelt and let them stand in a circle and check her out.

Their particular SEAL platoon tradition made them gather at the beach before a new deployment. All the wives, the kids, the close girlfriends, and occasionally parents were there. But only those on the inside, in the know. Some had lost loved ones. Some had been injured. Some had suffered too much. But these were the people who held them all together—who would hold Brandy together while he was gone.

The past two years with Brandy had been the hardest but most rewarding years of his life. When he was a younger SEAL, sometimes the ladies made him nervous since he didn't have anyone to come home to. But now that he did, now that he could actually lose something dear to him, it made this little celebration all the more special. He'd missed those evenings under the stars in Coronado, surrounded by life and the promise of living forever.

No one else would understand this kind of SEAL brotherhood, Tucker thought. You had to live it to know how it felt to be part of this family. You had to cry and celebrate with these people, tell them things would turn out, somehow. The miraculous would happen, because it always did. That's who they were. There wasn't any other group in the whole world he'd rather be a part of.

He'd tried doing without before. He knew better.

Tucker studied the beautiful, round face of his new bride and all her other curves that enticingly called to him by firelight. It seemed she grew more and more stunning every day. Her eyes met his, and he glanced down quickly, embarrassed that he might look like a teenage boy. But that's the way he felt. He was back to being the big, quiet kid the Homecoming Queen or head cheerleader came over to tease. It used to happen a lot in high school and he'd never gotten used to it.

Chief Petty Officer Kyle Lansdowne took up a seat next to him.

His chief was the most respected man on the team, even more than some of the officers, who were never invited to these events. Kyle had worked hard to make sure Tucker came to his squad. Although slightly younger than Tucker or Brawley, Kyle's experience leading successful campaigns through sticky assignments made him one of Team 3's most valuable assets.

"You nervous?" his LPO asked.

"You asked me that the day of my wedding, remember?"

Kyle nodded.

"I was nervous then." Tucker took a pull on his long-necked beer. "I know what I'm getting into this time." He smiled, which was reflected back to him.

"Well, you know what they say about leading men. Don't ask a question you don't know the answer to first." Kyle clinked his bottle against Tucker's.

"Hey, meant to give you a big congrats on making Chief."

"I have the best fuckin' platoon on the Teams. Makes it easy," Kyle said with a wink.

"Easy? You fuckin' said easy? That's B.S. and you know it."

They clinked glasses again and watched the children fawning over Brawley's daughter, still sleeping by the firelight, tucked in Dorie's arms. Kyle's two were right in the middle of them. Brandy gave Tucker a sexy wave.

"You got a good one, Tucker. I'm really happy for you," Kyle whispered, continuing to follow the ladies.

"You bet I did." Tucker meant every word he uttered. He'd always liked women he could grab onto and squeeze without breaking half her ribs. Brandy had the heart he did and that fierce joy of living, which also matched his own. And she'd earned that because of how she'd fought for every ounce of respect she so richly deserved. She spoke her mind. She loved with abandon, and he was damned lucky to have her in his corner. He was also grateful she let him go off and be a warrior again, just when most friends his age had wives ragging on them to quit.

And that was okay too. The SEAL teams were a revolving door of fresh and old faces, and internal dramas played out every day all over the world. It was sometimes hardest on the families. Men had to consider all of that when they played Varsity.

Kyle searched the crowd.

"I haven't seen him in about twenty minutes," Tucker mumbled. It worried him, too, that Brawley wasn't nearby. "I think he might have gone to get more beer, but that's just a rumor."

He knew Kyle suspected he was making up a safe story, which is why he didn't say a word. Then his chief slowly turned, facing him. "You let me know if he gets shaky, and I thoroughly suspect he will." Kyle's voice was low, avoiding anyone else's ears.

The two men stared at each other for a few long seconds.

"I got it, Kyle. He's not on his own."

"And you only risk a little. Don't let that go over the edge."

"We don't leave men behind." Tucker knew Kyle understood what he meant.

"No, we don't. I want you both upright. Both of you, Tucker."

"Roger that."

They gripped hands. Then Kyle broke it off and punched him in the arm.

"Dayam, Tucker. You can stop drinking those protein shakes anytime now."

Tucker liked that thought but dished some trash talk back. "Lannie, it ain't protein shakes. It's her," he said, aiming his beer bottle at Brandy. "You should see how she works me out."

Kyle stood up and then murmured, "I can't unsee that, dammit," and disappeared into the crowd.

Tucker hoped Brawley would show himself soon. His "ghosting" wasn't a good sign. He should be at Dorie's side. Tucker kept searching and then finally spotted Brawley pissing into the surf, which meant he was drunker than he should be.

Come on, Brawley. You're gonna get us both killed.

Brandy was still occupied with the women, and Kyle was having a little nuzzle time with Christy while carrying one of his two on his shoulders. Tucker scrambled to his feet and strolled toward his best friend, who was now throwing rocks into the ocean. His jeans were wet, and he was barefoot.

Brawley Hanks grew up alongside Tucker's family in Oregon. He couldn't ever remember a time when they weren't best friends. Always competitors when it came to sports and girls, even enlisting in the Navy the same day, they attended the same BUD/S class. They'd planned on getting out after their ten years, but close to the end, Brawley met Dorie, and, well, the poor guy couldn't help himself and got hitched up. She had pushed for the re-signing bonus so they could buy a nice house in Coronado. A beautiful, classy girl with all the wildness Brawley had, Dorie was missing his self-destructive bend.

Tucker wondered at first if their marriage would survive, but as Brawley showed all the signs of getting seriously embroiled in a lusty kind of full-tilt love that made him go stupid and do dumb things like buy flowers, Tucker became convinced his friend had finally been tamed and had given up his wandering ways.

Except that after his last two deployments, Brawley returned to his old ways—being the bad boy he'd always been before he met Dorie. He drank and chased too much. And although they had high hopes for his rehab, Tucker wasn't as convinced as Brandy or Dorie that his bad days were behind him.

"Hit any fish yet?" he asked Brawley.

"Fuck no," Hanks replied, slurring his words and letting go of another smooth, flat stone. It didn't skip like he'd been aiming to do.

"You know the more you hit the ocean, that ocean is gonna get you back, Brawley."

"I'm registering my complaint."

Tucker had to proceed with caution. He was at one of those turning points. But if Brawley lost it, at least he'd lose it here and save Kyle the trouble of having him sent home in shame. It sucked to be thinking this way just a day from deployment, but it was what it was. No sense sugar-coating it.

"I think your registration is going to the wrong department. Got your branches of service mixed up, Brawley. You should take it up with the man upstairs. Have you had that conversation recently?"

Brawley squinted back at him, as if the moonlight hurt his eyes. He did look like a big teenager, albeit a lethal one.

"I wear the Trident. Poseidon and Davy Jones are my buds. The man upstairs has given up on me."

His challenge hit Tucker in his stomach. *You dumb fuck. Where are you goin'?*

He walked to within inches of Brawley's hulking form. Inhaling deeply, he worked to calm himself down so it would be effective. He knew he only could say this once, so he made sure Brawley didn't misunderstand his steely stare.

"I'm going to remind you that you brought a daughter into the world. What kind of a world do you want her to grow up in, you old fart? You want her to grow up with an angry son-of-a-bitch for a father like you did, Brawley?"

His best friend started to interrupt him, and Tucker grabbed his ears and spit out his message.

"Or were you thinkin' you'd check out over there in that shit African red clay, making Dorie a widow and your daughter fatherless? Maybe causing the death of one or more of your friends who have pledged their lives to save your dumb ass. You willing to take us all with you? You want to be that kind of best friend to me, Brawley? Or are you gonna man-up?"

Tucker released Brawley's ears and pivoted like a Color Guard. He thanked his lucky stars he hadn't gotten clobbered with that delivery and called it good. Whatever Brawley did next was up to him.

It was just something that had to be delivered *before* they left for Africa. After they were there, it would be too late.

Tucker had done all he could.

CHAPTER 2

B RANDY HELD LITTLE Jessica, who began to stir and then fuss. She knew the toddler would sense she wasn't in her mother's arms, and it didn't take long. Jessica's blue eyes opened wide and then squinted, as if she considered going into a fearful cry, but then smoothed out as Brandy whispered down to her,

"You know me, Jessica. It's your auntie Brandy. And Mommy is right here, see?" She propped the child at an angle so she could see her mother standing next to Brandy. Dorie gave her another funny face and tickled her under her chin, which made Jessica giggle.

But when the squirming got to be more pronounced, Brandy handed her back to her mother.

"She's getting big. Can't believe how heavy she is now," Brandy said to her best friend.

"I know it. I fear she's going to take after Brawley's side of the family."

Both of them laughed.

"How are they these days?" Brandy asked.

"As weird as ever. Brawley's dad is having some health issues. She's trying to get him to give up drinking."

"Oh, Lord. I thought she was smarter than that."

"Brawley says it was a good talk with his dad, one of the best they'd had recently."

Brandy remembered the day of Dorie and Brawley's wedding. Mr. Hanks was so proud of his son for following in his Team footsteps, even if Brawley hadn't yet made it to twenty years like his father did. She remembered how tender Tucker was about the older man. The story had touched her, how this gruff old guy stood by his often cold and emotionally distant wife and two daughters. He was tough as nails with Brawley, but loved him intensely. She knew old man Hanks lived through Brawley.

She searched the crowd for Tucker and found him returning to the campfire, alone. He struck up a conversation with several newbie SEALs—froglets, as they were called.

Dorie was swinging Jessica around, singing. The firelight on her face melted the lines and dark shades her face had shown of late.

Honeymoon is over. Now the real life begins.

When Dorie took a bench, Brandy sat next to her and they swayed, shoulder to shoulder, like they'd done so many times over the past few years—before they were married, before Dorie's little girl, and before all the trouble that was brewing.

She wanted to ask her friend how things were going but didn't want to intrude or shatter what simple sense of peace the night gathering was giving her. The stars were out now. Someone was playing a guitar and laughter erupted as older children splashed in the evening surf, monitored by hovering moms and dads.

She remembered the 4th of July fireworks at the Santa Cruz Boardwalk her parents took her to once when she was a child. That night, they lay back on the blanket spread for all of them, holding hands, the three of them watching the night sky light up and sparkle as if it would go on without end.

Those were special summer days. Holding on to the hands of the two most important people in her life, inoculated against the screams of the Big Dipper coaster. She was never afraid when they both were there. It never occurred to her that these happy days wouldn't last forever. She made a mental note to enjoy what today, what tonight was and was not—to cherish it. And instead of the steady hands of her parents, she now had her big man with his basketball hands and arms the size of small tree trunks who could hold her tight if ever she was afraid and, in the most delicate of ways, hold her heart in the palm of his enormous hand.

She'd always been a woman to barge ahead and make space for herself, especially since opportunities weren't offered to her as often as they were for beautiful women like Dorie. Brandy had to work for it, yet, in Tucker's arms, she almost felt as fragile and delicate as a small bird.

Jessica had fallen asleep again, so Brandy offered to hold her, giving her mother's arms a break. The cherub leaned against her soft chest and grabbed the folds of her sundress in her sleep. She smelled clean. Her warm breath was soothing. Someday Brandy knew she'd like to hold one of her own, when the right time came along.

She glanced up and caught Tucker watching her rocking Dorie's daughter. His warm smile sent an electric spark down her spine. Her eyes watered as she inhaled and let her heart soak up all the love she had for this man. She was the luckiest girl in the world.

Dorie rested her head on Brandy's shoulder. "Look at that big oaf. He loves you so much. You can just tell the way he looks at you. I've never seen him so happy, Brandy," her best friend said, breathlessly.

"Who knew, right?" Brandy referred to the fact that he'd always been considered a permanent bachelor, just as she had fit the old cliché *"always a bridesmaid..."* He was strong as an ox and fiercely loyal but not the womanizing type, and so he had never been chased. That was something else they had in common.

Dorie noticed the tears in her eyes. "It's okay to cry, Hon. What you two have is special." She raised her head and angled it the opposite direction. "Sometimes, I envy you so much."

That was always how Brandy had felt, being Dorie's plus-sized friend, who was good-natured, positive, easy to talk to, but not the stunner Dorie was. She was aware that sometimes men befriended her just to get closer to Dorie.

All that had changed. And now Dorie was filled with envy of the love she shared with Tucker.

"Welcome to my world, Dorie. I used to feel that way about you every time we went somewhere. Then it was you and Brawley, the perfect couple. I wanted that so much."

"And see? You got it."

There was an awkward pause, and she found the courage to ask that question she'd been needing to. "So how's he doing?"

Dorie sat up straight. She pulled her oversized sweatshirt over her knees and wiggled her bare toes in the sand then re-clipped her hair, which she always did when she was thinking. "He's nervous. But I think he'll do all right. He just needs to prove to himself that he can handle the load."

Brandy nodded. "Tucker will keep an eye out for him. He looks ready," she said and then wished she could take it back.

They grew silent again. "He's got good meds, when he takes them. He'll be on them the rest of his life, the doctor told us. But he still is getting used to how they feel. I know he worries it will affect his reaction times."

"Performance anxiety. He'll shake it off, Dorie. You'll see." She wanted to be as positive as she could. She wanted to believe every word, but deep inside, she had some niggling doubts.

It was time to change the subject.

"You have plans for the two of you when they're overseas?"

"Mom wants me to go on a cruise with her, but I don't want to take Jessica, and I don't want to leave her."

"Let me take her. I'd love to help out. You just let me know. Go have that vacation with your mom," Brandy whispered.

Dorie smirked. "It's not a real vacation being with her, especially when she's between boyfriends. I feel like I'm the chaperone and she's the wayward teenager."

Brandy laughed. "Good point. You and your mom have always been like that, though. Take advantage of it while she's outrageous. I'd give anything to have just one more day with my mom. It's been over sixteen years and I still miss her every day."

Dorie put her arm around her shoulders. "Sweetie, you deserve a big hug for that one. We'll just help each other, then. And you should paint. Your sketches are beautiful, Brandy. Maybe this will give you time to explore that part of yourself you can't when he's around. And it might help you get your mind off worrying about what they're doing and if they're safe."

"I'll need some of that."

"We both will."

TUCKER WAS QUIET on the ride home. Brandy snuggled against him in the front seat, tucking herself under the protection of his huge wing. She could feel his thoughts.

They would have tonight together and all day tomorrow. One last chance for a perfect Sunday, and then it was early to bed for his four o'clock trip to the base for transport overseas. It was the first time she would be home alone knowing Tucker wasn't on a training exercise but an actual mission.

His chest began to rumble. "You're doing really well, honey. It will be over before you know it. The second and third time, they say it gets easier. After that, well, they'll be asking all the newbie wives to hang around you for advice and comfort. You'll see. Christy, Dorie, and the other wives will take good care of you."

"Thanks, Tucker. I'll try to check in with your folks and sister a bit too."

"They'd love that. But don't be surprised if my mom gets you worried. She's the worrier in the Oregon clan. Always was. Even worse now, I think."

"But she's so proud..." Brandy started to say.

"She doesn't favor the odds, the more I go over. It's just a fact of deployment."

Brandy knew it was one thing to be married to the love of her life knowing he was going over to a foreign and very hostile environment and quite another to raise a son going into harm's way.

"I totally get it, Tucker." She withdrew and studied his face. They had parked at her bungalow. "Only thing that makes it okay is that I know it's what you love. Who would I be if I tried to stop you from your desires?"

His grin shone in the moonlight.

"Speaking of those desires..." he mumbled then covered her mouth with his. "I want to make some memories in the next few hours we have left so I'll have things to dream about over in the jungle." His hand brushed her cheek tenderly. "I won't be sad if I focus on the homecoming," he whispered before he claimed her hungry mouth.

Their kisses turned into heavy petting. Her bra became un-hooked. His head barcly fit under the tight tee shirt until she pulled it up around her neck. He hoisted her up onto his lap after he slid beyond the steering wheel. She slowly pressed her mound over his groin and followed his hard edge then repeated the movement, back and forth, loving the stimulation. She was getting soaked with her own juices.

She framed Tucker's face between her hands. His wet lips and tongue had abused her nipples, which knotted and perked for him. His paw grazed down her rear, seeking entrance to her core with two long, probing fingers. She bent her knees at his hips and rose up just enough so he could feel her heat and the wetness of her desire.

"Baby, I want to do this right here, right now, so if that's what you want, I'm good with it," he whispered.

"Anytime, Tucker. Anywhere."

It was tight in the cab of his truck, but she managed to move down on him, eventually finding and covering his shaft, setting off the horn in only one staccato burst. She didn't even look outside to see if her father, who lived in the big home in front, had heard them.

And she could tell Tucker hadn't even noticed.

CHAPTER 3

TUCKER AWOKE TO the smell of bacon and coffee. Their Sunday routine usually meant sleeping in and staying in bed fooling around as long as possible, often until lunch. But he knew she was making him a memorable breakfast, to add to some of the memorable things they'd done last night in the truck and again in the bed until they both collapsed.

But today, he felt ready to go, ready to do it all over again. And he was starved.

He donned his American flag boxers and padded his way to the kitchen, where Brandy hummed a new country tune they liked. She wore her pink fuzzy robe, the one that was a tad bit small for her, not that he was complaining. The thing gaped open and only managed to keep her back and shoulders warm. It did nothing to cover up her luscious chest or that delicious triangle between her legs he was hoping to explore soon.

She was barefoot, her hair clipped atop her head, one hand holding a red coffee mug and the other massaging bacon with a red spatula. Brandy's smile could warm the North Pole. He especially liked the bruises she had on the right side of her neck.

"Look at you!" he growled.

She pointed the red spatula at him. "Look at *you!*" she returned. "All dressed up and nowhere to go."

He moved around to her backside while she continued to cook the bacon. He let her feel his hardness as his knees bent slightly, connecting their thighs. "I have something for you. Just take a seat," he said in a raspy whisper before carefully kissing an especially large reddish-purple bruise under her right ear.

"But I got bacon and coffee, Tucker," she murmured.

"I got bacon for you, sugar."

She wiggled her butt against him. His hands were inside her robe and, in one easy move, had turned off the stovetop and hoisted her up in the air, carrying her back to the bedroom.

"I wanted to make you something special," she giggled, still holding the red spatula.

"Oh, you are, honey. I can't wait to taste it."

He tossed her on the bed. She threw the spatula at him.

"So you want to fight? I can fight with you, honey." He pulled her ankles toward him, dropped his drawers, and was nearly inside her swollen lips when his phone rang. The ringtone meant it was Brawley.

"God dammit!"

"Just forget it. Put it in, Tucker."

"I'm going to, but I gotta take this call."

"Fuck me, Tucker. I promise to be real quiet."

He liked her spunk and her compliance, but he crawled over the bed, reaching for the phone at the side table. She was moving her body up to match him, pulling his butt checks down, trying to get him positioned for lovemaking.

"Brawley, your timing sucks," he said to his teammate.

"Oh, that's right. It's your fuck day."

Tucker held the phone out to Brandy while he began to give her another hickey. Brandy laughed.

"Hi, Brawley," she teased. "Go ahead and talk, but Tucker's sort of preoccupied at the moment."

She squealed as Tucker's tongue slid between her legs.

"You guys are both assholes," he squawked through the phone. "Guess I'll go do my PT by myself. No fun running with someone who can't keep up, anyway."

Tucker jerked to attention. "I can keep up. I can whoop your ass any day."

Next, they heard a tap on Brandy's bedroom window and discovered Brawley standing just outside, in the garden, with his cell phone to his ear.

Brandy screamed and dove for the bedcovers. Tucker lifted a pillow to cover himself then disconnected the call.

"Fuckin' jerk. I'll be right out," he shouted. To Brandy, he pulled aside the blankets. "I'm so sorry, sweetheart. Let me get a timed run in, and I'll be right back, if that's okay."

She smiled. "I'll get the breakfast finished and will put the eggs on when you get back. I got biscuits and blackberry jam my dad made last week. You could invite Brawley, if you want."

"No way," he said as he pulled on his running shorts and a tee shirt and then slipped into his running shoes. From the dresser, he retrieved his fitness watch. "I'll be back in about an hour, maybe a little longer. But I have plans for that blackberry jam." He wiggled his eyebrows.

She was still curled in fetal position, her tempting pink body parts peeking out from beneath the covers. "I'll be ready." Coming to her knees, she held up a sheet to cover her frontside and looked up to him with a sexy smile. "Have a good run."

Once outside, Tucker jumped into Brawley's truck, and the two of them took off toward the beach for their five-mile run and swim cool down. Brawley had music on loud, so a conversation was out of the question.

When they parked at the State beach, Tucker took advantage of the near-silence.

"You really are an asshole. Last morning before we leave. Did it ever occur to you I might have had other plans, you jerk?"

"Oh, I knew what you were probably doing or had just finished doing or were getting started doing. Look at it this way, I'm saving you from the excuse that you don't need to work out today. You're an old guy, Tucker. You don't have all the stores the younger ones have."

Brawley said the last bit while running quickly away from Tucker, over the sand dune covered in ice plant, and heading for the firmer sand by the surf.

Tucker had to work to catch up to him, and then Brawley turned on the speed, not giving him an ounce of respite. But Tucker had everything he needed, and the anger in his gut gave him a little more. He never let Brawley lead, not even by a nose.

At the conclusion of their run, they dove into the surf and paddled out into the inlet, doing a buddy swim in tandem. Tucker's swim stroke was the most challenging for him now at his age and weight. Although he'd kept up his timed runs and weight training, finding time for swim workouts had been difficult over the past ten years. His older body preferred a pool over the oily and dank inlet.

He considered trimming down his body size after this next deployment. Brawley was a natural swimmer, and Tucker could barely keep up to him until the last stretch, when he pulled away and left Tucker feeling like he was dogpaddling behind. Emerging from the surf, he found Brawley sunning himself on the sand, waiting. His eyes were closed, covered with the trim dark sunglasses they all wore that hugged his face.

Tucker kicked a little sand onto Brawley's chest.

"Ah, thanks for the catnap, grandpa."

"I'm only a month older than you are. Give me a session at Gunny's Gym and you'll drop that cocky attitude."

Tucker stood slightly taller than Brawley, but both of them

were two of the tallest SEALs on Team 3.

Tucker reached down to give a hand, pulling Brawley up.

"You game for a protein shake or coffee?" Brawley asked as both men retrieved their shoes and shirts and then ambled barefoot to the truck.

"Nah, I gotta get back. Brandy's got biscuits and her famous cheesy scramble and some homemade blackberry jam I'm dying to devour. I'm famished."

"Suit yourself."

Brawley covered the front seat with a couple of old beach towels he retrieved from behind the cab. Tucker rubbed the sand from his feet and ankles, dropped his running shoes on the floorboards and positioned his wet lower torso carefully on the fluffy towel.

"You have plans for today?" he asked Brawley.

"Dorie wants to take Jessica to the aquarium, so I think we'll head over there and have a picnic. We had a rough night with the little one up every two hours. When I left, they were both crashed, finally, so I'm going to let them sleep as long as they can."

"Good idea."

"You?"

"Just fooling around. Gotta finish packing, clean my Sig, and double check the rest of my gear. It's not second nature yet, but I know it will be, so I'm doing everything twice. You need anything for your kit in case I stop by the base?"

"I'm good."

They rode in silence until they turned onto the road leading to Brandy's bungalow. Her dad's truck was gone, so Tucker made a note to make a quick stop at the store to say good-bye.

"I meant to talk to you a little over coffee, so let me just get something off my chest, Tucker."

Brawley's arms and hands rested at the top of the steering wheel while he waited for permission to continue. He was focused on Brandy's front door as he pulled to a stop next to Tucker's truck.

"Shoot. I'm all ears, now that I'm fully awake." Sand was itching Tucker's backside as he angled his body, turning to partially face his teammate.

"I wasn't too proud of my behavior last night, Tuck. Had a real anti-social streak going on, and I should have stopped with the drinking much sooner."

"I wondered why you got so hammered. You're getting to be a mean old drunk, Brawley." It was awkward for Tucker to say this, but he wanted to make sure his friend knew it had been noticed.

"Yeah, Kyle said something too."

"We can't do it all, Brawley. You gotta meet us halfway. Just like boat crew. Everyone has to pull their own weight."

Tucker noticed Brawley flinched at those words.

"You have to exercise better judgment. What if something happens and you have to lead the team?"

Brawley looked away, nodding and staring out the driver side window.

"You brought your meds?"

"I got them packed. Went off them yesterday, because, well, I have trouble—"

Brandy had confided that Brawley had impotence issues sometimes when he regularly took the medication cocktails he was prescribed. He guessed this sacrifice of Brawley's demeanor went to no avail since the angry streak probably played havoc with his ability to be intimate. And Tucker knew it wasn't just about performance. Brawley wasn't that kind of guy.

"You can't do that."

Brawley shot Tucker a glare, winced, and rolled his right shoulder. His lips formed a thin straight line. "I wanted to show Dorie—"

"I know all about it, asshole. We've studied those meds in core school. But it's dangerous. You can't go taking risks."

Tucker wanted to leave the conversation alone until they had more time. But he adjusted his attitude and decided he'd give Brawley as much as he needed.

"Dorie's gonna love you anyway, sport. You know that. If you think about it, don't you figure she'd rather have you settled than hard, you dumb fuck?"

"Yup, you're probably right." Brawley's voice trailed off to some place distant.

"Doesn't make you less of a man. Besides, you can do other things, you know, work on it. Make it a project. Make it fun. I think you just need to get used to this new state. You'll figure it out. Only been about, what, four or six months now? But definitely using too much alcohol is a big mistake. That's on you, Brawley."

"I know. I didn't want to be there. I felt like everyone was watching me, looking for tiny cracks."

"You know that's bullshit, Brawley."

"And you're a terrible liar."

"I don't want to preach, but damned if I'm going to shut up, either. We get over there, and we'll be busy, and I won't have the time."

Tucker waited several seconds for the heavy words to clear. In the small space they shared in private, he continued in a whisper. "Brawley, the only way you'll get through this is to charge right through it. Who cares? You have a medical condition, like someone having a bum hip or a slightly sprained ankle. We watch out for one another. You make good decisions, Brawley, and people will stop watching you." He faced his childhood friend again. "Only way out is through. Right fuckin' through the middle."

CHAPTER 4

B RANDY HEARD BRAWLEY'S truck arrive and was glad she'd decided to shower and get dressed, since their run had taken longer than Tucker had promised. She knew her husband took the responsibility for Brawley's mental state of mind seriously. She had the rest of the day and evening to launch her first good-bye strategy. It was more important that Tucker see she could handle the separation maturely, like she had done when he went off to Great Lakes, BUD/S, and SQT. It was her job to give Tucker one less thing to worry about while he was on a real mission.

He headed barefoot to her front door, tapping sand from between his toes and on his shoes. He left his shoes on the stoop. Wrapping his arms around her, her big man nuzzled in her ear, and apologized.

"Is everything okay?" she had to ask.

Tucker sighed, scanning her face. He was thinking again—choosing his words carefully. Measuring. Waiting for something that would be revealed later. At last he gave the expected answer.

"I think so. We all just need to give him time. They had a rough night with the kid."

She felt the pang of disappointment, knowing that at some time in the future perhaps they too would have a day before deployment that wasn't ideal. Kids and other family members caused all sorts of chaos. Things get said. People get sick. There were bills to pay and other stresses on young SEAL families.

And there was never enough time to settle everything before they had to leave again. She'd heard the stories. Had happened to people everyone was surprised at. It could derail Tucker and Brandy too.

That's just the way life works sometimes.

"Why don't you go clean up, and I'll have everything ready when you get out?" She followed it with a kiss and a slap on his butt.

"Roger that. I'm off to the shower."

After breakfast, she threw in another load of clothes for his journey to Africa. She watched him search through his things—zip and unzip the packing sleeves and boxes he had organized, counting items in his medic kit, double-wrapping some articles in bubble wrap or foam wedges, and taping others together. He threw in two large rolls of duct tape, a box of disinfectant wipes, bug repellent, and a box of her lavender-scented dryer sheets.

His duty bag contained his specialized equipment, protection devices, and weapons. It would be carried separately with all the other team gear.

He left his clothing bag open as they headed out to run errands.

"Has anyone told you how long it will be?" she asked.

The traffic was blissfully light for a Sunday. He took a back route, away from the potential of distracted drivers unfamiliar with the little roads. It took longer, but it was worth it, he liked to tell her.

"At least a couple of months. It's something new, so we're not replacing another team who's coming home. A lot depends on what we find when we get there."

She knew this, but it was reassuring to hear him explain it again. It verified there was no camouflaged story, just consistent facts.

"Any last-minute instructions? Like when I'll hear from you, or can call you?"

"Not until we get there, Brandy. My phone will be off most of the time. But you can leave me some sexy messages."

He followed it up with a wink. She was going to miss those little half-smiles and winks.

"We're hoping we'll be able to do some face-to-face calls, but we have to be careful about the electronic footprint, so they'll lay it out for us when we get there. They'll establish a protocol."

He suggested she stay close with the other wives but be careful about repeating gossip or treating speculation as truth.

"Things can get blown out of proportion. We don't want to start any marital discord if we can help it," he added.

She'd never thought about that. "I can see why it's important to stay in touch."

"Yep. Christy will give you a call list, and just like the rest of us do when we're home, she'll tell you who you need to be in contact with on a daily basis. I'm guessing you and Dorie will be in the same grouping since you're already best friends. That way, we don't miss anything. Anyone has trouble with the kids or there is an illness, everyone pitches in. You know, life?"

"Yes, I do."

"You get any calls from overseas you aren't positive are from the Navy or one of our team, you disengage."

"You're kidding. You mean I might get calls from Africa? They'll know I'm alone?"

"It could happen. One of my early deployments, one of the wives actually got a telegram. Someone was asking for money, saying her husband had been captured. You know something like that is bogus, right?"

"Of course."

"It would never go down that way. You'd hear from the Navy if something like that happened."

Brandy noted her heartbeat was racing. "You're making me scared, Tucker."

"Good. If it makes you cautious and prepared, good. Be careful who you talk to. Don't volunteer anything. People will want to ask. You can't tell if it's innocent or not. You report anything suspicious to Christy right away, and she'll know how to handle it."

"Got it."

They approached her father's gourmet fruit and grocery store. Tucker continued.

"There is a plan for every eventuality for the families of deployed just like we have. This isn't a group think or rule by committee. Christy calls the shots, and she's the one who has to know everything that's going on at home that's important. You don't ask anyone else's advice or overrule an instruction she's given."

Brandy made the mental note she'd have to stuff down some of her stubbornness, perhaps dial back some opinions as well.

"As long as they're sending you over there prepared, Tucker."

He turned off the truck and chuckled. "Sweetheart. Let me say this one more time."

He took her hand. "Things *always* get fucked up. No mission ever goes as planned. We're trained for the unexpected and, hopefully, ways we can adjust to any eventuality. That's what we do. We don't get to come home just because they didn't get us the support we needed. We have to make do."

Her stomach rumbled. Tucker must have seen the fear now resident in her eyes and her heart, pulsing throughout her body.

"One thing you need to know that might reassure you. We're the best trained force out there. And I couldn't have a better platoon leader than Chief Lansdowne. Over a third of these guys

I've known for over fifteen years, like Brawley. I did this before. I can do it again. And every one of those guys would take a bullet for me without a moment's hesitation."

She began to shake.

Tucker leaned forward and whispered to her lips as he nibbled between words, softly replacing her worry with new flames of desire. "All you have to do is trust me. Trust that it will all work out. Think about the homecoming every single day and every single night. Feel how good it will be to be back together again, okay, honey?"

He pressed deeper. Then she broke it off, came up for air, wrapped her arms around his neck, and hugged him with everything she had. "Just come back to me."

"Nothing human could keep me away."

CHAPTER 5

T UCKER SHOOK THE hand of Brandy's world-class dad, the man
who he could count on to keep Brandy from jumping off the
rails. He liked that she had this gentle man to confide in. His wise
counsel was something not all the other wives had. And, if the
worst should befall him, Steven Cook would be a great help in
bringing Brandy safely through to the other side.

He didn't like to think about all these things, but now he had
more to live for than in his earlier SEAL Team years, and so he had
a lot more to lose. He wanted to make sure he did everything he
could to prepare them both for the possibility that he could come
home injured or worse. Being prepared, even for bad news, was an
important step in the grieving process, and it was every SEAL's job
to make sure the families had this.

He remembered the advice he'd given Brawley this morning.

Only way out is to drive right through the middle.

And that's what he was doing right now, hoping he'd covered
all the bases.

Steven Cook had been acting casual, appearing to accept Tucker's upcoming trip, but their handshake took far too long, and
when they disengaged, his eyes were watering. Tucker hadn't been
paying attention to a thing he was saying because he was reading
the man's handshake non-verbally.

"Just like a camping trip when I was in the Scouts, Steve. Mosquito repellant, sunscreen SPF over one thousand, moist towelettes, and extra underwear."

"Geez, didn't know they made sunscreen at one thousand SPF," Cook said.

"They don't. I lied." Tucker gave him a grin and winked at Brandy.

Cook laughed and slapped his arm. "If it was me, I'd do a mosquito dip. Those bloodsuckers are big as birds, I've heard."

"Amen to that. When they have to put bars on the holes in the latrines, you know there are some creepy things that can come up and get you. I'm gonna have to get used to spraying my butt with repellent."

Even Brandy laughed at that one. "I thought they have trailers, like shipping containers outfitted with bathrooms and kitchens."

"Yeah, DIY tiny homes," added Cook.

Tucker could only wish. "You remember what I told you about being prepared? If I'm visualizing using a hole in the ground and I got a nice air-conditioned trailer with air freshener, the mental adjustment is not as difficult as the other way around."

"Tucker, I admire how many details you have to pay attention to. Most you guys could run large corporations with the experience you've gained. And you work together as one unit, bringing the best and brightest to places in the world that sorely need it."

"Well, sir, that's why I've never wanted to go to OCS. It's really more like running a zoo, in my opinion. And it's never bothered me to take direction or orders, either, as long as I respect my superiors."

"We ought to make Congress go through your training, Tucker."

"Roger that. Love 'em, but they got one speed and one solution to everything."

"What's that?" Brandy asked.

"Plaster it with paperwork—so much paperwork that no one can move."

The three of them had a good laugh at the expense of some of the men and women who were sending Tucker on his mission tomorrow.

Brandy left to grab water from her dad's walk-in cooler, so Tucker took the opportunity to be frank with her father.

"Steve, you be close to her. She's not going to hear from me as much as she wants. That's going to worry her."

Cook nodded.

Tucker continued. "I think she'll be fine, but you know her. She'll also try to cover it up. Don't let her do that. She can't retreat. She has to stay engaged, connected, even if it means doing busy things to distract from the inherent dangers of warfare. Get her to paint, take a class, or help out more here. Make sure she fills up her days with things so she's not alone."

"She loves to read. I'm sure she'll get a lot of that done."

"Her romances will provide good diversion. I'm totally okay with her reading those." He felt his own cheeks blush at some of the things Brandy had read in her books, adding to her sexual education. He considered himself a very lucky man.

"Tucker, what are you guys doing over there?" Cook asked him.

"Can't say, Steve. The very poor and the very powerful with guns and money make for a deadly combination. Somehow, we're supposed to get between them without getting ourselves killed. Beyond that, we might see no action, or it might be pure hell."

"I'm so happy you're part of our family, Tuck. My daughter— well, I've never seen her so happy. You be sure to take care."

"Best is yet to come, sir," Tucker said, with a wink.

They said their good-byes. Brandy squeezed her father tight.

"Whoa, wait a minute. You're staying *here*. With *me!*" Cook said, unpeeling her arms from around his neck.

"I just felt like it. That's all," was her response.

They carted the two bags of groceries into the cooler in Tucker's king cab. He'd asked her if she wanted to grab something at the ocean in lieu of a big dinner she'd have to prepare, and she agreed.

Multi-million-dollar yachts, charter ships, and sleek sailing vessels spread out all along the waterway leading to the ocean. Over half of the berths were empty but would be occupied come sunset. They took a table overlooking the water and ordered clam chowder with bread. The warm, creamed soup was soothing on Tucker's stomach as he watched the afternoon sun dance in Brandy's red and mahogany curls, making her appear her head was on fire.

He let his mind wander. He didn't want to overwhelm her this first time with too many instructions. But when he came back, he wanted to sit down and lay down some plans, some future goals, like buying a house, saving their money, and missions they could accomplish together. He was starting late in life to be a new husband. He didn't want to waste any time, but he also didn't want her to feel pressure. He had to take it one step at a time, check this first mission off the list.

So tonight would be about him showing her how much he loved her. How much he was going to miss her. He wanted to thank her for letting him do this gig. He knew he was lucky to have a woman who loved him for what he was and what he wanted to do. Tucker was going to make sure she experienced his love every single day of her life.

He covered her hand with his. "You ready to go?"

When she turned her head and her face was bathed in sunlight again, he discovered she'd been tearing up.

"Honest answer? No. I promised myself I'd be brave."

"You are brave. You're incredibly brave, Brandy. Don't be afraid to show it. It's part of who you are and why I love you so."

He drew her hand to his lips. Their fingers wove together and gently dropped to the shiny shellacked surface of the table. He rubbed her fourth finger with the undersized wedding ring on it he was going to replace as soon as they could afford it, despite what Brandy said.

"Promise me you'll paint. Spend time in the garden and with Dorie and Jessica and your dad, okay?"

"I promise. Can you promise me something too?"

"Sure. What?"

"Write me some letters, Tucker."

"No, ma'am. I'm not a writer."

"I don't care if you think you're a writer. Write what's going on. Just tell me like we were here and you were describing your day. I mean, say the things you can say. Leave out all the—"

He knew what she meant but answered her with humor. "Leave out the bugs, sunburns, flat tires, and snakes, right?"

"Especially the snakes."

"Come on, princess. Let's get you home. I need to add a few things to my bags, and then I'd like to turn in early, if you don't mind."

SHE WASN'T LOOKING at him as she slipped his freshly laundered and folded red, white, and blue boxers into his bag. Her nimble fingers combed over his things like she was looking at them for the last time. Her breathing was a little ragged. She bit her lower lip and he could see the top of her chest was blotchy. Tonight, he'd be gentle with her, kiss every tear away and make her purr like a kitten. He was overwhelmed by her grace, the dignity with which she handled her fear, and the trust she had in him.

He set his phone alarm and then took her by the hand into the shower. As the warm water relaxed them, he kissed her neck and down her spine, rubbing the lemon shower gel over her backside, and then drew his fingers up the front side of her luscious body. When her head rolled back to rest on his shoulder, she moaned.

"Don't ever doubt that I'll return, Brandy," he said as he drew his tongue up and under her ear. He splashed the lukewarm water over her shoulder and smoothed his palm down her front, squeezing the fullness of her breasts, capturing her nipples between his thumb and first two fingers, pinching her.

Her eyes flew open. She turned around, facing him. Arched on tiptoes, she mated her mouth to his, while water cleansed them both.

"And I'll be here, Tucker. I'll always be here," she whispered back to him.

He handed her the fluffy towel scented with lavender. "I can hardly wait."

That brought a smile to her face, finally.

The room turned darker as they slipped into bed. Everything he wanted to tell her, he could do with his touch. He tasted her soft skin, savored the many textures of her body, and explored her dark and sensitive places with his probing fingers. He'd been noticing her effort not to cry, so he did everything in slow motion until he felt hot tears of his own.

As he filled her and held her shattering body in his arms, he wished for a fleeting moment he'd never signed up to leave her. Why had he agreed to risk something so precious he'd waited for his whole life? Why did he ask her to endure that as well? Was it sweeter this way, as he played her body, because he knew now life was so fragile? It all could be over in an instant. Would she ever forgive him if he was the one not coming back—something just an hour ago he was certain could never, ever happen?

Forgive me, Brandy.

After their bodies had cooled, they stared into each other's eyes. His thumb caressed her smooth forehead, and he wiped away the silent tears that streamed down her cheeks into the pillow. Somewhere in the distance, a sea bird was calling. A freight train blew its whistle, and car lights flashed by from the hills looking over the valley floor, quickly dimmed by the consuming darkness of their last night together. It was the eve of his first deployment as a married man. He was whole, complete, content. No matter what, wherever Brandy was, it was home.

Life continues. Everything moves to the rhythm of our hearts. Nothing stops. Nothing stays the same. I am yours forever, Brandy.

He knew now that he could write those letters and exactly what he would tell her.

Tucker was off before dawn, slipping quietly out before Brandy awoke, which was planned. All their good-byes had been done last night, softened with kisses and watered with her tears. To the end, she was strong.

The transport made a stopover in Norfolk for fuel. Once the team landed in North Africa, they took commercial flights to Benin, all of them operated by French and African charter flights used by private contractors and various U.S.-backed aid services. In this way, the team was split up, and arrived from different destinations, in case anyone was watching. Everyone posed as energy consultants working to improve the quality of the electrical grid in Benin.

Tucker's plane was the first to arrive. He and Brawley spent a whole day waiting for the team to assemble and helping to coordinate supplies they'd need for the overland convoy into Nigeria. He found the port village along the coast of Benin fascinating. Its history of the Slave Coast trade had brought tribal leaders much wealth in past centuries, but at a huge price for its people who were caught between waring factions.

The buildings reflected Portuguese and Spanish influences,

which gave way to French architecture during the colonial period of the eighteenth to early twentieth centuries. France gave Benin independence in 1950 and, after a couple of decades of Marxist flirtation, was a now a country with a duly-elected administration, sorely in need of foreign aid to keep the peace. The popular vote wasn't always peaceful. The most dangerous times were during elections, but Benin had proved to be a good neighbor to the U.S. and, with help from French intelligence, was deemed a safe landing spot and good cover.

The Team was put up in a tourist hotel overlooking the ocean, that catered to international businessmen. He roomed with Brawley. Kyle had arrived the day before and was off to visit with their French intelligence contact, as well as pick up the vehicles they'd rented. His LPO group took up the top floor of the hotel, but the iron balconies cascaded on the outside like a web of ivy vines. If they wanted to avoid the rickety elevator that was said to work intermittently or the stairs, they could always scale the building with ease. The rest of the team was scattered throughout the hotel.

Brawley was excited to discover an espresso machine in the lobby he didn't have to pay for. It wasn't long before they were talking politics, but they stopped just before they descended into the depths of hell—religion. Tucker knew he'd have trouble sleeping tonight with all the caffeine he'd ingested.

Former professional goalkeeper, Patrick Harrington, and his roommate, Jameson Daniels, had the room next door. The four teammates explored the city together. Patrick dubbed Porto-Novo the "African Riviera" with its old waterfront hotels and large residences of glory days gone by.

"Except a hellofa lot more dangerous. And that's a shame." Tucker knew that in today's world, the port city was far from safe.

"Not safe at the Riviera anymore, either," quipped Patrick. He'd lived and played throughout Europe during his professional days.

"I get you."

The four bought small trinkets from several tourist shops, including some local refined and scented shea butter, one of Benin's largest exports. They also wandered through a large open-air market that sold produce, fish, palm oil and other items, stocking up on assortments of nuts and dried fruits, including some incredible dates and figs.

Ships of varying sizes docked haphazardly along the waterfront. Most of the boats were for local fisherman and charter crews, but occasionally, there would be a huge yacht guarded by several men bearing semi-automatic weapons. Most the larger crafts were anchored farther out and used jitneys for travel to the town, which Tucker thought would be safer.

The odor of fish mixed with diesel fuel permeated the air, and at times, it was thick with black smoke. Narrow alleys snaked from the main coastal road up the ridge to clusters of colorful, metal-roofed shacks that fanned out in all directions, which appeared to be homes for workers employed in the town. While French was the language Tucker recognized the most, many African dialects that had adapted words from various languages he could recognize. "Cell phone" and "text me" were words he heard quite commonly.

Tiny coffee houses and bars were squeezed between larger stores and warehouses. A good number of the buildings were abandoned or in the process of being torn down and rebuilt. People were living under blue and green plastic tarps amongst the rubble. In addition to flocks of bicycles, human pushcarts and scooters were the most common forms of transportation.

The four teammates slipped inside a darkly lit coffee house to sit and observe and speak amongst themselves in private.

A barefoot waiter served them thick black coffee poured from a tall Samovar in the middle of their table. It poured like pancake syrup and was accompanied by a chipped bowl of sugar and shea butter chunks light brown in color. When Tucker dropped one into his small cup, it created a creamy foam on top.

"Amazing," gasped Brawley. "I'm taking mine straight."

"Wow!" said Jameson. "A couple of cups of this and my teeth will be permanently stained shit-brown." He smiled, and Tucker could see he was right.

"Not too bad yet, but your breath is foul," answered his roommate, Patrick. He glanced around and studied the two men smoking at the bar. "We got two military-aged males keeping an eye on us over behind you, Tucker."

"Hey, thanks. We all need to keep watch for causing too much interest. Because of where we're from and our accents, they'll be curious what we're doing here," answered Tucker.

"How many deployments did you do in Africa, Tuck?" asked Jameson.

"Not here. We don't use any specialized terms in public, okay?"

"Gotcha."

"But hell yes, I've been to the east coast several times. Mostly I went to the sandbox."

Brawley spoke up. "Kyle and several of the guys spent time off the coast, Cape Verde. Even took a cruise that was a bit exciting."

Tucker had heard all about those trips and about how they had to sneak the ambassador's body home in a food cart aboard another cruise ship.

"Our last trip next door was quite interesting," said Patrick. "I played on the League with fellow from Nigeria who had to flee as a child. This waterfront living is all different, really is like an African Riviera. Inland, it's a whole different place."

"Kind of reminds me of the Caribbean," said Brawley.

"That's a result of the slave trade. How the islands got populated." Tuck finished off his syrupy mixture and then leaned into the table. "This is where Voodoo comes from."

"You've got to be kidding me," mumbled Jameson.

"It was brought to the Caribbean and then New Orleans with the slave traders. The French, who were expelled from Haiti a couple hundred years ago, settled in New Orleans with their French-speaking slaves, and many of the slaves brought their religion with them."

"You've done your research, Tucker."

"I love history. Just read up a bit about Benin. Nigeria was settled by the Brits, but there's lots of crossover. We're supposed to know something about the country we're helping, right?" He grinned and could see he'd impressed the younger SEALs. "When you're home, read up on these places so you'll be prepared. Helps to know who we're dealing with."

Jameson and Patrick nodded. Brawley punched him in the arm.

"If you gents are done, I'd like to move on. Not a good idea to stay too long in one spot if you don't know the neighborhood," Tucker advised.

"Sounds good to me," mumbled Brawley, who was halfway out the door.

Tucker looked for shops that might cater to European contractors and found one fairly large hardware store that sold maps, camping gear, auto parts, and heavy clothing suitable for hiking and fishing. He bought a map of the port, as well as one for the entire country of Benin, and one for Nigeria.

Jameson and Brawley looked over the fishing equipment, which was sparse. Some of the rods were used.

"That's a good idea," Tucker said. "That would make a good prop to walk around with," he said pointing down at the bucket of rods in varying stages of disrepair.

Brawley bought a small hand-held net, some sisal string, and a small roll of wire. He said he liked the feel of the hunting knife in his hand, so purchased that as well.

Walking back to their rooms at the Hotel Classique, Tucker noticed they didn't draw as much attention as they had before.

Kyle, Cooper, Armando, and Fredo were waiting for them when they returned and were headed out to the airport to pick up the remaining members of their SEAL Team 3 platoon. Much of their specialized equipment was arriving with the balance of the team.

His LPO indicated they would be staying another two days, so Tucker set to re-packing his suitcase. He took a shower, washed out his clothes, and hung them up next to Brawley's laundry. When he reached for his patriotic boxers, something fell out onto the floor. It was a green leather journal slightly larger than the size of his hand. He opened the first page to read her inscription:

Tucker, my love.

I hope you find this easier to chronicle your journey and hope it helps fill the hours until you can return home. My heart is with you, as always. I know the men with you are lucky to have your experience and emotional strength. Enjoy what you can of the trip, and we'll bury or blow up all the other stuff when you get home.

All my love,
Brandy

He chuckled, which drew Brawley's attention. As he fingered through several sketches Brandy had made sporadically through-out the journal in watercolor pencil, his buddy had some choice remarks.

"I'm not checking my bag too closely. I might have gotten a dirty diaper."

"So that's what smells," said Tucker. "Make sure you bring her something nice, Brawley. I think she'd love getting some nice warm

Moroccan oil you can drizzle all over her body. It might be the miracle you're searching for."

He hoped Brawley would take it casually, but he wasn't sure. Brawley didn't speak to him the rest of the evening.

CHAPTER 6

TWO DAYS AFTER Tucker left for Africa, Brandy resumed work at her dad's store. She began training the new bookkeeper they'd hired. The little office had recently undergone a DIY makeover with a professional organizer Brandy found. It had been difficult to get anyone to even interview for the job, but after the decluttering and straightening, the space had been turned into a very efficient and sunny little office. No longer were boxes of invoices and books stacked to the ceiling, obscuring the window. She'd purchased attractive curtains and replaced the old AM radio with a new internet receiver and speakers installed around the store so they could stream upbeat music.

One of the things that didn't change was a metal bar of hooks behind the office door her mother had found at an antique store and attached herself. They were sacred, and they were like hands reaching out to hold hers and her father's green aprons. She nixed getting the door painted because it meant the hooks would have to be removed and then replaced. No one was going to do that to her mother's handicraft. She knew her dad would agree without even asking him.

Steve Cook arrived late, nearly Noon. He was wearing a long-sleeved, pinstriped white shirt and green bow tie. He noted her expression.

"Thought I'd start looking the part. I'm the green grocer now."

"The *gourmet* grocer, Dad." She hugged him. "How did you get the nerve to buy that bow tie?"

"I had a few things in my drawers I've not worn for years. I went through some stuff and got rid of tons of old clothes. Ratty with holes or things I was tired of. Decided to splurge on five new shirts, some jeans that weren't so baggy, and two bow ties. You like?"

"Definitely a good look for you."

Brandy had noticed he'd been losing weight, and he'd been using a belt with his faded blue jeans, cinching them up. Today, he looked ten years younger.

Studying his face, she also noticed he'd gotten a haircut and was allowing a bit of salt and pepper stubble to form on his cheeks and chin.

"I like this look, Dad."

He swung the green apron over his head, tied it behind his waist, and spread his arms to his sides.

"Showtime!"

Brandy watched him wander out onto the floor with a new spring in his step. He spoke to several customers before he started ringing in sales.

He was absolutely charming.

She wondered how long this change had been coming, realizing she'd been so preoccupied with Tucker's deployment that she hadn't been focusing on anything else.

As the day turned into late afternoon and early evening, she stopped checking her cell to see if there was a message that Tucker had arrived safely. He'd told her he could only call after their situation was settled and warned her it might take a week to get that established. But it was force of habit, and now she understood it was one more routine she'd have to learn to live without temporarily.

She'd made plans to have dinner with Dorie tonight and headed there after work. Before her best friend could open the door, Brandy heard Jessica's wailing.

"She's gotten hold of a red pen and marked all over our white leather furniture in the living room. Thank God Brawley is gone," said Dorie as she held the squirming child.

Jessica's arms were covered with long lines of red, and several also appeared on her cheeks. As soon as she was set down, the toddler began running full tilt. Brandy was worried she'd hit a wall and hurt herself. Her shrieking was ear-piercing. Brandy's words of sympathy were completely drowned out.

"Can't leave her unsupervised for a second. This all happened while I was in the bathroom, for Chrissakes," said Dorie breathlessly.

Brandy helped box Jessica off so her mother could pick her up. The toddler immediately wiggled and tried to pry herself loose.

"I don't even know what to use to get this off. It's permanent marker," said Dorie.

Brandy looked at the white couch Jessica had customized. "I'm not sure that will come out. But it will eventually wear off of her. Go put her in the tub. If you have nail polish remover, I can try that on the furniture."

"Oh, I'm not going to bother. I'll just get some slipcovers." Dorie brought the screaming toddler to the bathroom and drew the bath water, disrobing her.

Brandy watched as Jessica stomped her feet and tried every way she could not to cooperate. She fought Dorie as her mother tried to remove her clothes. Even after being placed in the tub, she splashed water and kicked her feet in protest.

"Is she like this all the time?" Brandy asked.

"No. She just gets stubborn. And she has so much energy,

Brandy. I blame it on Brawley's side of the family. She's just like him. Her switch is either on or off. Doesn't do anything half-way."

Brandy leaned over the tub and made funny faces. "Jessica, what's gotten into you, sweetheart? You're supposed to *help* your mama now. Don't you want to be a good girl?"

Jessica pounded the water with a resounding, "No!" which made Brandy laugh.

"Just wait, Brandy. You'll see."

"I've been to a few gatherings. Dorie, hate to say it, but a lot of SEAL kids are that way. Tucker calls them little action figures in diapers. I'm sure you've heard the stories too."

"Unfortunately, yes. I'm hoping it's just a phase. And I think kids can sense stress."

Brandy thought the same.

They got Jessica into her sleeper and set her up in a high chair in the kitchen while the two friends prepared dinner. Dorie poured some red wine as they ate their pasta and salad, sharing some of the plain pasta with Jessica.

Having a conversation was impossible as every sentence was truncated and interrupted by Jessica's demands. But as they finished, the toddler got tired and went down to sleep without further incident.

"At last!" said Dorie when she came back to the living room.

"Hope you didn't mind. Borrowed one of your brown towels to sit on."

"No worries."

Brandy didn't want to intrude on their personal life so asked a safe question. "Did you get the call from Christy?"

"Yes, I did. Already got a call from Luci Begay too. Did you know they have a couple of Navajo boys on the mission?"

"No."

"Danny's a peach. Met him at some parties in the past. Danny's cousin, Wilson, is with our guys. He's a SWCC boat guy. Their families are from Arizona, the Navajo reservation."

"Swick?" Brandy hadn't heard the term.

"Those are the guys they use for quick extraction or insertion by water. Wilson's new to the team, but Danny's been with Kyle and Brawley now for over four years."

"I'll make some calls when I get back. That's nice. So they live on the reservation there?"

"Used to. She was a teacher. Works part time now for a charter school here in San Diego. They have two kids."

"I'm guessing she'll be great help to you with Jessica. Wish I could be better support, Dorie."

"Don't be ridiculous. You're my best friend." She took another sip of wine. "Did you know they're related to one of the original Code Talkers? Their grandfather, I think. A real war hero."

"No, didn't know that. Don't think Tucker's met them yet."

"You learn lots of things. These guys, and sometimes their wives, come from all over. We had a gal from Germany married to one of the SEALs who got injured last time out. Man, did that woman like to go partying!"

"Do we get together as a group?"

"Christy is going to arrange something. When I first started dating Brawley, we all went out shooting! And we'll set up a babysitting pool so we kind of share the load. You don't have to participate unless you want to. She's talking about things like Karaoke too."

"Oh man. Rule me out. I can't carry a tune."

"Safety in numbers, Brandy," she said, holding out her wine glass. "No one can hear any one person when you do it in a group."

"I want to learn all I can. I want to do everything you do. But singing? That's not my thing."

"We got ourselves our very own Cowboy SEAL—Jameson.

Used to be a country western star in Nashville. You'll love him. He likes teaching the older kids how to play guitar too."

After a long pause, Dorie asked her how the good-bye went.

Brandy decided to face it head-on. "Broke my heart. I vowed I wasn't going to cry, but I did. Just not made that way. He was so nice. He's been through it before, you know."

"Yeah. Shayla. I never liked her."

"How did you meet?" A ripple of concern crossed her mind. Tucker had told her he'd been divorced over ten years. Had she come back to see him? Her earlier fears returned concerning Brawley's wandering behavior rubbing off on Tucker, though he'd denied it. She was sure she could trust him.

"Shayla came to one of the parties with one of the newbies about three years ago. Even tried to put a spell on Brawley, but he was wary of her. I don't think he ever forgave her for what she did to Tucker."

The information soothed Brandy's nerves but only slightly.

"She likes them young. I think she's a gold-digger. I don't think she stays with anyone very long. Tucker was fortunate he got out in time."

"Well, hopefully, he doesn't compare me too much to Shayla. He was so attentive. Very sweet."

"You're nothing like Shayla. I'm glad."

Dorie poured them more wine and then continued.

"We didn't get that nice, loving send-off. And that happens sometimes. Last time, I was big as a house and very uncomfortable. This time, Jessica wouldn't leave him alone. Almost like she knew he was leaving. Every two hours, it was something. We brought her into bed with us in the end, but neither one of us got much sleep."

"The boys probably got caught up on the plane," said Brandy.

"Hope so. They get pretty keyed up, though. They usually sleep when they get home. I've heard that a lot from other wives. Makes it hard on them sometimes when they need to catch up and crash, but everyone wants them. Just part of what causes the stress of being on the teams, I think."

"Tucker said Brawley looked good. He's expecting him to do fine."

"No comment."

"Dorie, he'll be fine. You gotta believe that."

"No offense, but you haven't walked in my shoes, Brandy. I was worried he wouldn't make it out of rehab." She sighed. "I'm waiting. Just waiting. I've done all I can. Now, it's up to him."

A cold chill descended on the room. Brandy was frightened for the first time in months. Perhaps she hadn't fully understood everything she was getting into. So much could happen to them and to the families at home. Brandy had been confident she had what it took. Yet Dorie had been one of the strongest women she knew and now was struggling.

The talk of Tucker's ex made her feel uneasy. He'd shared his intimate life with someone else, and that someone else could pop back into the brotherhood unexpectantly. She shouldn't feel jealousy, but that's what it was.

Maybe she should have asked more questions. Maybe Tucker had shielded her from some realities that would have made a difference in her decision. Because, if this could affect Dorie and Brawley, it could affect her relationship with Tucker too.

She didn't want to have the worries and thoughts she was having right now. She would have to deal with this because it would eat her alive.

Somehow, she'd have to find the answer.

CHAPTER 7

"**L**ISTEN UP, GANG," Kyle began. "We got a couple new members, so I'm going to make examples of them and give them a bit of shit, if you don't mind."

The group was assembled in the large suite Kyle shared with three others of his senior staff. Three platters of local foods and fruits had been spread out on the dining table, which they devoured in mere minutes. A pallet of bottled water sat on the floor nearby.

"First off, we got SO Tucker Hudson, trained medic, one of our boys from ten years ago. This is his first trip back, and I'm damned glad I could pick him back up. He put in ten as combat medic, and a hell of a good one, too. Now we're going for another ten."

Tucker was embarrassed at the hooyahs and water toasts.

"I intend to get even for those who I didn't catch the last time," Tucker barked. "I know who you are, so be ready," he said, aiming at Fredo, Cooper, Armando, Brawley, and Kyle.

"He rooms with Brawley, so take your complaints up with him," added Kyle.

The team chuckled.

"Okay, now we got some real newbies. DeWayne Huggles is a language specialist, spent a year at school in Monterey, and knows about ten African dialects. He'll help with some of our communications. His French is real sexy too."

A quiet, lanky black kid stood up and gave a shy wave. "I still can't get rid of my Mississippi accent in spite of all the training, but it's a real honor to be part of ya'll's team."

The group greeted him as warmly as they had Tucker.

"He rooms with Ollie," added Kyle. "Next, we got our two SWCC boat crew guys, itching to get you guys transported, if we go that way. Carson Philo here is from California, and he's been deployed with SEAL Team 5 several times and came highly recommended."

Carson gave the hang loose signal without standing up and didn't say a word.

"His roommate is Wilson Nez, who just happens to be Danny Begay's cousin, so don't fuck with him or you'll get a knife between your shoulder blades."

Tucker recognized his Dine features and shook Wilson's hand since they sat next to each other. Wilson got a proper greeting as well from the group.

"And, Wilson, you're in charge of the porn. That's a newbie thing."

Tucker could see the young boat crew guy was blushing. He'd forgotten that it was the job of the most junior member to haul the trunk with all the dirty magazines and CDs, in addition to their own gear. The crowd shouted "Hooyah!", putting him further in the spotlight.

"This isn't the Scouts, so we don't go around a circle and introduce ourselves and reveal our hobbies. So you get to know your brothers and their specialty on your own. We got the good to go this afternoon from the Headshed, so tomorrow at O-Eight hundred we convoy out, crossing the border into our base camp in Nigeria."

Kyle unrolled a map of both Benin and Nigeria and secured it with tape on the wall. "Our cover is that we're working for international aid—the French, in this case. The contractor is Areva Afrique, a mythical company based out of Paris with offices in Benin. You'll see the logos on our trucks. We'll be working on assessing and strengthening the electrical grid here in both countries, part of the aid package coming from the U.S. and Europe. We'll also help with some humanitarian aid distribution. Some of you medics will be working with the African Doctors' Corps at their various clinics along the way. Some of them are part of our intelligence network."

"Our French liaison is Jean Douchet, a former French Special Forces guy who grew up in Benin and knows many of the tribal leaders here and in Nigeria as well. He also knows those others that we need to stay away from too. He'll be by in the morning to hitch a ride with us. He has a highly skilled and specialized security crew with him at all times."

"Where is our gear, Kyle?" asked T.J. Talbot.

"Got it locked and loaded in the trucks, stored in the parking garage below. Jean has a couple of his private security detail guarding things to make sure they stay that way. We inventoried everything yesterday, and we're looking good."

Tucker was more than ready to start moving. It made him nervous if he had to sit in one place too long. He'd learned from previous deployments it increased the odds of being noticed by the bad guys.

"One other thing about using your cell phones. As I told all of you, we can't use them until we get to the compound. Good news is that we can make video calls by computer there, so some of you can touch base with your families. We'll keep those calls short and then have signups after that when everyone is back in camp. Very important you follow that protocol, so we don't get traced by hostiles.

"In case you didn't notice, you don't exactly fit in as locals, so everyone will be watched. We got lots of nationalities, races, and cultures. Most of the population is Roman Catholic, but those Baptists and Anglicans have been working missions all over the place here and have established mission schools. We got some stubborn Dutch, French, and Brits descended from old families during the colonial period. Even got a few Portuguese and Brazilians, if you can believe it. Jean says they can't always be trusted, so don't. Be cordial, but just be aware. Not everyone who looks American or European can be trusted, okay? You're fair game for petty theft if you're not from here. Some people don't consider it a crime, including some of the police."

Kyle scanned the group, grabbed another water bottle, and continued. "Stay hydrated."

Laughter broke out.

"Okay for the bad news," Kyle said, lowering his voice. The room fell completely silent. "I know some of you won't like this, but we're going to work together here. We may send some of you home earlier than others. We may switch off. But we're probably going to maintain a presence here for a bit, unless something changes, and it always changes."

Tucker heard sighs. Everyone knew not to ask questions at this point. He just hoped he would be one of the ones to come home early.

"On the coastal region, the bad guys are mostly smugglers, and we're here to learn about their human trafficking. There aren't as many religious zealots as there are in Central and Eastern Africa. Our bad dudes are your garden variety basic criminals dealing in human flesh, and they're very dangerous. Local corruption is rampant, especially among the police. The military here are loyal to their particular jurisdiction, and they're well-trained—some of them even by us, but many by French and Brit teams—so watch out for them."

Kyle continued. "We got African Union troops that will stay out of your way. A lot of U.N. aid goes to training and maintaining those peacekeepers, with some limited success. We got Chinese and Russians trying to curry favor with the traders, as well as the duly-elected politicians who make side deals benefitting themselves and their families. They also interfere with our humanitarian distribution, sometimes steering it toward the smugglers. The Chinese especially would like to get involved in setting up infrastructure partnerships in Nigeria in exchange for oil. There's talk about a huge Chinese port going in next door sometime in the near future. We'd like to find out more about that, too, if we can. As you can see, we got minestrone."

Several people chuckled, and it seemed to ease the tension.

"Drugs aren't as lucrative as the human sex trafficking. They go after mainly young girls, but lately, we've heard young children and older women have gone missing from several villages in the interior. Many of these bands also work out of the Congo or DRC to the south, as well as places farther north. These mini militia groups of bad guys hold up the highways and then sell their pirated goods closer to the ships docked at Porto-Novo and other places along the Nigerian coast. They use the rugged interior jungle region as cover for all their camps and operations, and they're extremely mobile. There's also some gun running going on."

"Make sure you don't look like anything but engineers and electrical contractors or medics. You will be allowed to wear your sidearms starting tomorrow, but keep them hidden and don't take them out unless you're gonna kill someone. Wearing a weapon is commonplace in this part of the world. Even the priests know how to shoot."

He turned to speak to Wilson and Carson. "You two are going to take a team upriver once we get to Nigeria, to explore a couple sites we're curious about. I'm gonna let Jean fill you in on that. We want to get those boats in the water ASAP and make sure everything is set for an emergency extraction should we need it. We need to check out the viability of a water operation."

The boat guys nodded.

"Questions?" Kyle asked.

"We working with any other U.S. operatives or CIA?" Trace Bennett asked.

"Not as of yet. That could change. I'll be in daily contact with State, as well as our ambassadors, as needed. They know we're here, and they've got their ears to the ground. It's very important to both State and our partners that we not escalate the tensions already existing. We get in, get the information about the operation, and then wait for further instructions. It would be great if we could get back to the U.S. without having to fire a shot. That's the goal. But as all of you know, these things change. And we'd like to make it so a few guys can stay behind to continue to collect information on the sex traffickers."

"Are we slated to do hostage rescue?" asked Lucas.

"Not at this time. But again, I wouldn't be surprised if this changes. A lot of these operations are under a cloud. If there is danger to any of our local assets, we might have to act. We're not at war. We're here to back up the people who are trying to negotiate and broker some relief and peace. Those guys are not soldiers. We're the good guys, as you know. We want to make sure we leave it that way when we're done. Got it?"

The room nodded.

"You're here in case we have to fight our way out."

BRAWLEY WAS LYING on top of his covers, staring out at the moon and stars through the tiny window in their bedroom, when Tucker returned from his shower.

"Sure is a fucked up world, isn't it?" He pulled on his water bottle.

Tucker felt the same way. "That's what we do. We do the stuff no one else can," he answered as he slipped on his boxers. Then he added, "But I agree. It's a mess."

"Makes you wonder if this is going to be our next big Desert Storm thing," said Brawley. His voice reflected disgust.

Tucker didn't agree this time. "Well, let's hope we learned a thing or two. It didn't turn out so well over there for anyone. If I can read what Kyle's told us, we're here to pick out the bad actors and make it so they are removed, arrange it so the rest can work together and get everyone to play nice."

"That would be a miracle. Feels like turf warfare to me. Centuries of it."

"You get enough water down?" Tucker asked.

"I'll be peeing all night long." Brawley held up his near-empty water bottle to show him. "And just in case you wanted to know, I've not missed my meds, either, Dr. Hudson."

"That a boy." He hung up his towel and laid out his clothes for tomorrow morning. "You mind if I do a little writing before I turn in? I got a book light I can use, but I won't if it bothers you. Or I could use the bathroom."

"Have at it. Won't bother me at all. We get up at seven?"

"That works. Make sure you look for that diaper, Brawley."

But Brawley didn't answer.

Tucker retrieved the notebook Brandy had left him, turned on the small penlight, and opened to a page opposite one of her water color drawings of a bowl of persimmons. He started to write.

Been here for two days now, although it seems like I've been gone a week. This place is very diverse—a splash of cultures, races, and languages. Very colorful, and also very poor. This is a place that has tried to heal over a scar created centuries ago during the dark Slave Coast period. Once powerful countries dominated the culture here, now being swept away and usurped by new tyrants and cultures all trying to impose themselves on this part of the African continent.

It makes me appreciate working plumbing, cell phone service, fast food restaurants, and highways I can drive at ninety miles an hour with the top down just to look at the landscape flying by.

I plan to have a seriously good time with you tonight in this lumpy bed, that is, if Brawley doesn't snore too loud. He's his usual self. I think he's going to be fine.

So while I'm dozing off, I'm going to remember our shower together on Sunday and the way your skin felt under my wet fingers as I rubbed shower gel all over you. I'm going to remember your laugh and the way your hair catches fire in the first light of the morning. I feel lucky to have you and our home to come back to.

Tomorrow we start our adventure, descending into the unknown. It's something that I remember doing before. I won't lie to you and say I'm not a bit fearful. But I'm vigilant. It's that healthy side of being scared—the part that will keep me alive until my time has come.

But, in my wildest dark imagination, I don't see how it's possible I could be given the miracle of loving you just to have it taken it all away. So that's the plan. I'm working my way back to you. And when I get there, I'll be all yours until the next time.

Loving you now more than I ever have, Tucker.

CHAPTER 8

B RANDY DECIDED TO explore her watercolor painting more avidly. She got out several of her old sketch books, looking for shapes and patterns that inspired her. She'd always loved the colorful fruit labels on the boxes at her dad's store and had experimented with drawing some in the bright combinations she'd seen.

She was taking pictures of baskets of red and green apples and vibrant oranges, when she noticed her father speaking with a young woman very privately. It dawned on her that perhaps this was that new element she'd been noticing about her father—his sudden interest in dressing better and his more active lifestyle. He'd been working out at the local gym, something he hadn't done since her mother passed.

At the end of the conversation, he gave the woman a chaste hug and then watched her get into her car and drive away. Before he could look Brandy's way, she turned and busied herself with her photography.

She had followed his actions all afternoon, sorting fruit, arranging bundles of asparagus, and pulling wilted greens, but since he didn't volunteer anything, she didn't ask him about his new friend. She caught him singing under his breath and smiling more to customers, and the other staff. He didn't even mind the constant interruptions by their new bookkeeper's questions and was patient and forthcoming with the answers.

Brandy knew that something or someone had caused this change in him, and she was dying to find out.

"Maybe she's just an old customer," said Dorie. The two of them had taken Jessica to the zoo. The toddler was excitedly watching pink flamingos who had gathered at the side of the path from the safety of her stroller.

"Not the way he was talking to her. And I've never seen him give a hug to a customer before."

"Did it bother you?" Dorie asked.

"No. It was nice." She wished she'd been able to see the woman's face.

"So ask him."

Brandy had to think about this for a few seconds. She and her father lived so close together. They'd both done their best to respect each other's private lives. She'd never seen him stay out late or have company at the house, but there was something different about the way he acted around this woman.

"I'll wait a bit. Maybe she'll come in soon, and I can do a little reconnaissance first."

"Brandy, you're so funny. Just ask him. Besides, you want to help him out with the vetting. You know there are ladies out there who prey on older men. You don't want him to be taken advantage of. So that's where you're coming from. Just ask him."

Dorie was right. Now that she had married Tucker, the roles had been a bit reversed. She was finding herself more and more the one taking care of her father than the other way around.

The next day, she found him stacking boxes in the back room cooler and asked if she could talk to him.

He closed the heavy metal door, removed his work gloves, and stared back at her with his hands on his hips. "I'm all ears. Something going on with Tucker and the boys?"

She found this amusing, and shrugged. "No, Dad, I wanted to talk about *you*."

"Me? What about me?"

The look he gave her back did have that small twinkle in his eye, like he had already suspected what she was curious about.

"Are you seeing someone?"

She knew she had hit the target when he smiled and looked down at his shoes, rubbing his hands together. His bow tie was crooked. She leaned over and adjusted it before he could step back.

His face flushed with embarrassment. "Thanks, sweetheart." He struggled for words.

"I was going to wait a little longer to say something, but I think this is okay. Yes, I've been seeing someone. Her name is Jillian. I met her at yoga class."

"Yoga? I didn't know you were taking yoga."

"Well, I decided to try it. I mean, I've been watching the class come and go for a few weeks now. You know, I use the equipment on the other side, and I figured they could use a man in there. Lots of ladies. And they didn't seem to mind."

"Didn't seem to mind? I'll bet they were all over you."

He leaned back on his heels, a sheepish grin on his face. "I don't know about that."

"Dad, you're a good-looking man. Or are you just figuring that out?"

Brandy was having fun at his expense.

"So tell me about her."

"She lost her husband only last year. She still wears her wedding ring, as I do. I don't know how the conversation came up, but we discovered we both had lost our spouses."

"Okay. So you like this lady? What does she do?"

"She sells real estate but is kind of part-time. Sort of semi-retired. Her husband left her in good shape, so she dabbles around with lots of things. Has two grown daughters on their own." He looked up. "She's a nice lady. Easy to be around. I guess you could say I'm rather smitten."

Brandy could see he was proud of the admission.

"Does she feel the same way?"

"I think so. Right now, we're just getting to know each other. I'm kind of slow on the romance scale, but neither of us is in a hurry. It's just nice to have someone to talk to, laugh with again. I've missed that, Brandy."

She was delighted with the news and grabbed him in a big bear hug. "I'm so happy for you, Dad. I knew there was something. You've changed, and I like it. I'd say she's a good influence on you."

"Would you like to meet her?"

"Absolutely."

"How about coming over tonight for dinner? I'm barbequing."

"Perfect. I'll bring the wine."

BEFORE BRANDY WENT next door to her father's house to meet this mystery woman, she called Dorie, telling her the news.

"Good old Steve. I'm happy for him. It's about time. He's paid his dues, grieved too long. I'm glad he's found someone. And you like her?"

"I do."

"Well, here's to another happily ever after."

"Indeed. You doing okay, Dorie? I didn't make my calls today, and I'm sorry."

"Well, I just came from the doctor, and I'm pregnant again. Not sure how Brawley will take it this time. God, I wish he was home."

"Me too."

JILLIAN BORDEN WASN'T anything like Brandy's mother, which surprised her. But she was very welcoming and eager to please. She liked to travel, something her father had always liked but her mother had been too ill to do much.

Watching the two of them prepare dinner together in his kitchen, showing her where he kept things and laughing when they bumped into each other, apologizing, Brandy could see they were a good match. She made him happy just by being there. There wasn't any real heavy lifting to do—they just seemed compatible.

It was the kind of relationship she had wanted with Tucker, but then realized she'd married someone completely different than her father. The choices they were going to have to make were much more complicated.

After dinner, she walked to the back of the property, back to her bungalow, took a hot shower, and then turned in early. The silent and empty house made her sad. She hoped very soon she'd be able to hear from him and know that he was well.

She allowed herself one last cry and vowed tomorrow she'd toughen up. But tonight, she missed Tucker more than ever.

CHAPTER 9

JEAN DOUCHET LOOKED *exactly* like a former Special Forces guy, Tucker thought. He was smaller in stature, like a lot of the European Spec Ops guys were, but he had powerful arms and shoulders and he moved with sleek speed. He could have been mistaken for an older mixed martial arts guy or even a world-class triathlete.

Kyle had confided in him Jean had gone through the BUD/S and SQT training and was one of the "special relationship" guys who could work out in the SEAL Team 3 building at Coronado. They'd met originally when Kyle's platoon was doing training for the French elite units, and the two had remained friends.

Jean's eyes picked up every nuance going on in the room. Tucker met several Eastern European Special Forces guys who embedded with them for brief missions in the past, and they'd told him knowing multiple languages fluently meant that they could practically talk to someone in one language and write a text message in another. Not the same message. So Tucker understood that Jean was a giant of an asset for their squad. He admired how detailed he studied all of the American SEALs.

Tucker was certain in less than a few hours Jean would know every team member's personality type better than a therapist would after a year of visits. He was *that* good.

Kyle introduced him without all the background Tucker was privy to, except for something the guys would appreciate.

"Jean has gotten some of our embassy staff out of some pretty prickly situations over the past few years, so you listen to him. He grew up here and then served under the BFST, French Special Forces command in the Middle East and in West Africa, Ivory Coast Command. When he retired, he went private, and we're damned lucky to have him." Kyle stepped away and allowed Douchet to take over.

"*Bonjour, mes amis,*" he started. In his clipped French accent, he explained where they would be traveling and what they should look out for. "When we arrive at the town of Lagos, which is after the border into Nigeria, we'll be heading inland, roughly following the Ogun River. Be sure you have your passports handy to show the border guards or they won't let you through."

Jean heard shouting outside and went to the window to check out what was happening four stories below. "We have demonstrations almost every day here. Mostly small ones, thank goodness." He grinned, and again, the team responded. Tucker could see how he could be charming when he needed to be. He was measured, cultured, and confident.

"I will take the lead vehicle with your chief. The rest of the trucks will be driven by my detail. It will cause less scrutiny that way, since I often accompany NGOs of various countries doing work in the area. My men know the terrain and most of the jungle. I trust them completely. We will all be armed. I'm assuming you are, but don't brandish them or draw attention to them. Just know that people will expect you have them for your personal safety, so don't show off. Be discrete."

Someone asked if his detail spoke English.

"But of course. Probably better than you."

The team chuckled.

"I trained most of them, all dual French and Benin citizenship. They are the best of the best, and they frequently have to turn down offers to work for lots of money in Europe or work as head of security for some of the contractors here. But they love their job, and I don't believe any of them would ever leave working for me. I want you to know who they are before we begin. Don't fuck with my men."

It took a minute for his smile to creep across his chops, but everyone in the room got the message loud and clear.

"Feel free to ask them questions. They will room near your quarters, but downstairs. Everything has been set up for your 'survey and site investigation'," he said, holding his fingers up in the air to show the quotes. "I have done this for others. We will have a secure WIFI connection. I am excited to tell you that this evening, after we arrive, you may be able to do Facetime with some of your families. However, at this time, I need you to stay off your individual cell phones, unless there is some emergency. I'll lay out rules on that."

Kyle had a question. "You expect we'll have to stop along the way? Or be stopped? And if so, what will we need to say?"

"That's an excellent question, Kyle. Only at the border. If we're lucky!" When no one laughed, he added, "That was a joke!"

Tucker felt his blood pressure rise.

"In otherwords, if you get stopped before the border, something has gone wrong."

"Gotcha. Thanks, Jean." Kyle retreated to the side and then took up a chair.

"I know I don't have to mention to you that you should not speak unless you are asked a question, and then you are very polite or say very respectfully you don't understand. Let my boys do the talking. *All* the talking."

After they were released, Tucker followed as he was directed, riding in the second seat next to Brawley behind their huge African driver, Leone. Trace and Tyler sat behind them, crammed into the third seat. Their truck towed a small trailer which contained the inflatable combat Zodiac and the small 55 cc super lightweight diesel motor that he'd been told had been customized for speed. The whole thing could fit into a man's backpack if need be.

Tyler retrieved waters from the back and passed them along up front. The convoy began to roll out and blended into traffic.

Tucker addressed Leone's eyes, visible in the rearview mirror. "How long will it take to get there?"

Leone shrugged, fanning the fingers of his right hand to show him it was an approximation. "We go about four to five hours. Depends on traffic, road work."

Tucker noted the man's perfect English. He nodded and thanked him.

Leone continued. "We always got road work. Lots of rain. Landslides. Big trucks. It's a constant problem. This time of year, not too bad."

Everyone was silent on the trip down the coast, where Tucker saw breathtaking stretches of white rocky beach snuggling up against blue waters like the Caribbean. Yet around the next bend could be dark brown granite cliffs without a hospitable landing area. At the water's edge of one azure blue bay, a hole had been dug and overflowed with reddish brown mud, which spilled out into the pristine bay, marring it with a brown stain feathering out to the ocean.

Occasionally, there would be iron security gates leading down to a luxuriously landscaped, western-style hotel or villa, but then next to it, they would come upon a crumbling structure or something that had burned and been repaired with metal corrugated siding and cinder block. Children walked dangerously close to the road on their way to school, dressed in their uniforms.

Clusters of tiny shops, gas stations, and wooden fruit stands roofed with palm fronds dotted the inland side of the coast, often accompanied by a couple of bars or liquor stores. Less than half of these were open. Groups of men sat together in the shade smoking, squatting on the dusty ground or sitting on oil drums or plastic buckets. The locals shared the ground with chickens who dodged traffic, bicycles, and scooters, while foraging for food. Fabrics in bright, bold designs and dresses blew in the breeze at wooden makeshift shops manned by women in colorful dress, often talking with one or two other ladies or children.

Their audiences, one by one, passively watched the caravan pass by and then refocused on whatever they were doing. Several scooters overloaded with as many as three children zipped dangerously around the traffic, pitching precariously and nearly spilling their precious cargo. Men and women balanced huge bundles atop their heads.

Tucker soaked all the visuals up, allowed the drone of the motor and bouncing of the Land Rover's squeaky shocks to lull him to near sleep. At one point, he did fall asleep and spilled water in his lap.

The patchwork of colors and textures was so unfamiliar yet strangely beautiful, even though the heat was oppressive. He could smell fires burning and felt the grit in his teeth from sitting by the opened window inhaling road dust. He was looking forward to a shower already and they had traveled no more than two hours.

At several points along the way they'd encounter a tall pile of debris—lumber, poles, broken bricks and chunks of concrete and plaster—with children and young men going through the rubble, mining for something they could sell. Advertisements for beer, sodas, political candidates long gone, and even cell phone and internet services were plastered to walls, fences, and sometimes, palm trees.

A billboard announced they were approaching the border with Nigeria. The picture contained the image of a black fist rising to the heavens with a green and yellow flag waving in the background. The convoy slowed and then stopped at the archway crossing. Everywhere Tucker looked he saw uniformed men in light blue shirts and navy or black pants, most of them with sub machine guns at their sides or long rifles strapped to their backs.

Tucker took his passport out of his vest pocket.

The two border guards at Kyle and Jean's vehicle slowly slid their sunglasses to their foreheads and peered inside their truck. Soon, two more did the same at Tucker's vehicle. Leone spoke an African dialect to the guard on his left, who then wanted to check out Tucker's passport and then handed it back. The guard on Brawley's side craned his neck and did the same, asking for Tyler and Trace's passports as well. Then both guards walked the length of the truck, studying what they could see inside the cab. Tucker was pleased to note someone had remembered to bring the two fishing poles they'd purchased, along with the net, which lay on top of their suitcases.

Jean and Kyle went inside the small border guard office secured with a glass door that had been taped back together with duct tape. Traffic coming into Benin was completely blocked off with barricades until the guards were done checking out all the Areva Afrique trucks and their occupants. Several other guards stood idly by and watched without saying a word.

The heat was oppressive with the complete lack of wind present. Leone tried to find a tune on the radio and finally gave up. He tapped his fingers on the roof of the truck, humming some Juju beat tune they'd heard in the city yesterday. A large tourist bus, which had been held up in the now-growing line of cars waiting to enter Benin, honked his horn.

"Oh, mister," whispered Leone. "Not a good idea, mister." Leone leaned over the seat, turned, and said to Tucker, "Chinese."

"Chinese tourists?" Tucker asked.

"No. Workers. They take them from the airport to their apartments. Then they take them to work, and back to the apartments. They do not wander in the villages."

"Are they held captive?" Brawley asked.

"You would say so, yes. But they are very quiet and very hard workers. If they cannot leave their compounds, they don't have a problem, right?"

"Where are they working?" Tucker asked.

"Mostly construction. They work on roads, even built a small private air strip."

"A friendship project, right?" said Tucker.

"Exactly."

They were given the green light to move forward, and their caravan continued down the coast until they encountered a fairly large city. Tucker read the signs and figured they would be heading away from the coastal areas, going inland. The road wove through various neighborhoods until it came to an expansive city center, designed with wide streets and fountains.

"Dada's folly," Leone said.

"Looks like Barcelona," Patrick said.

"This is Lagos. One of our early presidents, Dada, envisioned building a modern-day Babylon during the sixties. He nearly bankrupted the country with this project. But in the day, it was remarkable."

Once out of the city, they turned off the provincial highway and traveled a compacted red dirt road, which was slow and filled with potholes. Leone maneuvered as best he could, being mindful of the trailer they were pulling. Dust from Kyle's truck nearly obscured them. Lush jungle foliage appeared to have been burned back from the road to allow passage. They were coming to a small rise.

Once they hit the plateau, the view down to the coast was breathtaking. The air was slightly cooler but thick with mosquitos, especially as they approached the Ogun River. Dark-legged Sand-piper-looking birds with black and white racoon-like mask markings walked along the water's edge, wading several inches deep for food. Tucker observed a flock of bright red canaries and a bright blue bird the size and shape of a robin.

But the most amazing thing Tucker found was that he could hear the cacophony of bird calls, even above their groaning diesel engine.

They crossed the Ogun several times and, at last, came to a se-ries of small towns to the south of Abeokuta, the region's capitol. The district was heavy with two- and three-story industrial build-ings, mostly made of concrete and cinder block.

After several minutes traveling the narrow road through re-mote jungle, they turned off onto a crushed stone drive ending at a security gate without any signage whatsoever. The perimeter was fenced with heavy-gauge electrical fencing reaching over twenty feet tall. The gate automatically opened and closed behind them as they continued crossing what appeared to be a large private com-pound. A massive stone building loomed three stories tall, set in the middle of a grassy knoll, its rooftop covered in satellite dishes and several multistory antennae. They parked as directed by a security guard who greeted them.

Tucker could hardly get out of the Rover, he was so stiff. Every bounce, curve, and swerve had taken a toll on his body. Brawley laughed as Jameson and Patrick could hardly extricate themselves from the third seat as well.

All the Areva Afrique vehicles were lined up side by side, and the team was ushered around the front and up several steps, stopping at a massive porch overhang with a view of the knoll below and the Ogun River beyond the fencing farther down. Each member carried his own bag, and one by one, they dropped them to stare out at the beauty of the majestic scene.

"Holy shit," mumbled Fredo. "We the private guests of a king or something?"

Kyle shrugged.

"Nice, isn't it?" Jean remarked.

Surveying the lush green on the other side of the river, Tucker didn't see evidence of another structure. They appeared to be completely isolated.

Enormous carved wooden doors opened to the interior of the building. Inside was a nearly empty, two-story lobby containing a curved wooden reception desk that appeared to be hand crafted from a single tree trunk, skillfully carved in relief depicting leaves, vines and various symmetric symbols and shapes.

The almost black, highly polished granite floors echoed eerily. Several members whistled while others whispered astonishment. Tucker felt like he'd just walked into a brand-new museum.

Jean walked to the middle of the crowd and began his orientation. "This is probably the safest place in all of Nigeria, impervious to most rocket attacks and even perhaps some air strikes. The walls are made of reinforced concrete nearly two feet thick. As you probably saw, we have a satellite uplink and a dedicated, secure WIFI system, so you'll be able to call home as soon as we finish the activation tonight. In the meantime, there are offices upstairs that have been set up with beds. There's a large lounge area where we've got several big screen TVs so you aren't cut off from the world. We hope all the other things will be working by tomorrow."

"What was this built for?" asked Tucker.

"Originally, it was built with money from the Soviets about twenty years ago, designed to house the government safely in case of a military coup. Sort of a safe house. They chose the location because it's well away from the country's capitol but connected by a waterway to the coast. Even got room for a few helicopters in an emergency. You could easily stage an invasion from this place, and perhaps that's what they had in mind. It's nearly two hundred thousand square feet. We were able to purchase it several years ago to be used by our government and corporate clients."

Jean's men began unloading boxes of supplies, including all the duty bags containing their weapons.

"We have a large kitchen downstairs in the back, and we have one of my guys coming to prepare meals, so keep your equipment out of sight in your rooms."

"This is huge. Very unexpected," said Kyle.

"It's way more than you need, of course, but I'm afraid it's the safest place I can put you right now. You're close enough to the city, where a lot of your research will be done, and only a few paces to the river. Most people in this area don't even know this building exists, and those that do, understand it's a space rented out for corporate events. You probably won't be bothered here since this road is not on any map, by design."

"Are you staying here with us?" someone asked.

"I'm going to stay with my men. We're taking the downstairs right wing. You guys have the top floor. Go check it out, and then I need to get upriver with your boat crew before it gets dark."

The men explored the upper floor and set up their rooms, sticking to the original roommate list. Only thing Tucker could complain about was that there weren't private baths. But Brawley found the real prize.

"You guys won't believe this!" he shouted. He opened two six-foot glass doors behind him, revealing a multi-station working gym with newer equipment. Beyond was a full locker room complete with a row of stall showers, toilets, and even a steam room.

"I think someone slipped me some LSD," said T.J.

Tucker completely agreed. It was the most unlikely outcome to their hot and dusty road trip down the coast.

CHAPTER 10

B RANDY'S CELL PHONE rang as she was just about to put on her green apron.

"Hey there, beautiful!"

She couldn't believe her ears.

"Turn on your camera so I can see you."

She stared down into the phone screen and saw Tucker's smiling face looking right back at her. "Oh my god! I can't believe it's you!"

"Of course, it's me."

"What time is it there?"

"About five. I think we're eight hours ahead."

"So how's it going?"

"You wouldn't believe me if I told you. Trust me on this."

"Really?" He looked good, not at all stressed. She expected to see a sweaty and dirty version of him, like how he was when he worked in the garden or fixed things around the house, but Tucker was clean and appeared to be calling from a swanky office.

"You sure you're in Africa? I think you guys just took off for Vegas. That's what it looks like to me."

Brawley walked behind Tucker and waved.

"Hey, Brawley!"

"He's next. We got a line here. Anyway, I can't take too much time because a lot of us are lined up to check in at home, so this is just a quick one. Wanted you to know I'm alive, we are all situated, and so far, everything's been better than I expected. The real work begins tomorrow, though, so fingers crossed."

"Oh, thank you for calling, Tucker. I've been missing you so much, trying not to be worried, but I took your advice and have been staying busy."

"Good job. Well, I have to—"

"Wait a minute. I have news! I mean Dad does. He's met someone, Tucker. I had dinner with them last night. They are so cute together. I think you'll like her."

"Happy to hear it, sweetheart. But I've gotta go."

She threw him a kiss, which he returned. Just before he hung up, he told her he'd call longer tomorrow, if he could. "And I'm dreaming of you naked," he whispered. It generated some catcalls around him.

Brandy slipped her shirt over one shoulder to show him the only part of her bare skin she could. "You get your butt back here, Tucker. I mean it."

"Roger that, ma'am."

With that, he disconnected. She placed the phone in her center apron pocket and felt like she'd just had about a dozen cups of coffee. Then she wished she'd recorded the call and decided she'd ask one of the younger clerks how to do that for next time.

She was happy Brawley was going to get in touch with Dorie. She needed some cheering up. Brandy decided to check in with her in an hour, so she didn't interfere with Brawley's call. She wondered if her friend was going to tell her husband about the upcoming pregnancy.

Her father came around the corner with a cart filled with cardboard boxes of plump yellow peaches that looked delicious.

"I just got a call from Tucker, Dad. He's fine, got there safe.

And he looks great!" She hugged him so fast she nearly toppled the peaches.

"That's great news, Brandy. Must mean a load off your mind. Did he say anything about where he was or what he was doing?"

"He can't say. Even Brawley looked good."

"Makes me happy to see that big smile on your face. I'll tell Jillian tonight. She'll be thrilled."

AFTER BRANDY FINISHED going through the mail, she handed the stack of bills back to their bookkeeper for entry. She was going to call Dorie, but her best friend beat her to it.

"Brawley just called me. You got to talk to Tucker?"

"Yes! They look good, don't they?"

"Oh man, it was just what I needed."

"Did he get to talk to Jessica too?"

"No, she was sleeping. He told me it was going to be short this time. But we're going to try to get a schedule so she can be up for his calls. He said they're staying in this super-secret compound. Did Tucker say anything like that?"

"No. He wouldn't talk about it."

"Well, we've got to celebrate. How about I get a sitter and we go to the movies?"

"I'm up for that. Text me what time. I can pick you up."

Brandy met Dorie at Danny and Luci's house, where she'd dropped off Jessica. It was the first time she'd met Danny's wife. Her long shiny black hair was parted down the middle, framing her beautiful face with kind, dark eyes.

Brandy was introduced to Griffin and Ali, their two boys. Luci explained that Griffin was Danny and Luci's biological son, but Ali was an adopted Iraqi boy Danny had rescued on one of their missions. The team had tried to rescue both he and his father, but his father sacrificed himself to save the boy.

"The boys have been looking forward to it." Luci said. "I need to give them girl time, teach them some manners about being gentle with little girls. We don't get much chance to do that around here."

"Tell her about the sling shot," said Dorie.

Luci inhaled, first checking to make sure everyone was playing nice behind her. "Well, Danny made this sling shot for Ali over in Iraq and taught him how to shoot pebbles. Turns out, he's a crack shot! But the problem is, poor Griffin, who's not so adventurous, has had more goose eggs and black eyes than any other four-year-old around. Ali likes to lay in wait and pummel him. We've bought him some sponge balls to use, but he likes the real thing. Shoots jam and sugar packets at the waitresses, too, when we go out. Drives me insane!"

Brandy couldn't stop laughing.

They heard a loud, "No!" coming from behind Luci. No mistaking Jessica's voice.

"Oh boy. I better check—" started Dorie.

"No, they're fine." Luci held her hand out. "Whatever it is, we'll sort it out no problem. You have a good time and I'll call or text you if something comes up I can't handle, okay?"

"Thanks." Dorie gave Luci a hug.

"How's Danny?" Brandy asked.

"Thank God for that call. I was beginning to worry, but man, some of the places they go are mind boggling. Sounds like this trip won't be any different. It was great to see his face."

"Yeah, I guess next one we'll get more details," said Brandy.

"You may not know this, but Danny's cousin Wilson, is on his first deployment with them. He's a SWCC boat guy."

"Yes, Dorie told me."

"Thanks again, Luci," repeated Dorie. "We'll let you know when we're on our way home. I'm leaving my car here with the car seat. Do you want the keys?"

"No, I have two in mine. Have a great time."

AFTER THE MOVIE let out, Dorie checked on Jessica and was told they were all crashed, so the two of them stopped by one of the places on the strand for some soup.

Groups of young men, mostly Navy and not all of them SEALs, hung out around the outdoor fireplace, watching the girls sauntering by. It was a parade that had been going on for decades, ever since the SEALs had come to such public prominence. Brandy could see it was quite the show this evening. Young, skimpily-clad girls roamed between several of the local hangouts and especially flocked around the quiet tatted guys with the big arms. Brandy guessed by the difference in their demeanor they were probably SEALs.

Couples sat together at smaller tables around the perimeter. The air hadn't turned chilly yet, and the sky was clear. A large bachelorette party had taken up the long picnic table at the far side and were boisterous, at times drowning out conversations on the whole patio. The bride-to-be wore a short white veil with plastic penises attached, a crown, and a sash. Falling victim to drinks purchased for her by several of the guy groups, she was thoroughly smashed and had to be helped out when the party decided to move. Brandy sensed the entire place was relieved.

"Remember when we'd come down here in high school?" queried Dorie.

"Well, you came down. I was your comic relief." Brandy thought about how long ago it was. "And for the record, you weren't a sloppy drunk at your bachelorette party, either."

"Thank you," Dorie said, and clinked her water glass with Brandy's beer.

"You ever see the girls? The bridesmaids?"

"Not really. Funny how you know who your true friends are." She grasped Brandy's hand. "You've always been the one there for me, Brandy. I appreciate it."

Brandy remembered the wedding and how the other girls in the wedding party had treated her, made her feel excluded. How they stared when Tucker spilled the punch all over her. She'd been so embarrassed she almost left the reception. But she stayed, and it changed her whole life. She couldn't help but break out in a wicked grin.

"What the devil are you thinking, Brandy Hudson?"

She loved to gloat, especially when it felt like justice done. "They all went to the wedding to pick up one of Brawley's friends, didn't they?"

"Oh, it was the only thing they talked about!"

"Even your married bridesmaid—her guy is on Team 5?"

"Oh, Marsha. Yes, she's a slut."

Brandy pushed aside her soup bowl and leaned onto the table. "But I'm the one who went home with one. I'm the one who got the SEAL!"

"Poetic justice. As it should be. You got the best one of the bunch, too, except for Brawley, of course." Dorie winked.

Brandy was glad some of the darkness of their relationship seemed to be fading. She wished for more of that magic for Dorie and Brawley she'd envied when they first fell in love and became engaged.

A group of slightly older ladies sat at the table nearby without paying attention to anything in the room but the men scattered across the patio. Dorie studied them with a frown. Brandy could tell the ladies were trying to hook attention from one particular group of well-built guys she guessed were SEALs.

Dorie leaned forward. "You want to go?"

Brandy agreed and slipped her purse over her shoulder. One of the ladies at the next table called out to Dorie, who didn't look especially happy to see her. The woman scampered over and gave her a hug.

"You old married lady, you. Congratulations! Why didn't you invite me to the wedding? And how the heck is Brawley?"

The dark-haired woman was beautiful and very well-endowed, but she used a little too much eye makeup, Brandy thought. Her comparison engine had kicked in, and she sucked in her tummy, allowing anyone who wasn't blind to see that her chest was bigger than this woman's. Brandy also noticed that her eyes were hard.

"He's fine," answered Dorie, turning to go. Brandy thought it was odd she didn't offer an introduction but dutifully followed after her friend, turning to go, when they heard the woman ask a question.

"And how's Tucker?" Her sexy voice was laced with a growl.

Dorie closed her eyes, bit her lower lip, and then mouthed "sorry" to Brandy before she turned and addressed the woman. "Tucker married Brandy about two years ago, Shayla."

Shayla's head whipped to the side as she thoroughly studied Brandy up and down. After gaining her composure, the woman tilted her head back and whispered her reply. "Oh my." She leaned closer to Brandy with a smirk. "Tucker and I were married seven years," she said as she extended her hand. "I'm Shayla." The smile followed her greeting instead of preceding it.

"Nice to meet you." Brandy's handshake was short. In the next few awkward seconds, she had the urge to wipe her hand on her dress. Out of nowhere, she threw in a comment she knew she'd burn in hell for. Tucker would be furious with her, but she just couldn't hold her tongue—why she'd been fired from her last two jobs. Adjusting her stance, she said, "Thanks for divorcing him."

Before Shayla could respond verbally, Dorie interjected that they were late to pick up her daughter. She grabbed Brandy's arm and dragged her back into the protection of the bar.

As she disappeared, Brandy gave a taunting wave at the woman she knew instantly she hated. She suspected it would come back to haunt her.

But it was worth it.

CHAPTER 11

WHILE THE REST of the team was having dinner, Tucker was selected to take the river trip with Jean, Kyle, and the two boat crew guys.

The Zodiac was inflated while Wilson lovingly wiped down the compact motor he'd boosted, carefully attaching it to the craft. Everyone helped position the craft into the water, carrying it over the debris-laden and rocky bank. One tug on the starting rope and the engine kicked over and purred, sounding more like a small chainsaw than an outboard motor.

Everyone boarded, stashing their duty bags at their feet. They were instructed to pack light, which meant no heavy firepower and nothing a local businessman or government contractor wouldn't normally carry for a trip of this nature. Jean handed Kyle a sat phone for security since it would be impossible to trace and would give him direct access to the SOF command as well as Jean and his team, at all times.

They pushed off, heading upriver. Tucker felt just like when he and his dad went hunting in Oregon when he was a boy. The water was filled with debris, including plastic wrappers, floating foam cups, and occasionally an article of clothing. Depending on how close to the center of the waterway they were, the color of the river went from shit brown to brownish green. He was glad he wore his goggles around his neck, since, if he had to swim in the water, his eyes would most likely get infected.

Even though he'd applied repellant, the mosquitos had found him. He fought off the first few but then ignored them in time, like Jean did.

The French former Spec Ops guy searched the banks with his binoculars. Birds were at full play, chattering up a storm. They motored past a squabbling family of medium-sized brown and yellow monkeys moving along the treetops with ease. Several of the males began to follow along the trajectory of the boat and then broke off.

Carson was point, holding a long pole and sounding the river floor, on the lookout for large boulders or any other impediment to travel. Wilson manned the motor, steering to keep them in the center of the river and away from water plants that hugged the sides and could interfere with the small motor.

"I'm assuming we are to watch for crocs?" asked Kyle.

"To be sure," said Jean. "Not too many in these areas as many of them are harvested for their meat and sold at market."

"Appreciate the head's up, Chief," Carson shouted over his shoulder.

They continued upstream for several more minutes and then followed a sharp bend to the right.

Jean sat straight up with a command. "Carson, sometimes the Ogun dries up overnight, so be especially vigilant for shallow straits." he barked.

Carson gave him a thumbs-up in answer, not taking his eyes off the water.

Tucker took another admiring appraisal of the tiny diesel engine and smiled up at Wilson. "That thing sure does sound pretty," he said. "That a fifty-five?"

"Yup, but we got twenty percent more torque. Best little twenty-five-pound bundle out there. I can stick it in my backpack and carry the darned thing all day if I had to."

"I'm impressed. You do all the work?"

"I don't let anyone else touch this baby. Can't wait to demonstrate how she'll do full out. Covers the bank with waves about eight feet or more."

"Cool beans."

Jean was checking his phone and then spoke to someone on the other end in French. He put his binoculars up and checked the bank ahead while he continued the conversation, finishing it off with, *"Oui. Bon."*

Kyle was waiting for an explanation.

"We have a camp around the bend here that appears abandoned, but we're supposed to check it out on foot. Then I think we'll head back. I was going to try for the city, but I don't want to take a chance and get caught after dark."

"What kind of camp?" asked Kyle.

"My guy thinks they're smugglers."

Several minutes later, a clearing was visible where the jungle foliage had been hacked down and piled up. Evidence of off-road trails led into the thick foliage at the perimeter. Jean pointed to a fallen tree that was jutting out into the river, and Wilson positioned the boat to come in close, reducing the engine to a near stop. Jean searched the bank for evidence of inhabitants and then finally gave Wilson the okay to shut down the motor.

Carson guided the boat, acting as the bumper to avoid brushing up against anything sharp. He braced for the landing, secured the craft to the fallen stump, and then was the first to jump out into the shallow water where he attached another line.

Everyone hopped out, fanning into position around the clearing. Tucker first explored the tall grasses at the perimeter, looking through debris scattered in the brush as Jean and Kyle slipped in and out of the jungle, exploring the recently-made trails.

Carson called Kyle over to the riverbank.

"What you got?"

"Just showing you there's been another boat here recently, sir. It's a solid hull, probably a metal jitney. See how it left grooves in the mud?"

"Thanks for pointing that out, Carson. Good observation." Kyle returned to the camp perimeter.

Tucker found a plastic lidded box that had been tossed aside and then covered with branches. He put on his gloves and carefully set the container down at his feet. Inside were miscellaneous pill bottles, some vials of antibiotic, gauze, and some sports wrap tape. An opened box of latex gloves had spilled at the bottom. Kyle was at his side in an instant.

"I could use some of these things, leave them at the compound," Tucker advised.

"Are they still good? What are they?" Kyle wondered.

Tucker rummaged through the bottles carefully. "We got penicillin tablets, something for malaria, some aspirin, and these vials of antibiotic. Nothing to inject with and no pain killers, though."

Jean had joined the little circle.

"What do you think, Tucker?" asked Kyle.

"Looks like a medic kit, but without the pain killers and the needles. My guess is someone kept them and discarded everything else."

"Does the lid have a label?" asked Jean.

Tucker held it up, showing a label had been removed.

"You have a problem if he keeps this?" Kyle asked Jean.

Jean shrugged. "If you can use it, no."

Tucker set the box near the shore and moved on to the firepit, kneeling to see if he could recognize anything that had been burned there. He could still feel heat coming up, but there were no embers or fire. Jean dug around in the ash with a long stick. He hooked a wafer-thin piece of fabric a few inches long, holding it in front of Tucker's face.

"Someone's been burning bandages," he told Jean. "See the borders here? Those are blood stains."

Jean nodded solemnly. "See if you can find more. I'm going to alert the others."

Tucker removed the surface debris with his Ka-Bar then dug into the soft ash. He immediately encountered an article he thought at first was a piece of buried food, stabbing it with his knife. But when he laid it on a smooth rock and poured water over it, he discovered that what he'd uncovered was a charred human hand. It was small but not small enough to be that of a child. It appeared to belong to a woman and was severed cleanly. He noticed the smooth surface of the two cleaved bones above the wrist and associated circular saw marks, which confirmed his suspicions.

"Over here!" Tucker shouted.

Kyle and the others ran to join him.

"This was removed by a surgeon's tool, a portable circular saw," he told Kyle.

Jean knelt down to examine the hand. "Doesn't appear to be an amputation for an infected wound, am I correct?" he asked Tucker.

Tucker nodded. With his gloves still on, he examined the fingers, carefully. He noted a slight indentation, indicating the owner might have worn a ring on the fourth finger. "You see it?" he asked Jean.

The former commando agreed.

Tucker tried to straighten the curled fingers. The nails were charred completely off, leaving black flaky residue, but Tucker discovered that a portion of the little finger had been removed between the second and third joints. This was not done with precision but by hacking the end of the finger off with a small hatchet or knife, perhaps a pair of wire cutters. He looked up at Kyle.

"Proof of life," his chief murmured.

"Or, a trophy perhaps?" added Jean.

Tucker applied more water until he sloughed off the burned flesh and found enough remaining to make a stunning pronouncement.

"This woman, or young girl, was white."

The hand was wrapped in gauze and bagged after Tucker took pictures. The day's light was rapidly disappearing, and Jean requested they hustle their way home. Tucker tossed the bagged evidence in the plastic kit and carried it to the raft. Jean tapped his shoulder before they fired up the engine.

"Don't leave it in there. Put that in your duty bag and keep it zipped, just in case we get stopped."

"Roger that."

The images of the camp and the torture or possible loss of life haunted him during the return. He suspected it affected the boat guys as well. No one said a word, but they all kept a vigilant eye out for anyone in the brush. When the familiar shore and their building came into view, Tucker breathed a sigh of relief. Together, they carried the raft inside the gated compound, where it was covered in a large green tarp and strapped down.

"Tucker," Jean said after they unpacked their gear. "Go get some dinner, if you're hungry, but put your sample in the freezer for now."

"Will do."

"Oh and, Tucker, be sure to label it."

Tucker gave the former commando a grin. "I think I'll double bag it, too."

Jenn shrugged. "Would sure be a shame if your mates took that thing out and barbequed it, now wouldn't it?"

Tucker laughed on the outside, but privately recalled stories of some of their Desert Storm Ranger brethren who had gone over the bend in Iraq and created a whole ceremony surrounding roasting ears of the enemy. As a newbie SEAL, he'd had nightmares about it for weeks afterwards.

LATER THAT EVENING, Tucker was catching up in his journal when Brawley came to bed.

"Was wondering where you went," he said.

"Ollie and I watched a couple movies in the stash Wilson brought. Someone went to the trouble to bring us some world-class porn."

A red flag launched in Tucker's brain. Maybe it was his imagination, but he smelled alcohol.

"I hope Kyle didn't catch you drinking."

"Just a couple of shots of Jack. No biggie." Brawley didn't make eye contact.

Tucker decided to let it slide since the hour was still early for a normal working day. But he still didn't like it.

Brawley grabbed his towel and headed to the showers.

Tucker refocused on his notebook which had become a welcomed nighttime routine. He found it easier to write than to talk about his feelings. He figured it was safe, because if he got disgusted with himself for getting gushy, he could just burn the damn book. But without any way of knowing how to post a letter to her, or even knowing if it was allowed, it was all he had available.

He also wanted to purge his brain of the images of the severed hand they'd found today.

Today's trip made me feel grateful we live where we do. I see the violence, the way some people live, and the poverty. It's the same all over the world. One thing for adults to have to fend for themselves, but seeing the little kids having to live in these conditions really gets to me.

I used to think it would be a good idea to think of home and all the wonderful things I'd get back to, but I've changed my mind. I think about those barefoot kids, running around dirty streets, tugging at their mother's skirts, and playing with dusty plastic pans and sticks instead of toys. I think of the killings going on and the danger lurking in the jungle and wonder: when do those kids get to be kids? And it's not war that's doing it. It's desperate poverty and a power struggle that has been going on for centuries. Seems like a crying shame.

We're staying in a large bunker, sort of a safe house. I can't tell you any more about it, but you'd be pleased to know I'm safe at night, rather than hanging out in a tent in the bush. We even got hot showers and flush toilets!

But you don't care about all that. You just want to know how I'm doing, and let me tell you, I miss you more tonight than ever before.

Now, if I was king of the world, I'd command everyone to fall in love, like I have. I'd make sure they grabbed someone for a hug, not out of fear, but because they wanted to express that love. That would be a perfect world. And it has nothing to do with politics or power.

I guess I have to settle for the fact that what I'm doing is helping some place become more stable so those tiny flames of opportunity and freedom can get kindled, fostered, and become a bonfire. I don't want to run it, and God knows we shouldn't either.

Okay, enough philosophy. I know you can feel my words,

Brandy. There's no doubt in my mind about that. You're here with me.

Always.

He put away his light and the notebook, tucking it under his pillow, and slipped down under the covers just before Brawley returned. He tried to push the visions of today from his head, bringing Brandy's smiling face into view, but he fell asleep before her lips could touch his.

CHAPTER 12

T HERE WASN'T ANY amount of talking that could settle Brandy's nerves. Dorie explained several times how she should just focus on how much Tucker loved her. Her friend insisted he was a changed man, that she'd never seen him so full of life and happy. Dorie recounted what little she knew of Shayla, especially how manipulating that woman could be. She said not to worry.

Of course, she knew Dorie was telling her the truth. But Brandy still couldn't put it away. She was still fighting back for all the injustices that had been done to her in the past.

"Seriously, Brandy. You have nothing to worry about with Tucker. And, the more you let it get to you, the more she'll get permanently lodged deep in your head. She's not a nice person. That's why I didn't even want you two to be introduced."

"Logically, I know you're right, Dorie. But this obsession with her has got me caught in a rut. You know how it is when you can't get some damned song out of your head?"

"Maybe look at your past as your training, giving you courage to love a man like Tucker. As you've seen, this isn't an easy life, being married to a SEAL. Not everyone can do it. But it's worth it."

Yes, she'd told herself these very things over and over again. Still, she couldn't get the look of this woman out of her thoughts. The knowledge that someone had been private and intimate with her husband—yes, before he was her husband—was driving her crazy. She was so worried she would lose this wonderful relationship or that she could actually damage it just with her fears.

Brandy found no comfort in stacking shelves and clerking at her father's store since he was talking non-stop about all the plans he was making with Jillian. They were going to take a cruise. She was a wonderful cook. She loved to get dirty in the garden with him. All these things were now annoying to her, and it wasn't fair to him to be hanging around.

She asked for, and got, a few days off, so she took a watercolor class at the local community college. But drawing bowls of fruit and fruit labels only made her think about her father's store, which in turn made her think about her father's new romance. It did take her mind off not receiving another call from Tucker.

She knew it was wrong not to be happy for her dad's new relationship.

Dorie told her that Cooper's wife, Libby, had nearly completed her counseling degree, and her dad was the unofficial team head shrink, which Brandy knew. Dorie suggested Brandy call her.

Libby called her right back. "Let's get some lunch. I drop the kids off at school in the morning. Will doesn't get out until three, and Gillian's out at two."

"Perfect. Where?"

They agreed to meet at her favorite seafood place overlooking the harbor, where Tucker had taken her that last afternoon before he left for Africa.

Libby glanced around the wood-paneled bistro, decorated with surfboards, aloha shirts, and posters. "God, I haven't been here in years. We used to come here all the time. Coop had a motorhome he parked down at the beach a way south. The guys affectionately called it the *Babemobile*."

Brandy hadn't heard that story and asked her to explain.

"Cooper is very frugal. He stayed there for pennies, pocketing the Navy's housing allowance. And he could watch the sunsets, run or swim in the surf, and, well, meet girls."

Libby's blushing cheeks lit up her whole face.

Libby continued, "They change. I mean, they're the same person, but more settled with themselves. The first time I saw Coop I didn't want to have anything to do with him."

"Really? Now see, my reaction with Tucker was exactly the opposite, but then, you're like Dorie. Probably never had to worry about a date or about a guy not calling you back."

Libby took a sip of her iced tea and slowly looked up. "Brandy, that's not something you should keep telling yourself. I totally understand that you do…However, contrary to what you might think, I've had some problems with learning to trust men myself. I experienced sexual assault in college with a professor."

"What did you do?"

Libby returned an evil grin. "I got him fired."

"Good for you." She wanted to choose her words carefully. "I know Tucker's not interested in anyone else, and I also know he's glad they split up—"

"But? I know there's a but in there somewhere," Libby pried.

"I think his ex-wife still likes him."

Libby cocked her head. "I'd only worry if he's flattered by that. Does he give any indication it makes him feel good knowing she cares for him? Because a man like that can't be trusted. I don't get that about Tucker, and I barely remember his former wife."

"No, I think he wants to stay as far enough away as possible. I believe him about that."

"So it's not him that you don't trust. It's her? Is that what you're saying?"

"Exactly." As she thought about it further, she corrected herself. "No, it's *me* I don't trust, I guess. I worry I'll make a complete fool of myself on one of those long-distance conference calls. He deserves better, especially now."

"I think you're onto something there." Libby leaned forward and put her hand on Brandy's right hand. "But don't feel like you have to sugar-coat those calls. We're not all happy, happy, happy all the time, are we? Just be honest yet respectful of the pressures he's under."

"So I should focus on trusting myself instead?"

"Here's what I'd tell you to do, and take this with a grain of salt, because I didn't sit for my test nor do I see patients. Think about all the things about you Tucker loves. Remember those things. You are unique. He loves that about you. You speak your mind. He absolutely loves that about you, I can tell! He doesn't want a doormat or someone he has to battle with all the time. He's battling bad guys every day at his job. And he doesn't care about what other women from his past think of him. He just cares about how *you* love him. That's what you show him."

Brandy could tell she'd received very well-timed advice.

Libby continued. "There's a story I hear the guys talk about all the time. They say there are these two dogs. One is a mean dog and the other is a loyal and good dog. You feed the good dog, so he's big and healthy. Don't feed your fears, Brandy. Feed what's good in your life."

BRANDY WAS OVERWHELMED with Libby's gift. She could hardly wait to talk to Tucker the next time and prayed it was soon.

CHAPTER 13

K YLE AND JEAN gave a team update at breakfast. Jean's men had joined them.

"Honest to God, gents, I've been asked three times already this morning about *The Hand*. Well, here it is." He held up the bundle Tucker had wrapped in a tea towel. Tucker hoped it was still frozen.

"You guys are sometimes are like a bunch of teen girls with your gossip. If you weren't told about this, then don't read anything into it. We're doing a lot of stuff here. Nobody is being left out, okay?"

Several of the men nodded. Tucker wondered who had talked about their excursion last night, because he didn't say a word. By the way Wilson had hung his head, he guessed where the leak came from. Not that it was a leak.

Kyle continued, "But just to set the record straight, we found this hand when we went upriver to go check on some intelligence about a group of possible smugglers set up nearby. We confirmed that they had indeed been there and recently."

Jean barged in. "Kyle was tasked with this larger group for a reason. Our efforts might go in several directions. As he has explained to you, it might even take more than one trip for your guys. We figured the more guys we expose to the mission, the better chance we have of long-term success. With that comes some inherent problems. Information that is 'guessed' about can be damaging and downright inaccurate. We want to be able to make split-second decisions based on good intel. We're asking your help with this. That's the reason for this meeting."

Tucker sensed that, by now, Wilson was feeling pretty bad. He'd never served on a SEAL Team before, didn't know how they operated and how easily feathers could get ruffled, especially when there was so much down time. He knew the men were trained, programmed to be ready to go. Boredom was one of their enemies. They were men of action.

He decided to talk to the young boat guy and give some encouragement he might appreciate. For that, he didn't need Kyle's permission. It was just helping out a fellow team member.

He glanced at Brawley, who sat next to Ollie Culbertson, his arms crossed on his chest and his gaze off to the side, which was worrisome.

"Here's the deal," Kyle continued. "Today, Jean and I and several others are going to drive up to Abeokuta, which is the local provincial capitol here. It's a fuckin' huge city of some half mil, a hub for the trans-Nigeria railroad that connects neighboring Chad, Niger, Cameroon to the west coast, Benin, and beyond."

"May I add something, Chief?" Jean requested.

Kyle stepped aside and motioned for him to take the floor again.

"There are things that happen up north in the capitol of the country, which is Abuja. But there are also business interests that flourish and enjoy being *outside* the capitol, especially with access to good transportation, the Gulf, and the Atlantic. Growing up, we always knew the multicultural aspect of our society was greatest at the coast, naturally, due to old trade routes and alliances. And believe me, there are those who appreciate being farther away from the politicians and their cronies." Jean turned and gave Kyle the floor. "Continue, Chief."

Tucker understood the dynamic they were talking about. If people wanted to conduct business without political interference, they'd do it as far away as possible, until their activities drew attention and brought them out of the shadows.

A trade in human trafficking or smuggling might be one of those businesses.

"We're going to send this in for analysis." Kyle held up the bundle and unwrapped the towel from the double bagged package, still frozen. "We believe this to be the hand of a young woman. And there is evidence part of a finger was removed, for some reason. It's common in ransom cases as a verification. It also scares the pants off loved ones and increases the size of the payout. But we're puzzled as to why the whole hand was removed and then discarded. And we're not sure if a subject could survive such a procedure if done out here in the jungle. So we're going to see what we can learn in town today."

"We'll take two trucks and two men with the boat crew. The rest of you will hang out here, ready, should we need you. You can use this time to contact your families, sleep, do PT, or watch some movies. You are to stay indoors, and as of today, you can use your cell phones. Right Jean?"

"It's set up. Yes. I have the passcodes posted in the lounge up-stairs. Again, do not make your calls outside this building. And always safest to use the equipment here, which is hooked up to our satellite link."

"Questions?"

"How long will we be gone?" asked Ollie.

"Ollie, you're staying here. But the teams going north are the following: Cooper, Armando, Fredo, T.J., Rory, Jameson, Patrick, Danny, Jake, and Tucker. DeWayne, you and one of Jean's guys will go with Wilson and Carson by boat. That leaves the six of you to yourselves, but you'll also have two of Jean's men guarding the perimeter."

"So how long, Chief?" Ollie asked again.

"We'll be back before dark. Anything else?"

"We pack light?" asked Armando.

"Leave your long guns here, Armani. Take your sidearms. You heard Jean yesterday. Never be without your sidearm."

The team was dismissed. Kyle shouted above the rumble of the crowd, "Leaving in thirty minutes."

Tucker waited for Brawley, but when he couldn't find him, he sought out young Wilson, pulling him into the hallway.

"What's up, Tucker?" the young Dine warrior asked.

"I just wanted you to know you're doing a great job. I'm so fuckin' impressed with you. You did good today. And if you wanted to crow a little bit about the adventure, well, everyone understands that's a newbie mistake. Not anything serious."

"Yea, I only told Danny and one other guy—"

"I get it. And Danny should have told you so, but keep your mouth shut until you're asked. Just don't offer. All new guys go through this. You want to make a good impression. Don't worry about it, kid. In no time, someone else will be new, and you get to help them."

"Thanks, Tuck. I appreciate that."

"I still got the same things going on, Wilson, and I'm an old fart. But I'm still new to this rotation, because the Navy changes, the Teams change. We're doing things way different than even ten years ago."

"Thanks, man." He fist-bumped Tucker.

"No problem. And remember, they look like big tough guys, but they're really pussies at heart."

Wilson had a deep chuckle over that one.

"Gotta split."

Tucker took the stairs two at a time to their second-floor room to gather his gear.

He checked his medic kit and double-checked his clips. He slipped his Kevlar vest over his long-sleeved tee shirt. Like most of the other Team guys, he'd customized the Velcro pockets that held his smaller gear. He was applying a repellant towelette to his neck, face, feet, and lower arms when he heard Brawley walk in.

He raised his head just in time to see Brawley head straight for him. When his buddy's palms smacked flat against his upper torso, Brawley pushed Tucker into the adjacent wall.

"What the fuck was that, Tucker?"

If it wasn't Brawley, Tucker would have immediately answered the assault and with lethal force, if necessary. But it was *Brawley*. The guy who'd been there for him his whole life. The guy who'd suffered and was not quite fully recovered. Tucker stuffed down his anger and responded in a cool, measured tone.

"You fucking get your hands off me, Brawley. Get your shit together, and then we can talk." He held his arms to the side, which he hoped Brawley would see as a submissive move. He made sure the eye contact was anything but.

Brawley bunched up a couple of his vest flaps, curling his fingers, then pushed off Tucker, and swore under his breath.

"You wanna tell me what's going on?" he asked Brawley. He was hoping the choice would be made to keep their interaction from escalating. "Talk to me, Brawley," he nudged further.

Tucker could hear several other guys gathering downstairs. Someone was playing some rock-n-roll, mentally gearing up for the mission. He hoped Brawley got that he was trusting him to make the right choice. It was clearly up to him now.

"You said something to Kyle," Brawley barked through his teeth, not making eye contact.

"And told him what? I've barely talked to Kyle since yesterday. What the hell do you mean?"

"Is there a reason why I'm not going on the trip to the city?"

"Fuck, Brawley, there are six of you not going! I don't think anyone else feels that way. Your time will come." It was obvious Brawley was short on the emotional reserves. In the old days, he'd have never thought of it this way.

"How'd you get favored treatment, Tucker? You tattling to the chief?"

"Is there something I should be telling him? You ask yourself that right now, Brawley, because you're bordering on some psycho shit. Now get your head out of your ass and wake up. You can't be prepared when you have all this garbage floating around in your head."

Brawley looked away, deep in thought.

Tucker extended an olive branch. He touched his shoulder and squeezed. "Get some rest, man. Perfect time to get caught up. And stay off the booze. Next time I smell it on you, I will tell Kyle. Don't make me do that."

Brawley nodded solemnly.

"Remember, it's not about you. It's the *other* guy. He deserves you at one hundred percent. You owe that to the Team."

"You're right, you fuckin' asshole." After a tense couple of seconds, Brawley followed it up with a wide grin.

"You forget your meds?"

"Didn't take the one last night. It was an oversight."

"Another reason to stay completely sober. Brawley, you gotta get turned around about all this. Talk to me tonight if you need to. We gotta handle this shit right now. I love you, man, and don't want to see anything happen you'll regret."

They embraced quickly, following it up with a pat on the back, then separated.

"Hooyah," Brawley whispered.

As Tucker ran down the stairs to the waiting group in the reception area, he knew it was only a matter of time before he was going to have to make a major intervention. He'd give Brawley one last chance. And if it didn't improve, he'd make sure he got declared medical and would get Kyle to ship him home. He was kicking himself at the decision made to allow Brawley back on the team.

His best friend was still not whole. Tucker vowed Brawley's condition wouldn't cause anyone else on the team to suffer. This was on him, and it was up to him to make sure everyone else was safe. Tucker knew it was his responsibility to protect the Team.

He knew he could fix it.

DEWAYNE AND THE three others gingerly carried the raft to the water and took off. The rest of the team loaded their bags into the two vehicles and began their trip to the rendezvous point designated. Tucker's last sight of their compound was through the rear window of the rover he was in, watching Brawley, Ollie, and others standing inside the compound gates with their hands in their pockets. Just before they disappeared from view, he watched Ollie give Brawley a backward kick to the butt, sending him to the ground.

They wound through the dense foliage on the dirt trail, passing trading posts, clusters of huts, and one make-shift school which had not been repaired from a recent fire that had engulfed one of the classrooms on the end. There were several children playing in the yard, but the school appeared to be closed.

The trail crossed a two-lane paved road, traffic going in both directions and congested with a variety of small trucks filled with people riding in the bed and seated on the side rails, busses and scooters. Leone skillfully blended into the flow of traffic behind the other vehicle. Though each direction had a single lane, in most cases, three vehicles occupied that spot, jockeying for position and avoiding contact.

In the minutes that followed, more and more commercial properties came into view. Bus stops with brightly colored advertising and gas stations started to appear. As they rounded a gradual turn to the left, they could at last see the huge city sprawling up the gentle slope, literally covering the entire landscape. Spires of churches were prevalent, as well as several prayer towers and domes. As they entered the city proper, the traffic came to nearly a standstill. Along the side of the road were sellers of various wares, including water bottles. Once, when they were stopped, a small boy tried to sell Tucker a baby crocodile no longer than a foot, its mouth secured shut with a rubber band.

Chickens dodged cars, carts, and bicycles. Dogs slept in doorways and under concrete benches. Tucker also noticed rows of unemployed men sitting on their haunches, watching the noisy procession in front of them.

The temperature of the city was cooler than where their bunker was. Most of the larger buildings were covered in red clay tiles, but smaller single-story structures like homes and shops were covered in rusty corrugated metal, patched and repaired numerous times. The roofline looked like a colorful patchwork quilt. Here and there, a large banyan-like tree arched above the buildings, but in general, there was very little landscaping.

Leone followed the Areva Afrique truck ahead as it turned west and headed toward their planned meeting point. Tucker read several signs directing tourists to Nigerian museums, frequently dedicated showing off artifacts of the slave trade. A large customs house was located a block away from the river bank, the area surrounding it paved with brick, making it a huge open-air marketplace filled with vendors stalls. A painted green and white sign on the building indicated it was the old slave marketplace, with a date chiseled in a stone block below it of 1502. Beneath that were the words *Point Of No Return*.

The vehicles pulled to a stop while Leone gave out instructions. "Follow Jean through the marketplace. We have a few minutes before the boat guys should arrive, so feel free to wander but not too far. Stay in groups of at least three."

"Can we use our dollars?" Tucker asked.

"They love dollars. That's more than a day's salary, but show your money cautiously, and be very careful about pickpockets. The locals don't figure it's illegal to cheat or steal from you. Do not use any of the cash machines, if you can find them, and don't exchange your money at a Chinese trader."

Danny asked for the exchange rate.

"I think roughly three hundred sixty Naira to the dollar."

"So where do we meet up?" asked Tucker.

Leone pointed to a small gate next to the custom house. "We'll be meeting them as they come through there. We have a place where we can leave the boat undisturbed, and Obe will guard it. You can leave your bags in the vehicle for me to guard. Be at the gate no later than,"—he checked his watch—"eleven hundred. That would be about right."

Tucker's group stuck together as they wandered through the marketplace. There was a section that sold fish and meats and another that sold local vegetables and cheeses.

They came upon a stall selling handmade stringed instruments of all sizes that attracted Jameson's attention. He drew quite a crowd when he pulled down a long stringed instrument looking like a banjo, consisting of stretched skin over a calabash, and tried to play it. The neck on the instrument was nearly a foot longer than a classical banjo, and it had only three strings. The owner asked Jameson if he wanted a demonstration.

The musician began a series of repeating refrains varying slightly in syncopation but keeping to the same time. With that background, the musician chanted, his voice picking up notes in harmony to the stringed beat, cutting in and out at half-intervals similar to a blues performer. Several small children instantly appeared and started dancing in a circle at their feet, each one trying to outdo the other. Another shopkeeper picked up a thumb piano and joined in the song and dance.

Kyle's group heard the music and turned to see what the ruckus was all about. Tucker threw his arms to the side, and Kyle closed his eyes, shaking his head in disbelief.

As soon as the music stopped, several shopkeepers ran to the circle, pushing their instruments in Jameson's face, holding out their percussion bells, wooden xylophones, reed flutes, and animal skinned drums, as well as every size of stringed instrument imaginable. He was overwhelmed and overridden with vendors all wanting his dollars.

Tucker helped extricate him from the crowd, purchasing the thumb piano from the original vendor, which seemed like the only way to get Jameson free. The transaction cost him ten bucks.

They located Kyle's group very close to the gate and stayed focused on catching up. Several of the men stopped along the way and bought beaded bracelets sold by children but passed up the dried fish heads, snakes and mummified baby crocodiles.

Jean was on his phone and then approached Tucker.

"We have to return the specimen to my contact at the local Civil Guard, since it's an internal matter. I'm going to ask him some questions, and we'll go from there."

Tucker retrieved it from his backpack. The package was dripping and was starting to smell. He gingerly handed it over to Jean, who reluctantly took it.

The small Jeep-like vehicle with blue lights arrived and pulled some distance away as Jean ran over to meet him, clutching the package and letting it drip in his hand. Just then, DeWayne and the two boat guys came through the rusty gate to greet them.

"Uneventful trip?" Kyle asked.

"We had some traffic just before we came to the city limits. But the river looked pretty deserted today," said Carson.

"How'd you like the ride, DeWayne?" Tucker asked.

"Cool. Felt like I had become my daddy in Nam. It was a time warp," DeWayne answered.

Jean returned with news there had not been any kidnappings reported for nearly two weeks. But the policeman suggested they speak with the aid agencies and one of the pastors.

After their guide rinsed his hands in the fountain, he asked them to join him in a quick tour of the city.

They stayed to the main street, detouring down only a few side streets. Jean noted the police stations and the emergency pharmacies, letting them know what could be purchased there. He pointed out the government offices, most of them in their own separate, gated compounds. He recommended which restaurants to stay away from and which street vendors had food that would not make them sick.

He showed them the great houses of some of the civic leaders and which homes were owned by their own African-Bollywood celebrities and wealthy businessmen.

Kyle split them into two groups. Tucker was in the group that made the trek to the Baptist Foreign Mission Church, to speak to the new, young reverend. T.J. and several others went off in search of the Africa Corp Administration building.

Reverend Gordon Schusler was picking up bibles and hymnals left in the pews, being helped by a couple of young boys who chased up and down the rows of seats, dropping books and chattering with excitement.

Schusler looked like he was fresh out of seminary. Tucker noted a bulge under the back of the pastor's shirt, and assumed he was probably carrying a firearm.

"We're here on a humanitarian mission, assessing some electrical grid issues for Areva Afrique," Jean began. "We came across evidence of a campsite and discovered a severed body part."

The reverend turned pale. His eyes shifted nervously amongst the group.

"The local Civil Guard told us to check with you to see if you were aware of any disappearances, especially perhaps any white woman?"

The reverend quickly scanned his little chapel, swallowed hard, and appeared not to have hardened to the realities of the region. He checked the area behind him before he spoke.

"Oh, that pains me to hear. There is so much talk of violence now that the elections are coming up. But no, I'm not aware of anyone missing amongst our ex-pat community. But I can ask around on Sunday, if you like."

"Would you, please?"

"You hear any talk about active human trafficking groups lurking in the area?" Kyle asked him next.

"The locals trust me. We discuss many things," he said as he set the books on a table in the narthex. "I was just telling some of my colleagues in other regions that it appeared to be quieting some. I was hoping that perhaps the Civil Guard were doing a good job with apprehension." He shrugged. "But you never know here. These people could be members of my church. My understanding is they blend in very well with the local population."

Tucker could see fear written all over the young reverend's face.

"I know you're going to think I'm insane, but there was a rumor earlier in the year that a local dentist was conducting raids. One of the teachers recognized him. Can you believe that?"

Jean handed the clergyman his card. "Call me anytime if you hear of anything."

THEY REGROUPED AN hour later, the boat crew team returning to the shore and the rest of the team heading for the vehicles. T.J. was quite animated with his discovery at the medical mission.

"They've got three new teams just arrived to do health evaluations and give vaccinations at the schools, which start back up in two days. They've had a national holiday."

"And?" asked Kyle.

"They've lost contact with one of the teams, who were supposed to check in day before yesterday."

Kyle and Jean shared a look.

"This is out of your jurisdiction, Kyle. We have to let the locals handle it, and I'll get my trusted friend on it. But it means we've stumbled onto one of the cells, I think. We're close."

CHAPTER 14

B RANDY GOT THE call from Tucker just before she was leaving for work. His handsome face was such a welcomed sight.

"You look great, Tucker!"

He gave her a crooked smile and winked. "I could say the same. How are you doing, sweetheart?"

"I've been busy painting, spending some time with Dorie and Jessica, and had lunch with Libby Brownlee. And of course, there's Dad with his schoolboy crush."

He chuckled. "I can only imagine what that's like. He probably feels like he's starting over."

"At first, I think he wanted to hold back, you know, because of my mother. Now, well, I finally had to take a couple of days off he was getting to me so much."

"Ah, let him have his fun."

"So how have you been? Anything interesting you can tell me?" she asked.

He rolled his eyes. "Nope. But I'll have lots of stories when I get home. Very different over here. I spent most of my time in Iraq and Afghanistan before, so this is a change in one way and not so much in others."

His voice quieted and Brandy sensed he wasn't anxious to go into detail, even if he could.

"You staying safe?"

"I think so. We're in a pretty good spot. Oh, and you'll love this. We went into the market today, and I bought some trinkets, but you should have seen the instruments. They have this long banjo-looking three-stringed thing that Jameson loved. Course, he couldn't play it worth a damn, so we got a little concert from the shopkeeper. The kids were dancing all around us. A real Sound of Music moment. You would have loved it."

"That's totally not what I expected! So did he buy the banjo?"

"Nope. Way too big to lug that thing home. But I bought him what's called a finger piano. It's got—well, next call I'll get it out for you. You can search the internet too. There is a metal plate carved into fingers that are different lengths. The whole piece is nailed to a wooden bowl, and they use soda pop bottle lids to hold it in place. Very different and makes a beautiful sound. He's driving us all crazy with it."

"Sounds cool. Is the weather okay?"

"Muggy. Bugs. Dusty. I'm sure you get the picture."

"How do you feel being back in the Scouts?" She knew he'd pick up on the code word for Teams.

Tucker shrugged. "Work is work. Some fact finding today. Got a tour of the city, visited a little mission chapel, saw some unbelievable houses owned by the wealthy, too. It's just different. Lots of lucky chickens and lazy dogs. Parts are incredibly beautiful, and then there are other parts that break your heart."

Brandy saw a wrinkle develop on his forehead.

"How's Brawley doing?"

"Fine. He's doing fine."

Tucker's smile was flat. Fine was not a word he used very often, and Brandy sensed there was something deeper behind it.

"Have you eaten any of the local food?"

"We have a cook, if you can believe it. He's made some tasty stuff. They use coconut yams and peppers in everything. Make a red and green curry-like sauce and eat it over rice or potatoes, like a chutney. A lot of seafood. Some of it reminds me of Cajun food, like jambalaya. There's this red oil that takes your breath away. So far so good. Not had any stomach issues yet, but it's early."

"How long will you be, or do you know?" she asked.

"We're just getting started, really. I can't say, even if I knew." Tucker turned around to speak to someone. "Hey, we got another line tonight, so I need to sign off soon."

"No problem. I'm thrilled we got to talk. Always makes me feel better when I can see your face. So glad we get to do that."

"Me too. I've been writing in the journal you packed for me. Kind of my evening routine before bedtime. Wish I could write a letter, but you'll get caught up when I bring it home."

"Can't wait. Well, you take good care of yourself. I'm proud of you, Tucker. They're lucky to have you. Just remember what you promised."

"I think of that all the time. I'll be home before you know it. I really appreciate being able to see a little bit of home. Not enough, of course, but it will tide me over for now."

She kissed her phone screen. Tucker gave her the peace sign and disconnected.

She was left standing in her living room, her body shaking. She hoped they'd have longer next time, and she kicked herself for not asking when he'd be contacting her again. But she was grateful for the call. She sensed he was covering a little for Brawley but knew better than to get a report over the phone.

It was just good to hear his voice, feel that connection.

After work, Brandy had made an appointment with a personal trainer Dorie recommended. It was to be a trial, complimentary session. She met Cory in the equipment room. He was a much shorter and more compact version of Tucker, and he eagerly showed her a routine she could follow, marking machines and numbers of reps on a card he created for her. She wanted to show him how strong she was by pushing herself to the limits of exhaustion, though he cautioned to take it slower.

"I want to have guns like yours by the time my husband comes back," she announced.

Cory gave her a goofy scrunched up expression and responded, "Doesn't work that way, Brandy. Just be consistent. You don't have to push yourself, experience all that pain. Besides, if you do that, you won't enjoy it."

She went ahead and booked another three trainings at their introductory discounted price and was feeling really good about concentrating on her health. She could also feel the effects of her exertions and knew she'd be a little sore tomorrow, but put it out of her mind.

Instead of going home to a heavy dinner or eating fast food, she sat in the juice bar and ordered a healthy green drink that was gritty and tasted terrible. She was about to dump it and leave for home when three of Dorie's bridesmaids walked into the spa, dressed in their designer workout sets, complete with headbands and fancy shoes she knew cost hundreds of dollars.

The ladies attracted quite a bit of attention as they sauntered through the lobby. Marsha, the one who was married to a Team 5 guy, recognized her and came bounding up to say hello, her perky ponytail flapping behind her like a school girl.

"Brandy? Is that really you?"

The initial blast of Marsha's perfume made Brandy's eyes water. She drew down a large slurp of the green drink, trying to look as if she was enjoying it, before she answered. "Oh hi. You're Marsha, is that right?"

"Come on over here, girls. You remember Brandy? From Dorie's wedding?"

The other two floated to Marsha's side. "Who could forget that wedding?" one of them said.

"And I'm so glad we finally got that bustier on you, Brandy. How embarrassing it would have been if we'd torn the material or we couldn't get it on," the other girl said.

"That would have been a good America's Funniest Videos, for sure," answered Marsha.

Brandy wanted to throw the drink in her face. Instead, she laughed at herself with the rest of them and slurped. The seaweed and grass something-or-other drink was starting to grow on her and didn't taste as bad the third time.

"So how is Dorie? We haven't seen her here in ages," Marsha asked.

"Jessica takes up a lot of her time now that she's walking."

The other two squealed their O.M.G.s and surprise that they'd had a baby. "I'll bet Brawley is a *divine* dad," said one of them.

Brandy wanted them to just go away and leave her alone. But she was surrounded by other people, including her new personal trainer. "How's married life treating you, Marsha?" Brandy figured that would be mean enough.

"Gone." She held up her bare ring finger.

Brandy wasn't surprised. She wrapped her fingers around her straw, taking another sip and showing off her very small diamond. But it was a diamond given to her by a man who truly loved her just the way she was.

"Brandy!" Marsha whispered. "When did you get married?"

"About two years ago now. Met him at Dorie's wedding."

"You married a Team guy?" one of the girls remarked.

"Yes. Tucker, Brawley's best friend. You remember him, don't you?"

"The one who held your hair back while you were throwing up? That was so sweet of him, Brandy," Marsha said with a sad, long face.

"Yes, that was very touching. We all watched. Such a sweetheart!" said another.

Brandy's nails dug into the Styrofoam cup. She took another long pull, which made a loud slurping sound when she hit bottom.

"Well," Brandy began. "I just finished my workout with Cory, and I'm off. Hope to see you here again, ladies."

The three friends gave her a hug, one by one, and then disappeared into the women's locker room. Brandy tossed her cup, swung her bag over her shoulder, and headed for her car. She knew she was angry and wished she had the courage to go all Ta-Wanda on one of their cars. But she closed her eyes and thought about the life she had now.

She was the lucky one.

CHAPTER 15

THE TEAM SORTIES began to pay off. Several sightings were made of a group of men who had traveled from the north. There had been a recent skirmish, and several villagers had been killed after the Africa Corp caught a similar band of men trying to abduct a classroom full of young girls. Reverend Schusler had an older member of his congregation he wanted the men to interview.

Brawley had been chosen to accompany Tucker and a small group, including Danny and DeWayne, to interview her. Kyle and Jean were off to a meeting with the Civil Guard. Ollie and several others were sent to visit the school that had been fire damaged, since school had re-started in the region. T.J. and Coop visited the aid workers office to see if they'd made contact with their missing team. All the groups had a man from Jean's team accompany them and were to assemble at noon near the river.

Reverend Schusler introduced his parishioner to Tucker and the others. DeWayne helped with the translation. She spoke French but little English. DeWayne had studied Yoruba.

"She has a granddaughter who has gone missing," Reverend Schusler said in a whisper.

DeWayne gave an introduction, first in French and then shifted to her native Yoruba and got better results.

She was animated, rocking back and forth as she sat in the pew, then waving her arms as she spoke. Tucker could see DeWayne was having a little difficulty at first understanding her dialect.

"She says her granddaughter works for one of the big houses, I assume those are the houses on the hill, as a houseworker," translated DeWayne. He stopped to listen further and then added, "She says sometimes that does involve a little sex, as her granddaughter is a pretty girl."

Brawley tensed, and Tucker knew he was stuffing down some choice words.

"Unfortunately, this is common," added Reverend Schusler.

"Do you know who she works for?" Tucker asked.

"No, but I can have her show me later, if you want." Reverend Schusler patted the woman's shoulder and spoke gently to her in French, encouraging her to continue speaking.

Tucker's stomach boiled. "How old is she?"

Dewayne waited for the answer back. "Fifteen," he said, his eyes downcast.

Brawley's eyes were red with anger. Tucker felt the same way. They listened to the woman tell the rest of her story. She drew a cloth from her bodice and wiped her eyes as she began to sob.

DeWayne paused. "Her daughter was kidnapped several years ago, and since then, she's been raising her two granddaughters. This one is the youngest. The older one was able to go to a boarding school in England sponsored by the mission."

Schusler nodded. "Yes, yes. Bimi. Very bright. She's doing well, we hear." He hesitated, "So she is Bimi's little sister? I don't recall seeing her at church."

Dewayne asked the grandmother about that. "She says Sunday is the only day she has to sleep. She works very hard, very long hours for the big man. It was on Sunday she went missing. At first, she thought she'd been called to work, but when they sent a messenger around on Monday when she didn't show up, her grandmother knew something was wrong."

Tucker asked Dewayne to translate. "Your granddaughter, does she attend school?"

The woman shook her head.

"So she's been gone how many days?"

She held up two fingers.

"When was the last time she saw her?"

DeWayne came back with the answer. "She was asleep when she left for church Sunday morning."

"Ask her if she has a picture of her," Tucker instructed.

The answer came back, "No."

Reverend Schusler spoke to the woman in French again. He listened and translated her answer. "She says she doesn't think her big boss has anything to do with her disappearance."

"Do you believe her?" asked Tucker.

"I do."

"Ask her to show us to the house. We can drive her there. We'd like to ask her employer some questions."

As the Reverend spoke, the woman got agitated and refused, shaking her head. She continued explaining something in Yoruba.

DeWayne gave them her answer. "She says she can point to it. You can see it from the front steps of the chapel. But she says she will not go there, because she does not want to offend the big man."

Tucker thanked the Reverend and shook the grandmother's hand. *"Merci, madame,"* he said over and over again, as he bowed to her.

She led them to the street, faced the rise in the distance, and pointed to a bright pink house with lots of vines covering the outside. It was one of the largest ones in the neighborhood.

"Do you know this person, pastor?" asked Brawley.

"No. Probably a foreigner. Could be a local official. Your friend

Jean might know who he is, but I don't. My flock isn't from there," he said and then turned back inside the chapel.

Tucker took a picture of the house with his cell phone camera. They headed to their rendezvous point to report their findings.

Kyle and Jean were waiting for them. When Tucker showed Jean the picture of the house, he was rewarded with an answer.

"Dutch businessman. Makes cell phones and electronic components. He's white. He doesn't fit the profile."

"So the Civil Guard will interview him, then?" said Kyle.

"That would be best. I'll get someone over there now." He was walking away, talking on his cell as Ollie and his group returned.

"Anything at the school?" Tucker asked Ollie.

"We talked to a couple of the teachers. Everything so far has been normal," said Ollie. "No one missing, no one hanging around, and they haven't seen anything unusual. But we gave them Jean's card."

"What about the fire?" asked Kyle.

"They attributed the fire to a faulty extension cord."

T.J. and Coop were jogging toward them. Tucker knew they'd found something.

"Any word?" Kyle asked.

"They're MIA," answered Coop, catching his breath.

T.J. added, "They get their supplies in those plastic bins, like what Tucker brought back. I have a gut feeling our girl was from that team." He handed a sheet of paper to Kyle, still gasping for breath. "Here are the details of the missing aid workers. We got three women and four men."

Kyle took the paper and began scanning. His face grew pale as he stared back at T.J. "One of these is American."

CHAPTER 16

K YLE OBTAINED VERIFICATION from the State Department that Sheila Coburn was indeed a twenty-three-year-old nurse from California. The Africa Doctors' Corps had inserted three new teams after finishing their training in France. They were to work primarily with children in the schools, since they could perform their examinations and vaccinations easily without having to travel all over the bush. And it needed to be done before the school year got out. The hope was that they'd be on the front lines of any further Ebola outbreak, as had occurred in the DRC.

Back at the bunker, they received a photograph of the young nurse, as well as pictures of the other six members of her team. The two other women were from Belgium. One was a nurse and the other a doctor who had been working off and on in Africa for nearly ten years. Two of the men were from Italy, one from Norway, and another from Algeria. The medic from Norway had served in the Special Forces. This was his first humanitarian gig.

Tucker eyed the picture of Sven Tolar with his intense cool blue eyes. He'd served in Afghanistan with several Norwegian SO troops, and he had high regard for their abilities.

"If this man's still alive, he'll be a huge asset for us," he said.

"I agree," said Jean.

"So this changes things," started Kyle. "State's made the request, and the SOF Africa Command has given us authorization to do a rescue or recovery. There are other embassy personnel in the region here for a conference, but at present, we don't think they're in danger. So our main goal is to locate and return these aid workers safely, by lethal force, if necessary."

Tucker knew that the other SEALs were as excited as he was about finally getting their hands dirty. He knew no one outside the community could ever understand that.

"We're getting some satellite infrared feeds after sunset. Once we locate the group, we'll launch. So get locked and loaded, get some sleep, check your bags and be ready when we get the call." Kyle turned to Jean. "Anything else you want to say?"

Jean studied the hostage pictures before he turned them over to Cooper. "My guys don't have identification yet on the hand, but I wouldn't hold my breath from the Civil Guard. At this point, we should assume we have a severely injured female and six trauma-tized hostages. Good news is that we have a combat medic and a doctor in this group. That bodes well."

It wasn't great news, but Tucker decided he'd take it.

After the team was dismissed, Wilson approached Kyle. "Sir, are we a go?"

"Depends on where we have to get to. We will leave a few men behind here, and who knows, maybe you'll have to come rescue us?" Kyle grinned.

Wilson and Carson tore upstairs. Tucker was right behind them.

Brawley had showered and was quickly getting dressed and gearing up. "It's showtime, Tuck. Didn't come all this way to spend my afternoons at the bazaar."

"Roger that. I'm going to shower, and then I'd like to get some shuteye. You okay with that?"

"No complaints here."

Tucker quickly cleaned up, rinsed out his shirt from today's trip, and hung it with the pants he'd washed earlier over the chair in their room. He finished getting fully dressed, including his vest and his boots with doubled up socks. He lay down, Brawley serenading him with his snoring. Just before he fell asleep, he heard the faint tune from Jameson's finger piano. He knew that from now on, every time he heard that sound, he'd think of this moment, getting ready to hopefully save the day.

BRAWLEY BARKED IN his ear, waking him from a sound sleep. "It's a go. Get up, Tucker."

The sky was black. He followed Brawley to the lounge and then down the stairs to where the rest of the team waited.

Kyle had sheets of paper spread over the countertop in the kitchen. "Help yourselves, and then take a seat." He pointed to the large tub that held bottled waters. Next to it was a box of energy bars, nut packets, and meal replacement shakes.

"Our satellite images show they've been moving around in a circular fashion." He showed the clip that had been downloaded to him earlier. "We're here."

Several men swore.

"Yeah, they're close, really close, and probably heading our way. So we're leaving a small force here at the bunker with the Zodiac. They've stopped moving, so we're guessing they've bedded down for the night. Jean and his guys are going to get ahead of them in case they run back to the city. The rest of us are going to meet them on the road. Going to spread out in three teams. We have to stop them before they get to the river," said Kyle. "And we don't have any time to coordinate local help, but the Civil Guard have been notified. We're on our own."

Kyle demonstrated the route they'd be taking on the map. "Wear your night vision, of course, and we're going to take our

Invisios. I'll give a com to each team. Coop, you lead one. I'll get one, and, Tucker, I'd like you to lead the other."

It hit Tucker in the gut that he'd been given a lead the first time out. He chanced a glance to Brawley, whose nod was nearly imperceptible.

"Snipers take your long guns, and Fredo, you and your guys make sure you load up on percussive and flash devices. Once we get a count, all three teams will hit at once, after Fredo tosses the percussive blast."

He called out the teams and the men staying behind with Wilson and Carson. He handed Tucker the sat phone, which he attached to his vest in the Velcro pocket he'd made especially for that purpose. Fredo passed out the Invisios so the team leaders could communicate.

Two of Jean's men were dressed in black sniper gear to guard the compound from the outside, with one man on the roof. The gate was opened, and the three teams jogged into the night, following the road. Jean's men left in one of the Rovers.

Along the way, Tucker's NV picked up the reflective gold eyes of small animals in the brush.

When they arrived at the launch point, they assembled one last time to coordinate the strike. Kyle's tablet showed the latest heat signatures of more than a dozen people clustered in groups. It was impossible to make an accurate count. None of the images were moving. He motioned for Tucker to take his group, which included Ollie and Brawley around to the right, sending Coop to the west, on the left side of the encampment. Kyle would attack the middle.

"We are a go." said Kyle. "Check in, and wait for my mark."

Tucker's group was able to follow a trail for several hundred feet and then came upon the campsite. A bright blaze from the campfire temporarily obscured his night vision, so he turned it off and flipped the scope up out of the way. His eyes slowly adjusted until he could see the sleeping forms ahead.

"We're in place," he whispered and heard the confirmation from Coop and Kyle.

"We can't get a count," said Kyle. "Tucker?"

"Checking now," he returned. Tucker moved closer. The fire gave him good visual advantage. He made out three forms tied together surrounding a small tree. They all appeared to be males. Another form sat in the driver's seat of an older Jeep-type vehicle, a rifle of some kind lay across his lap. He appeared to be the lookout, but his head dropped, and Tucker determined he was asleep.

"Got three males tied together right, sentry asleep in the Jeep, armed." He inched closer. "Troop convoy has no movement but can't see the back. We have eight, no, nine sleeping forms on the ground. I can't see the women."

"Shit."

Tucker froze, holding Brawley from moving forward.

"That's two unaccounted for," whispered Kyle. "Armani, anything?"

"I got eleven on the ground."

"On my mark. Three...two..."

Tucker waited, breathing slow. Then someone stumbled right over the top of them, coming from behind. As he fell, the man fired and woke up the whole camp. Fredo's blast went off simultaneously.

Tucker heard a thump and thought perhaps he'd been hit, but he remembered he'd worn his Kevlar. Brawley hit the shooter once in the head, the dark spray indicating it was a kill shot. Rounds started flying toward them, scraping the ground, tearing apart leaves, and pinning them down. "One kill," he whispered into his mic.

Cooper's team hit the group from cover behind the vehicles. The sleeping driver had been taken out, but two panicked shooters started spraying the whole perimeter.

"Two," he heard in Coop's distinctive voice.

Tucker knew it would be nearly impossible for the automatic fire not to have hit someone on their team. There wasn't any cover, and they'd planned for a coordinated stealth hit on the whole group. Gunfire ricocheted off the vehicles, sending sparks flying. "Three, four," he heard, and the automatic spray in front of him was still.

He had to extinguish the fire so the team could use their night vision scopes. He hoped Brawley would cover him as he ran into the circle, grabbed a blanket which had been covering a bloody body, and threw it over the fire, stomping it down until there was darkness again. He felt a sting on his upper right arm, which spun him around. He dropped to his belly again, firing in the direction of the shooter, and heard him hit the ground. "Five," he whispered hoarsely.

Tucker repositioned his scope and noted the body next to him had a heat signature. He touched the face and knew it to be a woman. She groaned. "One woman hostage, alive but wounded."

From behind, Brawley cut down a dark form he'd missed, running straight for him. "Six," he reported.

They heard a woman's scream then a single shot. "Seven," said Armando.

"Eight and Nine," he heard Kyle count off.

"Danny's got ten," said Coop.

Tucker heard movement near where the three men had been tied up. He saw the outline of a man using them for cover, as they stomped their feet and tried to scream through gags. Before he could take aim, Ollie came up behind and slit the man's throat.

"Eleven."

Everything was silent until he heard Kyle's voice over the com. "Gather the wounded. Lights on."

Tucker flipped up his scope just in time before the high intensity lantern illuminated the scene. Coop and T.J. checked for signs of life and re-confirmed the body count. Brawley scanned the perimeter.

Tucker knelt by the wounded woman and was aghast that she was still alive. Her body shook from a raging fever. Her right arm was bandaged where it ended at the wrist and was soaked with blood. She had multiple other wounds on her legs and around her neck. Barely conscious, he brushed the hair from her face and checked her pulse, which was weak, but she was still alive.

"Hang in there. We got you. We're bringing you home," he whispered. She said something in French he couldn't understand.

"Got one of the Belgium girls," he barked. "Serious. Gonna need immediate attention."

Brawley cut through the binding on the three men and reported, "Kyle, they say there are only three. One lost, and they lost one of the girls, too."

He could hear the American girl talking fast in English, crying between her words. Ollie went over to her and helped her walk.

"I got you, sweetheart. Just lean on me." He kept her at the outside, helping her to sit on a boulder as she clung to him, sobbing into his upper thigh. "No worries. You're safe now."

The three aid workers raced over and began to help the Belgium woman. Tucker dropped his bag and handed them his medic kit. They worked with skill, giving her an injection of antibiotics and had the dressing changed in seconds. Those cool blue eyes stared up at him, but this time, they were smiling.

"Thank God you came when you did. She would have been dead by morning," he said in his Scandinavian accent.

Tucker answered him. "Nice to meet you, Sven."

"Jean? You guys out there?" Kyle barked without getting an answer. "Jean, we got eleven dead. We're going back with three males, a seriously injured female, and the American nurse relatively unharmed. We've been told the other two perished."

Tucker saw Kyle double checking the sat phone, swearing as he still didn't receive an answer.

Danny, Coop, Brawley, and others checked for I.D.s, notes, or maps from the dead and presented Kyle with a very sparse pile of papers. Kyle tucked them into his jacket.

"We can't wait any longer," whispered their chief into his In-visio. "Let's get everyone and the firearms in the lorry. Coop, can you get these puppies started?" Kyle said, pointing to the two vehicles.

"I'm on it," said the big SEAL, running.

Before anyone could move, a twelfth shooter appeared around the back of the troop transport, drilled a shot to the back of Ollie's head, grabbed the American nurse from behind, and screamed, "I'll shoot her!" He aimed his pistol under her chin, hauling her into the tiny Jeep while using her as a shield.

The Team was temporarily stunned as they watched the body of their brother slumped against the transport. As the sound of the open-air Jeep took off into the night, the distinctive crack of Armando's sniper rifle fired after him, but the Jeep continued.

Ollie's body pitched and fell to the ground like a limp rag.

CHAPTER 17

BRANDY WAS HEADED to the gym when Christy Lansdowne's number came up on the car's dash as an incoming call. Her heart immediately began to pound in her chest. Her hands got sweaty. She temporarily couldn't find the answer button and almost disconnected the call. Her mouth was parched.

"Christy?" she rasped.

"Hey, Brandy. There's been some trouble, and I wanted you to hear about it from me first before you see it on the news."

"Is Tucker—?"

"We have one fatality, but it isn't Tucker."

"Who?"

"I'm not allowed to say, but please don't breathe a word to anyone. Stay off your phone but have it by your side. More to come."

"You need help calling people?" Brandy asked, relieved that at least Tucker was alive.

"Oh thanks, sweetie, but I got this. I gotta run, but stay off the phone, and if anyone on the outside tries to contact you for details, you haven't heard anything. Understood?"

"Yes, ma'am. Thank you."

Brandy pulled over to the side of the road as hot tears slipped down her cheeks. Still in shock, she took several huge gulps of air to calm her nerves. But just when she was getting control of herself, a wave of pain flooded over her, and she lost it again. The proximity to danger, to the fact that Tucker could have been killed, had knocked her so hard, she was reeling from the aftermath, gasping to wrap her mind around it.

What does all this mean? Is he alive but injured in some way?

After regaining her composure, she turned her car around and headed home.

First thing that hit her was that the place looked so empty without Tucker there. Everything was the same as she'd left it, but now she saw it through a different set of eyes. She was desperate for information.

Who is it? Brawley?

She wanted to call Dorie but turned on the TV instead and sat watching the news, clutching her cell. She flipped the channels, hoping for some commentary on trouble in Africa. After nearly an hour, one of the stations finally broke for a special report that Special Forces had been engaged in an altercation in an unknown location in Central Africa and that there were multiple fatalities.

Multiple fatalities?

Could Christy have not gotten the latest news? Were more members of the team injured—or...? She had to stop herself.

She ran to the kitchen and poured herself a tumbler of Tucker's whiskey, feeling it burn all the way down her throat. As she flipped from station to station, there wasn't any further detail.

HER CELL PHONE rang, waking her up. She'd fallen asleep on the couch, the glass tumbler was on its side in her lap, the TV still blaring in the background. The room was dark as the sun had set hours ago. She didn't want to look at the caller I.D. before answering.

"Hello?"

"Brandy. It's Dorie. I just needed to call someone. Did you—?"

"Is Brawley okay?"

"Yes. Tucker?"

"Yes, thank God."

She heard Dorie collapse on the other end of the phone. "I know I wasn't supposed to call. Please forgive me."

"Nonsense, Dorie. You want me to come over while we wait?"

"Could you? Jessica is down for the night, but I could sure use some company."

"Be right over. You need me to bring anything?" Brandy asked.

"No, I'm good. Just come."

BRANDY WAS AT Brawley and Dorie's house in twenty minutes. She turned off her car radio, annoyed at the news hypes and all the advertising. The clock said one A.M when she arrived.

She knocked at the front door but let herself in without waiting. Dorie ran straight to her, wearing a long nightgown, and collapsed in her arms. Brandy immediately felt comforted wrapped in the arms of her best friend. Dorie's body was shaking in compulsive sobbing she couldn't contain. As she held Dorie, images of their years of friendship passed by her eyes as she relived and recounted all the happy days, all the big joys and trials they'd shared together, and prayed for a happy ending.

This cannot be!

"Come on. Let's sit. Have you tried watching the news?" Dorie's eyes were puffy, a vein in her forehead pulsed, and her chest heaved as she tried to get her breath.

"I—I haven't been able to find out anything, but I stopped watching. I just couldn't."

Brandy understood how she felt.

"Well, we've heard both Tucker and Brawley are okay, so let's be grateful for what we know and pray for the families of all the others."

It broke her heart to think of the bonfire on their last weekend, all the wives and kids sitting around together. She finally understood why that was so important. Someone would get some bad news tonight—something she never wanted to hear.

As if she could will it so, she pushed all those thoughts out of her mind. Dorie lay curled up against her as she pulled a throw over both of them, and they held each other.

This was unknown territory for Brandy. Brushing the hair from Dorie's forehead, she tried to think of something that would soothe her.

"At least this time he's not missing like the last deployment. It sounds like they are safe. Just remember, Brawley isn't missing. He's coming home."

"Yes. This is different, but, Brandy, he had to work so hard to come back. It took him all that time in rehab. What's going to happen now?"

Brandy didn't have any answers for her but tried. "You know him, and you know he's strong. And this time, Tucker's with him. He also has you and Jessica. It's a whole new family he comes back to. He did it before. He can do it again."

After searching the news outlets again, they decided to go back to bed and wait out the word. Brandy left a message on her dad's cell so he wouldn't expect her for work and promised to get back.

Dorie insisted she stay over and offered her the bedroom, but Brandy needed to be on her own.

"Go take a shower, Dorie. It will relax you. And then turn in. I'll just borrow a pillow and sleep in the couch in front.

"Thank you. I have to get stronger about all this, or I won't survive."

"You don't say things like that, Dorie. You've got the baby and Jessica now to take care of too. He's going to need all the strength you can muster. I know you can do it."

"You're such a good friend, Brandy."

They hugged and retired for the night.

MORNING LIGHT HIT her across the face as her cell rang. It was Tucker!

"Tucker! Oh my God. Are you okay?"

"I'm fine."

There was that word again. She waited for further explanation.

"Um, we're coming home early. We lost a guy, and we're bringing him home."

"Christy told me. Who, Tucker?"

"Ollie Culbertson." Dead silence followed his whisper.

"I'm so sorry, Tucker. Are any of you injured at all?"

"Just a scratch. A few of us got banged up, but we're used to that. Just tough dealing with it. It will be good to get home. And, look, I can't stay on the line long. Just wanted you to hear it from me."

"Thank you. I've got you, Tucker. I'm going to dedicate myself to making you feel better."

He didn't answer back, which told Brandy there was much more he needed to say and couldn't. Then he whispered, "I'm not going to be very good company, Brandy. Just warning you. But I'll try."

"No worries. Don't even bother about that."

"And there's Brawley. He's a mess."

This was what she was expecting. "I understand. I'm at Dorie's house right now."

"Good. Listen, Kyle's going to call her, but don't mention that because she probably wants to hear from Brawley, so just tell her we're having to take turns here. And give her my best. I'll text you when I'm in country."

"Thank you, sweetheart. Love you, Tucker."

But he had disconnected the call.

CHAPTER 18

KYLE HAD MANAGED to get the Belgian doctor a medivac to the new trauma center at the capitol until she could be stabilized and then sent home to Belgium. The bird was to meet them back at the compound.

The decision was risky, but the Hajere Trauma Center was the closest available medical facility capable of handling her injuries. The capitol was about to become destabilized, and Sven and the other medics doubted she'd survive the trip back to Benin. It was hoped she'd be ready to be flown home to Belgium in two days' time.

The State Department confirmed that there was an impending coup about to break out any day and that Jean, through his contacts with the Civil Guard, had been detained until the SEALs were removed. There was worry that an armed government militia was on its way to prevent their leaving.

"Someone wants trophies," Cooper said.

"I'm guessing their timing was off, and they expected to intercept us on the way," said Kyle. "So, we have to get out of here immediately."

"Suits me fine. Can't wait to get out of this shithole," muttered Brawley. He wandered off into the dark, mumbling.

Everyone had to fit inside the only form of transportation they had: the one lorry. T.J. and Tucker wrapped Ollie's body in a blanket, securing it with rope, and loaded it on top of the canvas cover. Then they climbed up top with him. The doctor was laid out over the laps of four men in the second seat, and everyone else was jammed into the back. They also loaded up the weapons and tossed them in the back.

"Shit, where's Brawley?" asked Kyle.

"Goddammit," Tucker said as he jumped from the roof and switched on his light. "Brawley, where the fuck are you?"

Kyle chimed in. "Brawley? We gotta go? You want to wait for the bad guys?"

They heard someone across the firepit. Brawley was sitting cross-legged, rocking back and forth, mumbling something over and over again.

"I got him. Can I get some help?" Tucker shouted.

Several men hoisted him up, dumping him into the back. "Someone secure him if he tries to get out," Kyle barked.

They heard a "Roger that."

Brawley wasn't making any sense, and Tucker knew it was spooking the Team, but he could count on them to keep him restrained. Tucker jumped up top again, as the two others repositioned themselves and they headed out.

Cooper drove at break-neck speed, even though the night was still pitch black.

When they arrived at the compound, Jean's men had indeed pulled out, leaving the entire place unguarded. Wilson, Carson, and the other SEALs had convinced them to leave behind two of the four vehicles, which they had already packed, including the Zodiac and Wilson's precious engine.

Tucker was grateful they wouldn't have to hike out, especially now that they'd have to restrain Brawley and perhaps carry him.

The helicopter arrived and took charge of the doctor, as well as evacuated the two Italian workers. Sven Tolar agreed to accompany the SEAL Team to the Benin border and beyond to the coast where he could arrange transportation home.

"Before we head out, make sure you find your passports for the crossing. I don't want to fight our way back, if we don't have to."

Tucker had to find his in the bag that had been thrown in the back of the Areva Afrique truck. He also found Brawley's.

"Everyone legal?" Kyle shouted. There were no complaints.

"I have mine as well," said Sven from the back.

Kyle eyed Tucker, leaning forward and giving quick glances to Brawley sitting between them. "Everything good?" Kyle asked.

"Perfect," returned Tucker. Brawley continued staring straight ahead, thankfully, without saying a word.

Several of the team had injuries, which Sven, T.J., and Cooper had treated, but nothing that couldn't wait until they got stateside. The idea was to cross the border at dawn and make it to Benin to catch a charter flight home. Tucker's job was to keep an eye on Brawley and keep him from wandering off.

The three trucks roared out of the compound and headed straight for what they hoped was the fastest route, the highway, since getting out stealth mode wasn't a priority. Cooper had DeWayne up front with him as a translator, while Kyle, Tucker and Brawley took the second seat. Sven sat behind. T.J. drove the second truck and Fredo the third.

They passed a convoy of military trucks heading north to the capitol, but the road otherwise was empty both ways.

Kyle ended his long call with his State Department liaison and shook his head.

"Sons of bitches said this caught them off guard. I'm not buying that," Kyle cursed.

"Excuse me, Chief Lansdowne," Sven inserted, "but we're always on alert here for potential coups. We have an election coming up in two weeks. You know how it works. If they think they're going to lose the election, they have a coup, and then there's a civil war. They couldn't have known for sure."

"Well, we were sent here to find the smugglers, not save the country."

"We did," said Coop. "We rescued four out of seven. If it was going to be easy, they'd have sent in somebody else."

Tucker agreed. But in the silence, he knew everyone was thinking about the man they lost.

TWO HOURS LATER, they'd raced through the crossing, which was oddly unmanned. The sky was growing pink as they traveled toward a coastal town, where State had made accomodations for them at a crumbling hotel.

Tucker snuck in his quick call to Brandy from his own cell to let her know he was coming home.

Relieved at least to have a bed and the possibility of some sleep, he felt more human. He laid Brawley back on his bed, removed his shoes, and gave him a shot so he'd sleep the night without wandering off. He suspected the PTSD diagnosis he'd had nearly two years ago had now flared up.

Sven stopped by to check in and say good-bye. They whispered so as not to disturb Brawley.

"Just wanted to say thanks. I was hoping I'd get to spend some time with you guys. Maybe take a raincheck?" His forehead was wrinkled as his eyebrows rose.

Tucker gave him a hug. "Not anytime soon."

"I understand," muttered Sven.

"I wanted to talk to you about your Spec Ops tour. We trained with some of you guys last gig, over ten years ago. And I served with a couple of your guys in Afghanistan. I got tons of respect, man."

"It's mutual."

"So how the hell did you get back here as an aid worker?"

Sven leaned against the doorframe, exhaled, and then began. "When I came home, there was no family left behind to welcome me back, and after I got out, I just couldn't focus. I tried applying for some private security, you know, contracting jobs. But when I read about the Doctors' Corp, I got inspired. I knew I could help protect the workers, and I wanted to give something back."

"See the other side of suffering and war."

"Exactly. I was saving lives overseas, but I just wanted to use my skills for good. This was my first one."

"And did it help?"

"I feel like the work's not finished. But yes. I'm needed here."

"So, you'll come back?"

"I will. When the violence allows us to re-insert. They want me back in Paris until then."

"Let's stay in touch, Sven. If you ever get out to San Diego, stop by. I'd like to hear about your travels."

They shared contact information.

"Thanks again," said Sven as he started to leave.

Tucker had an unanswered question. "Why did they remove the doctor's hand?"

"One of them had been badly injured. They originally came to us for medical treatment. We couldn't refuse, of course, but the man was near death. Lisle did everything she could. We had to amputate the man's leg, and he still died. It was her punishment. They were crazy with hatred for her. When they came to take the body home, I thought they'd kill us all."

"That's tough."

"You survive. We just stuck together to survive. I had her pretty well drugged up when they did it. Nothing I could do because they threatened the other women. We tried to fix her up, but without proper supplies, I feared for the worse."

"The American girl. She tough enough to deal with all this?" asked Tucker.

"You want the truth? She was a spoiled brat. Should I feel bad for saying so?"

"No, I understand."

"Her first trip. It's not fair."

"What were their intentions?"

"They were looking to hook up with a larger militia. The girl was for their General. I think they'd have executed us when they met up, but that's just a guess."

Kyle arrived. "How's he doing?"

"I gave him some Ativan. He'll get a good sleep."

"Okay, good." He turned to Sven. "When do you take off?"

"Waiting to hear, but soon. I fly back to Paris."

"Gotcha. Thanks for your assistance. Jean told me about your background. Sure you don't want to come join us? We could always use a good man," Kyle said.

"It's a long story. I told Tucker here. We'll stay in touch." Sven shook Kyle's hand, waved to Tucker, and was gone.

"How're you doing?"

"I'm hanging. I snuck a call to Brandy after we got here. Hope you don't mind."

"Nah, that's good. Get some rest. Just stay with Brawley. I'll bring by some food later so hopefully you can get a couple hours of sleep, okay?"

"Thanks. What about you?"

Kyle leaned over and looked at Brawley again. "I'll get my sleep on the plane. I promised I'd call Dorie, so probably do that now."

"Right."

"Welcome back, Tucker. You did good."

"Then why am I not celebrating?"

"Because we lost one. Remind me next time not to plan a mission a week before the country is going to erupt into civil war, okay?"

"It's the first thing I'll ask, Kyle."

"You think he'll sort out?"

It hurt inside to lie to Kyle. "I think so. But he's going to need more time."

"And maybe he's done," said Kyle.

"He's only got two and a half more years to his twenty. Would be a shame."

Kyle nodded. He placed a hand on Tucker's shoulder. "Get some rest."

CHAPTER 19

THE NEXT DAY, Brandy got the text that they were about to depart Africa. It would take nearly twenty-four hours for him to get home. She was filled with relief and a growing anticipation. She knew that Tucker had done his job. Now it was time for her real job to begin.

Brandy was relieved that Dorie's frank call with Kyle had helped her deal with the future she was going to face. She contacted Dr. Brownlee and asked his help again to have Brawley admitted to the same clinic he'd been at before. Dr. Brownlee took time to walk her through what would be going on this time and generously offered to underwrite whatever the VA wouldn't cover with the hospitalization, as his family had done before.

She'd spent the day yesterday with Dorie and Jessica, but now was home, preparing for Tucker's return. She'd spoken with several of the wives on her phone list and offered to babysit or run errands. Everyone was in the same boat: waiting for their men to come back. She got many pieces of advice, some of it not helpful, but she felt mentally strong and ready.

THE AIRFIELD AT Coronado was windy as Brandy lined up with the other wives, waiting for the transport to arrive. Kids were decked out in their finest, some of them pulled from school so they could welcome their daddies home. Following tradition, the families occupied a small hangar away from the rest of the public, and the kids, who had grown up with each other since infants, had completely taken over the facility.

Dorie smiled to her as she waited with two attendants, who would be assisting Brawley to the clinic. Jessica sat close to her mother and was playing with items she found in her diaper bag.

As she scanned the little gathering, Brandy did feel part of this very large, growing family. It was the part of being with Tucker she hadn't expected. She had never felt alone during the short deployment and didn't feel alone now.

At last, the plane arrived. A hush fell over the room. Within minutes, men began to deplane. Kids were pointing, wives were crying and holding onto each other, and others were chasing their kids around the hangar. The men stood to attention, forming two lines as Ollie's flag-draped casket was lowered from the cargo bay, and several of the men carried it to the black waiting hearse. Ollie's mother was helped out of the hearse and then shook hands and hugged the men who had been with her son. She gave a long endearing hug to Brawley and spoke to him briefly. Brandy watched Brawley's arm slowly draw up to the woman's back to return part of the hug.

As the vehicle pulled away, Tucker looked strong, his jaw firm with resolve. He had an arm around Brawley, who walked clumsily as if his shoes were made of concrete. Tucker had both duty bags over his shoulder until Armando relieved him and remained in step. Brawley was working hard to keep up with the group. Many of the other men ran for the hangars as the families spilled out onto the tarmac in celebration.

She waited for him to be free before she saw him look for her. That's when she ran into his arms, colliding so hard they nearly toppled.

"There she is," he whispered in her ear. "I couldn't wait to get that body slam."

She drew back to search his face. He was back. He was totally back.

"Are you making a comment about my weight again?" she teased.

"Hell yes. I've always told you. You're perfect the way you are."

"So glad you're home, sweetheart." She was going to say more, but Tucker had covered her mouth. She tried to mumble through.

"Shut up, Brandy. Let me kiss you proper."

HAVING TUCKER HOME was like starting out all over again. She found herself shy undressing around him until the familiarity returned. She was surprised it had changed so in the brief time since he'd been gone. But their routine returned. They talked at night and slept in late.

She'd been prepared for a lack of enthusiasm for sex, which was part of the advice some of her friends had given her. Tucker was the opposite. He was obsessed with her, driven to follow her around with a perpetual hard-on. She wondered if it would start being annoying after a while, he was so much under foot. If they bumped into each other in the kitchen, it turned into sex. She got partially dressed, only to have it turn into sex. She found herself wondering if she was keeping up with him, his need had grown so.

He read her his journal in little excerpts but kept it privately tucked away. Brandy was overjoyed he planned to continue writing, though. His entries made her feel like she was right there with him.

"You could be a writer, Tucker. Your writing is very clear. You paint such vivid pictures. I'm so happy you've learned to enjoy it."

"Didn't know I liked to write. Now that I've found my voice, I'm going to explore it further. It's like second nature, something that I find easy to do. Who knew this big guy could do it? Gives me something to think about when the time comes after I'm off the Teams."

"Oh, you could write thrillers!"

"Sexy thrillers," he whispered.

Even the discussion about writing led to sex.

AFTER A WEEK, she started going back to her father's store, giving Tucker some alone time. He also wanted to schedule a visit with Brawley. It would take a few days to arrange.

As if the knowledge of this visit coming up added a burden, the happy veneer of his homecoming began to fade slowly in the weeks that followed. He became less interested in her work at the store or in helping her dad with the garden. Their sexual encounters became less frequent as well. He'd spent time with Kyle and others, and she could see he was worried the Navy was considering medically discharging Brawley. Tucker wanted to defend his best friend with a burning desire she'd not seen in him before.

He'd had discussions about their mission and she learned from Dorie that the Navy had been unhappy with the Team's performance. Not only had they lost a man, but the Navy questioned Kyle's judgment about bringing Brawley on the mission, as well as the mission itself. There was a chance Kyle himself had lost favor with his superiors. She knew Tucker took it hard, like he was partially responsible for it.

She felt the Brotherhood was pulling Tucker away from her.

As the days drew closer to his first visit with Brawley, Tucker's demeanor became more reserved.

Little arguments cropped up. She became worried, and asked if everything was okay with his position on the Teams. Tucker reared up and spat back a question.

"Where the hell did you get that? You think there's something wrong with me? That I didn't do my job well?"

"No, Tucker. I'm just trying to help. In case you want to talk."

"About what? There are some things I have to keep to myself. Quit trying so hard, Brandy. It pisses me off."

It was impossible to even talk about little things without her comments causing offense. Finally, on the morning he was to visit the clinic, the two of them had a major fight.

"Quit asking if I'm okay. You act like you're afraid of me, afraid of what I've done. You're walking around on egg shells, Brandy, asking too many dumb questions. Do I do anything that makes you think I'm not okay?" Tucker shouted at her.

"You're misunderstanding me, Tucker. What I'm asking is what's going on with you? Because I see a change. That's all. I see a hardness in you I didn't see before."

Tucker's body reacted. His fists balled, and he held his jaw clamped down tight, without a glimmer of anything soft. She knew she wasn't going to like what he had to say next.

"I'm not going to even dignify that comment with a response. Does everything have to be happy, happy, happy all the time? Why do I have to keep reassuring you? This isn't about you. It's about standing for my teammate, defending him, because right now, he can't do it himself. I won't leave him behind, and if you can't understand that, then you never really knew me, Brandy."

His hard stare scared her. She was on shaky ground and didn't want to escalate the tension between them, but she was confused, worried why he was reacting so personally.

Tears collected and began to stream down her face.

"Don't do that!" He barked. "That's not fair. You've got to stop hovering around me like some butterfly and just let me handle my own shit."

She knew he felt bad for her. But she could also see he wasn't going to back down.

"Brandy," he said as he softened his voice, "there are some things about me that you can't be a part of. There are things you have to just trust me on. Stop prying. Stop needing to know everything about every thought and emotion I have. I don't like or want that."

She remembered the conversations they'd had when they first met, about how he'd never let anyone into his life before. Had that all changed now? And why so quickly?

Brandy's insides melted. She felt the barrier between them, that a line had been crossed, and knew that he didn't trust her with some of his secrets. It would be a mistake to try to reason, convince, or otherwise try to manipulate him, but she was deeply hurt.

The best thing she could do was not make it worse. It didn't feel right, but she stuffed down her emotions, took a deep breath, and found some backbone. She wiped the tears from her cheeks.

"Well, you let me know when the other Tucker comes home. I'll be waiting. You go ahead and be the way you have to be. I'm not going to apologize for my tears or try to change the way you're feeling. It's like what you told Brawley. I can only go so far. You have to meet me halfway, Tucker."

She watched his truck pull out of the driveway on his way to see Brawley. She hoped that the man she loved would be the one coming back after the visit. He hadn't said good-bye or given her a kiss. He didn't notice she was standing there, her heart worried— not broken, but drained.

This sudden change between them was harder than the concern she had when he was deployed.

Should I feel this way? What is happening?

CHAPTER 20

T UCKER CRANKED THE music up in his truck and tried to set aside their argument. He didn't want to figure out what he was feeling. Best to just push it out of his mind. He needed a blank slate when he talked to Brawley. He needed to be ready for anything he observed with his friend. Today wasn't the day to analyze the argument with his wife.

The clinic was bright and clean, not like some rehab facilities he'd been to in past years run by the VA.

He asked for Brawley at reception. The young attendant batted her eyes at him, making an obvious flirtation, and it pissed him off. She'd pushed a clipboard across the counter at him.

"Why do I have to fill this out?" He'd worked not to use any smacktalk or swearwords.

"Well," she said in her pert little way, "we keep track of all our visitors. As I'm sure you're aware, this is a mental health clinic, and, well, we're very protective of our clients."

Tucker thought it laughable she regarded Brawley as a client. He nearly threw the clipboard at her.

"But I *have* an appointment! It took like two weeks to get that appointment. You have to examine me as well before I can go in there?" He pointed with his thumb down the hall. Several people in the waiting room stopped their conversation and looked up.

An older, matronly woman appeared behind the young receptionist. She angled her head closer, noting his SEAL Team 3 shirt, speaking in a low tone so the audience around them wouldn't be further alerted. "Don't take it out on her, sir. She's just doing her job." The woman gave him a spiteful sneer, whispering through her teeth. "And I don't care who the hell you think you are. Even as a Navy SEAL, you won't get to see him until you fill out the paperwork. Navy's rules, sir, not mine."

She stood back a step, straightened her form, and plastered a smile on her face. Tucker never had hit a woman, but he wanted to hit this one. He knew it wouldn't be smart, and he did his practiced deep breathing technique until his ire dissipated. Clutching the clipboard, he took it over to an armed chair and prepared the form. He nearly shattered the pencil gripped in his hand.

As he was signing the bottom, a young woman appeared in front of him, wearing a white lab coat.

"I'm Dr. Christen Saunders. You must be Tucker Hudson?" She held out her hand.

The doctor had a firm handshake, her bright blue eyes peering deep into his. Her attractiveness was probably her secret weapon as Tucker found it hard to stay angry standing before her.

"Yes, I'm here to see Brawley Hanks," he mumbled as he stood.

"Can I have that?" She pointed to the clipboard. Tucker gave it up.

"We've been expecting you, Tucker. May I call you Tucker, or would you prefer another term to address you?"

"Tucker's fine," he answered. He shifted his weight and felt exposed, speaking to the doctor in front of so many prying eyes.

"If you could follow me?"

He walked beside her, looking over his shoulder at the large woman behind the desk who was still protecting her turf and her protégé.

"Carmen can be a little harsh at times, but we've recently had some issues with some of our patient's rights being violated. I understand Brawley has been here before. These are new procedures."

"No problem."

As they continued down a highly polished wide hallway decorated with paintings done by patients and some by staff, he asked her how Brawley was doing.

"He's moving forward." She stopped. "Most guys like Brawley will be fine outside on their own, and can live normal, effective lives, eventually. But he's going to always react to stress in ways perhaps you or I wouldn't react. And I want to warn you, I doubt you'll be able to take him on future missions. I tell you this," she lowered her voice as a patient slipped by in a wheelchair, "because he's spent a lot of time talking about you two. He's very concerned how you think of him."

"Understood. Thank you, doctor."

They began walking again. "So my admonition is to make this a very light meeting. Don't stay too long, but come back soon. Tell him things he'll like hearing. Just reconnect. It will do him a world of good."

Tucker recalled his argument with Brandy this morning, especially the "happy, happy, happy" comment, and it annoyed him. "You want me to lie to him?"

"No. Just steer the conversation so you don't have to, and keep it to things he likes."

Tucker stopped this time. "But he likes the adventure of being on the Teams. He lives for that."

"Then you'll have to find something else he likes just as well. Just as intensely." Her pretty eyelids fluttered, and in his single days, he'd have found her attractive because she had an edge to her he liked. This gave him an idea.

"Do you get along with him?" Tucker asked.

"Oh yes. I think we have a very frank relationship. He's really coming along well. I've seen his chart from before, and he doesn't have any of the memory losses."

"Okay, good. Thank you, doctor."

When they arrived at Brawley's open door, Dr. Saunders greeted him cheerily. "We have a surprise for you today, Brawley."

"Oh yea?" Brawley smiled back at her and then looked to the side and made eye contact with Tucker.

"Fuckin' A! It took you long enough!" Brawley crossed the room in one leap and grabbed Tucker in a big bear hug.

Dr. Saunders turned and headed for the doorway. "Hey, you don't have to go. We could have a threesome," yelled Brawley.

Tucker saw the pretty doctor blush, examining the two of them. "Back in the day, you two would have been exactly the kinds of bad boys I'd have been delighted to sit with. But that was then. This is now. This is about you getting well and going home, Brawley." She looked down briefly and then whispered, wrinkling her nose, "But thanks."

She left the room.

Tucker knew his brief discussion with Brawley was going to be all about the doctor.

TUCKER AGREED TO meet Brawley again in a few days and asked him to get the doctor to expedite his appointment so he didn't have to wait so long. Brawley was in near tears at the prospect Tucker had to leave.

"I don't want to do anything to jeopardize your stay and treatment here. We want you out."

"But we didn't get to talk about the guys. What happened to everyone? I barely remember it."

"Next time. Promise," Tucker said as he left.

He reported in to Kyle who told him a few of the guys were getting together for beers at the Scupper. Tucker was all in for that one.

The two boat crew guys were there, which was a surprise. He hadn't seen them since he got back. "Amigos!" he shouted as they greeted him. Several others sat at their favorite table next to the fire pit.

"Kinda feels like old times, right?" said T.J. Talbot. "Nice fire, stars out tonight." He broke into a grin.

Several of the team clinked long-necked beer bottles, and Tucker shivered. "Not anxious to do another one of those campouts."

"I agree. The rangers are fuckin' mean," quipped Fredo. "I'd have to say downright nasty."

Kyle asked him about his visit with Brawley.

"Well, hey, not sure if this is the case, but I'd say he's getting better because of his doctor. Kyle, have you been by yet?"

"Nope. Wanted to see how it went with you first. But she briefed me by phone."

"Well, I don't know if her phone voice is sexy, but man, she's a looker. Very nice too. A little tough, but fun." He winked and the guys cheered.

"Now, don't get ideas, Tucker," said Cooper. "Old married man means just that, my friend."

"Hey. I was doing it for Brawley!" said Tucker.

One by one, he made eye contact with the team and one by one, he saw in their faces that in his first mission, he'd passed with flying colors.

"You knock up that pretty wife of yours yet, Tucker? Now would be a good time," teased Jameson.

"Some are working on it harder than others, I hear, Jameson," added DeWayne Huggles. "He's got the finger piano action going on!"

Again, a chorus of cheers let out. Someone poured a beer on the Nashville SEAL.

But the comment had struck a nerve with Tucker and he'd lost his lightheartedness. He'd left Brandy in a state he wasn't proud of. He'd have to watch that, he noted.

It felt good to be with the guys, in the warm night in San Diego, and it even felt good to get a bit of a buzz on. Tucker knew he'd have to order something or he'd have to take a cab home. The waitress was overloaded, and the wait would be extensive. So, while everyone was jabbering on about being back home, Tucker slipped into the bar to order a burger.

"We can bring it out to you," the bartender told him.

"Thanks."

Tucker was on his way back to the table with four new brews when he nearly ran into Shayla, his ex. Her eyes widened as she hungrily devoured the sight of him in front of her.

"Well, look who got out of the cage tonight. My favorite sailor." She glanced over to her bevy of friends sitting in a dark corner.

Tucker wasn't having any of it. "Not in the mood."

"If you change your mind, call me." She put her hands on his chest, sliding them down his jacket, yanking and tugging on his pockets. Tucker nudged her away.

"Shayla, why do you do this? It's totally beneath you. I have absolutely no interest in having anything to do with you ever again, so do me a favor and butt out of my life."

"Well, sailor, didn't mean to get you all hot and bothered." She leaned into him and whispered, "You do remember those days, don't you?"

"I honestly don't," Tucker said and walked outside.

An hour later, the group had pared down to just Tucker, Kyle, Cooper and T.J. As he hoped, the burger had helped take the edge off.

"You hear anything from Sven?" Kyle asked him.

"Not yet. I will. I think you will too," Tucker answered. "You hear from Jean?"

Kyle frowned. "Yea. The guy's whole world has fallen apart. They seized all his property, and he barely got out with his life before the militia came through. Some of his men defected."

"That surprises me," said Coop.

"They had families they had to protect. It's the story of Africa, Middle East too. They'll fight for whomever will protect their family."

Everyone agreed.

"So he's back in France?" asked T.J.

"He is. For now. He's still looking into what happened with the American nurse. But he doesn't have much hope, and there's not much he can do from Paris."

The conversation got sober in a hurry. "Crying shame," whispered Tucker.

"You think they'd ever send us back in to get her?" Coop asked.

"Maybe another team. Not sure I'll get that chance," Kyle said with resignation. "Although this *is* our deployment window. Depends on when they find her. Jean told me not to hold my breath."

Tucker didn't want to ask if Kyle was considering leaving the Teams or if he felt his career in the Navy was on hold. He wanted to have that private conversation with him about Brawley without other ears. He asked about the Belgium doctor.

"Understand she fully recovered, and has a prosthetic hand, Jean says. He was encouraging her to get a hook!"

"Serve anyone right if they tried to mess with her," said Tucker.

Everyone laughed.

Tucker knew it was time to leave. Before he was tempted with another beer, excused himself and said his good-byes. "I like this. Let's do it again, sooner," he suggested.

"We were just talking about that when you arrived," answered Cooper.

THE DRIVE HOME felt longer than the trip over. The house was dark, but Brandy had left the porch light on. He removed his jacket, tossing it on the chair, and kicked off his shoes. He sat on the couch and stared at the blank TV screen.

Normally, Brandy would have greeted him just as soon as he came through the door. But after their argument today, he figured he deserved what he got. So he sat in the dark and just thought about things. He thought about taking a shot of Jack, but lost interest.

So much was out of his control. He thought about the poor American nurse, about the misfortune Jean had gone through. Brawley, he wasn't worried about any longer, or at least not for now. Getting the Navy to keep him in might be something Kyle could help him with. The guys were good. He knew Sven was probably enjoying Paris.

But that left Brandy. She was the glue that made everything hold together. He realized that loud and clear when he saw Shayla at the Scupper. The differences between these two women were like the two sides of the moon. He remembered what Kyle had told him at the bonfire before they left, *'You got a good one there, Tucker.'*

It was true.

But it also wasn't fair to her if he couldn't get as close to her as she needed. He'd been fine with long distance friendships and casual hookups. But Brandy wanted everything, wanted it intense. Believed in the happily ever after. She wanted every part of him, and he wasn't sure he could give it. Sometimes, he was all on.

Sometimes he was just switched off. And it could happen quickly too. Maybe he'd been lying to himself. He never wanted to lie to her. She deserved so much more.

He knew it was time to go back and apologize. Maybe that would help him remove all the rough skin and the worry. Nothing was ever one hundred percent perfect, especially a homecoming.

Just like no mission was.

He opened the door to the bedroom a crack just to watch her sleep. Moonlight showered her arm and shoulder with silver. Her hair splayed all over the pillow. He vowed he'd try harder. If he couldn't get to where she wanted him to be, like she said, she could go only halfway. If he couldn't go the rest of it, well, he'd go as far as he could, out of honor for how hard she was working. How devoted she was.

He sat on the bed and removed his pants, trying not to make noise. He took off his SEAL Team 3 shirt and slipped into the sheets with just his stars and stripes boxers on. The warm mattress melted the kinks in his shoulder and thighs. He crept closer until he could spoon behind her, trying not to wake her up.

Her smell filled his nose as he lay his head down in the nest of her hair, his lips so close to her neck he could kiss her. And then his hand was on her hip as she slowly moved, pressing her backside into him and letting him feel the length of her body. His hand slipped down her thigh. She turned to her back, drawing up her nightgown so his fingers could feel her flesh. Her smooth inner thigh was magic to touch. She inhaled, arched back, covered his fingers with her hand and drew him up to her core.

She dropped her hand while he felt her wet heat, slipping through the petals of her labia. She moaned, and he lost all his control. He climbed on top, pulling her to him with one arm under her waist. Her beautiful breasts called to him in the moonlight. He didn't take the time to remove his boxers, or her gown, but found himself inside her, thrusting deep, and desperate to be deeper.

She writhed beneath him, already feeling an orgasm blooming and sending rivulets of passion down where their thighs slid against each others'. She reached between them and felt their joining, tears streaming down her cheeks, dropping like diamonds into the pillow.

He was going to spill, and he felt awful it was so quick. That's not the way he'd wanted it to be.

"Brandy," he started to whisper.

She covered his mouth with her fingers. "Shhhh."

"But Brandy—"

She stopped him again. As he started to come inside her, she held his face between her hands and whispered, "It's all perfect, Tucker."

CHAPTER 21

W HILE LAST NIGHT'S lovemaking was a gift, Brandy also knew that it didn't necessarily mean everything was back to normal. But it did encourage her that he sought her engagement, that he came to her, instead of the other way around.

She made coffee, leaving Tucker to sleep in as long as he wanted to. She sat on the sofa with her knees pulled to her chin. She stretched her nightgown over her legs, grasped the coffee mug to her chest and sipped the warm mixture.

She knew some of her friends would disapprove of her actions last night—just jumping right back in bed with him without getting things aired out first. Maybe that worked for most marriages. Maybe it was the healthiest way. But that might also be the way she'd lose him. She knew men of action were different and that she'd actually married two men, not one. Now that he had gotten re-acquainted with his other self, she'd have to accept the other side of him if she wanted their marriage to work.

Brandy always wanted to understand the why of it all, to feel things, figure out situations and people. Tucker was different. He was act now and think about the consequences later. Maybe he never doubted himself like she did. Or, maybe he just did a better job of either covering it up or charging ahead anyway.

Tucker cracked open the bedroom door and padded out to the

kitchen for his coffee. His stars and stripes boxers were bunched up in his butt crack, but he was still a delicious package with his enormous shoulders, muscled back, and bundled thighs. He had more scars on him than she'd noticed before. He turned, his body facing her, but continued to look down at his coffee. She glanced away and waited for him to say something.

"I want to apologize, Brandy."

That got her attention.

He took another sip and collapsed his enormous frame in the nearby arm chair, dwarfing it. She could tell he was thinking, choosing his words carefully. She decided to test his capacity for a little humor.

"Well, to be honest, I didn't think the sex last night was all that bad."

Tucker's head whipped around, his expression one of shock.

She continued, "don't apologize on my behalf. I had a good time." She tried to keep a very straight face as she peered at him over her mug.

His grin was slow to develop, but when he finished, she enjoyed just looking at him sitting there with his knees spread, nearly bare, the enormous tent in his pants extremely prominent. Suddenly, she was dripping with desire.

"I can do better."

She sipped her coffee quietly and ignored him, again working hard not to smile.

"Did you hear me?" he repeated.

"I'm ignoring you," she said. She knew she had piqued his interest big time.

"Okay, so I deserve this. I'm sorry, Brandy, for the argument yesterday morning."

It was a good start. "I'll try not to ask so many questions. But will you do something for me?"

"Within reason," he said as he finished off his coffee and set it on the coffee table.

"If you want to be left alone, just tell me. Don't snap at me. Give me a heads-up, and I'll learn to deal with it." Her eyes teared up, but she fought to make sure they didn't overflow. "Don't push me out like that, and I promise to put away my butterfly wings."

"Come here, Brandy," he said softly.

She knew that he wanted sex, but as she sat in his lap and curled herself against his chest, she felt his careful, protective arms surrounded her. There were no strings. They sat together in the early morning space that was their life.

It wasn't perfect, but it was what they had. And that was indeed quite enough.

THAT EVENING, BRANDY and Tucker went out to dinner with her father and his new girlfriend, Jillian.

"I've heard so much about you," Jillian said as they were seated. "What you do is incredible, Tucker. I have nothing but respect."

Tucker was polite but dodged questions about what their last mission had been, except to say they were in Africa and there had been a hostage rescue operation. He stopped short of calling the mission successful.

Steven Cook held Jillian's hand. "We've got some news to share with you."

Brandy held her breath, having a good idea what it was about.

"Jillian's agreed to marry me, Brandy." He smiled as Jillian snuggled closer. "We'd like your—" He backed up to correct himself. "We'd like both of your blessings. It's important to us."

"Oh, Dad. I'm so happy." Brandy stood, and danced over to hug her dad first, and then Jillian.

Tucker put his hand over theirs and said, "Way to go, guys. I think that's a wonderful idea. Brandy and I are both on board."

"And there's more," her dad began. "We've been giving a lot of thought to the store. And I think I want to sell it," he added. "The way things stand, we're awfully tied down. We could do more travel, and you know, Brandy, that's what I've wanted to do for years."

"Can you find a buyer?" Tucker asked.

"We think we have one," said Jillian. "There's a family from Mexico, second generation Americans, and they'd like to convert the store to something that caters to the Latino population. They can carry specialty foods, keep some of the deli items and the fruit, but add other ethnic things. They own two catering trucks already. It would be perfect for them."

Brandy was delighted. "Sounds like the perfect plan."

"One more thing. Jillian has the house by the ocean," her dad began. "So why don't you two move into the big house? I'd like to deed half of it, your mother's half, to you, Brandy, before we get married. It's something she'd want me to do. You can do whatever you want with it. Sell it, refinance it and pay off my half, buy something else—anything you want."

"Dad, I don't know what to say." Brandy was overwhelmed with her father's generosity. It was nothing she'd ever imagined would happen.

Steve Cook laughed. "I know it's a lot to consider, so you guys think about it. You don't have to let us know tonight. You might want to go get something of your own. In that case, I'll sell the property and give you half."

ON THE WAY home, Tucker asked her if she had any thoughts about her father's proposal.

She watched his strong profile, lights from the highway splashing colors inside the cab of the truck. "What do you think?"

"I think it's your decision." He kissed her hand. His eyes briefly connected with hers. "Okay?"

She thought perhaps she'd need more time, but all of a sudden, it became clear. Because of her dad's generosity, they were living in the bungalow behind the big house that her parents had lived in. That big house would always be her parent's house long after they were both gone.

Tucker arrived home and sat in the driveway, turning off the engine. He put his arm around her and let her think.

"Tucker, this property was chosen and belonged to my parents. They've moved on with their lives." She looked up to his face. "I think I'd like to move on with ours. I'd like to find *our* house. Together."

"So be it," he said, just before he kissed her.

IN THE WEEKS following, the store ownership papers were drawn up. Brandy's father put the property on the market and it sold in one week for way more than they'd ever thought possible. During the escrow, Brandy and Tucker packed up their household, put some of their belongings in storage, and temporarily moved into a rental near Brawley and Dorie's home until they could find their perfect place.

Tucker also spent time with Brawley, who improved so quickly he was released from the clinic. Dorie's pregnancy was progressing, and Brawley was looking forward to the new little one.

But still unresolved was Brawley's future on the Teams. Everyone held their breath and waited.

CHAPTER 22

TUCKER WAS AT the Scupper with several of the other team-mates when he got a call from Brawley.

"They tossed me," Brawley said.

"No way."

"Yup. Got the letter when we got home tonight. I'm to get a medical discharge."

"But your pension. You get that?"

"Yes, but I'm a secretary or some shit until I get my twenty years in. I'm a desk jockey."

"No harm in that, Brawley."

The more he thought about it, the more relieved he was. The Navy had taken away the possibility Brawley could go out and get himself killed, or worse, get someone else killed. He remembered what Dr. Saunders had told him.

This was actually good news.

"You could go become a BUD/S instructor, Brawley."

"I was thinking about that."

"Take all your frustrations out on those froglets. Would you have the heart to do that?"

"The way I look at it, if they'd have me, I'd be saving their lives. Those brothers would be solid, kick ass."

"Well then, let's work on it tomorrow. We'll get Collins on it.

SEALED FOREVER

With Kyle's recommendation, I think you'd be a shoe-in."

Tucker didn't want to push, but he sensed there was something else Brawley wasn't telling him. "Dorie's got to be relieved, man."

"She's in shock. But yea, I think she's pretty cool with it. As long as I am. Tucker, I can't be pushing papers around."

"Why not? It's all support. You'd still be helping Teams operate. It's just that you wouldn't be stuck in the jungle, getting shot at, getting sick, or walking into a trap."

"I wanted to get those motherfuckers who took out Ollie."

"How many Team guys retire and feel like they've gotten all the bad guys?"

"Nobody does."

"Exactly, Brawley. And it wasn't your fault."

Again, there was a pause. Tucker got annoyed.

"You're not drinking, are you?"

"Nope. No more of that. I'm on my meds regular, too."

"You tell your father yet?"

"Nope. I'm going to bring you along when we do that."

Tucker completely understood. "I'll be there for you." He kept listening for something more but finally gave up. "Well, if there isn't anything else, I gotta get home to the wife." He tried one more time. "Brawley, are you sure there isn't anything else?"

Tucker heard him exhale. "Well, we got another piece of news today as well."

"At last! I knew there was something. Spill it."

"We had a fun visit at the doctor's. Dorie and I are having twins."

A WEEK LATER, Tucker took Brawley to his interview with the Commander on base. Kyle stood up for Brawley, he said. They'd asked that he retain his SEAL rank, and do his last two years as a BUD/S instructor.

"I was surprised, because you know, he's a bit on their shit list."

"That's totally misplaced, in my opinion," Tucker said.

They were watching the BUD/S class running drills on the beach. The pickup with the DOR, Drop On Request, bell was slowly making its way in front of a crowd of about twenty young men, running in sand with their combat boots on. And it was a race. One of the instructors, who sat on the tailgate was yelling something with his bullhorn.

Tucker punched Brawley. "You gotta think that would be fun."

"Yea, well, we'll see what they say. I might be processing DORs too."

"Even that wouldn't be too hard. You did it. You made it and served, stuck out eighteen years."

"Don't remind me. That's two short of my dad."

"I'm sure he doesn't care about that. He wants you alive, and whole."

"He does. We had a good talk."

"Excellent. So what do they think about the twins?"

"Biggest smile I've seen my mom sport in about three years. She was almost giddy, Tucker."

"No shit?"

"Honest. Even my old man mentioned it. Said she looked ten years younger."

"Holy smoke. Happy for you, Brawley."

"How about you guys. Still looking for a house?"

"Yup. Brandy has been busy with all that. Christy has been helping her look. Soon. I think it will be very soon now."

"Don't you have a say?" Brawley asked.

"Are you fuckin' kidding me? I had one friend who picked out the house for their family when they moved east, and they fuckin' got a divorce. I'm not that stupid, Brawley. A house is a house. I've lived in a bunch of them. If she's happy, then I'm happy."

"Tucker, you're a smart man."

He chuckled. "It's because of all the mistakes I've made."

They spent the rest of the evening over at the Scupper, meeting several of the Team. It was still Tucker's job to keep Brawley connected, and that was the best way to do it. He had to cut out early, because Brandy said she was trying out something new, some kind of special dinner.

Tucker was looking forward to it.

CHAPTER 23

BRANDY HAD PREPARED this special evening in her mind for months. She'd had several close calls, but at last, she confirmed with the doctor that she was pregnant. She'd been worried, since she was certain she'd been pregnant a couple of other times but wound up with a late period, dashing her hopes. He estimated she was nearly four months along. She had no symptoms whatsoever, except for her expanding chest.

The two of them hadn't discussed the timing of having a child, but they weren't using protection, either. Now they'd have to start looking in earnest for a new home. She was tired of living in the tiny studio, looking for things in boxes nearly every day.

She bought Tucker's favorite red wine and a ribeye from the specialty meat market that had just opened up on the island. She was making his favorite garlic mashed potatoes. She hoped he'd still be hungry and made him promise to be home early.

The table was set. She lit candles around the kitchen and living room, plus one in the bedroom. The salad mix was chilling, and the wine had been opened. Tucker was fussy about his meat, so that part would fall to him, but the lean steak was peppered just the way he liked it, waiting on the grill.

She had just a few things to finish before he was due home. She picked up a load from the laundry and sat on the bed, folding. She hung up two of his shirts and discovered a jacket he'd misplaced during their move had fallen on the floor of the closet and somehow had gotten shoved to the back corner.

She shook it out, gave it a smell, and decided it didn't pass the test. There was no question the last time he'd worn it was at the Scupper. There was only one place that had that aroma in all of San Diego County.

She checked his pockets because Tucker was forgetful, often leaving cough drops or pieces of gum which made a mess in the dryer. In his front pocket was a slip of paper, which she removed.

She thought perhaps her eyes were deceiving her. Her body began to shake, and so she sat down on the bed. Between her fingers, someone had written in blue pen the name Shayla and included a phone number. It wasn't Tucker's handwriting.

Brandy felt she might become sick, so she put her head between her knees and took several deep breaths.

How did I miss this? Is that where he's been going lately? How could I have been so blind?

This wasn't going to be the happy evening she'd planned. Could Shayla have come into their life during those weeks when he was so aloof? Did this woman swoop in and steal her husband back from her at his most vulnerable time?

Or, and this was worse, was Tucker pretending to be the loyal husband, while he fooled around and played the field. Except he'd made a mistake. A grave mistake.

There was a tiny voice in the back of her head trying to tell her something, but she hit it with a baseball bat. Except for her heartbeat pounding in her ears, the chatter was gone.

Think! Think! Should I pack? Should I lock the door and make him go away? Or should I listen to his explanation, even if it was a lie?

She heard Tucker's truck pull up. She checked her face then brought the jacket into the living room, to wait for him to walk through the door. She left all the lights out and the candles on as she heard his footsteps, and, at last, the door handle turning.

"Whoa! This is nice," he said, turning around to find her. He dropped his keys by the door and removed his shoes. "Something smells heavenly with lots of garlic." He paused and then called out again, "Brandy? Are you here?"

"I'm here, Tucker," she said.

"What's up, sweetheart?"

He came over to her and bent down. She turned away.

"Hey, what's up?" he said as he sat beside her. "You found my jacket, I see."

When she looked at him, he suddenly recognized what kind of an emotional state she was in. Brandy wondered if he knew yet that he'd been caught. His forehead wrinkled as he frowned.

"You're upset. Tell me." He reached for her hand, and she withdrew it.

"I found your jacket. Inside one of your pockets, I found this." She held the slip of paper up in front of his eyes.

"May I?" he asked politely.

She gave him Shayla's note. His eyes were angry as he stared at the note and then searched her face. "You don't think—?"

"I don't know what to think, Tucker. How about you explain this to me?"

"I've never seen it in my life."

"It was in your *jacket*. Why would you have her phone number, and I'm thinking she wrote it there for you. Isn't that her handwriting—?"

"I have no idea. Honest, Brandy, I've never seen it. You certainly don't think I've been seeing her? Is that what you think?"

"Give me a better explanation, Tucker. I'm all ears."

"I can't stand the bitch. I don't know how—" He stopped, leaned back into the sofa, and hit his forehead with his palm. "My first night out at the Scupper after we got back, she was there with her little witches' harem. I bumped into her in the bar."

"You were flirting with her."

"I was trying to get out of her way. I had four beers I was trying to take out to the table. She practically slammed into me and—" He stopped again. "She reached out, but I pushed her away. She must have slipped this into my pocket. I never saw it, Brandy. Honest. Since we've been together, I've never called her. I don't want to ever see her again."

Brandy heard all the laughter of her childhood years, when the kids at school teased her for being larger than the rest of the girls. She remembered the bridesmaids and how they gossiped at the wedding, how they treated her at the gym. Her defenses were strong, her reaction hard to the suspicion that perhaps she couldn't trust Tucker, that perhaps he too was a part of that crowd.

Her perfect life had gone up in smoke. She wasn't even hearing what Tucker was telling her, until she felt his hands on her arms as he turned her to look at him. He was asking her to look into his eyes.

"I swear to you, Brandy. There has never been anyone else since we met. I've not even considered this."

She blinked, watching him in slow motion say words she couldn't understand.

"You've imagined something that never happened, Brandy. I would never do this to you. Please, honey, trust me."

At last she heard him. Her body began to thaw. His pained expression broke her heart.

No, I've broken my own heart.

"You've never called her once?"

"Not once. I didn't know this was in my jacket. I'd lost my jacket, remember?"

She nodded. Her lower lip began to pucker.

"Man, do you have an imagination." He pressed the hair from her forehead. "I love you, Brandy. I always will. But please, when you think something like this has happened—I don't care what it is. Just ask me. You wanted me to give you a heads-up when I wanted to be alone. Can I ask you to give me the benefit of the doubt?"

She nodded again. She was ashamed. She placed her palm against his cheek. "Tucker, I'm so sorry I doubted you. I made a fool of myself."

He held her to his chest. "No worries. I want you to trust me completely. I'm going to work hard to make sure you know you can." He smiled and then kissed her. "But you do have a wicked imagination!" He followed up his comment with a chuckle.

"I wanted this to be a special night until I found this."

"I was thinking for a moment I'd married an ax murderer. It was very gothic, Brandy. The whole scene was very dangerous. All these candles, with you sitting there in the dark giving me daggers."

Brandy found a little humor in this.

"Geez, honey. You kind of gave me a scare."

"You want some wine?"

"I think I'll have something stronger. So what's the special occasion?"

Brandy had really messed up her planned evening. As Tucker ran to the kitchen to get a drink, Brandy came up behind him, wrapping her arms around his waist. He stopped, turning around to face her again.

"I've got a nice ribeye steak, green salad mix and garlic mashed potatoes."

"This is unbelievable. You did all this for me? Or was it the ritual you needed to kill me?"

She bowed her head, feeling shy.

"I'm pregnant, Tucker. I went to the doctor today and verified it. You're going to be a father."

"Holy crap."

"That's not exactly what I was expecting."

"Well, look at all this. Do you think I was expecting this?"

She gave him a couple of minutes to let it sink in. He poured two glasses of the opened wine, and when she declined, he drank both of them.

"You know that evening we met? I knew right then and there my life would never be the same. I was having a miserable time, wishing I'd not come, and then you waltzed right into my life." He gave her another hug.

"I won't do something like this again, Tucker. You can trust me on that."

"I don't believe you, Brandy. But whatever it is, I'm going to love the hell out of it."

THE EVENING WAS indeed perfect after all. There was so much to live for, so much to look forward to. They celebrated with the wine, the food, and the ice cream afterwards.

They were headed to their bedroom when Tucker's cell phone rang. He hesitated.

"Should I see who it is?" He winked.

"Up to you. Go ahead, I'll meet you in bed."

She removed her clothes and put on the lacy bright red nightgown she'd purchased. Leaving one candle on, she slipped into the lavender-scented sheets and thought about what their child would look like.

A little Tucker?

Tucker's voice silenced. He stood in the doorway with his cell phone still gripped in his hand.

"That was Kyle. They found the American nurse."

SEAL'S RESCUE

Bone Frog Brotherhood Book 4

SHARON HAMILTON

CHAPTER 1

NAVY SEAL TUCKER Hudson woke up to his rosy-cheeked bride's snores. And she drooled, which had been one of the most remarkable things he'd discovered about her that first night they slept together. He watched the look on her face—totally engrossed in a dream of some kind, as spaced out as if she'd fallen asleep in a drunken stupor. Her plump upper lip folded and curled into a little sexy peak, showing a few of her front teeth. Brandy's hair scattered all over his chest, lovingly entangling him. Her right arm draped across his shoulder and hung free, her cheek pressed against his right upper chest.

It was deliciously hot and sticky next to her pink flesh. Carefully, he slipped his arm under the covers, reaching across his abdomen to pinch her right nipple.

She awoke with a squeak. He did all that for a squeak, that momentary tiny shock of terror before she realized he was ramping up to play with her as passionately as she wanted. And she usually liked it intense.

She moaned when his fingers searched below and found that little garden of delights. He lifted her knees then wrapped his arms around her waist and pulled her on top of him. She arched backward and gave him that view of her enormous breasts, which formed his growing erection.

"God, sweetheart, look at you. Look at us together," he said as he dug his fingers into her hips hoisting her above him long enough to position his shaft. She shuddered on the way down, her eyes rolling as he gently bounced her then clutched her breasts, hungry for their taste. Maybe it was his imagination, but she was bigger there than before the deployment, even though it was still very early in her pregnancy.

"You're gonna kill me seeing you all ripe and,"—he sucked in air as she formed a ring around his member at their joining—"big with my child."

"Oh, Tucker," she whispered as she stopped, and with her elbows squeezing her tits together, she allowed him to feel her flexing internal muscles.

She liked to get that first little one out of the way before they got into the heavy tussle that would leave them both breathless. And she could sustain her little ripple orgasm for long minutes until he was ready to explode.

He placed his thumb on her clit, and her eyes sprung open. "Suck me," she begged.

She really didn't have to ask.

THE MORNING SUN woke Tucker, blasting a laser over his brow, through a crack in the curtain. He'd go out and splurge for some blackout shades today, even though this was a rental. He was sad that with the upcoming deployment they wouldn't have time to do a proper house hunt and get Brandy situated before he had to leave. He was awaiting orders that could come any minute.

That part of his job really was the pits. It interrupted everything. Unlike a regular job where birthdays, holidays, and family events were sacred, his job ignored all those things and he was supposed to not let that upset him. He'd done it before with his first ten-year stint. But it was harder this go-around. When he was out, he spent the next ten years wishing he'd never left the Teams. Now he was back to square one, trying not to think about leaving Brandy again.

Except this time, he was newly married and expecting a child. And that made all the difference.

Brandy was probably awake and thinking too, because her breathing was surface and barely audible. He pondered yesterday's events. The day had started out okay but had turned into some gothic freak show during the evening with Brandy's discovery of a note his ex left in his jacket pocket. It surprised him how wounded she'd felt. He reminded himself to pay attention to that and not to see it as a defect in her character, for her past made her the lady she was today. She was kind, because she knew how it felt to be on the other side of cruel. She knew the difference between right and wrong with a backbone as strong as any he'd seen on the teams. That's why he loved her so much. If it meant he had to watch her insecurity about being his one and only, he'd do that. In spades. That was the key to her happiness.

It was also the key to his.

"Are you awake, Tucker?" she whispered as she snuggled into his neck.

His arm slipped around her waist again, as if it permanently belonged there. Her head tucked under his chin, and as he inhaled and exhaled, he took her body up and down with his rhythm.

"I am. Thinking about you, sweetheart." It was true.

"When do you think the call will come?"

"Have no idea. I'm guessing soon. We have to expect that, Brandy."

"I know." She propped herself up on her arms folded across his chest. One long finger traced down his slightly crooked nose, following over a scar he'd received from the last trip to Africa, and then across his lips, first the upper then the lower. She kissed him softly and examined them as she continued to trace.

"Say it." He knew she liked to tease like a little girl when she had something important on her mind.

She angled her head, as if to let the thoughts drain to somewhere she could speak about them. "I was thinking when you go, perhaps Dorie, Brawley and I could go on a road trip, if you think he's okay."

"I'd prefer that he go. I don't like the idea of you and Dorie on a road trip by yourselves."

"And yet we used to do it all the time."

"Before you were with me. Before Brawley. But you're both pregnant. She has a child, is getting ready to have twins, and Brawley's just recovering. Don't you think it's a little much?"

"You're probably right."

His fingers laced up her spine, enjoying the smoothness of her delicate skin. "I know you're looking for things to take your mind off the waiting. Maybe you and Christy could do more house searching?"

"But she's Kyle's better half, and she has the kids and so much responsibility while you and the Team are gone."

Kyle was their LPO, their Team leader, and as his wife, Christy Lansdowne was unofficially in charge of the wives, fiancés, and families.

"Maybe it will help her too. You could offer to babysit in exchange. She might appreciate that, since she does still work."

"I'll think about that." She smiled, staring down at his lips again. "Tucker, you have so many great ideas."

"I have another one I think you'll like," he whispered, raising up to meet her lips, then gently folding her beneath him in the bed.

CHAPTER 2

BRANDY LOOKED FORWARD to officially telling Dorie about their pregnancy and seeing how her best friend was coming along with her own. Most of the time since Tucker's return had been taken up with getting back into the routine of being home, assuming something of a "regular" life, which was never really that regular. Part of that was making sure Brawley had a station and job he could look forward to so Tucker wouldn't have to worry about him while he was gone again. So, under the dark cloud of that phone call letting them know the deployment was a go, they opted for a visit to Dorie and Brawley's home.

Jessica, Dorie and Brawley's toddler, was even more of a handful than she'd been a week ago when Brandy last saw her. She was tall for her age, taking after Brawley's side of the family, and not yet willowy like all the Hanks women with her baby fat still present. But she operated just like Brawley, like a tank crashing through life—breaking toys, furniture, and everything in her wake. Dorie looked exhausted, and Brandy noticed her center of gravity was changing with her showing belly.

Her beautiful friend pushed her blonde locks off her forehead, straightened her back with her right hand on her hip and blew out air with the stretch. "I keep thinking this is supposed to be the easy time. Imagine what it will be like when I have the three of them, all in diapers."

"You'll get lots of help, sweetie," Brandy said as she hugged Dorie.

"And then with Brawley. Well, it's like having a toddler, and a teenager to raise all at once, and me with a broken knee or foot or something."

"Now you're scaring me, Dorie. You mean being pregnant is a handicap?" Brandy gave her a wink.

Dorie stood taller and smiled. "Point taken. Not fair of me. It won't be like this for you. I apologize."

"Silly!" Brandy quipped back. She appreciated the comment and thanked her lucky stars she didn't have the same situation as her friend. "You're allowed to tell me whatever you like."

"Something tells me Tucker will be much more help around the house than Brawley is. My guy doesn't mind things in chaos, and he encourages Jessica to be fearless. She loves her daddy so much. Really cute to watch. My parenting style is slightly different."

"As it should be. After all, you're more delicate."

Dorie stared off to the side, giving a hard look at Brawley wrestling with Jessica in the backyard while Tucker stood beside them laughing. Brandy noted a slight frown. The snapshot of the two men, one a SEAL and one a former SEAL, "doing family" as Tucker called it, would forever be embedded in her memory. It was a reminder that life passed by at breakneck speed and that she should enjoy every moment for what it was. The future for these men and their families was always dangerous. But one thing was blazingly evident. They loved their families with a fierceness and loyalty unlike any other.

"Thank goodness I fell for him hard. Their bodies take all the scars, but they're in their element. We have the harder job, Brandy." She aimed her clear blue eyes toward her friend in an unwavering message of understanding they both shared. "We're the ones who pay the price."

A chill drifted over the room with Jessica's screams in the background. For the first time, Brandy saw fear resident in Dorie's eyes.

AFTER THE STARS came out and they had cleaned up the barbeque mess, Brawley put Jessica in his carry pack and the five of them drifted slowly down the beach. Not much of the blush of the spectacular rose-colored sunset was left. Brandy's hand felt tiny gripped and protected by Tucker's huge paw. They swung their arms in the cadence of their gait, listening to the waves break on the shore and the call of late sea birds looking to settle down for the night. One or two small bonfires were lit, couples snuggling under blankets to stay warm, even though the breeze was mild. The ocean smoothed its way over the sand, erasing footsteps of long-forgotten travelers, rendering afternoon sandcastles into a melted mess.

Tucker drew his arm around her shoulders. "Are you warm enough?"

"I am now," she said as she leaned into his hulking frame.

"Watching Brawley and Jessica this afternoon, I was thinking about what our beach parties coming up would look like. I think we're going to have a water baby. We both love to swim so."

"I'm going to enroll her in swim classes as soon as her eyes can focus!" Brandy admitted, tugging on his tee shirt.

"Her, is it? You mean that? You think it's a girl?"

"I honestly have no idea. And I don't care. Maybe we could have a boy. Then he could marry Jessica and our families could be even more close."

She giggled as he squeezed her shoulder tight. "Wouldn't that be something?" he whispered.

He continued walking, his head now downturned, watching their feet before the night erased them. "Tomorrow I'm going to the flea market with Brawley, and of course you can come too, if you want."

"This the big one or the auto one?"

"It's the big one."

"Of all the things you could do before you go overseas, why do that?"

He shrugged. "Just something normal."

She stopped in her tracks. Brawley and Dorie kept walking ahead. "*What?*" he asked.

"And just what is spending time with me, then?"

"Or," he began to stumble on his words, "I was about to say we could spend the whole day in bed. If it's safe for the baby."

"You were *not* going to say that." She watched him turn, then pull her to him.

"I just wanted to do something mindless. Our bedtime escapades are anything but mindless. I'm aware of every wiggle, shudder and moan. I am wide awake and loving every second of it, Brandy. You know that."

She felt herself blush from the top of her head all the way down to her toes. Her heart skipped a beat, and her palms grew hot. She touched his cheek. "It's the same for me, Tucker."

They ran to catch up to Brawley and Dorie. Jessica had fallen asleep, and her little head was bobbing at an uncomfortable angle, so the four of them said good-night, and they returned to their respective houses.

It felt like the quiet before the storm.

CHAPTER 3

THE LARGE SATURDAY flea market drew crowds from all over Southern California. It was a mixture of cultures and languages, ages, sizes and personalities. The saying went, "If you can't find it at the flea market, you don't need it." Of course, one person's junk was another's treasure, and so the bartering and haggling going on rivaled any good bazaar in Marrakech and some of the open-air fruit and vegetable markets Tucker had visited in Europe.

Brawley was entranced with piles of slightly used and occasionally broken wooden toys he might be able to fix up for Jessica. That didn't interest Tucker in the slightest. But he was tempted by several large garden tools, mulchers, and chippers he could tinker with.

They met up with several other groups of Team guys who acted surprised to find each other but weren't, really. Wasting the day looking over discarded things was something many of the other brothers liked to do.

Fredo had bought a bag of flat soccer balls for the playground they were still sponsoring down at the old Catholic school they had converted to a neighborhood center. Cooper was giving him grief for not testing them first with a ball pump.

"They can be fixed, even if they do leak. Besides, doesn't make me feel so bad when they get 'borrowed', man. Right?" he told his lanky best friend.

"Still a waste of money," Cooper mumbled in return as he looked over a plastic bin of electrical cords, cables, and appliance chargers marked "One dollar each."

Fredo nodded toward Coop and squawked to Tucker. "You remember, Tuck? This is the guy who doesn't like to use more than one dryer sheet at a time. Who measures his dishwasher soap with a teaspoon?"

Tucker remembered their colossal fights back in the days when he was a newbie.

"It's not good for the dishwashers to have too much soap. Gunks up everything," Cooper said in his own defense.

Fredo couldn't be silenced. "He has to check his packets of ketchup by their expiration dates he has so many."

"I don't do that anymore. Libby—"

"Libby has made a regular guy out of him. But she doesn't know he rents two storage spaces full of junk," Fredo continued.

"Like I said, I have enough parts to fix anything. And who is the one who fixed your blender? Who found all the handles Ali was using as projectiles for that sling shot Danny made for him?"

On and on it went. Tucker and Brawley and several others just fell in line behind them. Brawley found a vendor with handmade drums, and flutes, and crude instruments shaped and pounded out of coke cans. Another vendor was selling hand-loomed rugs from Central America and carved black lava figurines from Mexico.

At the first sign of a bicycle pump, Tucker sat and quietly demonstrated that about half of the balls did indeed leak. But they still fit into the net ball bag.

"This bag alone was worth the ten bucks," Fredo insisted.

Nearby, their group ran into Jackie Daniels and his two daughters. Jackie had been their Iraqi interpreter on missions Tucker had been on the first time around and over one thousand missions after Tucker had left. He'd fought bravely with the SEAL teams and was responsible for saving many lives, both US and Iraqi. In a narrow escape, he and his family had been allowed to immigrate to the US, and he'd just taken his Citizenship Oath. Jackie's code name was selected because of his love of whiskey, as well as an easy way to mask his real name to avoid retaliation on him and his family. Some of them still lived there.

"Jackie! So great to see you!" Tucker said as the two men embraced. Brawley, Fredo, and Coop, as well as several others, followed suit.

"Tucker, you're a braver man than I. No more for me." He lowered his voice to a whisper. "You can't get enough of all that shit over there?" Jackie said in his heavily accented but perfect English.

Tucker always admired Jackie most for his fondness for American swear words. He'd taught many of the men on Kyle's team how to swear in Pashtu during his early rites of diplomacy.

"Not over there. Hope we don't have to go back there. But yeah. I guess I just wasn't done. I'll know when that time comes."

"Yes, you will, my friend." He placed his arm on Tucker's shoulder then introduced the men to his two daughters, who dutifully looked downcast and wouldn't touch any of the Americans. Both wore their headscarves, an odd addition to their overworn faded jeans and high-top tennis shoes in red, white, and blue. Tucker guessed if Jackie wore shorts, his would also be with stars and stripes, just like the ones most guys on Team 3 donned every day.

"Got myself married and a little one on the way, too," Tucker informed him, holding his belly as if he was the pregnant one.

"That will make a real man out of you, Tucker."

"She's trying real hard."

Brawley barked the understatement, addressing Jackie's daughters. "Your dad's a hero, ladies. You gotta know that."

The group burst out in Hooyahs like a colony of sea lions, attracting attention from the flea market crowd surrounding them. The girls shyly tucked behind Jackie but smiled. Tucker knew Jackie was too high profile to continue with the adulation in public, for his own safety.

"So what brings you out here? What could you possibly need in all this junk?" asked Fredo, who scowled when Cooper pointed to his bag of soccer balls. The Latino SEAL leaned in. "Coop wants to find a good deal on another Babemobile," he finished off with a whisper, which earned him a major punch in the arm from his Nebraska best bud.

Jackie laughed at all of them. "You guys never change, do you?" He turned to his girls. "Hands." He demonstrated by cupping his hands over his own ears and watched his daughters mimic the motion. He addressed the men, "I miss all the shit-talk. I've almost forgotten how to swear." He grinned, showing off his white teeth. "It does my heart fuckin' good!"

Jackie nodded to the girls, who removed their hands.

"Heard you took the Oath. Welcome to the good old US of A," said Coop as he shook Jackie's hand.

"You bet. Very proud. A very proud day for me, indeed."

"You still haven't answered my question," asked Fredo.

Jackie gave a respectful gaze around the open-air market, examining faces, stalls, piles of goods, and plastic bins full of everything imaginable. He nodded and then gave his answer. "The first thing I did when I came to America was to take the girls to go buy a hamburger and milkshake with my crisp new American dollars. I'd dreamt about doing this my whole life."

The group around him remained silent. Even his girls listened with rapt attention.

"The next thing I did was to come here, to these bazaars. I

wanted to see what you Americans discard. Many of these things that are being sold off or given away I'd never seen before. I know some people think I'm crazy. I ask them, 'What's this?' and they look at me like I'm from Mars. I've learned so much about your country by looking at flea markets and the people who come here."

Tucker examined his shoes. Several other men cleared their throats or adjusted their shirts.

Jackie added, "I first learned about your culture from you SEALs. You guys did a terrible thing, igniting the fires of freedom in my soul but giving me a very warped sense of what it's like to live here. Thought I'd get a little more perspective. Get the *whole* picture."

No one seemed to have an answer to Jackie's heartfelt comments. Tucker knew the rest of the team felt just like he did. The cost of freedom was very dear. But looking into the face of this brave Iraqi man and his beautiful family, Tucker knew the price was worth every drop of shed blood. They'd all do it over and over again, until they couldn't. But they'd never forget what they'd tried to do and how they served.

CHAPTER 4

T HE CALL CAME in at midnight. Late night interruptions were always jarring, but Brandy was adjusting to the unexpected, and this call wasn't exactly a surprise. She'd been in a deep sleep when she heard Tucker's whispers as he cupped the cell to his ear and tried to get out of bed without disturbing her.

Tucker confirmed what she already knew. They were going to deploy in two days. At least she had two days with him. It wasn't enough, but she'd make it stretch just like the rest of the month felt when Tucker's check had been nearly spent.

"So it's back to Nigeria, then?" she dared to ask as Tucker slipped in to spoon behind her.

"Mrs. Hudson, that's on a need to know basis," he said as he kissed her shoulder and then settled back into the pillows. "But the answer to that question is yes and no."

She pondered this briefly then fell asleep with Tucker's over-sized hand palming her belly.

Next morning, Tucker took them down to the harbor to have breakfast and walk along the pier, examining the boats, both large and small. Crews who took tourists out on the water were at work early washing and polishing their crafts. A variety of music blended in the early morning moist air—classical, reggae, and some oldies rock.

"Maybe we should take your dad's money and just buy a boat and sail away, never come back, Brandy," Tucker said as he pulled her jacket collar up around her ears.

"I'm not going to have a baby on a deserted island somewhere or on a boat in the middle of the Pacific without good medical equipment and staff."

"Hey? What am I?"

She smiled, never passing up the opportunity to tease him about his work. "You're good at removing limbs and stopping the blood spurting everywhere, but have you ever delivered a baby?" She looked up at his expression of surprise.

"Why yes, I have."

"You never told me that."

He shrugged. "Part of the medical course at Bragg. And first tour I delivered twins in Afghanistan to one of the village girls. We had to improvise."

"I'll bet. Honestly, I never knew this. Did it make you nervous?"

"Hell no," he said as they entered the diner and were shown to their table. "In Oregon, we had animals. I'm actually better at hatching chicks."

Brandy frowned as they sat. "Don't chicks hatch on their own?"

"Yes, and so do puppies, goats, horses, and little pink Brandy and Tucker babies."

"Good to know. Geez, I hope ours isn't born with a shell."

"Very funny." He grabbed her hands and held them from across the table. "But I agree with you. We want the best. And being alone on a remote island might sound more romantic than it would be. It's one thing to put myself at risk, but now that someone else is coming to live with us, well, that's a different story."

Tucker dropped his eyes, deep in thought. He watched their fingers entwined on the wooden tabletop, his large thumb rubbing against hers. She waited, now recognizing the signs of something he wanted to say he was having trouble putting into words.

"When I was on the Teams last time, our deployments were regular. We worked up for it, trained, re-trained, and studied what the job was. Then we went over, and usually, the length of deployment was about equal to the workup. Afterwards, we'd have that amount of time to be at home, or go to a specialty course, or heal, depending on how we came home."

His brown eyes stared deep into hers, and for a second, a shudder came over her. It was part excitement and part fear. Her pulse quickened. She loved Tucker's intensity, even when it was bad news.

"Now, things have changed. Things are active all over the world. It isn't in one or two theaters. It's all over the world. We used to train Special Forces from other countries, kind of the "Show and Tell" brigade. We were supposed to demonstrate why we're so awesome, and, to be honest, part of it was propaganda so other bad guys wouldn't fuck with us."

"Okay," she said, drawing it out, answering his focus with a smile. "Where is this going, Tucker?"

"So now we don't always get much notice. That means sometimes the training is limited. We go over more often, I'm being told, and this is what I wanted to speak to you about."

"About what?"

"Well, we'll be going over to those hot spots more frequently. Maybe not staying as long, but more missions. Perhaps more time away from home than I originally thought. I wanted to prepare you for the possibility that you could go into labor when I cannot come home and be with you. They try to work it out, but it might not be possible, honey."

Now she understood what he was trying to tell her.

"I think I understand. What you're telling me is that the SEAL Teams don't give you paternity leave."

He chuckled. "That would be the day. If I was an officer, perhaps. But not for a regular Joe like me."

She leaned across the table and nearly collided with their food and coffee. After the waitress left, she answered him. "Tucker, there isn't anything regular about you. Everything about you is *supersized*, including your heart. I'm going along with whatever it is that you want to do. It's all good."

"So you won't miss me?"

"I didn't say that," she said as she threw a napkin at him which hit him in the face.

"You'll pay for that," he growled.

"I was counting on it." She felt her cheeks turn bright red.

CHRISTY LANSDOWNE CALLED on their way home, telling Brandy that she found a house she wanted them to look at, if they had the time.

"How can we buy a house when you're overseas?" mumbled Brandy, her arms crossed.

"DocuSign."

"Excuse me?"

"DocuSign. I did it for one of my deployments. I even got a car loan once that way."

"You mean electronic signature. Is that safe?"

"Depends on where we are."

"You said yes-or-no-Africa. I meant to ask you what the heck you meant, Tucker."

His GPS directed them to a little green two-story house that was taller than it was wide, tucked behind dense gardens and several brand new or majorly remodeled mansions. The house address was on Flora Avenue. He knew he'd get a load from the Team about that. But then, Cooper lived on Apricot, so what the heck.

Tucker shut off the truck's motor and glanced down the street both directions then eyed the home carefully. "Kind of cute. I like that it's off the road. And only what three blocks to the beach?"

"Oh, no, you don't. Tell me."

"Tell you what?"

"You know. The mission."

"We're going to the Canaries off the west coast of Africa. Island cluster that's part of Spain. Definitely feels more Spanish than African. And it's a lot safer too."

"Wow. Sounds exotic." Brandy noticed Christy's car pull up in front of them. She was wearing a light blue suit, which looked stunning with her blonde hair and athletic build. Christy motioned for them to follow her.

Tucker continued. "It's nice. Great vacation spot for Brits and others from Europe. I've been there once before, briefly. Come on. Let's go see the house."

Tucker helped her from the truck.

Before they reached Christy, he added, "Mum's the word, Brandy. We don't talk about this in front of Christy. I'm not supposed to tell."

"Roger that, Mr. Hudson."

"Oh, you have a smart mouth today, Mrs. Hudson. I know just what you can do with that mouth a little later."

Tucker took hold of her hand, and before she could give a snappy retort, he pulled her down a narrow path through lush foliage about ten feet behind Christy.

"So one of the ladies in the office listed this just this morning, but it hasn't been put on MLS yet. We're the first to see it." Christy beamed. "Now prepare yourself, because I've been told it's a little plain, nothing done to it in like sixty years. It might be pretty bad. I suspected so when Danielle told me the listing price. Don't be mad, okay?"

"But geez, Christy, it's nearly a million dollars," gasped Tucker.

"But we're totally cool with it," said Brandy. "Thanks for thinking of us."

"Is it vacant?" asked Tucker.

"The owner has been living in a rest home for over twenty years. Family members have kept the jungle at bay and, I think, kept the house clean. But all his things are supposedly still in there. He never got to go back home."

Brandy felt sad for the owner.

"I know it's at the upper limits of your price range. I just hope that the work it needs doesn't blow it out of the park," Christy continued and then opened the front door.

It felt like they'd just stepped back in time about forty years. The kitchen had real wood cabinets—knotty pine—with vinyl countertops trimmed in stainless steel edging. Brandy felt instantly in love with the charm. As she walked down the hall and heard the hardwood floors squeak, she giggled. "I love that sound!"

Tucker and Christy exchanged glances.

The bathrooms were lined in blue and black four-inch tiles, trimmed in diamond-shaped edging pieces with art deco designs. One bath had a real porcelain tub and an etched glass medicine cabinet like the one Brandy remembered from her grandmother's home. The other bathroom, the master, was totally tiled in the same blue and black colors, but with a tiny stall shower and a doorway barely large enough for Tucker to step in.

"We'll get a bid on what it would cost to remodel these. This will never work for you guys," said Christy.

"So if there are two bedrooms downstairs, including the master, what's upstairs?"

Christy's eyes sparkled. "Just wait. Now be careful."

The stairway was way too narrow but passable. At the top landing they came upon a great room the size of the house footprint with wall-to-wall model trains. It was a replica of a tiny village, complete with a main street of Victorian houses, a post office, and several stores that looked like they were from the early nineteen hundreds.

"This is amazing," whistled Tucker.

"His daughter told their Realtor that he was a member of several model train clubs. This village, of course, doesn't go with the house. It's being left to the heirs and probably will go in a train museum somewhere. But isn't it fun?"

"What would you put up here?" asked Brandy.

"A gym," said Tucker.

"A new master suite with nursery?" Christy added.

"We could convert it to a separate unit, Tucker. Make it into a duplex. We'd have to add a kitchen and bathroom, add outside stairs, but what do you think?"

Christy interrupted her. "Great idea. I'm not sure the zoning will allow it but definitely worth asking."

Tucker was focusing on the detail of the village, studying the miniature locomotive and cars. "If I ever brought Coop here, he'd never leave," he mumbled.

Brandy walked along the four walls, since the stairway came up through the middle of the room. She noticed the ring of windows, which would let in sunlight all day long. "I could paint here. Tucker, you could write." Brandy's voice trailed off softly as she luxuriated in the visualizations coming at her so fast it was hard to remember them all.

Christy turned and faced Tucker. "You write?"

He shrugged without answering. He rolled his right shoulder and searched the room as if he were looking for a vacant desk. "I've been keeping a journal, but yes, thought I'd tell some tall tales of danger, adventure, and valor." He rolled his eyes and winked at

Christy.

"I think that's really cool," said Christy. "Good for you."

"And not a word to Kyle, either. They'd tease me to hell and back."

"Your secret is safe with me. A hobby room, then, is it?" said Christy.

"That's it."

"You think they'd allow some seller financing?" Brandy asked. "I don't want to use up all Dad's money and not have anything left for the remodel this would require."

"I can ask," said Christy. "But if you're interested, we'd have to jump on it right away. Good news for you is that you've already sold your father's home, so you can be a non-contingent sale. With fifty percent down, you qualify for a four hundred-thousand-dollar loan, right?"

"Yes," answered Brandy. She was trying to get Tucker's attention.

"What do you think, Tuck?" asked Christy.

"You know we're leaving day after tomorrow, right?" he mumbled, still focusing on the model trains.

"Yes. That will present some problems, but I think we can work it out, if you like the house. There are only a handful of houses on Coronado under a million—I think less than five. There might be multiple offers if you wait too long."

Brandy hung on every movement Tucker made. Her mind was filling with ideas. She thought about removing some of the shrubbery in front and expanding the yard space, since the lot was so small compared to the surrounding homes. After a few silent minutes, she noted Tucker wasn't making eye contact.

She waited until he looked up at her. His eyes betrayed something he was trying to hide. At last a smile drew across his face. "You always grab the first thing that comes along?" he whispered, following it with a little smirk. He was too damn sexy for his own good.

"I know a good thing when I see one," she replied. "And, yes I go for it. I grab it and never let go."

CHAPTER 5

TEAM 3 GATHERED in their building on base so the mission could be explained. They were scheduled to leave at Zero-Four-Hundred the next morning for their mission to the Canary Islands off the western coast of Africa.

Tucker's bags were already packed at home. He settled between Coop and DeWayne Huggles, their language specialist from Mississippi.

Kyle began the presentation before he turned the floor over to the young State Department Special Agent, who would be accompanying their group. Kelly Fielding looked like she had just graduated from high school, but Kyle told them she'd already worked in Africa for nearly eight years and had a master's in International Relations with an emphasis on the African continent. He also told them she was fluent in about a dozen languages.

Huggles swore under his breath. "This is going to be fucked."

Tucker knew many of the men already started out with a bias against the "brains" in the State Department who often overruled action with diplomacy. But when their lead was a woman, as well, it made for a double strike. He knew the SEALs weren't necessarily there to fix the problem but to get everyone out safely when it became one.

Tucker whispered back, "Give her a chance, man."

Huggles' eyebrows nearly got lost in his scalp, his eyes wide with feigned shock.

When Kelly began to speak, half the back row barked that they couldn't hear her voice, so she repeated her introduction much louder than her normal timbre, and it made her face turn red from the stress. She was probably nervous as hell, Tucker thought.

The problem with doing missions when females were on hand was that half the younger men would need to have everything explained to them all over again, since the sight of such a beautiful, red-headed peach-skinned creature made their brains malfunction. It was simply a lack of blood to the right organ, having been diverted elsewhere.

Tucker wasn't worried for himself, even though he could admit she was attractive as hell. It was the violation of their Team building, their private space, that worried him the most. It rarely happened, so this was a big deal, according to his superiors. He was used to the cold smell of firepower, explosives, and metal, not the exotic floral scent of her perfume. It somehow diluted the man-cave, tradition and, besides that, felt all wrong.

"Thank you, Chief Lansdowne," she began. She took a moment to scan the room, making eye contact with everyone sitting before her.

Kyle took his seat in the front row and crossed his legs.

"I'm familiar with this group who managed to smuggle Jenna out of Nigeria. And I also know her family," began Agent Fielding. "Her father's a well-known philanthropist in the Northwest. Although this is a joint State and Special Forces operation, we've been authorized to let you know no expense will be spared. We believe she has been trafficked, and the group perhaps does not know about her famous and very wealthy family. We want to keep it that way."

Tucker didn't like the idea that special treatment would be

happening, which was just another way of saying he and all the other team guys were more at risk than usual. Secrets were never good. They always cost lives of the "little" people.

"It looks like she was sold to a Dutch billionaire who does a fair amount of business with the raiding Nigerian militant gangs. He gets drugs and conflict diamonds from them and, in exchange, sells the militants guns. He's been on the State Department's radar for about three years now. Much of his business is disguised as building roads and wind generators, which he claims he doesn't do for profit. We know otherwise, of course. There have been rumors he's begun to dip his toe into the lucrative human trafficking business."

As the agent continued, her voice got lower, and she became laser-focused on identifying pictures of various characters projected on the wall of their buildings, explaining who the organization was and how it operated.

In the lull after her presentation, Cooper asked, "So where is this place where they're holding her, or do you know?"

"Oh, we know," Agent Fielding answered. She threw up another slide of an enormous white building that looked more like a commercial lab than a residence. It was heavily fortified, a regular fortress guarded by roughly one hundred men, she told them.

Kyle uncrossed his legs and sat up straight. "The militia groups may not know who her father is, but what's the chance this billionaire slave trader doesn't know?" he asked.

"Well, the State Department has not allowed him to obtain a US visa. Most of his trade is with Europe, United Kingdom, and South America. I'd say of all the countries of the world; he knows least about the US. But it's always possible, Chief."

"So what's the plan for getting into the compound?" asked a heavily-accented voice from the rear. Tucker recognized him immediately. Several other SEALs turned around to confirm Sven Tolar had indeed made it to San Diego, and, apparently, would be tagging along.

That was great news.

The agent deferred to their LPO for the tactical details. But while Kyle explained his plan, Tucker noticed the room's energy, with the addition of Sven to the Team, had suddenly exploded in chatter and crosstalk. One by one, members shook Sven's hand and then stood next to him in a group while they listened. For the first time, Tucker was filled with happy anticipation. He turned to the frowning Huggles.

"What do you know? I actually think we have a chance here."

AFTER THE MEETING, Tucker greeted several men he hadn't seen in months, as well as Sven Tolar, the retired Norwegian Specialist they'd met on the previous mission to Nigeria. Although he didn't know Sven back then, he remembered their grueling joint training operations back some ten years or more. Tucker always had a great deal of admiration for these men, considering them to be the best-trained team in survival tactics, no matter the weather. They'd been legendary for fighting the Nazis, the Russians and anyone else who thought they could defeat their much smaller numbers. Tucker had learned they could live in snow caves virtually undetected for months at a time.

"What a huge surprise and a boon for us all," Tucker said as they briefly embraced.

"I said I'd look you up."

"Well, damn, didn't know it would be this way. Nonetheless, glad to have you aboard. Are you part of the intel here?"

"Nope. Just a private contractor. I guess I got listed on some asset sheet," Sven added.

Tucker knew that was probably Kyle's doing. Kyle had extensive files and contact information on good men they'd worked with in the past outside the SEAL community.

"How's your friend?" Sven spoke softly. "I don't see him here."

Tucker took a deep breath at the mention of Brawley. "Nah, he's retired. Going to begin being a BUD/S instructor until he can get his twenty in." He looked down at his feet and then up to connect with Sven's deep penetrating eyes. "It was a close one."

"I'll say it was. We've lost a few too. They would just walk off into the forest, and we never see them again."

It broke Tucker's heart to hear of a warrior, a man of action who chose to end his life. Suicides were on the rise in the military, even on the Teams.

"I guess we can't save them all," Tucker whispered.

Several other men joined their circle, ending the conversation. Tucker said his farewells and headed for home.

His happy mood had turned, and he wondered about that. It was a good thing that they'd have Sven's help. This wasn't going to be the kind of deployment that would be months long. They were to go in, grab the nurse, and get out. So why was he so blue all of a sudden?

Tucker thought about the house they were trying to buy, and how happy Brandy had been when they found out their offer had been accepted. But he wondered if it all was too soon. Should he take one step at a time? Should they have the baby first, learn how to be good parents, then take on the financial responsibility of the house payments? Being a SEAL was more rewarding than being a regular Navy guy, but he still didn't make nearly enough money to own a close to million-dollar house. He was having second thoughts about allowing her to talk him into it. And his pride was a little bit dusted up that it was Brandy's money—money she got from her father. Tucker had always paid for everything with his own funds, earned with his own hands.

You're thinking too much, Tucker. You've got to keep your head on straight. Concentrate on what's ahead of you. Be grateful for what you have.

That was it. He'd not been grateful enough lately. He was going to be a father. He was married to a wonderful woman. He'd successfully gotten his buddy home safely and seen to it that he was positioned right for the best possible results. His family was going to plant roots, own something that would keep them close to the beach, ensconced in the community he loved.

Next time he opened his journal, he was going to write about that—all the good things coming to him, not the things that were at risk.

But the thought of a man walking into the woods to purposely end his life still chilled him. It had happened to Brawley. He hoped, if it ever happened to him, he'd recognize the signs in time.

CHAPTER 6

B RANDY KNEW TUCKER should be home early from the meeting, not have a pitstop at the Scupper. But when she heard his truck, she was relieved. It was going to be their last night together, and he had to be at the base by three.

"Hey there," he said as he tossed his keys and grabbed her for a smothering bearhug. "Wanna miss dinner and fool around until I have to go?" His eyes sparkled as that little smirk crept across his lips.

"I could be up for that. Anything you need to do first?"

"Think we could take a shower? Then I won't have to shower in the morning."

"That sounds nice," she said as that familiar tingle tickled all the way down her spine. "But maybe you'll be too hot and sweaty and—"

His big mouth covered hers, making words impossible. His hands were already digging into the top of her pants, and then those pants were down at her ankles.

"I think I'd like to taste you a bit first, maybe," he said through his teeth, not giving her a chance for a reply. "Then I might want to slather some of that lemony gel all over your body so I can have a nice, lasting image of what I'll be coming home to."

When his fingers breached the elastic of her panties and penetrated her core, she inhaled sharply and pressed herself into his hand, raising one thigh to rest on his hip. He quickly disposed of her panties, kneeled, slipped her knee over his shoulder, and licked his lips as he examined her sex. His quiet deliberation and his slow movements had her breathless with anticipation. Finally, his tongue was on her clit, making its way inside her opening.

She gripped his shoulder with one hand while the other sifted and tugged at his hair. Her pelvis quivered as his tongue explored and set her on fire. He took his time, giving tiny love bites extending into the soft tissues of her upper thigh. His thumbs pressed as his lips drank from her and had her begging for a night of lovemaking that would never end.

Maybe it was the sweetness of knowing that he'd be gone for a few weeks—hopefully only a few days. Maybe it was because she was more sensitive now because she was carrying his child. But whatever it was, the fire in her belly grew, filling her with cruel need. She was completely his.

He gently rose, taking her hand, and led her to the shower where he stripped. Her breathing was ragged, and her desire for him so great, she hungrily stared at his beautiful, chiseled body with his enormous cock teasing her. She didn't remember how she got undressed, but when she stepped into the warm spray, his arms were about her, his mouth on her mouth, pressing deep, moving her to the slick tiles at her back. Effortlessly, he hoisted her up, hands under her thighs as she rocked against his hips. He bent his knees and angled himself and then pushed his way deep inside her.

She nearly fainted. There was so much she wanted to say, but he had total command over her mouth. He begged for her hands on his shaft. He drank her moans. He kissed her neck. She felt the hard muscles of his chest press her such that she could hardly breathe. Her hands slid up his lower back, feeling his huge muscles deliciously ripple as he thrust hard and deep, repeating and picking up the intensity until her bones were made rubber.

After several minutes he quickly shifted. He held her under the spray and, as her orgasm peaked, he spent inside her and then stroked her back. His chest heaved and then let out an enormous sigh, but he held her still, lovingly brushing down her shoulders and arms, finding her mouth and placing soft nurturing kisses there. At last he moved from side to side, cuddling her in his enormous arms as the water covered them both.

They didn't speak the rest of the evening, and Brandy knew there was so much to say that it would take weeks to get it all out. But she didn't want to spoil the sacred night. It was that little pretense, like they'd be separated forever and this would be the last time they could make love, making them so desperate for each other. Gallows sex, it had been called in one of her romance books.

She was filled, consumed with him, loving him in the flesh here and now, because time was so precious and unpredictable.

SHE HAD THOUGHT she was still awake, still dreaming about his powerful body, when she felt his kiss whisper over her skin, "Don't wake up. Don't open your eyes. It's time."

But she couldn't help it and opened them anyway, giving him a tug as he was trying to stand up. He took her with him, squeezed her body and then settled her back down on the bed.

"Hold that thought, Brandy. I'll be back before you know it. Maybe the next time you wake up."

She smiled through her tears. "I vowed I wouldn't cry, and I'm so sorry, Tucker."

"Honey, don't ever apologize for showing me how much you'll miss me. Don't ever apologize for that." He kissed her and then left the bedroom.

Naked, still breathing hard from what she felt like was hours of uninterrupted sex, she listened to the front door close behind him and the roar of Brawley's truck pulling out of the driveway.

She was filled with wicked thoughts like running outside and begging him to come back, of making a scene, but she tucked herself in the wet and warm sheets that smelled of him, rubbed her belly softly and allowed sleep to take over.

THAT AFTERNOON, BRANDY signed the confirmation to the escrow instructions for their future home over at Christy's house. Her beautiful realtor was a mess just like Brandy was. She could see the traces of tears, and she knew that, even after what must have been a hundred missions, it still affected Christy the same way.

Her kids were playing in the backyard as she handed Brandy a tall glass of ice water. Even in sweats with her hair up in a scrunchie, Christy Lansdowne was one of the most beautiful women she'd ever met. She had the kind of classic beauty that Dorie had.

"Now, when we get time to sign the final papers, you'll have to get your power of attorney out so you can sign for him."

"Yes, I understand." It had been one of the things required when she married Tucker. She had the durable power of attorney for illness, finances, everything. The Navy required all these things in case of the unthinkable. And for good reason, too. It would minimize the further pain of losing a loved one to have the "affairs"—meaning the things one had to do with the rest of her life—in order.

And everything else could be done with DocuSign, everything but a grant deed.

"So, I'll order a pest inspection on Monday. I'll get a home inspection contractor out there, and I think we should get one for the roof too, what do you think?" Christy re-tied her hair up atop her head.

"That sounds good. You have people you like to use?"

"Yes. But you can choose."

Brandy had some poor experiences with the inspections for her father's home and didn't want to repeat that. "No, the guy that the buyers used was horrible. Remember?"

"Oh yes, the old guy who wouldn't go under the house and called out tiny rips in the window screens? We didn't get a choice, but don't worry. We'll not use them."

"Great."

Noise was coming from the backyard, and Christy was out the back door in a flash. Brandy heard a major scolding going on just before she returned to the kitchen.

"We have a couple of their friends over. It helps the kids to keep their minds off the fact that daddy is gone."

Brandy understood the wisdom of Christy's words. There was so much she needed to learn. Here she thought buying a house with Tucker being overseas was difficult, yet families did this sort of thing every day, with kids, illness, and all sorts of things going on at the same time. Brandy and Tucker's life was rather uncomplicated in comparison.

"You're so great with those kids and with all the Team wives too. And you work. I don't see how you do it."

"I did it just like you're going to do it, Brandy. Bit by bit. I had great teachers. Kyle being a leader meant that came with the territory." Christy stopped, took a sip of her water. "You know, Kyle thinks Tucker has some potential as a leader. Have you two ever considered sending him to OCS?"

"He thinks he's too old. No. I don't think he wants that. But he loves being one of the ones the Team guys, especially the younger ones, look up to."

"It's the healing side of him, the medic side. I can see that," said Christy.

She was right. There wasn't anyone else who could have helped save Brawley but Tucker. "He's one of the guys you can count on.

Always."

"Then we're all lucky to have him. Hang onto him, Brandy."

"Oh, I intend to!"

They both laughed.

After she left, Brandy wandered through several large home improvement stores, looking at countertops, cabinets, and appliances. She picked up brochures for window coverings and paint samples.

She stopped by her favorite art store and purchased some new water color pencils and acrylics, along with several new paper tablets and two canvases. She'd taken the time to select colors she remembered from the house, as well as the color of the blue and white surf, and the beach. She wanted to do some sketches of color schemes for a new kitchen and a decent-sized bathroom. Making love in the shower was almost a routine for them now. That tiny one would have to go.

Before she returned home, she stopped by the house they had in contract. With the memory of Tucker's kisses still fresh on her skin and her sex swollen from all the lovemaking they'd done last night, she slowly walked down the green path toward the front door.

This would be the home they'd raise their baby in. This exciting new chapter was the start of something bigger. She was ready for it all. She wanted to remember every sight and smell of it all.

She had thought her life had started when she met Tucker that New Year's Eve at Dorie and Brawley's wedding. But this was the real start. This is where it would all begin.

CHAPTER 7

T HE HARDEST PART of any trip was always the transport across the Atlantic. They usually rode in a troop transport plane that lacked any amenity but a bathroom, and some didn't even have those, which made a ten-hour flight even longer. But this sleek jet had been chartered, and Tucker knew it had something to do with the girl's father.

So far, so good.

There were ten of them who went this time, a smaller number than those who went to Nigeria last month. It was thought that the extraction would be quick, just like some of those snatch and grabs they used to do in his early Afghanistan deployments—before the rules of engagement had changed, when you could actually do those. Now those poor guys had to practically post it on the front page of the Times and then try to go in by "surprise." These days, you had to get permission for something you knew you weren't going to do, so you could execute Plan B, which had been the real plan all along. Or so Tucker had been told by some of the older guys who remained in after Tucker left.

He took a window seat, placing his bag on the spot next to him. He was hoping to be able to get his large frame comfortable and then catch up on some of those erotic dreams he knew he'd have. He wanted to imagine what it would have been like to extend their lovemaking session another three hours or more. Nothing wrong with the way it went, though.

Absolutely nothing fuckin' wrong. Last night was perfect.

One by one, the rest of the Team wandered down the aisle. Several people noticed his bag, taking up the seat space, but most just kept walking past him. Kelly Fielding hesitated for a second, but when Tucker didn't move his bag, she kept going.

Behind her was Sven, who whispered in her ear, "Sorry, darlin', but he was saving it for me. Hope your feelings aren't charred."

Tucker actually saw that Sven was kind of sweet on the Special Agent, which was a big surprise. He didn't like himself for trying to be too wary of a woman on the mission, but he was grateful for Sven's save. Personal politics was never Tucker's strong point, unless he was the teacher, of course.

He pulled his bag off the seat and let it hit the floor with a thud.

"How about we do this like adults, Tucker." Sven picked up the pack and placed it in the overhead bin—also something not usually found on their transport plane. Sven loaded his pack up next to it.

"Thanks, man. I guess I wasn't very nice." Tucker turned his head around to see if Agent Fielding could hear him. She was way to the back of the plane.

"I was saving you from pissing off the most important person on this plane," said Sven as he sunk down hard in the seat.

Tucker was shocked. "Excuse me?"

Sven lowered his voice until Tucker could barely hear. "She's the nurse's sister-in-law."

"No shit? Don't you think Kyle should have mentioned it?"

"I don't think he knows."

Tucker let his head hit the back of the seat. The take-off instructions were announced, and within minutes, they'd taxied and were in the air. Tucker looked down with pride at the Navy's fleet, some of the finest ships and equipment in the world and the men who were dedicated to using every gadget to keep the world safe. Being a Fleet Commander was like running a small foreign country but paid far less.

So this was going to be another mission with secrets. They were walking into something and even though they were to put their lives on the line, they were still not good enough to be made aware of all the little minute details that could blow the whole thing sky high.

"Question for you. Are we the hired help, or working for Uncle Sam?"

"Depends on who you ask. If you asked her father-in-law, he'd say the POTUS works for him. But I think he exaggerates a bit." Sven scrunched up his nose with that last comment.

Tucker searched for Kyle and found him up front with Cooper and Fredo and several of the others. Par for the course, Kyle wasn't letting them sleep, but laying out maps and showing them pictures, while the person with all the information was sitting in the back near the bathroom. He started grinding his teeth.

"Don't even think about it," grumbled Sven.

"I have to tell him. He'd do the same for me."

"When the time comes. When we have to. Right now, we need him raw. You don't know Kelly like I do," he said as he wiggled his eyebrows up and down.

"Oh, really?" Tucker said with a grin.

"Well, almost. I like to move slower than the ladies. You'd be surprised what the result gets you."

Tucker knew what he was talking about. It was exactly what happened with him and Brandy. If he strung it out and then let her take the lead, he was in for a mind-blowing experience.

Sven chuckled. "I thought maybe she liked ladies. So I asked her, and she took it on herself to prove me wrong."

"Son of a bitch. I rescind your invitation to visit us in San Diego. Consider yourself disinvited."

They both had a big laugh over that one. Tucker was pulling down tears he laughed so loud.

"You Viking assholes have some moves, I'll give you that."

"We have to. We're smaller than you Yanks. When have you ever heard a lady boast of balling a Norwegian? But how about an American SEAL? I'm just trying to catch up. My heritage is on the line."

Tucker found he liked Sven more each time he was around him. He was smart as well as good at his job. Not good at his job and stupid like Brawley was. He'd always thought the SEALs attracted men who had major flaws and needed their demons excised. The type of guys who could defend a whole village and then go home and have a salami sandwich and a beer and fall asleep in front of the TV. Those guys would wake up someday broke and alone, hardly speaking to their grown kids, and after they were out, they never were the same. Sven's guys could probably do their jobs and then go back to being preschool teachers and think nothing of it.

American SEALs did the things everyone else was too damned scared to do, and for good reason. That was the real payoff for them.

"So I'm surmising you and Kelly spent some time together in Paris, then?"

"Actually, I visited her in the Canaries. We're the ones responsible for the surveillance."

"Now I'm really interested. Between the time we left Nigeria and now, you hooked up with Kelly on the Canary Islands—"

"We hung out in Morocco too. Spent a couple of days on Capri. That was strictly fun."

"So you posed as a couple? Taking pictures?"

"Yup," Sven said as he nodded.

"Drinking wine and wandering around the streets at all hours of the day or night?"

"Yessir! That's exactly what we did."

"A couple?"

"I already said we did. We made it convincing too."

"I'll just bet you did."

"And the nurse's dad, he knew about this?" Tucker asked.

"He paid for the trip."

"But—Sven, I don't want to ask you how you arranged all that. I'm assuming Kelly's married to his son?"

"*Was.*"

Tucker looked straight ahead. "I'm not sure I want to know the rest of this story, Sven. You're kind of creeping me out."

Sven shrugged. "There's a simple and perfectly logical explanation, Tucker. Kelly's husband, the old man's son, and Jenna's brother, died of an overdose two years ago."

"And he thinks this Dutch guy had something to do with it?"

"Indirectly. It doesn't wrap up too pretty like that. But, Tucker, he's already lost one son to drugs. Now his daughter is sold into some kind of sex slavery. If you had all the money in the world and no family to leave it to, what would you do with it?"

"I'd go find the bad guys and make them pay."

"Exactly. And if your daughter-in-law is a Special Agent working for the State Department and has contacts and you have some cash for some fundraising parties for the President, don't you think an accommodation could be worked out?"

Tucker was amazed Kelly had spoken to them and kept a straight face. She was good. Really good. But the situation still bothered him, and he had to bring it up.

"Sven, our Teams aren't a private for-hire group that go in and do things for influential friends of the present administration."

"Apparently, they don't put that in your textbooks. There have been world wars fought exactly for that purpose, my friend. But make no mistake, these are the real bad guys. And if they could, and with enough time and money they'll achieve it, they'd destroy any Western nation who tries to interrupt their income stream. Maybe I see it differently because we're sort of neutral. Not really neutral, but we don't have the money to go overseas and start or end wars. We give token support to the good guys, we hope."

Tucker pondered this. *How did they decide where to send the Teams in the first place?*

"We're helping one man get his daughter back. We're helping to interfere with some bad elements preying on innocents and American interests in Africa, obstructing, among other things, their importation of drugs that are killing off your American children. I think it's a fair trade-off, Tucker. Don't you?"

Tucker knew he was right. But he didn't want to admit it. He didn't want to know what was too far below the covers. He just wanted to do his job.

"And as for who hires whom, doesn't this happen all over the world? You think we live in some perfect world where only the good guys win? You know that's not true. I guess that's the advantage of living in Europe. We can't save everyone. So we don't even try."

CHAPTER 8

BRANDY HAD CHRISTY take her, Dorie and little Jessica over to the house they were buying. Dorie loved it. Jessica tried several times to escape, heading straight for the narrow stairs.

Dorie's pregnancy was really starting to show, even though she was only five months along. But her body was skin and bones, and the dark circles under her eyes were worrisome. Even Christy noticed and asked Brandy about it while Dorie went out to the car to change Jessica.

"Everything okay at home?" she asked.

"He's waiting on the Navy to get his paperwork processed. At this rate, she said the re-assignment might come just as he is finishing his twentieth year. She's worried the discharge gets processed before his new job comes through."

"That's the Navy for you," signed Christy. "But with so many on Brawley's side, they'd get it fixed. But I get it. He wants to feel useful."

"Now that he's on outpatient, he has a lot of free time. Unsupervised free time. I just wish he'd help out with Jessica a bit more. I try, but you know."

Christy gave her a hug. "You're a good friend. I'm sure his doctor has explained that he might not be able to be there emotionally for her, to know what to do or how to help her. He's disabled and not himself."

"She knows it, but she's tired, Christy. And they're having twins."

"Yes, well, you let me take some of the burden off your hands. Don't try to help her out alone. Let me get some of the wives and we'll see if we can be more present. You'll see. We stand up for each other, Brandy."

Brandy's heart was beating full of gratitude when Dorie returned to the kitchen area, chasing Jessica.

"Well, that makes six for today. Honestly, she's got the same appetite as her father," said Dorie breathlessly.

"Well then, seems only fair to make him do the cooking, then. If you're supposed to do the changing, I'd say that's a fair tradeoff," laughed Christy.

Jessica had turned several knobs in the kitchen, and they smelled gas. Christy was quick to turn them back to off. Jessica was on to pulling open the drawers and slamming them shut.

Dorie raised her shoulders. "Christy, you re-thinking about having Jess come over to play with your two? You'd better put a helmet on them."

"No, that only happens when we have little Ali and Griffin come over. Our rules are that Ali's slingshot has to be checked at the door like any other weapon."

Dorie touched her belly. "Oh, I just felt one of them move again. Wow."

Brandy knew she'd been concerned about not feeling movement, even though her ultrasounds had been normal and she was reassured the babies were kicking. She hoped that would give her some relief.

"Let me see," Brandy said, placing her palm against Dorie's belly. She felt a slight movement like someone had moved an elbow or heel against the insides of her stomach. "I feel it too! That's cool!"

Christy had taken Jessica outside to the backyard, holding her hand. With the gentle guidance, Jessica walked calmly beside her, her arm outstretched, chattering partial words as she pointed out grass and flowers and followed the motion of a bird.

Dorie turned. "I think you and Tucker are going to be really happy here. What a great neighborhood. You're surrounded by much bigger homes."

"I know it's the right thing to do. Maybe eventually make this a separate unit up top. Give us a little income."

"Good idea. If not, what a great room to paint in."

"I know. Already got the paint!"

When they headed out to the yard, Christy was on the phone but still holding Jessica's hand. Dorie quickly took over.

Christy hung up and then addressed Brandy. "Can you come in to see my loan guy tomorrow morning? He wants to take the application and run the credit."

"Sure."

The three women took turns holding or walking with Jessica as they got to the beach, until she fell asleep in Brandy's arms.

"Today was a good day," said Dorie.

"By now, the guys are probably having coffee and waking up, if any of them slept," added Christy.

Sandpipers escaped from the fast moving surf as they foraged for sand crabs and other little burrowing creatures. The western sky was turning bright pink.

"Never gets old, does it?" asked Brandy. She rocked from side to side and then took a seat on a large log that was stuck in the sand. Jessica repositioned herself.

"Looks like she's completely out," whispered Dorie.

Brandy gave her a thumbs-up.

Christy surveyed the empty beach and the pink glow of the horizon. "When my mom moved here, this was the first thing she showed me. She'd bought one of those apartments at the Millennium complex. One of the first owners. She loved it here."

Brandy agreed. There was something magic about this place.

THE NEXT MORNING, after filling out the paperwork for her home loan, Brandy called her Dad and invited herself to their house for a quick lunch. She was anxious to hear from Tucker, so spending time with her father and Jillian, his fiancé, would keep her worried mind active with other thoughts.

As they sat down, she told them about the house.

"Only a couple blocks from the beach, and everything around it is huge and remodeled. Dad, I think we stole it," she said.

Jillian smiled as she dished up salad. "That's what I thought when we bought this place. And I was right. Even if it's small, hang onto it and use it as a rental. Don't sell it."

"Not planning to," Brandy returned. "Dad, you've got to come see it one of these days."

"Just arrange it. I'm pretty free."

Jillian brought up the topic Brandy had been avoiding. "When do you hear from Tucker?"

"Actually, we're expecting a call anytime now. Everyone's on pins and needles," she answered.

"Where are they going this time?" her dad asked.

"Not sure," Brandy lied. "But we're not supposed to talk about it, either. All I know is that they are going back to get someone they didn't get before."

"You mean like a bad guy?" her dad asked.

"You know I can't talk about that. Honestly, we've been through this, Dad."

"Steven, stop that. You know the rules."

Her dad patted her hand. "Sorry, kid."

"You been to the doctor since we saw you last?" Jillian asked.

"Tucker and I saw the baby's heartbeat last week. It was so cute to see such a big guy cry. Kind of touched the little technician, too."

They ran out of things to talk about if they were going to avoid talking about Tucker being gone. She promised she'd arrange a time so they could inspect the house.

ON THE WAY home, she got the call she'd been waiting for.

"Hey there sweetheart. We're here, safe and sound."

"That's great. How was the flight over?"

"Private first-class jet charter. I recommend it highly," Tucker said. "Of course, it would probably mean we couldn't buy that house."

"I'm glad. But I'd rather have the house than the ride."

"Probably the only time in my life I'll get to fly that way. Sat next to the Norwegian Special Forces guy, Sven, remember?"

"Yes. I'm glad he's going with you."

"We are too. So how was your day?" he asked.

"I took Dorie over to the house yesterday. Jessica was a handful, but between the three of us—"

"Three of you?"

"Christy was there too."

"Right. I forgot."

"Anyway, she fell asleep on me as we were walking down the beach. Then this morning, I had lunch with Dad and Jillian and told them all about the house. Tucker, I'm even more convinced it's the right place. It's just magic."

Tucker was quiet, more than she expected. He presented a big yawn and apologized.

"You probably didn't get any rest on the way over, did you?"

"Nope. Sven and I got to talking about stuff. So, honey, if you don't mind, I'm going to sign off and hit the sack."

"No problem, Tucker. Great to hear your voice."

"I'll try to check in again tomorrow, if I can. But there's a chance we'll be dark for a couple of days, so don't worry, okay? Just not sure what the schedule is."

"No worries. Now get some rest. Think I'll turn in early too. I hope Kyle gives you the day to catch up."

"Oh, forgot to ask, anything about the house I need to know?"

"Not yet. Inspections are in about a week. We might have to make some decisions after we get the reports. I filled out the loan papers this morning, and the broker doesn't think there will be much problem."

"I still can't tell anyone here what we're paying for it," Tucker whispered.

"It's none of their business anyway."

"Okay, well, it's in your capable hands. I'm exercising for all the work you're gonna make me do when we own it." He yawned again. "Hey, I'm gonna have to cut out, or I'll fall asleep here on the phone."

"You go. Get some rest. I'll talk to you tomorrow or whenever. Thanks so much for calling, Tucker. It means a lot to me."

"Nite, sweetheart."

Brandy pulled up to her house, parked the car, and headed to her front door. There was a small package left on the landing step addressed to Tucker. Someone had written on the outside of the box "Baby Gift."

Bringing it inside, she sat on the living room couch and tore open the paper. Inside was a shoebox. When she opened the lid, she found a doll dressed in a sleeper. It wasn't the type of doll she'd ever seen anywhere for sale in the large local stores, and she was surprised by the fact that it wasn't really babyproof, either. Plus, it looked slightly used. She scrounged around the packing paper for a card but found none.

She pulled the doll out of the packing and held it up. The eyes opened and closed when she lay it down and stood it up. She spread the doll's legs so that it would sit on the coffee table in front of her. She went to straighten the arms up into a searching position, like she wanted to be picked up.

But one of the hands on the doll was sliced off.

CHAPTER 9

TUCKER NEVER LIKED sleeping during daylight hours, but he was used to forcing himself. He finally gave up two hours later.

The Team had been housed in a large home not too far from the compound they were going to invade this evening. In fact, Kyle had insisted they drive by it early this morning when they landed.

The lush island was a favorite for Brit vacationers but wasn't as well traveled by American tourists. Parts of it felt like the Caribbean, and other parts, like the crumbling older parts of the city, looked Portuguese or Spanish with the red tiled roofs and stone fencing. He recognized the Spanish Civil Guard uniforms, all well-armed and very visible.

But on top of the hill, where the blue water of the Atlantic contrasted with huge puffy white clouds and overgrown vines with tons of flowers in bright shades of fuscia and coral, it wouldn't take much of a stretch to understand why—for some—it was paradise.

Several of the team had doubled up, but Tucker got a bedroom to himself. Instructions went out that all cell phones were to be turned off and there would be no calls home until after the raid. Kyle told them to try to get a little sleep, and then they'd have a meeting to go over the plan.

He asked Kyle for a moment of his time and was asked to wait. He was waiting for an update from Spec Ops.

The conversation on the flight over with Sven bothered him greatly. He knew he had to inform Kyle, and he was glad Sven didn't make him swear he wouldn't, so that was what he was going to do first chance he got. He couldn't stand the thought of bringing his brothers into a situation they weren't one hundred percent up-to-date on. That was always the problem, getting accurate intel. The relationship of the Special Agent to the victim and her father was something his team should know about.

Now he had second thoughts about Sven. Perhaps he'd been played. Though he liked the guy, perhaps he wasn't the dude Tucker originally thought he was. He was telling the truth when he told Sven he never liked the politics of the job. He was just there to get it done. Politics was a dirty word, as it was for most the team guys. It was just not a factor, even in today's situations. It muddled the decision-making dangerously. A fighting man got orders. He wasn't supposed to think about the consequences. Likewise, it wasn't fair to make him fight with one hand behind his back or without accurate information. Having to think too much about the consequences gave a tactical disadvantage to the team on a mission.

Tucker tried to lie back again to get some sleep but gave up after a few minutes. He got up, changed his tee shirt, slipped on a pair of pants, and ran downstairs barefoot in search of his LPO.

Special Agent Fielding was still up, having a cup of coffee and studying a topography map. It completely caught him off guard, and before he could retreat back upstairs to find Kyle, she spotted him.

"Morning, Tucker. You can't sleep either?"

He looked for something, anything to focus on other than her young face. He knew she was going to try to extract questions of him, and that's not what he wanted until he talked to Kyle.

"Nah. Your old friend, Sven, kept me up." He poured himself a coffee that had been freshly brewed.

"So I heard." She slowly rose and walked into the kitchen with her mug in hand, extending it for a refill. He obliged, still not making eye contact.

He turned his back on her, looking for some milk or cream in the refrigerator and was happy to find it well-stocked with everything, including chilled wine, beers, fruits and vegetables and milk. There also was a quart of half-and-half, which he grabbed to top off his coffee.

The warm liquid felt like vitamins this morning. He took another long gulp and nearly finished off the mug. She was watching him, not letting go. Now he'd have to deal with her, and he felt ill-prepared.

"Tucker, I—"

"Save it," he barked, which he could see surprised her. "I don't like what Sven told me, and this little act you two are playing is very, very dangerous."

Her eyes filled up with water.

"It's not an act. These are horrible people, Tucker. My only hope for getting Jenna out is your team."

"Tell me how that works. You disable the team you say is your saving grace? Just how are any of these guys, who you've weaponized to be your family's fighting force, to put their lives on the line for someone who doesn't give a damn about giving them the truth? I'm all ears, Kelly."

She sucked in air as if he'd punched her. Here was another example why having a woman on a mission was a bad idea. Tucker grew more furious as he talked to her. She wasn't the hardened, seasoned professional he was used to seeing in combat zones, the CIA operatives he'd seen do interrogations. Those ladies were tough and mostly well-respected. It was obvious she had no military training like the CIA gals did. Even the language specialists could defend themselves and had lots of marksmanship and combat training.

This lady looked like she read Cosmo and had her nails done regularly.

"I get it. What I was about to say was I wanted to tell Kyle. And I think we should, this morning first thing."

"You think?" Tucker spit back. He poured another cup of coffee and added more cream.

She followed him to the living room but they both remained standing. He glanced around him to make sure no one else was up to overhear their conversation.

"What's this thing with Sven?" he asked.

"You jealous?"

Tucker nearly threw his coffee at her. His blood boiled. He inhaled, closed his eyes and waited for the anger to fade away.

"That was cruel of me. I'm sorry."

"Your attitude sucks, lady. You think this is some kind of game? How the hell did you get your little ass on this mission? Now we have to protect you, as well as get your clueless sister-in-law."

Kelly sat down and focused on her knees. After a few tense moments, she murmured, "You're right."

Tucker wasn't a complete asshole, and he realized perhaps she'd been drawn in with the best of intentions, but it was a plan created by a non-combat type individual, and it was a very bad idea.

"Jenna lacks common sense. She ran off to Africa without her father's permission. She's never been smart. If she survives, life will change for her."

"But she has a father with billions to waste on operations he thinks he can plan. This kind of world, this arena is not one you can do this in. This isn't a corporate takeover or some boardroom proxy war. These are big-time major drug and human trafficking, cartels. Heads of governments are all in on it, even the police or armed forces. What I've seen over in Nigeria and what I've been told is horrible. You have no idea how those people live. You can't just go in there and be a 'nice person.' These people—" He stopped because he could see his point had already been made. Kelly was nodding her head.

"I get it."

"So Sven. What's up with that? I need to know."

"He's the one who found Dad. Sorry, I call Mr. Riley dad. I know that's offensive to you."

"Oh, cut the crap, Kelly."

"When he contacted him, that's when Mr. Riley told him about me." Kelly looked up at Tucker, and, although he was still boiling with anger, he did feel sorry for her. Just a smidge.

"Go on."

"He agreed to bankroll an operation on the condition that I was to remain part of the team and was to be protected."

"And?"

"And because of my language training."

"But you don't know anything about these people."

"But I do. My husband—he got involved with some guys I thought were just locals. He used drugs recreationally. I was just getting started with my State Department final phase. I was worried I'd not pass a background check. I moved to Washington D.C. to complete my training, and we separated for a short time. That's when he overdosed. I was devastated, and I thought it would end my position. Turns out, they knew all along."

"Geez. Who the hell is running things, anyway?"

"We agreed to go forward, and I reverted back to my maiden name so there wouldn't be any taint. I'd study the drug and human trafficking businesses, and eventually help them identify the bad actors. I was to provide background and research for our diplomats who were risking their lives to try to work out arrangements with leaders in foreign countries, specifically African countries. And I'm still motivated to do that. I feel I owe it to Jack."

Tucker sat across from Kelly. The wheels were turning. Tucker found her convincing, but he knew this information had to get to Kyle without delay. "Do you think Jack was targeted at all?"

"You mean, because of his dad?"

"Exactly."

"I wondered about that, but I have no real way of knowing for sure. That's always been a question Sven's had too. He asked it in the briefing, remember?"

"Yup, I do."

"Jack's father was always a heavy anti-drug guy. He's contributed to many organizations to combat opioid abuse in the Northwest. I think Jack was a bit naive about what he could handle. He always wanted his dad to set him up in a business he could run, but Mr. Riley was lavish with the donations and stingy when it came to his kids. They'd had a falling out. Who knows who knew what was going on there? He went downhill fast, after I left."

Tucker thought about his own parents in Oregon, who had attempted to run a medical marijuana business, a grow farm, and decided to give it up because of the inherent dangers. He was never so relieved when he found out his dad went back to work as a mechanic. But they still had the land.

"Kelly, I think it's beyond time we need to get this information to Kyle." He leaned forward, placing his elbows on his knees. "It's his call. He might want to abort."

"I understand."

"Tell me about Sven. You trust him?"

"With my life. He's solid. I didn't even know about what you guys did. I think he wants them as badly as I do. He sees this as an opportunity to make a difference. Honest."

Tucker still didn't like it, but he knew exactly what he had to do next.

CHAPTER 10

"STAY RIGHT WHERE you are, Brandy. I'll be over in five minutes." Brawley's voice was low, nearly a whisper, and she could tell he was trying to hide their conversation from Dorie.

Brandy checked her phone and still hadn't received a message from Tucker. Instinct made her lock all her windows. She didn't know the significance of the doll, but the fact that it had been addressed to Tucker and had been designated "baby gift" led her to suspect there was some history involving the last mission, and Brawley would know about it. She still trusted him enough to believe he'd understand what next to do.

True to his word, Brawley steamed into the driveway and burst through the front door as soon as she unlocked it without saying a word. He stared down at the doll on the table, instantly used the box to scoop it up, and then threw it out the back door—as far away from the house as he could. He waited. Nothing further happened.

"What's going on?" she asked, standing beside him.

"Pack. You have to get out of this house right now, Brandy. I'm going to take you over to our place, and then we'll figure out where we'll go."

"We? What do you mean we?"

"I don't have time to explain it, but get your clothes packed right now. Take anything you care about but quickly."

She ran to the bedroom, pulled out a suitcase and started throwing things in. It struck her as she was putting underwear and tops into the bag she didn't know what kind of trip she was packing for.

Brawley had removed the carpet in their closet, accessed Tucker's gun stash, and started loading up things he hadn't taken with him on the deployment.

"Why are you doing that?"

"So no one else will find them."

"Who are we talking about?"

"Just pack, dammit."

Brandy was instantly in tears, confused, afraid, and heaving for breath. Brawley ran to her side, gave her a hug like he'd never done before, and whispered, "We have a problem here. You have to remain calm. I'm here to get you out of this house ASAP and to someplace safe. I promise I'll explain everything when we get there."

She managed to nod her head against his chest and untangle herself from his grip. She felt the cold realization that the dream world she was living in had been shattered by the real world. Something was out there trying to take it all away. She wasn't going to second-guess it. She'd just act. That's what Tucker would do.

"Birth records, marriage certificates, your passport, bank records? You have them in one place?" Brawley asked.

"Yes, in the box in the pantry. Everything's in there. I have a file drawer for paid bills—"

"Leave them. I'll get your box. Do a double check and make sure nothing too personal, too important is left behind."

He tossed the extra duty bag over his shoulder on his way to the pantry. Brandy stood in the middle of the bedroom, searching, then started going through drawers. She found a filled journal of

Tucker's and decided that should come with her. She scanned the bed, her eyes filling with tears again. Bending down, she lovingly straightened the covers and plumped the pillows, as if it would be the last time she would touch that place that had brought her and Tucker so much delight. If Brawley wasn't with her, she'd just curl up into a ball and stay there under the covers, where it was warm and where it smelled like the man she missed so much now.

Now Brandy understood how people felt when they had to pack for a natural disaster and hoped she hadn't left anything behind.

Brawley grabbed her suitcase as she locked the front door. "Everything's locked, even all the windows," she said hurriedly.

"Good." Brawley tossed her suitcase into the back seat of his truck as she climbed into the cab.

He checked both directions on the street before he pulled out. Brandy didn't see anything out of the ordinary. There were several vacant cars and small trucks parked along the curb, and one turning into a driveway. It was nearly dark, and most of the families living there would be having dinner, she thought.

He raced down the street and headed for the freeway, checking his rearview mirror constantly.

"Where are we going?"

"I'm just going to make sure." Then he dialed someone, still checking the mirrors. He mumbled to himself, "Come on. Come on, pick up."

They entered the freeway, which was clogged with late commuter traffic, causing them to slow down. Brandy heard squawking on the other end of the phone. Brawley began leaving a message.

"Collins. Hey, we got a situation here. I'm with Brandy. I'm taking her over to my place. I gotta talk to you, man. Like pronto."

Brandy had met this mysterious Collins man at one of the graduations. He was their team handler, the go-to guy in case they needed anything done for them by the Navy or to help locate an asset.

Brawley finally relaxed as they weaved in and around slower traffic until they passed two exits. At the third exit, he veered off and doubled back toward the direction of his house, using smaller streets that threaded along the freeway. He turned to her, asking, "So, you tried calling Tucker, right?"

"Of course. I called him first." She knew he didn't want questions, but she didn't care. "What is it with that doll? What's going on, Brawley, or what do you think is going on?"

"I'm not sure. And I can't explain much, but that doll was very clearly a warning. Like a night letter."

"What?"

"Over in Iraq and Afghanistan, the bad guys would leave notes on the doors of some of the people they were targeting, or on a school door, warning the kids and women to stay away."

"Because?"

"Because, in many cases, that house, that school was targeted for an attack. Not always, but the night letters put the fear of God into the villagers. It was very effective that way."

Brandy sat still and swallowed hard, staring out the windshield of Brawley's truck, her stomach churning. Why would anyone target her, or her house, or Tucker? She felt the heavy thumping of her heart, and the way her mouth was parched. She knew she had to calm down, for the sake of the baby she was carrying.

"But that's over *there*. This is *here*. This is the US," she dared to whisper, knowing Brawley wouldn't like her question.

Brawley shrugged, checked his surroundings again, and then began to slow down. He exhaled then repositioned his hands on the steering wheel. "I don't mean to scare you, but a lot of the team guys have thought for some time that the enemy is trying to bring the war to us. At least to show us that they can. With all of our border issues, San Diego would be an easy place to infiltrate, get in the country, and conduct mayhem. They won't win, Brandy. They'll never win, but they want us to know they're coming. They want to invoke fear. That's what that doll is about."

"But what's the significance of it—of that missing hand?"

"I can't really talk about it until I have permission, but I promise you, I'll do it just as soon as I can. You'll just have to hang on a bit. Can you do that for me?"

Brandy nodded.

"And I need you to keep Dorie calm too. That's a tall order, but I have to focus on something else first, and I've got a couple other calls to make. I need her to remain calm until we figure out the next step."

"But—"

"Please, Brandy. I can't give you any more than that, but I need your help. It's that important. Tucker would do the same thing if it was reversed. You gotta trust me."

Brandy was suddenly felt grateful, no matter what Brawley had been through, that he was with her and not with the rest of the team overseas. She never thought she'd feel that way about his breakdown, but right now, she could see that all his training had kicked in and he was totally focused, thinking clearly, and was someone she could count on.

And that's exactly what she intended to do.

When they arrived at the Hanks' home, Dorie had set the dinner preparation aside and was reading a story to Jessica. Her eyes got huge when she saw Brandy enter the room right behind her husband.

"When you said you had to go pick up something, well, I didn't expect this, Brawley."

"Hey Dorie," Brandy said as she wheeled her suitcase through the front door, then bent and gave her a kiss on her cheek, giving another one to Jessica.

"Dada!" The little one outstretched her arms, and Brawley picked her up. While Jessica was playing with Brawley's beard, her dad tried to explain the situation to his wife.

"Brandy got a package delivered to their house. It was a warning that she's not safe. I brought her over here, but Dorie, honey, we got to pack up too. If they know where she lives, they're going to know where we do too."

"Oh my God! No!" Dorie stammered as she stood, her hand over her mouth. "This can't be happening."

Brandy threw her arms around her to calm her down. "We hope not, but Brawley's just trying to be careful. Apparently, you may be in danger here. You need to get things put together just like I did. He's trying to find out what's going on. Even if it turns out to be a false alarm, we have to plan to get someplace safe for now. Help me, okay?"

"Is Tucker okay?"

"They've gone dark. No word from him yet, so he doesn't know," said Brandy.

"As far as we know," inserted Brawley. "Let's get some clothes packed for all three of us. I'll get some other things we might need, and then I'd like to be out of here in like ten minutes. Can we do that?"

Dorie nodded, walking like a zombie to their bedroom. Brawley handed Jessica to Brandy when his cell rang.

"Thank God, Collins." After a brief acknowledgement, Brawley continued, "A package was delivered to Tucker's house, and Brandy picked it up. It was a doll wrapped in paper. Labeled as a baby gift."

He paused for Collin's comment.

"No, she opened it. And yes, I'll tell her. When she called me, I raced over and tossed the thing in the backyard. It's still there now, the paper it was wrapped in, the box. Everything. Someone needs to go check it out. I didn't see any wires, powder, or anything suspicious, but who knows? You need to get the bomb squad."

Brandy tried to get Jessica interested in the book but wasn't having much luck. She saw Brawley remind Dorie to pack certain things while he was on the phone with Collins.

"Listen, sir, the right hand was cut off the doll. It wasn't a new toy, but rather like something from a used toy store or charity store. And in light of what went on in Nigeria with the doctor, I just know these assholes are somehow here. Can that even be possible?"

Brawley listened to some further instructions and then hung up.

"Okay, we're to get to a motel nearby until we get more details. I'm going to call Christy right now. Let's complete the packing and take off, okay?"

Both Dorie and Brandy nodded. Even Jessica did so.

"He told me to pack banking information, passports or marriage licenses, anything legal, personal, too," Brandy reminded her best friend in a whisper.

Dorie stood before her in tears. "This doesn't make any sense."

"But thank God we have Brawley."

Dorie went back to her search while Brandy walked Jessica to the living room again. She overheard Brawley on the phone with Christy Lansdowne.

"—No, absolutely not, Christy. I'm not going to put you or your family in danger. Collins instructed me to get a couple of rooms at the Marriott. But if Kyle calls, be sure to tell him to contact Collins. He's arranging a team to go over to the house, and then they'll come here and do a quick search. Do not open the door for anybody. No parcels, got it? And he'll want you to alert the other wives when the time comes, so be ready, okay?"

When Brawley hung up, she asked him again about the package. "You told Collins you'd tell me something. What's that?"

"That wasn't your fault, but if you ever get something like that mailed or delivered and you don't recognize who it's from, you don't open it. You call someone who will get in touch with Naval Security."

She must have been shaking because Jessica was touching her cheeks, looking for tears.

"Brandy, a lot of these rules are changing. It didn't used to be this way. Same reasons we want you off social media, not posting anything on Facebook. The bad guys are out there, and unfortunately, the families are targets."

Jessica was squirming in her arms, so Brawley took her. "Let's get this show on the road." He called to Dorie. "Are you ready?"

"The passports. I forgot where I put them," she answered.

"I got 'em in my duty bag. All set?"

"I know I'm forgetting something, but I can't even think right now." Dorie passed him and headed to the kitchen. "Let me just clean up these dinner things, and—"

But Brawley was right behind her, gently taking a pan from her hands and speaking to her softly, "Sweetheart, leave it. We gotta go. No one cares about that right now. We gotta get out of here."

As they ran to the truck and placed the bags inside, Brandy slipped her phone out from her purse and noted there still was no answer from Tucker.

She wasn't even sure what to tell him.

CHAPTER 11

K YLE WAS STUDYING diagrams and maps when Tucker entered his room.

"Kyle, I think we have a problem," he said.

His LPO looked up, gave him a frown, and then went back to looking over a floorplan, probably of the house they were to invade tonight.

"What's got you bothered?" his Chief mumbled.

"There's something you don't know about Sven and Kelly."

That got Kyle's attention. "Oh yeah?"

"First of all, Sven and Kelly spent time together gathering all the surveillance on the Dutch guy's house."

"I know that. So?"

"But you don't know that Kelly is Jenna's sister-in-law."

Kyle was cool about it, pretending to get occupied with the maps. Then with one sweep of his arm, he wiped everything off his bed. "Fuck me."

"Exactly."

"How did you hear this?"

"Sven told me on the ride over. Kelly was married to Jenna's brother, who was our benefactor's son."

"*Was?*"

"As in he died of an overdose."

"I get it now. It would have been nice if someone had told me. So what you're saying is all this help we're getting is partly personal—well, that part we knew, but we didn't know members of this team had a personal stake in the outcome as well. I fucking don't like this."

"What are we going to do?"

"A little late for that, don't you think? Unless you don't feel you can trust her or Sven?"

"That's a tough one. I just don't trust anyone who isn't honest right out of the box, Kyle. That's not how we roll."

"Yeah, but it's what we get sometimes, right?"

Tucker chuckled darkly. "It's not the first and won't be the last we get faulty intel. Story of our job, right, Kyle?"

"Amen to that."

"So, what's next?"

Kyle stood up. He stretched his arms above his head and behind his neck then rolled down as if to touch his nose to his knees in a yoga stretch. He let out a big exhale and grumbled, "We come to Jesus."

TUCKER'S JOB WAS to get everyone assembled in the great room off the kitchen. Not many were happy about this. Sven nodded respectfully toward him, standing in the shadows at the corner of the room. Kelly was making another pot of coffee.

"Okay, guys," Kyle began. "We've just been updated on some information on this mission I want you in on. Sven and Kelly have a little secret, it turns out. And let me say, for the record, if one of you guys ever does anything like this to me, I promise I'll get you busted, and off the teams. I'll make sure you spend the rest of your miserable Naval careers peeling potatoes on a sub."

"What the hell?" Fredo remarked. "What happened?"

"No, man. What you doin' fuckin' with our LPO?" grumbled

T.J., looking around the room. Several others, including Jake, Armando, and Jameson agreed.

DeWayne Huggles pointed to Kelly. "I never liked you!" Tucker could see all his earlier concerns had come crashing back to haunt him. Haunt them all.

"So which one of you wants to tell the team?" barked Kyle.

"I'll do it." Sven stepped from the corner and studied all their faces before he began. "I got a tip that the American nurse was being held here on the island. I did some digging into her family background, because I was getting nothing from the Africa Corp folks. I was on hold, and, well, I got tired of waiting. I knew time was of the essence and they were dealing with something much bigger than they were capable of handling. And the big problem is that they don't pay ransoms, not because they don't value their people, but they never have enough money."

Tucker watched the faces of the men remain hard. So far, Sven hadn't cracked their veneer.

"I discovered who Jenna's father was. He's a very wealthy investor, did well in the tech industry in the Pacific Northwest, and was semi-retired, donating his vast fortune to worthy causes. The man's a good guy."

Sven cocked his head and looked across the room at Kelly, who didn't return his gaze. "I contacted him and told him I thought I could lead a team to rescue her. He didn't know me from Adam, and I'm sure he didn't trust me, either, so I flew out to Oregon and had a sit down. And he introduced me to Kelly, who happens—and this is the part you guys didn't know until now—to be his daughter-in-law. Kelly was married to Jenna's brother, the old man's son."

The swearing would have been stronger if there hadn't been a lady present, even though Kelly was part of the source of irritation.

Kelly interrupted Sven's story. "Jack died nearly two years ago while I was finishing my State Department specialty training. Prior to that, Jack and I had worked lower level jobs in Africa together for State and other departments. It's how we met. Jenna heard the stories and always wanted to go there. My qualifications still stand and are true. But you didn't know that Jenna is related to me by marriage. And I feel very responsible for her capture and demise. My father-in-law is a very rich and powerful man who wants to save the only child he has left."

"We have a say here, Chief?" asked Coop.

"You can try. I'm not sure what good it does," answered Kyle.

"We're kind of fucked," whispered Armando.

"But I will say this. If any of you want to abort, I'm not going to stand in your way. I owe it to you, though the Navy would think otherwise. You were brought here under false pretenses, and I didn't want you to think I did it. You gotta trust me. But most important is the question of do you trust these two?" Kyle added, pointing to Sven and Kelly.

"What about the Headshed?" Tyler asked.

Kyle stood up and rubbed the back of his neck with his hand. "Well, I received the go, and told them we're going silent for twenty-four hours. I could just not call them. They're not expecting to hear from me until tomorrow morning, and with good news, too. We have no backup, so nothing had to be coordinated."

Tucker and everyone in the room knew it was a career-ending decision.

"Not fair you taking that risk, Kyle. I don't like it," said Coop.

Armando agreed. "Something goes wrong, maybe we all get tossed, but this will come down on you hardest. I don't like it either, Kyle."

Kyle smiled back at two of his oldest friends on the team. "Then we don't screw up."

That generated another level of swearing in several languages.

Over the next few minutes, everyone had their say. Some spoke to themselves. Some spoke to the person sitting next to them or to the room. But by the end of the few minutes, the decision had been made, and everyone was on board as a team. This was how the boardroom of a spec ops team functioned.

The mission remained a go.

Sven and Kelly took over the discussion, showing floorplans of the house and the position of the posted guards and what kinds of firepower they were carrying. They detailed the security cameras and electric perimeter fencing.

The good news was that even though the Dutch billionaire had spent a lot of money on security, there were huge gaps in his coverage and safety precautions. The bulk of his protection was his reliance on the men he hired. Tucker knew that any one SEAL on the team was worth at least twenty of them, so the odds outweighed the bad guys significantly.

Tucker asked another question of Kelly. "What kind of mindset will she be in? Did you see her or observe her condition at all?"

Kelly took a deep inhale. "Yes, she's being chained to a bedframe in the bedroom. She doesn't have the freedom to roam the house. She gets to shower, use the bathroom, but she doesn't go anywhere outside the bedroom. And,"—Kelly's breath hitched— "he beats her. I think he's given her drugs too. Other than the obvious sexual abuse, which must be horrible, I think she's physically fine. But the sex, judging from how she looks, is nowhere near consensual."

Several of the team guys swore. People who abused women were always at the top of their kill list.

"We both thought, based on how Mr. VanValle was acting, he was going to tire of her very soon. She's a mess, really. We need to tell it like it is, Kelly."

"Of course," she whispered back.

"But she's strong enough? I mean, she can walk, run on her own?" asked Coop.

Kelly and Sven nodded.

"Part of the reason I didn't want you to abort this mission is, well, I don't think she has much time left. She has no value to him." Sven again surveyed the room. It generated lots of head nodding. Her life expectancy was short. They all understood this.

Kyle re-traced what their positions would be. He ordered his snipers, Armando and Jameson, to find a good vantage point to cover the front door and the vehicles. Fredo would pass out Invisios. The whole team was ordered to carry everything they brought, since there might not be the chance to come back to the villa. Kyle showed them the best escape route by road and a secondary road, if they had to hike out, where they could get somewhere and commandeer a vehicle, if necessary.

"We got about five hours until it's dark. I recommend everyone do a power rest. Change your clothes, re-pack your bags, and check your equipment." Kyle's command was well heeded.

Kyle divided the men into two groups for transport to the Dutchman's house and then hopefully beyond. Their villa came with a ten-passenger Opel van, and a larger Jeep SUV, so there would be plenty of room. Sven volunteered to load up the vehicles with waters and things from the house they might need during the stakeout while everyone else rested and prepared.

Tucker went upstairs, set his alarm and was going to take a quick nap. He got out his journal to write a few sentences to Brandy.

Not exactly what I was expecting this time around, but then I'm supposed to handle anything that's thrown at me. Good news is I doubt we'll be here longer than an overnight and that makes me real happy.

I hate sleeping during daylight hours, but I'll be working at night, so that's just how it goes.

Learned some things about family dynamics I don't ever want to see in our family. It's like there's us and then the rest of the planet. We're here to fix a mistake we didn't make. That's always the job, though. If we're lucky, we'll be able to get information on the operation we're fighting so the next group can go further with the cleanup.

The islands are a mixture of cultures, not unlike Africa. But this place is part of Spain, and though it's close, it doesn't feel like Africa at all. The buildings are colorful, like the Caribbean, but they use more rock and stone, and many of their streets are cobblestone. Lots of churches tolling all day long. It seems a little more prosperous and not as many inhabitants.

We're up high where it's cooler, and if I concentrate, I can smell the saltwater way down below. Where we're staying, the homes are for wealthy world travelers or vacation rentals for the jet-setting crowd. We have two nearly new vans, more bathrooms than bedrooms, and a refrigerator the guys are going to regret they won't even begin to tackle.

I miss Brawley. Doesn't seem like a mission without him. My thoughts are with all of you. Tell my son (I know you think it's a girl, but I don't) to be nice to his mama and to let you sleep. Hope Jessica is behaving. I owe you all a nice, long walk on the beach when I get home. That's what I'm going to think about while I turn in for a bit.

Then it's showtime.

Love you more each day, Brandy.

Right on time, Tucker was awakened and was ready to go in minutes. He double-checked his bedroom and bath for anything he'd forgotten.

Downstairs, the group stocked up on food from the refrigerator. There were energy drinks on the counter, along with granola bars and peanuts. Tucker grabbed what he could, stashing things here and there in the pockets he'd fashioned.

He piled into the Opel with Kyle, Armando, and several others. Sven and Kelly rode in the Jeep with Jake, Tyler, and DeWayne.

They passed the house as they had coming up the twisting road, driving farther down to a wide driveway with a metal electric fence from a neighboring house behind the shoulder. They listened for traffic and heard none. Quietly, they grabbed their duty bags and exited the vehicles, staying to the sides of the road in the shadows. As they approached the compound, Armando and Jameson split off to position themselves on two carport rooftops that would give perfect vantage.

The rest of the team advanced, splitting up into groups as planned. Kelly and DeWayne were to get closest to the house to listen and check on Jenna's condition, so Tucker and Kyle helped her up into a tree that hovered over the wall so she could climb down. Huggles followed behind.

They split up into two groups on either side of the large gate entrance. Two guards smoked cigarettes and engaged in whispered small talk. Silently, the two groups scaled the outer walls, carefully cutting the razor wire installed at the top, and dropped into the compound yard. A dog barked, which made them freeze. Coop threw a small rock in the opposite direction, away from the house, which distracted the dog. They heard voices coming to check, two flashlights sending beams through the cactus and other exotic plants in the yard. Tucker's group lay flat on the ground until the lights were turned off and the dog lost interest.

The tiny squawk in Tucker's ear told him Armando and Jameson were in place. Kelly whispered she had a visual on Jenna, who was sleeping. Alone.

Huggles confirmed the location of the Dutchman in the house, watching TV in the living room. "He's got a big dog with him, dammit," Huggles whispered.

"I got Dutchie. Jameson's got the dog," Armando confirmed over the Invisio.

Kyle gave the instructions. "On three, two, one."

Tucker quickly disabled one of the sentries, while T.J. did the other, tossing their semi-automatics into the bushes. Two high-pitched bursts tore through the night as the man with the flashlight fell next to the patrol dog, who had also been hit.

"Sentries secure," said T.J.

Tucker heard several other comments, and then Kyle gave the perimeter secure call.

They were expecting an additional four men on the inside, but Tucker could only count two. DeWayne responded that two bodies were sleeping in a bedroom off the back.

"And Jenna?" asked Kyle.

"Still asleep. She's alone," answered Kelly.

Cooper indicated he'd dismantled the sliding glass door lock on her bedroom. Fredo had picked the front door.

Again, the count from Kyle, "Three, two, one, go!"

The whine from Armando and Jameson's long guns was followed by the tinkling of a glass window being breached. It gave VanValle just enough time to look up as his forehead exploded. Simultaneously, the dog, sleeping down at his feet, was hit without waking up. The team entered the house from all sides. Tyler and Coop disabled the two sleeping men. The two who sat at the dining room table stood with their hands up when they saw their employer and the dog die in a burst of red spray. Their wrists and ankles were secured, and their heads were covered with two bloodied pillowcases from their teammate's bedroom.

Kyle's team had managed to breach the house then disable or kill everyone without a single shout out or sound of a weapon firing. All Tucker could hear as various rooms in the home were declared clear was the whimpering coming from the back bedroom. Jenna was sobbing uncontrollably. As Tucker approached, he saw Kelly take out a pair of jeans and sweatshirt and tennis shoes and hurriedly got her dressed.

Jenna's lip was split and she had a black eye. It made him want to throw up.

Kyle instructed them to look for cell phones, any laptops they could take. Six were found and zippered into duty bags. On the table were some papers, and all of them were confiscated. Pictures of the bodies were taken, including the two dogs that unfortunately had to be sacrificed. Kyle gave the message for the shooters to come in with the all clear.

Just as quietly as they arrived, the team left, this time using the main gate entrance. They left the TV on, as well as all the house lights. They ran back down the road by starlight to their vehicles and waited for Armando and Jameson to catch up. Then they were on their way.

The whole operation had taken no more than ten minutes. With any luck, they'd be at the airport in three hours and back on that nice jet, perhaps drinking champagne, before daylight.

Tucker monitored himself and discovered his blood pressure hadn't risen more than a few clicks. It was just like the old days. The job was done. The only thing he focused on now was getting home.

CHAPTER 12

THE CHEERFUL DESK receptionist inappropriately smiled and asked them how their day was going. Brawley couldn't resist. "Fucked."

The young brunette fluttered her eyelids several times and then responded with, "I'm sorry to hear that." She clicked a few keystrokes and then regrouped, adding, "Now I'll need your driver's license and one form of payment for incidentals."

Brawley didn't quibble or ask to make sure the Navy was picking up the tab. He just gave the young girl what she wanted.

Still holding the sleeping Jessica, Brandy noted all the places in the lobby where someone could hide and not be detected. She looked for anyone who had more than a passing interest in them and found none.

The smile was still plastered on the desk clerk's face as she directed them to the elevator and asked if they needed help with their luggage. Brandy guessed she received a "special" look from Brawley, because the young girl stepped back from the counter and then just watched as they scampered toward the tower elevator.

Dorie struggled with one suitcase and a duty bag. Brawley had the heavy one with the guns and two others strapped across his chest and could easily outrun them all. Brandy was able to tow her wheeling suitcase without problem, but Jessica was getting very heavy. The elevator dropped them at the fourteenth floor.

Two rooms had been provided, which connected. Brandy lay Jessica down on her bed and instructed Brawley and Dorie to take the other room for privacy.

Brawley made sure Dorie got off her feet. Her skin was pale and a bit clammy.

"She doesn't look too good, Brawley."

"I know it. I think I should get some food. She missed dinner."

"Let me order something. Maybe some soup, a sandwich or something. You want anything?"

He shook his head. "Go ahead. I'm going to see if Collins has anything yet. And I'll tell Christy where we are and let her know we got out without incident."

"You owe me an explanation. You know that, don't you?" Brandy wasn't going to let Brawley off the hook until she was given as many details as he could give.

"Make the room service call. I'll get done with Collins and Christy, and we'll talk."

Several minutes after the food was delivered, Brawley closed the adjoining door behind him and took up a seat at the desk in Brandy's room. Jessica was snoring soundly. The two of them shared some potato wedges and two bowls of hearty soup.

"She didn't want anything, but I left it by her bed. I think she just needed water," he whispered.

"Good." Brandy waited for him to fulfill his promise.

"Last time over, we were to check on groups that do human trafficking and run drugs and guns. We were just there to get information and set up a base camp so we could go back and forth for a bigger operation to be done at a later date. But what happened was that we ran into a small militia group who had already ambushed a team of aid workers trying to give vaccinations and medical treatment to the villagers and several schools. They're international aid workers, partly sponsored by the U.N."

"Okay."

"So our safe house got compromised, and we became a rescue operation. We were able to free three medics and two females, one of whom was a doctor who gave aid to a dying rebel soldier. The kid didn't make it, after she had to do an emergency amputation to try to save his life. They blamed the doctor and cut off her hand."

Brandy's stomach lurched and she had to work to keep its contents down.

"Someone who knows about that mission sent the doll, I'm convinced. Collins thinks so too. They're inspecting it now, but we didn't have any chatter or warning that something like this was being planned. But it clearly is an attack on Tucker, through you."

"Is Tucker safe, then?"

"Well, they're not in Africa now, so I assume so. But now I'm not sure what information they have. If they know you're alone, then they know something."

Brandy checked her phone with no result. "If I could just talk to him."

"Believe me, the SOF Command is trying to get hold of Kyle."

"How did they know where we lived? How could that be? It's not like he wears his uniform everywhere. I mean, does this mean that someone has been following us? Could they be following me?"

Brawley stared back at her, his lips in a straight line, no expression to his eyes. He was masking. She knew it well. Brandy looked away.

"Honestly, some days I feel like we should be housing families on base, for protection, like they do outside the U.S. But these are different times, and the enemy is getting resourceful."

"Has this happened before?"

"Here and there. More like incidents with locals who had some kind of an axe to grind. That's why we ask all the families to be careful. It's also why I never go anywhere unless I'm armed. None of us do."

Brawley's cell rang. "Christy must have gotten my message." He put the phone to his ear. "We're safe. Haven't heard anything yet. How about you?"

He listened. Brandy wasn't able to make out Christy's words.

"I promise you'll be the first to know, Christy. I'd get the kids ready, just in case. Just put a couple days of clothes together if they ask you to leave."

The phone call was brief. Brandy planned to call her later, after she'd had a good night's sleep. Right now, buying a house was just not high on her list of priorities. Keeping everyone that she loved safe was.

JESSICA HAD MIRACULOUSLY slept through the entire night, and it frightened Brandy so much she woke the child up herself. After the little one got her bearings, and realized she wasn't in bed with her mother, she began crying for her. The door between their two rooms was still open, and Dorie stepped through in seconds.

"I'd check the bed. More than likely, you are sleeping in a puddle, Brandy."

"Oh geez," she said as she felt the wet spot nearly a foot in circumference.

"Better get used to it, sweetie," Dorie said in farewell as she exited to the other room, the toddler in her arms.

Brandy left another message for Tucker and then decided to shower and get dressed. Afterward, she joined the other room for the breakfast they'd ordered.

"So there's nothing yet, I take it?" asked Brandy.

"Nada. Collins told me to expect some investigators this morning. Navy Intel."

"I tried calling Tucker again. I didn't leave any detail."

"Are we just to stay here all day? In the motel room?" asked Dorie.

"For now."

"Sure would like to know if my house is okay," she mumbled as she fed Jessica.

"What if they know we came here?" Brandy wondered.

Brawley's cell went off, and Collins told him two officers from NCIS Domestic Terrorism unit were on their way.

The two Special Agents, one an older woman and one a young man looking fresh out of college, presented their cards and both showed their shields. Brawley introduced his wife and Brandy and mentioned that Tucker had been on the mission with him to Nigeria but was overseas now.

"So, Mrs. Hudson," asked the woman, "did you see anyone at your residence earlier in the day? Someone perhaps hanging around the street somewhere, or someone you've not seen before?"

"No. I left in the morning. Came back at night. I wasn't expecting anything, so I really didn't look."

"How about your neighbors?"

"I didn't talk to them. Brawley came over and got me out of there. I didn't have time. Haven't you questioned them?"

"I believe we have, Mrs. Hudson, but was wondering if anyone had said anything about someone checking out your home."

"No. Tucker has a sixth sense about things like this, and he said nothing. I mean, he always checks out a room wherever we go. Just his habit, I guess."

"We didn't find any video surveillance on your front door, Mrs. Hudson, or did we miss it?"

"No, we don't have anything like that."

"What did you find out about the doll?" asked Brawley.

"In a minute, Mr. Hanks." The female agent flipped through a tiny notebook and stopped at a page. "Were you, Mr. Hanks, in any public places recently where you could have been identified as a member of the SEAL community?"

Brawley thought about it but shook his head. "Nothing out of the ordinary. I mean, we go to the Scupper. We don't announce who we are, but we sit together. Everyone kind of knows it's tradition. Tourists and people we don't know are in there all the time, too, but we never really talk to them or make much out of the job. Mostly people just watch, and if they get curious, we leave."

Both the agents nodded. After a series of further questions, the female, more senior of the two, began to reveal small portions of the investigation. "The doll is loaded with prints. Must be fifty or more. Nothing came up that we have a record of. We found carpet and clothing fibers, spilled juice and food. It's a used doll, plain and simple. Harmless. With your permission, we need to take your prints, Mrs. Hudson, to exclude yours."

"Sure."

"Brawley, you didn't touch the doll, did you?"

"No, ma'am. I picked it up in the box and threw it in the back-yard. But I don't believe I touched it. I probably did touch the box when I tossed it."

The younger agent took a set of prints from Brandy while they talked.

"You'll probably be relieved to know it came up negative for any toxins or explosives of any kind," she said.

Brandy found some relief in that. "Do you think this was a message? What did you call it, Brawley, a night letter?"

"Yes, a warning letter—"

"We know what a night letter is, Mr. Hanks. I'd say that's pretty spot-on. What it does mean is that either one of the people in-volved in the incident in Nigeria has come here to San Diego or has talked to someone who lives here."

"So why send it?" Brandy asked.

"To scare you. And it looks like it did," the female agent answered.

"And what do we do next? We have our houses, our lives. Brawley is supposed to start a new job here in a few weeks. Are we supposed to stay in a motel room or go back to our houses and wait for the other shoe to drop?" Dorie's frustrated voice wavered.

The two agents looked at one another.

"We're not really set up with a witness protection or relocation program, not for this, anyway. We have limited resources. We can put surveillance on both houses, coordinate with the locals, have regular patrols. Maybe have someone stay with both of you, but beyond that, yes, it's a waiting game," the female agent said.

Brandy could see this was a wholly unworkable situation.

The younger agent posed the question. "Do you have family or relatives you can go stay with, either of you?"

CHAPTER 13

O N THE WAY to the airport, Coop tended to Jenna. He cleaned and put sterile pads on several surface wounds and put a strip on her cut. Kyle had Tucker drive so he could make contact with Collins. Traffic at this early hour of the morning was non-existent, except for an occasional delivery truck.

Cooper complained, so Tucker slowed down. "Sorry, man." He turned to Kyle. "You asked the jet to stay, right?".

"I did, but you never know. With a small airport in a foreign country, things happen. He could be directed off, or they charge a huge retainer for layovers."

Tucker watched Kyle switch his phone on. The small screen lit up like Christmas.

"Holy shit, Collins has been calling me every half-hour. Something's going on back home." He dialed the number and then put it on speaker. "Hope you don't mind."

There was nothing but silence in the back two seats.

Collins' voice cracked. "About fuckin' time Lansdowne. You guys okay?"

"Right as rain, and we got the package. A lot of computers and other stuff someone in Washington is going to want to take a look at."

"Okay, here's what's up. We got a big problem."

Tucker held his breath. He could see T.J. and Fredo had pulled themselves awake and were hanging over the seat. Cooper held Jenna against him, wrapped in a blanket. She was drinking a bottle of water.

"Hey, Collins, I've got you on speaker. I've got half the team in the van, just so you know."

"That's okay. Everyone needs to know. Last night, I got a call from Brawley. Someone delivered a package to Tucker's house, and Brandy opened it."

Tucker squeezed the steering wheel and shouted, "Is she okay?"

"Yes, yes, she's safe. They're all safe."

Tucker sighed with relief.

"Who is they, Collins?" asked Kyle.

"Brawley, Dorie, the little one and Brandy got moved to the Marriott until we could inspect the package, and check out both the houses. Inside the box was a doll with a hand cut off."

"Fuckin' perverts," Fredo barked.

Tucker's mind was winding around itself. He tried to grasp for answers he couldn't find.

"So, they're attacking at home, then," said Kyle. "They're in San Diego."

"The girls must be scared out of their gourds," said Tucker.

"Actually," sighed Collins, "I've been told the girls are pretty good. This morning a team from NCIS came over to get some information. They've just started working over the doll. It's been handled by everyone under the sun, and so far, we've got nothing."

"You getting us home this morning? That better be a yes, Collins." asked Kyle.

"I wanted to hear from you first, but yes, I'll make sure the jet is there. Does the girl need any medical attention? Should she go to a hospital? Or, I could find a private clinic."

"I think she's good till we're stateside," said Cooper. "You know, the usual testing for what she's been through."

"I want to go home!" Jenna shouted.

"Under the circumstances, Collins, we need to get off this island as soon as is possible," added Kyle. "One thing you'll need to arrange for us is a passport for Jenna. They'll check ours at the airport. In her condition, and she's a little beat up, I don't want to involve the local authorities. That would be a ticket for a week's delay, or worse."

"I'm on it. So what about the Dutchman and his body guards?"

"All but two are done. It was very quiet and quick. We left everything the way we found it, but took the laptops and cell phones, which ought to be a treasure trove," reported Kyle.

"Okay, well, I've got some calls to make. I'll be in touch. You guys head for the airport. What's your ETA?"

"Two, two and a half hours."

Tucker needed to be in touch with Brandy. "Collins, I gotta call my wife."

"You better, or you'll be getting a divorce next month," quipped Collins.

"And does Christy know?" asked Kyle.

"Yeah, she was the first one I called. Solid as a rock, but she'll want to hear it from you. Tucker, all of you, go ahead and call your families to give them a heads-up. We don't want anyone opening up packages."

Tucker didn't know what this country's laws were, but since it was night, he doubted anyone would catch him on the phone. Brandy picked up at the first ring.

"Tucker! Thank God. Is everything okay?"

"Comin' home, baby. You hang on."

"Listen, the Navy guys thought perhaps we should drive up to stay with Brawley's folks in Oregon."

"That's a no, Brandy. I'm going to be home in a day."

"But shouldn't we leave the area?"

"Maybe your dad's, but no long road trips. Absolutely not."

"Brawley and Dorie really want to go."

"I think it's a bad idea. You stay right where you are until I come. No moving around. Stay put and let everyone do their jobs."

Tucker knew they'd lose control if everyone scattered in different directions. And if something should happen, it would be too hard to get there in time. They were better off as a unit, families and all. He cursed the investigators for having put the idea into their heads.

One by one, each of the men talked to their wives and families. Coop let Jenna briefly talk to her father, who was screaming for joy.

Tucker wound through the city center, where traffic became congested, though dawn was still several hours away. Most of the congestion was due to large vans and early shop deliveries. There wasn't a building above three stories, and most of them looked at least two-hundred years old. With no public streetlamps, the going was slow, and Tucker had to be on guard for motorbikes and small lorries that buzzed in and around traffic like motorcycles did on the California freeways. By the time they came to the two-lane approach to the airport, Tucker's armpits were drenched, and he was reminded he'd not showered like some of the other men had.

He mulled over and over in his mind how the elements they'd fought against in Nigeria had been able to infiltrate their border. Could this militia group be more mobile than they assumed? In all his years of service, it was the first time consequences of his actions over in the arena actually followed him home. Or the first time that he knew of.

They'd not talked about their last job except to their liaison, and Kyle did most of the coordination with the CIA and prepared their formal mission papers, which were on file with the Navy. Yet something had slipped through the cracks.

He wondered if he should call Brawley but figured he wouldn't be so stupid as to take off with the family. But he wasn't the SOF Command's responsibility any longer. He was in that limbo land between having been formally detached from the Team and not yet picked up elsewhere. Tucker decided to wait, perhaps give his best friend a call when his boss wasn't sitting right next to him.

He was grateful, nonetheless, in the wisdom of getting Brandy out of the house and finding her the safe place to spend the night. Brawley would fully protect her; of that he was sure.

The Jeep passed them by, so Tucker followed them all the way to a gated entrance near the hangar. The sentry made note of the sticker in the driver side window, and they were allowed to enter the secure compound. The gate closed behind them. Tucker parked right next to the other vehicle. Kelly dashed from the passenger side to check on Jenna, who was being helped out by Cooper.

But the jet was nowhere on the tarmac and not on the horizon. Tucker doubted that they'd land now until morning, but hopefully it wasn't too far away.

"What do you think?" Sven asked him.

"I don't think they can land at night. But I guess it depends on the bird," Tucker answered. They all stood in a huddle, waiting for instructions.

Kelly got off her phone. "Good news. Mr. Riley has made the arrangements for a backup plane, in case they can't cut the other one loose. It will take about three hours to arrive," Kelly said to Kyle. "We can wait in the Net Jet building until we know. There's food and coffee in there."

Kyle directed the team to unload everything from the vehicles and deposit their things inside the hangar.

"I imagine he must be one happy fella," Tucker said to the special agent.

"That phone call from Jenna will be something he remembers

for the rest of his life. He's greatly indebted to you all."

Kyle stepped up. "We're supposed to get a passport for Jenna. You don't happen to have one, do you?"

"I do not. But perhaps her father has a copy we could get delivered. You want me to try?"

"Wouldn't hurt. Collins is working to arrange it, but that could take a while. You got any other Department contacts here on the island?"

"Nobody I trust. I think your man is our best bet, but let me see if we can get a copy of the original one."

She sat Jenna down in the middle of the group. Except for a handful of staffers preparing food and stocking vending machines, the place was empty. From several paces away, she made another call and then waited. About ten minutes later, her phone pinged with a message. "Got it!" she shouted to Kyle.

"Thank God. I hope it's enough."

Tucker was looking for someone official. "If the jet arrives, maybe we just board and forget the permission."

"Never happen. As soon as the plane lands, customs will be here in a flash," answered Sven. "They're notified of incoming."

Kyle sent the picture of the passport to Collins for added ammunition.

A large black van stopped at the gated sentry and was allowed in. The seals on the sides doors were not readable, but it was apparent an official of some kind had arrived. Before the two suited gentlemen got to the entrance of the hangar, they could hear the buzzing of a plane overhead.

Kelly Fielding introduced herself and showed her credentials. The gray-haired gentleman with the large moustache gave her a long perusal before he decided to show his identification. He spoke in Spanish, and Kelly continued in the same.

Kyle stood next to Fredo to get an unofficial translation.

"They're asking about the girl."

"Uh oh," whispered Kyle.

Kelly showed the man a copy of Jenna's passport, and then she said something quietly Fredo couldn't hear. He took a picture of the passport image with his own phone and walked away to make a phone call.

The jet, twice the size of the first one, landed with a boom and then taxied until it got within a hundred yards of the building. Tucker could make out two pilots, who waited.

A stretch Mercedes with diplomatic flags appeared at the sentry gate and was granted entry. The two officials jogged over to greet whomever was sitting in the back seat.

"Not sure about this," said Kyle.

Sven shrugged his shoulders. "I'd be more concerned if it was a troop transport truck. I think we're about to be given the golden ticket."

The older official bowed, gave a salute to whomever was in the vehicle, and headed back to the hangar. The Mercedes, with its mysterious passenger turned around and left the compound.

In broken English, the gentleman with the moustache spoke to their group. "We have been given assurances by the Brazilian Consulate General in person that your papers are in order. He was entrusted to get everything ready, but he apologizes for the delay. He says it was all his fault. And he's promised us he will deliver the necessary documents to my office this morning. So you are free to go."

Tucker exchanged stares with Sven.

Kyle monitored a text that pinged his phone. "Collins," he said, waving the screen in the air.

The two officials were on their way back to their car.

"That sonofabitch," Kyle whispered, shaking his head. "The old man came through for us."

The bags were loaded aboard the plane with haste. Kyle remained on the tarmac while everyone else boarded the gangway. He waved to the officials standing beside their car, boarded the plane, spoke to the pilots, and then took the first vacant seat in front.

Tucker sat behind Sven. As the plane began to taxi, Cooper called out, "Just where are we off to?"

"Norfolk. We'll be on US soil in ten hours."

CHAPTER 14

"**H**E SAID NOT to go, Brawley." Brandy had pleaded with them not to leave. "They're on their way home. Just wait. One more day," she pleaded.

"Brandy, we don't know if we're any safer here than in our own home," said Dorie.

"Well, first of all, there's no evidence that they even made it to your home. And secondly, this is a big hotel. The Navy knows we're here. I believe Collins. This is the safest place we could be, like he told you."

Jessica had been fussy all morning, and Brandy could see it was stressing Dorie out. Without her toys and her regular routine, keeping a toddler amused in a hotel room was next to impossible.

"Why don't you take her for a swim?" she suggested. "There's a big indoor pool here."

"How is that any safer?" Brawley spat.

"I didn't bring my suit," mumbled Dorie. "Look, if we just left now, we could be up past Eugene in ten, twelve hours. About the time they land. And they still have to catch a flight to California after that. His folks' place is like a bunker. Nothing could touch us there."

Tucker had told her the stories. Brawley's dad had been a SEAL, on the teams over twenty years before retirement. She imagined he'd have enough firepower for an independence movement.

"You really should come with us, Brandy. It's the smart thing to do," Brawley insisted.

"I'm doing what Tucker asked. I'm going to stay right here."

It sucked that there was no protocol, no procedure for these types of situations. Her husband was unreachable again. If she stayed with one of the other wives, she might bring attention to them as well. It wasn't safe, but there was no definite plan. The hardest thing for her to do right now was wait.

Dorie and Brawley were showering and preparing for their trip, which would leave Brandy without a vehicle, but she didn't mind about that. She was more worried about being left all alone. She decided to give Christy a call.

"I'm glad you called. I got a chance to talk to Kyle and they're on the plane. Won't be long now. How are you holding up?"

"Christy, I'm wondering if I'm doing the right thing."

"You mean about the house?"

"Oh God no!" She found herself giggling despite herself. "About waiting here. I feel like a sitting duck."

"But they're checking in. You know they are."

"Yes, that's what we were told. The NCIS guys were not very reassuring."

"I wish they'd let you come to my place, but I've been told not to. I think that's smart, too."

"Yes, it's the right thing."

"There really isn't any alternative, Brandy."

"Well, Brawley and Dorie are driving up to his folks place in Oregon. They think that's the safest right now."

"But you're supposed to stay together and stay put."

"I am, but they're leaving, Christy. Nothing I can do to change their minds."

"Dammit."

"Should I go with them?"

"No. Please, Brandy, just stay there. There won't be any help if you leave the protection of the motel and the people they have watching over you. You don't see them, but I'm sure they're there. You have to trust in that."

"I'll be all alone."

"What about your father?"

"I can't involve him. To be honest, I'd feel safer with Brawley. At least he can shoot."

"Well, there is that. But you have a gun, don't you?"

"We brought some of Tucker's. He's trained me on his SigSauer, enough so I know how to use it without shooting myself. If I'm left alone, I'm more likely to shoot the housekeeping staff if I get too spooked."

Her eyes began watering. The whole situation was confusing and dangerous. There was no leader, no one's instructions to follow, except the man who was fifteen hours or more away.

"Look, I've got to go check on the kids. Keep your cool. Call me as often as you like. We can stay connected that way. I'll let you know if I hear anything, and you do the same. Okay?"

"Okay. Thanks, Christy."

"I'm here for you. If I didn't have the kids, I'd be right beside you with my .38. And you know I can shoot too."

The call cheered her slightly. But then the quietness of the room descended upon her. She took their breakfast tray to the door, checked the hallway to make sure it was deserted, flipped the doorstop, and laid the tray to the side. Again, surveying the area, she listened. It was quiet, too quiet. There was absolutely no sign of anyone guarding them.

"Is anyone there?" she called out. After several seconds, she repeated the question. "Anybody out there?"

Her answer was complete silence, which confirmed her suspicion. No one was on guard, watching out for her and her growing family.

Closing the door, she sat on her bed and made a decision.

Brawley stepped through the adjoining opening. "We're ready to go. Last chance, Brandy. I still think I'm your best bet."

She looked up at him and nodded. "I'm ready. I've decided."

"Smart cookie," he said as he winked.

They again struggled with the bags, Brawley taking the heavy ones and loading Brandy's suitcase with the diaper bag and Dorie's soft shoulder satchel. As before, she held Jessica and the rolling suitcase while Dorie helped Brawley with the duty bags.

She almost left behind her phone charger and managed to run back in before the door closed for the final time.

They walked through the lobby area, filled with guests waiting to check out and a girls' soccer team waiting to check in. Brandy nearly tripped over a bright yellow ball that was skimming over the granite tile floor.

The valet brought the truck and helped load the heavy bags into the bed. Brawley gave them twenty dollars, and with Dorie in back with Jessica, Brandy sat up front with Brawley. They were off.

Instead of heading for the interstate, Brawley doubled back onto the island.

"What are you doing?"

"I'm picking up a few things Dorie needs for Jessica. Some toys, some extra diapers, and snacks. You know, stuff."

"But we could buy those on the road," Brandy protested.

"Which would take more time. This is simple. We'll just be in and out in five minutes."

Brawley knew she was fuming inside.

"And if you need a little courage," he flipped open the glove box in front of her knees, "this should do the trick."

She could see the butt of a snub-nosed revolver. "I'm not trained on this," she said in shock.

"Don't need to be. It's loaded with five rounds. You just point and shoot. You do know how to do that, don't you?"

"You know I do."

All this discussion of guns made her nervous. She quietly closed the lid of the box and tried to calm her nerves. She found herself observing everything as they made their way to the house. Two cars passed by while Brawley was pulling into the driveway. Several other vehicles were parked in the street: A green and white landscape truck, a yellow VW Beetle, and a bright green compact pickup with something tied to the back.

She remained in the car while Brawley and Dorie dashed to the house. Jessica had already fallen asleep in her car seat.

"Just you and me, kid. Off on an adventure. Sure wish we were on our way to Disneyland or some place fun, instead of running away to 'The Compound.' Tucker had made fun of Mr. Hanks' game trophies, which covered most of the available walls in the living area. He even had several in their bedroom. He'd told her about when they used to shoot at them with their dart guns and, later on, B.B. guns. On more than one occasion, Brawley had gotten a spanking so hard he couldn't sit down for a couple of days.

"What have I gotten myself into?" she asked to the cab.

At last, the couple came from the house with another suitcase and a large what looked like a baseball bag with a logo she didn't recognize. Dorie also brought another soft beach bag and waddled along next to Brawley. Brandy noticed how pregnant she looked.

The suitcase had to go in the bed of the truck next to Brandy's. Brawley was able to stash the ball bag behind the second seat. Dorie clutched her satchel on her knees, climbing into the rear seat next to the still-sleeping Jessica.

"My dad used to say when we'd go camping, 'If it's not in the car, we don't own it.' That pretty much sums up how light we pack," Brawley boomed.

Dorie sighed. "Brawley, quiet. You'll wake her and hurry up. I'm getting the creeps sitting here. Let's get on the road."

Traffic was light since they were between commute runs. They made good time for the next two hours until the truck needed gas and Dorie wanted to get something healthy for lunch. Once again, Brandy stayed behind with Jessica while her two friends went inside to pay for the gas and make their purchases. The truck stop teemed with customers, creating a small line for gas. Brandy counted and observed cars coming and going. Something caught her eye, but as she turned and scrutinized the parking lot, she didn't find anything of interest. After gassing up, they were on their way again.

"Does your dad know we're coming?" she asked Brawley.

"Yup. They're pretty excited too. You've never been there, have you?"

"No, but I've heard a lot about it."

"Dad retired at thirty-eight. I'll be a couple of years older when I retire, God willing."

"How did he manage to be on a west coast team and live in Oregon?"

"He didn't at first. Then when he met my mom, well her Mennonite roots are here in Oregon. They bought a place up there when I was born. My mom's kin thought they'd make a farmer out of him. It didn't take."

"I can imagine. Your mom doesn't drink, is that right?"

"No coffee, smoking, alcohol. I'm sure it surprised most of his friends when they hooked up."

"So they bought a farm and he still deployed. I'll bet you missed him."

"I honestly don't remember. The last six years he stayed down here during the week and came home most weekends, and we did stuff the whole time. There are always lots of guys who do that, lots of divorced guys who room together. I think he also saw that my mom wouldn't fit into the wives' club, if you know what I mean."

"She seems nice, Brawley."

"Fiercely loyal but definitely an acquired taste, like my dad."

Brandy appreciated the light-hearted conversation and, for a few minutes, forgot the peril they were running from. The farther and farther away from San Diego they got, the more she began to relax.

Maybe Tucker wouldn't approve of her decision, but she definitely felt it was way easier on the nerves. Plus, being beside another man of action, someone she'd known well and knew would do anything to defend his turf and his ladies, brought comfort to her soul. It was just one long road trip. By the time they got up to Oregon, Tucker would be only a few hours from home.

And then everything would be perfect again. She knew he'd figure out a way to make her feel safe.

CHAPTER 15

S VEN TURNED AROUND in his seat to address Tucker. "You still mad?"

"Yes." Tucker glanced out the window, studying the blackness and the grey clouds hovering above the ocean. He was going to hold it over Sven for as long as he could get away with it.

But what was the point? It was going to be a long flight, and the mission had been accomplished, which was the most important thing.

"No," he murmured, still not making eye contact.

Sven quickly slipped from his seat to the one next to Tucker. "Didn't take you for holding grudges."

Tucker glared at him. "Wasn't there another way? Did you have to go all Spygate on us? Do you know what that could have cost?"

Sven's blue eyes smiled even if the rest of his face didn't. "That was my idea. I wanted the plane to be in the air first."

"We could have turned around."

"Sure, but you know that wouldn't happen."

"So you weren't sure if we'd abort if we knew all the connection? See, we do things differently on our team. We trust each other."

Sven punched him gently in the arm. "I trust you all day every day. I don't trust your government. I don't trust the upper crust of your Navy. Remember, we're the 'little country' people. We get squashed. We're careful."

"So get the big brown bear angry and then watch him take out the whole block."

"Pretty much, yes."

"Well, you've had your bite. Don't ever do that to me again. I'm not so sure there is a place for you on our team, in case you were thinking about it. We just don't do this to each other. We die for each other. Don't take my life for granted, and I won't take yours."

Sven held out his hand for a shake. Tucker took it, and they both looked off in opposite directions.

The Norwegian kept prodding. "It sounds like you have some problems at home. Something about a doll delivered to your wife? What's that about?"

"It surprised me. I'm trying to figure out how those assholes in Nigeria came to find us in San Diego."

"It's been all over the news. Your border?"

"Don't remind me. We could fix it. Everyone just has to learn to talk to each other without picking fights." Tucker didn't really want to talk politics. But it came out anyway.

"So let's think carefully. You honestly believe someone from that group flew over to the US and lay in wait for you or your wife? They would have had to know where you came from, even what team you were on. I'm not sure even Jean's people knew all that information. Not that they couldn't have found it."

Tucker thought he had a point and nodded his agreement.

"So the second-best explanation is that someone who is sympathetic to their cause actually lives in San Diego or nearby. Someone they could have talked to by phone."

"But again, they would have to know where we were stationed," Tucker posed.

"Unless they were already there. What if they were positioned there not for you specifically, but because it was close to the Naval base? What if that was the intended eventual target, and you guys just walked on stage?"

"You mean like a sleeper cell?" Tucker asked.

"Exactly that. Can you tell me if incidences like these are more or less frequent?" Sven waited eagerly for Tucker's answer.

But Tucker didn't have to say a word. Then the question popped up again.

"Sven, how exactly did we 'walk on stage' as you say?"

The Norwegian shrugged. "I have no idea. I wasn't there. You were, though. Because they targeted you."

After several minutes, the two warriors fell asleep.

SUNLIGHT MOVED THROUGH the portal window as the jet banked left and lowered altitude. It roused Tucker from a dream he was having. He kept hearing the words, *she'll make a man out of you!* over and over again. Laughter fluttered all around him. He remembered laughing too, holding his belly.

Immediately, he sat up. He remembered exactly the event that triggered the dream. It was his conversation with Jackie Daniels at the flea market in San Diego.

"Holy shit!" he whispered.

Sven opened one bloodshot eye nastily. "Excuse me?"

"I remember now. I think I know how I got singled out. Excuse me, Sven. I gotta talk to Kyle."

Sven stood and repositioned himself across the aisle in a vacant row. Tucker dashed to the front of the plane. Kyle was asleep, his legs resting on the pair of leather chairs in front of him. He slipped onto one of the seats and touched Kyle's right knee.

His LPO jerked awake. "What the hell?" When he saw Tucker,

he relaxed back, rubbing his eyes.

"What time is it?"

"I think it's about zero-five-hundred. But, Kyle, I remember something that might be helpful."

"Shoot. I think I'm awake."

"You remember that day when we went down to the flea market with Brawley? Fredo bought those soccer balls and everyone was making fun of him?"

"Yeah. I remember."

"We met up with Jackie Daniels?"

"Okay, yes. What's up with that?"

"Do you remember I told him I'd gotten married—"

"And you slapped your belly, and he told you it would make you a man—" Kyle interrupted.

"—and Brawley told Jackie's girls he was a war hero and we all cheered for him?" Tucker completed.

"That's what happened. Someone overheard. It was someone from the flea market. Tucker, they must have followed you home."

"That's exactly what I think happened. They waited until we weren't home and left the package at the doorstep. Could have bought that old doll there somewhere too."

"Totally makes sense, Tucker. They targeted you because they saw you talking with Jackie." Kyle stared back up at him a vein in his forehead thumping. "Wonder if Jackie is in any danger."

"We gotta talk to him. We gotta tell the NCIS."

Over the next few minutes, both Kyle and Tucker questioned the other men who that day were there, asking if they remembered any of the crowd around them at the flea market, particularly their faces. Everyone remembered the incident, but no one recalled their audience.

But they all agreed that Jackie might. As a frequent attendee of the swap meets and flea markets in the area, his eyes might pick up something the rest of them would overlook.

TUCKER HAD BEEN told the plane would be given special clearance for landing at Norfolk, since they were on an official mission. They were also warned that the next leg wouldn't have them sitting in such luxury.

Kyle was on the phone with Collins, who would relay the message to Jackie, not only to ask for his help in finding whomever might have left the package, but for a heads-up for his own family's health and safety. The two men were still on the phone when Tucker decided to call Brandy.

"Tucker!" she answered. "Are you back on US soil?"

"I sure am. Can't wait to get home. How's the Marriott?"

He heard a pause at the other end of the line.

"Brandy?"

"Um, Tucker, I didn't do what you asked. I'm so sorry. But I'm with Brawley and Dorie. We're headed to Oregon. We're nearly halfway there, just left the Sacramento area."

"What?" Tucker gripped the cell so hard he actually saw the case bend in his hand.

"I decided to stay with them, to stay together. I didn't want to be alone in that hotel. Figured I'd be safer with Brawley."

"No, no, no! Dammit, Brandy. How am I going to get to you?"

"You can take a plane to"—he waited while she conferred with Brawley—"He says Salem would be the closest. You let us know, and we'll come pick you up."

"Put Brawley on the line." Tucker was ready to explode.

"Hey, glad you're back, bud."

"You fuckin' asshole. I asked her to stay put where they could keep an eye on her."

"Wait a minute, Tucker. You're exaggerating it all out of proportion. We're fine. We've had a very whole day on the road.

We've been able to gas up, get food. Everyone's happy, Tuck. No stress here."

"Brawley, can you put this on speaker?" Tucker begged.

"It's not synced, but yes we've got you on speaker now. Brandy's holding the phone up so we all can hear."

"We're working on a couple of leads, but we don't have anything definite yet. Just clues, places we're starting. We think we know the source. What that means for all of you is that you have to be very, very savvy about what's going on around you at all times. Don't make any unnecessary stops, don't go shopping or wander away from each other or away from other people. Don't allow strangers to get close to your car or to strike up a conversation. Keep your distance from everyone but stay in populated areas. You don't want to be caught alone anywhere, in case you're being followed."

"You really think this could be happening?"

Tucker couldn't believe Brawley was still in denial. "Always possible, Brawley. Until we find someone to detain. Please, please be careful. Since you're halfway up there, I won't demand you return to San Diego, but you took a big risk streaking out on your own. Brawley, you weren't smart."

"Look, Tucker, that's B.S. First, we don't really know if someone's trying to cause us harm or just scare us. And they've done that. Best we're out of the way completely so you guys can tear up the houses or lay in wait for a suspect to do something. But let's be clear. No one has been harmed yet."

"Yet," repeated Tucker.

"When do you arrive in San Diego?"

"Early in the morning. Before sunlight. We're waiting for our flight now."

Brandy cleared her throat. Tucker felt the strain in her words. "Tucker, I'm sorry. I was so scared. There was no one to talk to. I didn't see any of the people they said would be watching over us. I felt like I was totally exposed, and I had to take the only option I felt comfortable with. Please, it wasn't an easy decision to make, sweetheart."

"I understand." Her words melted some of his anger, and he softened his voice. "I'm frustrated, too, because there's nothing I can do. You probably made the right decision, in hindsight. Brawley will guard you with his life, as I would all of you. Just pay attention. Be smart from here on until I get there and we have this figured out and catch someone."

"Thank you for understanding, Tucker."

"Always, Brandy. I don't want anything to happen to you. Any of you."

He let that sink in, hoping they understood the gravity of the problem ahead of them. But then Brawley spoiled it.

"Any other tips you wish to share with us?" he said flippantly. Before Tucker could respond, Brawley quickly apologized. "Okay, that was unfair."

"Damn right. I'll call back when we're back in San Diego. Go straight to Oregon. Don't veer from the path. Stay together."

"We will," Brandy agreed.

Tucker added, "One more thing. Stay armed."

CHAPTER 16

N O ONE SAID a word as the day turned into evening. The I-5 California freeway was nearly deserted. Weather was dry and had started to cool from the heat of the day. They'd been on the road twelve hours when they came to the town of Redding, which lay at the bottom of the Shasta summit, a long desolate stretch of the highway very treacherous in the winter. But without rain or snow, it was easy for Brawley to go over ninety miles an hour, as he had during much of the I-5 stretch.

Brandy had switched seats with Dorie, who talked to keep Brawley awake. She was rooting for having them stay overnight some place, but Brawley was not having any of it.

Jessica had been chattering and awake for a large portion of the trip. They'd let her run around at their various pit stops before the call with Tucker. Now that they had been warned, their stops were quick and efficient.

But thankfully, Jessica was sound asleep when Brawley announced he needed to get gas and the large truck stop just south of Redding was full of truckers and cars going in both directions, clean rest rooms with showers, and a huge restaurant serving homemade pie. It was a trucker's haven where they could use the internet, rent a computer and printer, drop off or pick up music CDs, videos and audiotapes. It even had a self-serve laundry and a twenty-four-hour diesel mechanic. So at midnight, it was probably the busiest stop between Sacramento and Eugene.

"How's your bladder?" Dorie asked her.

"Probably not as bad as yours is. You go first. Both of you go. I'll stay in the car with Jessica."

Brawley handed her the keys. The couple walked arm in arm to the restaurant as Brandy adjusted herself, anxious to get out and stretch. But, as promised, she kept the windows and doors locked.

She should have told them to have a shower, a little alone intimate time together. She knew Dorie could use some warm water and loving kisses. Brawley was probably stiff as a board from all the driving. He was as stubborn as Tucker was and, though Brandy had offered several times, refused to even take a short nap, allowing someone else to drive.

She looked at her feet and found a plastic bottle with about an inch of water left. She sipped it down then allowed her hips to slide over the vinyl seat so her head could rest on the back. Her knees hit Dorie's bucket seat ahead of her. She planned on taking a long, long nap and then volunteer to spell Dorie again so she could do her part to keep Brawley awake and mentally occupied. The energy drinks he was knocking down practically non-stop were helping, but soon, he was going to have to get some real rest. She guessed he'd be purchasing some 5-Hour Energy concentrate inside.

Cars lined up on one side of the pumps, the large rigs on the other. Occasionally, an idiot driver would take up a whole lane and make the huge trucks wait for him to get his diesel from the truck side. But by and large, it was an orderly transition with people washing the bugs off their windshields and checking their tire pressure in between their fill ups. There was a drive-through vehicle wash in both sizes—one for trucks and one for passenger vehicles, which was operating non-stop.

While Brandy watched a couple of truckers with matching beer bellies sharing a soda, and waiting for their rigs to fill, a bright green truck with a black carpenter's rack pulled ahead and parked parallel to Brawley's truck. Two lanky youths exited the truck and peered at the restaurant with binoculars, sharing them back and forth, pointing.

She'd seen that truck before, she was sure of it. Blinking several times, she finally remembered seeing it on Brawley's block when the two of them were inside gathering their additional things before the trip. What were the odds the same identical truck would be way up here in Redding, stopped at the same rest stop?

The odds were too great to calculate.

She tried to dial Brawley, but he didn't pick up. When she dialed Dorie's phone, the cell chirped in the front of the cab. With barely any battery left she tried to dial 911 and her phone died before it could connect.

She continued to watch the men as she started to type a text to Brawley, but again her phone's screen went black. Then one of them pulled a rifle from the cab and balanced it on the roof. He was lining up a shot.

Brandy knew she only had seconds. Scrambling, she nearly fell from the back seat, gripped the passenger side door handle, ripped it open, and lunged into the front of the cab. She pressed on the glove box, and it didn't open. She used a fist and banged on the metal flap. Again, although it was now dented, it didn't open.

Jessica was stirring. She was directly in the line of sight between the youth with the rifle and the toddler. She'd have to distract him, make herself a target to keep Jessica safe. She took a darting glance at the restaurant entrance and still didn't see Dorie or Brawley.

One last time, she kicked the glove box, and finally, it gaped open like the tongue of a robot. She clutched the police special and found it lighter than she was used to. Her hands were shaking so hard she nearly dropped it on the asphalt.

The youth with the rifle was using his scope, fixing on something inside the restaurant. With adrenaline pumping full force, almost enough to make her explode, she held the gun at her side, like she'd seen Tucker do many times.

"Hey!" she yelled, moving to the right, waving her arms above her head. "Are you looking for me?"

Several pedestrians nearby scurried out of the way, and one woman shrieked and ran inside the building, dropping packages behind her.

The two boys whipped around to face her. Their eyes squinted in the overhead lights. The boy on the right began to reach behind him. The one on the left repositioned his rifle—bringing it up to his eye, taking slow, careful aim—while the other began running directly toward her and briefly blocked the shot. She knew what the kid was reaching for because she was doing the same thing herself. But she'd practiced this many times at the shooting range with Tucker. She'd shot with the other wives when they first were dating. It all came surging back to her.

With a last glance at the building's entrance, she took one more leap to the right, away from the truck, raised Brawley's police special from her side, just as she saw the revolver appear in his right hand. Brandy aimed slightly low to the boy's body mass, preparing for recoil like she'd been trained, and pulled the trigger.

She heard Brawley scream and items hit the pavement, but she didn't see him. Her focus was on the trajectory of her round, which lodged in the boy's forehead. The kid with the rifle took a quick shot in her direction, but it went wide to her right and cracked a windshield behind her. Brandy returned fire, and again, her aim was true. It caught him right in the center of his chest, and he dropped.

That's when she heard the screaming, and for a second, she wondered what they were yelling at. Someone tackled her hard, but he was soon pulled off by the angry Brawley, who drew her to his chest in a tight bearhug. She leaned against him like a limp rag and tried to breathe. On the third try, she squeaked, with just enough energy to punch Brawley in the chest.

"I can't breathe!" she gasped, and immediately, he released the pressure, but kept his arms wrapped around her, not letting her fall.

That first delicious inhale felt so good. Then everything turned black.

CHAPTER 17

TUCKER GOT THE call as soon as they landed in San Diego. Sven told him Riley had secured a private jet to get him up to Redding as fast as possible. Collins confirmed the Navy granted him the time to go bring Brandy back. Kelly and Jenna had arrived in Portland for the reunion with a very grateful Mr. Riley.

Brawley met him at the Redding Jetway terminal alone. He explained his wife and daughter were at the hospital with Brandy.

"When you're up to it, Tucker—"

"I'm not up to it."

"She was amazing. Talk about grace under fire. Just sayin'."

"Not fuckin' now."

Tucker had been told about the shootout, of course. He didn't doubt for one minute she was capable of heroic behavior, but he still needed to see her for himself. He knew she would be okay, but he wanted to make sure she understood that this would never happen again. He never wanted her to be in harm's way like this.

He'd done lots of thinking during his long plane trips home and was on the verge of making some big decisions, based on Brandy's frame of mind. He was done with the texting, the Facetime calls, the writing in journals to let her read perhaps some day after he was dead. He was done with it all.

Everything revolved around her. If something had happened to her, if she'd sacrificed herself to save Jessica or to protect Dorie or Brawley, he would be inconsolable. He'd be a shell of the man he once was. And this was too close. Way too close. He couldn't ask this of her ever again.

He and Brawley had formed a kind of mental bond during their growing up years and it was still there right now, even though they didn't say a word. He was furious at his best friend for allowing his wife to get in the middle of something she had no right to be involved in. At the same time, he knew Brawley had just done what he thought best. She was the one who chose. Thank God it worked out.

He'd loved Brawley like a brother. They shared everything together in those days playing against each other in basketball, soccer, and baseball. They shared unmentionable bad dates, and great first dates, breakups and heartaches. Brawley was there for him when he got divorced, when he thought he'd never have a woman again by his side. Now look at him. Now the both of them were expecting babies. It was another life event he shared with Brawley.

And though Brawley couldn't be on the last mission they completed, he'd been there during the first part of it. He'd gotten it kicked off. By accident, Brawley had created the bait that allowed the elimination of the bad guys.

Everything in his life was connected to Brawley. Brandy relied on him, trusted him. He'd made sure she knew where the gun was or the outcome would have been much different. Everything contributed to the result that had the possibility of a happy ending.

After all was said and done, what he thought of Brawley's decision or Brandy's lack of following directions was small potatoes compared to what was really important. They were all safe. They would make it out together, alive. Even the unborn babies would be safe. Life would go on, as long as he protected it. That's what he'd commit the rest of his life to doing.

Brawley drove carefully, as if juggling him around in the cab of his big truck would cause him to explode. But Tucker knew he wasn't that fragile. His conscience was beginning to irritate him. It was time to make his peace.

He glanced over at Brawley, who gave a tiny smile Tucker could see in profile. His eyes remained pinned to the road.

"You know what really bothers me more than anything, Brawley?"

"I think I have a pretty good idea."

"I couldn't control any of it. Not one fuckin' thing. No one did what I asked. And yet, somehow, everything worked out."

"Well, you have the little issue of a hearing on the shooting, but I think she'll be cleared, don't you?"

"I'm not even thinking about that."

"I know. I'm just as much at fault as you are, Tucker. Going all big man at the flea market. You did hear the story, didn't you?"

"I think I missed it."

"When Collins asked Jackie about that day, the terp remembered having conversations with an older couple at the flea market. They compared their immigration process. The couple made their living selling things from their West African heritage, and were very excited about becoming Americans, just like Jackie. The one thing they had a problem with were their two youngest boys, both radicalized by recent trips overseas. The boys were caught up in some false idea they were freedom fighters. He remembered they were distressed the boys were out of control. Just as they feared, the investigators found out the boys were being groomed for something very public and very big, a massive show of force against the Navy."

"I feel sad for them. How is that possible, Brawley? Does that make me a wimp?"

"Because you're a decent human being. Because you're trying to help the innocents get away from being preyed upon. If you weren't a man with honest feelings, you'd kill with a coldness that would repel anyone who knew you. You're not that guy. You care about people. And you find home with others who live as intensely as you do."

Tucker thought about all that. "You do a pretty good job of buttering someone up, Brawley."

"If you're saying you're strong enough to accept the truth about yourself, well then, yes. You could call it buttering you up."

The Redding hospital was straight ahead, perched on a hilltop overlooking the deep green valley forged by the Sacramento River. They parked near the Emergency entrance and Brawley walked Tucker past the nurses' station to the rear elevator and up to the third floor.

He stopped to address his best friend before entering Brandy's room. "For the record, Tucker, I'm sorry. I made a mistake, and it almost cost me the life of my best friend's wife. That's unforgiveable, but I'm still asking for it."

Tucker grabbed Brawley and the two hugged because there wasn't anything else that could be said or done.

"I appreciate that, Brawley. Now, tell me what I'm getting into."

Brawley put his hands on his hips. "Nope. I'm going to let you walk in cold and figure it out for yourself."

She was sleeping with Jessica tucked into her arm. Tucker didn't think he'd ever seen her so beautiful, even though it appeared she'd roughed up her face a bit. He was going to have the ass of the person who did that to her, if he was still alive.

Her long hair had been brushed and wasn't the usual tangle on the pillowcase he was used to seeing. Dorie was bent over on the wheeled table that held her water. She was also fast asleep.

He turned to let her sleep, when Brandy opened her eyes and

gave him a big smile. Her expression changed as her hand came up and felt the bandage that had been placed there.

In two long strides, he was at her bedside, suddenly ashamed he hadn't brought her anything like flowers she so richly deserved.

"Hey, sweetheart," he whispered and kissed her even though she whimpered. He didn't care and kissed her harder.

Tucker positioned himself on the edge of the bed as Jessica started to stir but then found another comfortable position in Brandy's arms.

"You look so beautiful. You are so amazing, Brandy. And I'm so sorry you had to go through all this."

She was just staring up at him, tears streaming down her cheeks. "Never in a million years did I think when you taught me to shoot that I'd need that training. I really hesitated, almost didn't do it. That was what I was the most scared of. I thought, if I didn't get over this hurdle, I wouldn't live to regret anything or to see you or our daughter."

"Son."

"Whatever."

"You did good. Brawley is over-the-moon impressed with your tactical skills," he said through his chuckle.

"There was nothing tactical about it. Point and shoot."

"The decision to shoot the right person is always the biggest thing, Brandy. That's what I meant. No one else was harmed." He touched the bandage on her lip. "Who can I punish who did this?"

"Oh." She started to giggle, which woke Jessica up in earnest. Dorie rose, craned her neck, gave Tucker a hug, and took the toddler from her, exiting the room. "It was some good Samaritan thinking he was stopping a crazed hormonal woman from shooting at her boyfriend or something. I think I chipped a tooth."

"He beat you up?"

"No, he tackled me! Knocked me unconscious."

Tucker did begin to laugh behind his hand, in spite of himself.

"It wasn't funny, Tucker," she barked.

"No, I understand. But he was being brave."

He loved the flash of anger in her eyes, that fighting spirit that wanted justice. If the gentleman hadn't knocked her out, she'd have gotten the better of him, Tucker was certain.

"I'll show you how to fend off an attacker next," he said through his laughter.

"No, don't! Because that's what will happen next. Don't you dare!" Her eyes were huge, her cheeks had pinked up, and in all her fiery loveliness, she was speaking honestly.

He loved her more today than he ever had.

"The baby's fine?"

"Yes. They said you can listen to the heartbeat again, if you want."

"Okay, let's do that," Tucker responded. He was anxious to replace all the nasty images in his mind of what she might have lived through.

An aid entered the room, bringing in a tray. "We've got breakfast here," the young girl said.

Brandy shrugged. "They had pancakes."

The tray was set on the wheeling cart and moved closer to Brandy.

"Should I order you some?"

"I don't think so. I've had more coffee in the past ten hours than I get in a month. What I really need to do is get you home, get you in that shower, and then get you in my bed."

Brandy stared lovingly at the pancakes. "After my breakfast?"

He stood up, shaking his head.

"Mr. Hudson?" a voice from the doorway announced.

Tucker saw one of the nurses standing there.

"I have someone who would like to speak with you."

He followed the nurse to the hallway and then several doors down to a meditation room/chapel. A white-haired man in a modern, gadget-encrusted electric wheelchair sat in the aisle, his back turned.

"You wanted to speak to me, sir?" Tucker asked.

The wheelchair turned effortlessly. The disabled gentleman was disarmingly handsome, with the brightest blue eyes Tucker had ever seen. He wore an expensive deep blue suit with a designer shirt and tie. His shoes were highly polished and appeared never worn.

The man's heavily veined hands worked the controls of the electric device until he was close enough to extend his hand.

"I'm Colin Riley, Jenna's most grateful father, Mr. Hudson. Can I call you Mr. Hudson?"

Tucker shook the man's hand. He was surprised to feel the strength of Mr. Riley's firm handshake.

"Of course, Mr. Riley. Nice to meet you too."

Several other things began to surface as Colin Riley started speaking. He was measured. His eyes were friendly and warm but far from weak. Tucker could even say that the man was driven.

"Sit down, Mr. Hudson. I won't take much of your time." He smiled. "I know this is a special day, as mine was yesterday, and I have you to thank for that."

"It was our job, really. I'm not the team leader. That would be Kyle Lansdowne."

"Yes, I'm well aware of that. But you had more skin in the game, shall we say."

Tucker bristled at this a bit. "Sir?"

"It's a vulgar term, I admit, especially since you nearly lost your wife completing this mission. Many important games in business use athletic competitions to characterize them. I'm going to have to learn a more appropriate way to describe them."

Tucker's intuition was firing red hot. He wasn't sure which ledger of the scale the man sat. But one thing was evident. He was an extremely powerful man and was used to wielding it.

"Just what did you want to speak to me about? I'd like to get back to my wife, if you don't mind."

"I wanted to thank you in person."

"Well, you've done that, sir. We just did our job."

"No, you did my job."

Again, the hackles on the back of Tucker's neck began to stand up.

"Excuse me, Mr. Riley?"

"You did a very personal task for me, even though, technically, you work for the United States Navy. I helped with some of the logistics, but I would not have used these resources if it weren't for the fact that my very foolish daughter had followed in the footsteps of her unfortunate and equally foolish brother. She's flawed. But she's all I have left. Other than my billions, of course."

Tucker was getting annoyed with how heavily laced with power and privilege his conversation was. It wasn't an arena he was familiar, nor was he comfortable with.

"You trying to impress me, Mr. Riley? Because billions of dollars don't impress me. People do. And bad people motivate me to want to squish them like a bug, like a pimple on freedom's ass."

Colin Riley beamed, his eyes filling with water. "I've grossly underestimated you, Mr. Hudson."

"Whatever," Tucker said, finally at his limit. "Look, I'm glad it turned out. I'm happy you're reunited and sorry for the loss of your son. Now I gotta leave, and I'm not going to argue anymore with you. My wife is the most valuable thing in my life, and that's where I'm going."

Tucker turned around and stormed out of the chapel. He could hear the wheelchair whining behind him. He wasn't going to stop for anything. His hands balled into fists.

"Mr. Hudson, please take my card," Tucker finally heard.

He didn't bother to turn around. "No thanks, sir."

"What if someone paid you to go take care of those bugs and made it so you never had to worry about money again?"

Tucker stopped. Wheelchair or no, he was about to deck the guy, stomp on his nice blue suit, and rip some of his hair out. He inhaled deeply three times and then faced the man again.

"One last time, Mr. Riley. My services are not for sale. The U.S. Navy owns my ass. They trained me and believed in me, twice now. They've given me a job I wake up loving to do each and every day. I get insurance. My wife's pregnancy is covered, I'm covered, the kids will get college paid for if I die, and I own my life."

He lunged forward, his face not more than a foot away from Mr. Riley's face. The man was still smiling in rapt adulation, and Tucker wanted to smack the smile right off his mug.

"I *own* my life."

Riley sat still, raised his hand and presented his card.

"We have much to discuss, Mr. Hudson. And much to learn from each other. I suggest you think about it. You can have all that and your dignity and your soul and your profession. Let me help."

Tucker ripped the card from the man's fingers, whipped around, and headed through the doors to Brandy's ward.

Brawley and Dorie were standing at the nurse's station, watching them bounce and play with Jessica. His best friend took one look at Tucker's expression and stood to full attention.

Tucker ignored them, addressing the nurses. "Can I take my wife home, *now*?"

CHAPTER 18

T HE LAST OF their boxes were loaded into the driveway. The college kids they'd hired were happy with the sandwiches and the extra twenty dollars Brandy gave them apiece. She promised to let them know when they had a work party to rid the yard of much of the shrubbery, which gave privacy but ate up too much territory. She wanted a play structure, a nice perimeter fence for both the front and back yards, and a lawn. She wanted a puppy for the baby to play with some day. Her list of plans for this house was never-ending.

Dorie was nearing her term as Brandy was just beginning to show. Ever since the close of escrow, the two friends had been busy wallpapering one of the bedrooms for the nursery and painting the kitchen and most of the rest of the house. But Dorie wasn't going to be available any longer. Getting up and down a ladder was becoming too much of a risk.

Brandy drew up sketches of what she wanted the front of the house to look like and what the rooms would look like with their very sparse furniture. She calculated and planned for future buys when things went on sale. She scoured the free used furniture listings and picked up some nice finds.

Tucker arrived with drawer pulls, towel bars and new light fix-tures from one of the big home improvement stores.

"Got some things I think you'll like," he said as he passed by her with his shopping bags, giving her a peck on the cheek.

"Oh, show me!"

He brought the new hardware into the kitchen and spread everything out on the old Formica countertop. "This old stuff is kind of growing on me, Brandy," he said as his hand brushed over the mottled "space age" themed surface, complete with silver flakes and elliptical circles circa the 1960's.

"I know. It's the character of this house. When we re-do the kitchen, then I'd like some granite. But nothing wrong with this the way it is. I hate throwing out something that can still be used."

"Exactly. And we'll remove everything carefully so Coop can sell it at the flea market." He laughed. Then he remembered that day before he left on deployment, the day that had changed everything.

The purchase of the house had taken up most of the money her father had given her from her mother's estate, so they were being frugal. They knew it would be a few months before another deployment came up, so they did what they could and planned everything else out in stages.

"Come, let me show you," Tucker said as he picked up several brushed chrome light fixtures and two long boxes of towel racks, entering the master bathroom. She followed him.

He held up the light bar that would be installed over the sink.

"I saw some mirrored medicine cabinets that would work great and will fit here. I'd like you to see them first," he said.

"Sure. I like the way that looks. I totally approve. The racks go nice with all that too."

"I got one that matches for the guest bath. I think I found a plumber at the store who said he could install a shower over the tub there. We're kind of stuck with this thing," he said as he pointed to the tiny tiled shower.

Brandy came up behind him and hugged him. "Mr. Hudson, this will be the nicest tiled closet anyone has ever seen. It's the perfect size. All we need is tension shelves."

Tucker gave his approval.

They liked to eat dinner upstairs in the "observatory," as it was now labeled. Brandy found the narrow stairwell comforting and knew it would be even nicer once she was further along. Tonight, she ordered some Italian food and had a nice bottle of red wine breathing on the folding table that was their fine dining area for Tucker. She had a bottle of cranberry mineral water for her.

It was getting to be near time when the food would be delivered. She took out a clean tablecloth, some silverware and two wine goblets from her boxes downstairs and set the table with some roses she'd found growing wild in the miniscule back yard. Tucker followed her up.

"I'm starved. When does it arrive?"

She checked her smartwatch. "About twenty minutes."

"Let's get this wine poured. Is it ready?" he asked.

"Whenever you want."

She stood in front of the large picture window that faced the Pacific Ocean. The sun had begun to hang, but it was still an hour until sunset.

"My queen," he said as he handed her the goblet with her fizzy cranberry juice. He toasted them and, before he drank, gave her a long kiss. "Who knew, Brandy, we could live this way?"

"You've come a long way, baby." She giggled. "Remember that dumpy apartment with the Big Booby magazines on the coffee table. Those things were awful!"

Tucker took a sip of his wine. "Guilty as charged. That was before I had the real thing."

His kiss this time lingered down her neck, headed toward her cleavage.

The doorbell rang. It sounded like an apartment buzzer.

Tucker stopped and grimaced. "That's the next thing I'm going to fix. We need a decent doorbell. I'll be right back."

Brandy watched from above as Tucker paid the driver. He pointed to two wooden crates containing young palm trees that had been placed at the side by the front stoop.

The driver shook his head, waved and returned to his car with the plastic "Flo's Pizza" sign attached to the roof.

"Hey, Brandy," Tucker called out while he was climbing the stairs. "Where did you get those palm tree?"

"I never saw them before. They must have just arrived."

Tucker set the food on the table, but they both went over to the window and examined the boxes, and then looked at each other.

"Not another package," Brandy said.

"Fuck."

In a flash, he was drilling down the stairwell. Brandy carefully followed behind him at a much slower pace.

An envelope was affixed with a piece of stretchy gold twine. On the outside was written,

To Brandy and Tucker, from a grateful friend.

Tucker let the note drop back against the palm tree base.

"Well, open it. You can't be serious to think it's a night letter, now, do you Tucker?"

"I don't want to touch it."

"Well then, I will."

She reached for the envelope and Tucker stopped her, holding her wrist tight and then putting his body between her and the trees.

"Tucker. What's going on?"

"I think I know who it's from. No, it's not a night letter. But it's not something I want to accept."

"Tucker, it's one of those fancy palm trees. You know how much they cost? Like one hundred dollars a foot. And there's two of them! No, wait, they're the cluster type, so we got, what Five? Six palm trees in each box?"

"I'll get something to wheel them out to the street, and someone else can enjoy them."

"Tucker, you're being an idiot." Brandy struggled to remove her arm from his grip.

"I'm protecting my tribe."

Something odd had come over her husband. A dark mood lingered from something she knew was being kept as a secret.

"Look, I'm sorry." Tucker gently slipped his arm around her waist. "Let's eat first, and then we can have a chat. I'll open the envelope up after that, okay?"

She was moved by the softness in his voice and agreed.

They ate silently, watching the roses and peaches of the sky above the ocean, until at last the sun set and a bright green light formed at the last minute before it fell below the horizon and out of view.

"We got the flash!" he said.

His face was bathed in an orange glow as he continued to watch the sunset.

He was the phenomenon in the room, she thought. He was the handsome warrior who had brought life and love to her world, who had turned a life of frustration into a fairytale.

Green toads and danger along the way, of course.

She smiled at her own internal thoughts.

"What's got you laughing?" he asked.

"You. I'm so grateful I met you, Tucker. I can't imagine what my life would have been like without you."

"Nah, someone else would have swept you off your feet." He leaned across the table and gave her a kiss. "You're so easy to love, sweetheart. I think I'm the lucky one."

"When I think of what I was trying to be, it was like stuffing my personality into the mold of what I thought a girl should want and have and dream for, just like that bustier at Dorie's wedding. You remember that contraption?"

"Who could forget? To see you trussed up like that, it was such a turn-on."

She frowned.

"Don't be that way. I'm all mixed up, I admit. I love all the ampleness of your body. I always have. You're perfect for me."

She sipped the last of her mineral water and then set the glass down. "Okay. So now we're having that chat?"

Tucker looked up at the ceiling, rolled his head, and sighed. He leaned forward, put his arms on the table, and fiddled with the roses, causing a couple of petals to drop.

"At the hospital, Colin Riley came to visit."

"Who is he?"

"He's the benefactor, the one who helped out with the trip. He arranged the special flights, rented the big house on Gran Canaria, arranged the cars, everything. We couldn't have done it without his support."

"Okay. And?" She knew there was more to the story.

"We rescued his daughter. You know that."

"I do. You guys did a great job."

"Yeah, well, it spilled over, of course. You got dragged in, and—"

"And I shot them."

Tucker winced. "Yes, Brandy, you shot them. Thank you very much for that."

The cat-and-mouse conversations they had were so much fun for her. She loved seeing him spill something he didn't want to tell. It was impossible for him to tell her a lie or to hide his fear, although he tried.

"What about the hospital again?" she said, angling her head.

"He came to thank me. And he did."

"End of story? Somehow, I don't think so."

"He gave me his card and said sometime he'd like to talk to me, share ideas, and that stuff."

"And?"

"Well, you know, Brandy, I can't share what I do with anyone. I'm not supposed to have those conversations. I could lose my clearance, be out of a job, and I love my job."

"He offered you a job. I knew it."

"No, he didn't. He wanted to talk."

"So talk to him. He's a billionaire."

Brandy had suspected something had happened that night at the hospital, because Tucker had been hell-bent on renting a car and driving her home. He'd practically fought the nurses on staff to get her released. He made quite a scene. She knew something had caused that. And Brawley wasn't talking.

"I want to see the envelope. If it's what you say, there shouldn't be anything you can't show me. Or is there?"

"No, Brandy. I have no secrets."

"But you do."

"No, I don't." He wrinkled his brow. "What are you talking about?"

Brandy stood up and walked to a bag of groceries and plucked out the Big Butt magazine she'd pulled from his gun bag when they moved. It was frayed and dog-eared. But it was one of his, and she knew he'd been saving it as one of his favorites.

"Geez, Brandy. I didn't know I still owned that."

She loved the look on his face as she slowly placed the magazine in front of him. "Consider it dessert," she whispered in his ear.

She headed for the stairs and then stopped.

"Are you going to join me on the front porch?"

Tucker leapt to his feet and slipped past her, running down the stairs ahead of her. She met him on the outside. He removed the envelope, opened it, and took out a cream card. Brandy looked over his shoulder at the distinctive handwriting.

Brandy and Tucker,

As I've said before I can't thank you enough for your wonderful gift of my daughter's life. These trees should reach the height of thirty feet or more, so I hope you will plant them where you can enjoy watching them grow, as you grow your family and enjoy your new home. But don't place them anywhere they will spoil that fantastic view.

I'm glad our paths have crossed. I hope someday to be able to be more a part of your lives. During the time these trees grow, and hopefully before they get to be thirty feet, and I'm gone, I'd like to sit down and thank you in person and talk about a future that could be for all of us.

Thank you again,
Your friend,
Colin Riley.

Tucker's eyes were filled with tears.

"Honey?"

"Well, I was just thinking. Can you imagine how he feels, losing a son and nearly losing a daughter? And let me say just this, knowing he gets to spend the rest of his life with her is payment enough. He doesn't need to thank me. I've lived with death before, and it's terrible. I've had people die in my arms. I thought we lost Brawley at one point. I thought I lost you."

She hugged her big man with the big heart.

"No, Tucker, you'll never lose me. Not ever."

SEALED PROTECTION

Bone Frog Brotherhood Book 5

SHARON HAMILTON

CHAPTER 1

TUCKER HUDSON, DECORATED Navy SEAL from legendary SEAL Team 3, spent the entire weekend in San Diego hacking and pulling up old vines and shrubs that had lost their shape from plantings more than thirty years ago, as well as obliterating escaping bamboo invading from neighboring properties. He'd started with hand clippers, then moved on to large tree nips, electric hedge trimmers and finally a small chainsaw to remove the stubborn foliage. It was Brandy's vision that this area become a combination garden paradise and vegetable garden, even though it was technically the front yard of their new home.

If it was what Brandy wanted, Tucker was going to make it so, regardless of how sunburned and sweaty he got, or how much noise and dust he created. It was vegitative warfare this willing warrior was fighting for the bride of all his dreams, mother of his soon-to-be born son.

Well, that's what he was counting on—a son.

Of course, if Brandy wanted a girl, it would probably be a girl. He no longer marveled at how many of her dreams became reality. His job was to follow along the gilded path she created with her zest for life and her overall exuberance for living to the fullest.

She'd keep him young, with their over fifteen-year difference in age. When he was hobbling around on a cane, he'd still be her knight, fixing things and balancing himself on dangerous ladders to hang pictures or change light fixtures or drapes, just because Brandy wanted it that way.

Each time he stopped, gulping down half a quart of ice water, he'd glance over at the large boxes containing the gift palm trees they'd yet to plant in the ground. It was on his daily honey-do list, to water those plants, and every time he did so, he thought about the man who gifted them, Colin Riley – a man he met on his last mission.

As I've said before, I can't thank you enough for your wonderful gift of my daughter's life. These trees should reach the height of thirty feet or more, so I hope you will plant them where you can enjoy watching them grow, as you grow your family and enjoy your new home. But don't place them anywhere they will spoil that fantastic view.

I'm glad our paths have crossed. I hope someday to be able to be more a part of your lives. While these trees grow, and hopefully before they get to be thirty feet, and I'm gone, I'd like to sit down and thank you in person and talk about a future that could be for all of us.

He'd memorized nearly every word, having read the card over so many times—something he never would admit to Brandy. He noted the many-fingered branches fluttered in the breeze as if saying hello. If he put those roots in Brandy's Secret Garden, they'd grow. That would mean the man who'd sent them would become more and more a fixture in their lives.

He hadn't decided whether or not that was a good thing.

TUCKER KNEW HIS next deployment was coming up in another thirty days. He'd promised Brandy that he'd be home for the baby's birth, and he hoped he could keep that vow. But the short trip back to the Canary Islands required his leadership, since their normal team leader, Chief Kyle Lansdowne, was off on special assignment to the State Department. Although technically still a newer member of the squad, he'd done ten years previous to his re-enlistment and re-qualification. At forty-one years of age, he was one of the oldest members. Outranked by nearly everyone, the guys still looked upon him as the unofficial LPO in Kyle's absence. And that's why Kyle wanted him on this mission.

The job would revisit some of the bad guys they'd encountered several months ago, when they rescued the daughter of the man who gave him the potted palm trees.

He'd tried to get billionaire Colin Riley's face and the squeak of his wheelchair out of his mind, but the man was a stubborn memory. He knew why. Riley had scratched an itch that was now inflamed. He'd dared to offer Tucker a job lining up a secret security force for good. But that would mean that Riley would *own* Tucker. He wasn't going to even let the man give him a proper presentation. The answer was no before Riley could finish his first imaginary PowerPoint.

No one, not even a billionaire offering a lifestyle he could only fantasize about, was ever going to own Tucker Hudson. He hadn't become a SEAL for fame or fortune. He wasn't about to change that all now.

But on days like these, when he was working in the yard and trying to get the house into shape to prepare for the new baby, it would have been nice to rent some equipment to make it a little easier on his body. Unlike Colin Riley, Tucker and Brandy's funds were precarious. They were living on one salary, and even as a SEAL, the pay wasn't great.

They'd just bought a major fixer on the island, overgrown, neglected and mercifully hidden from the other large homes in the neighborhood. Their furniture came from second-hand stores. The new refrigerator they bought had a six-inch dent in the door and was missing handles. The new stove had a cracked black glass door. These were all things that could be fixed, of course, but after they finished purchasing the new vanity and toilet for their bathroom. Everything they bought came from some Asian warehouse where not a word of English was spoken. The damned place smelled of fish, reminding him of some of the villages in Africa and South America. All the cabinets, appliances, and fixtures were cosmetically damaged but deeply discounted.

It was a delicate balance, calculating where their next paycheck would be spent. With luck, it would all be complete before the new arrival.

He was expecting some help from his childhood best friend, Brawley Hanks, as well as T.J. Talbot and several other guys from Team 3. Brandy was off getting things for a "thank you" barbeque after a few hours of work and drinking beers until the stars came out. He'd made a firepit, lined it with bricks, and found an old grate he could use as a spark catcher. He wanted to have a bonfire without setting the neighbors' houses on fire.

But damn, he heard that mechanical whine from Riley's wheelchair again and wished he could wipe his memory, because now it was becoming really annoying. He turned up the music on his second-hand paint-spattered boombox, which successfully masked the noise by blaring country music from a local AM station.

He dug out several deep roots of shrubs he'd castrated and tossed them to the side. He skimmed the top hardpan layer with a shovel and discovered a soft sandy soil underneath that could eventually be habitable for Brandy's garden.

His whole life had changed dramatically after that fateful New Years' eve, two and a half years ago—the night of Brawley and Dorie's wedding, where he watched Brandy walk down the aisle behind the other bridesmaids.

He never was able to recover from that vision of her and that damned bustier, which accentuated the features he loved most in women: their bosoms and curvy hips.

That brought a smile to his face. They'd both been running away from something that night, he remembered. He was running away from loneliness, not on a Team at that time but desperately needing the connection. Brandy was running away from the same thing but was the only one being honest with herself. She wanted one perfect night. Well, hell, he happened to be there and available, and the attraction was instantaneous, even when he had to hold her hair back as she threw up. She was dosing. Tucker was just fishing. And like two shooting stars in the night sky, they slammed into one another. And that was it.

It was a simple case of undeniable chemistry. Not a damned thing he could do about it, either. Not that he wanted to.

Now he was going to have a little "orbit" of his own. That's what he and Brawley had called children when they were growing up. Little annoying things who got in the way. Except now he had a whole new appreciation for offspring. He'd been given a miracle, even though he was a poor, dumb frogman. He wondered why God had trusted him to become a father. But he had a fierce love for Brandy that loomed larger than a battleship. And that gave him hope for a bright future.

Although he would never tell a soul this, he believed in the healing power of true love. He was a big, tough SEAL, but he was a hopeless romantic.

Brandy drove up in the Hummer, following the driveway on the right side of the property. She stopped close to where he was standing, and he threw his shovel down to help her get out of the truck. Before he could get there, she'd slid out until her dangling feet touched the ground. Her belly must have been infringing on her lungs, because just as he arrived at her side, she paused, closed her eyes, and took several slow, deep breaths.

"I could have helped you. Next time, don't be so impatient, Brandy."

She gave him a sweet smile, her cheeks pink and plump, like the rest of her.

"Oh, stop it, Tucker, I'm not an invalid."

"But I want to help you, sweetheart."

She patted her palm against his cheek. "Silly man. Women have been having babies for thousands of years and managed quite well."

He wrapped his arms around her and forced her to hug him back, as he whispered in her ear, "But they don't drive Hummers that they have to HALO jump from. Don't do that anymore, okay, sweetheart?"

Brandy's VW bug was in the shop until Monday. But she'd not been able to drive it the past couple of weeks because she couldn't fit behind the steering wheel. He didn't have to mention that at all.

She relaxed and squeezed him back. "My protector."

"Always." He meant it.

He rounded the truck, retrieving the two grocery bags, and then walked beside her into the house.

"Where's your help?" she asked.

"Delayed." He set the bags on the countertop and sorted through the contents. Finding two five-pound packages of marked down hamburger meat, he quickly placed it in the refrigerator then examined her other purchases. He was delighted to find a half gallon of rocky road ice cream. "Nice!" He held the package up to her smiling face.

"Not sure if we have any more of that chocolate syrup, but I bought whipped cream."

He shook the metal can and wiggled his eyebrows. "Danger-ous!"

"Uh-huh. I think that's where the chocolate syrup went." She blushed, grabbed the whipped cream, and slipped it next to the hamburger meat. Tucker put the ice cream in the freezer.

She handed him three six-packs of beer bottles, one at a time. Then she handed him a large pre-made salad with dressing and a dozen ears of corn.

"If everyone comes, we'll have to split the corn in half. And I got some fresh cherry tomatoes, but I'd like to go to the Farmer's Market tomorrow, if you're game to get more veggies."

"Sure thing. Let's go early."

"I miss not being able to run over to Dad's store and just pick stuff up."

Tucker wrapped his arm around Brandy's non-existent waist. "But now he's free to travel, and he's happy, babe. Jillian's taking good care of him."

"Not complaining," she sighed as she leaned into him, placing the side of her face against his chest. "I can't wait to *not* be pregnant. I want to see her little face. I'd also like to be able to see my toes again, take a bath, put my own shoes on—stuff like that."

Tucker snickered softly but didn't correct her. He accepted the fact that she was probably right—they'd be having a daughter. How women knew these things mystified him.

"Hello?" Brawley's booming voice nearly vibrated the windows.

Tucker walked into the living room and found his best friend carrying a large brown shopping bag. "What did you bring?"

"Some energy drinks, beer, water, more beer, and a pie."

Tucker noticed Brawley's skin was tanned, his eyes were clear, and he appeared to be in about the best shape of his life. These days, he no longer smelled of alcohol, either. He'd spent several months in a private brain clinic while he slowly came back to the living, becoming more and more the man Tucker used to know. He'd just transitioned to work support for the Teams as a BUD/S instructor until he could get his twenty in. Alcohol wasn't restricted but closely monitored. Tucker could see he was following the program.

"You look like you've been enjoying the beach," said Tucker.

"Only this time I'm *watching* the wet and sandy. Were we ever that dumb, Tucker? Those little tadpoles don't know shit about anything. They look like they've just begun to shave."

"I think we were the same," Tucker disagreed.

"Nope. You never looked like a boy. You were built like a man from the first time I hurled that pitch at you and you hit it over the fence. My coach said we were going to have to check your birth certificate. All that black hair all over your body when you were ten. Fuckin' ten, damn you!"

Tucker ducked so Brawley's punch didn't connect. "Dorie coming later on?"

"Yup, I'm supposed to text her when you're ready." He leaned around Tucker to speak to his wife. "Brandy? She's sorry she couldn't get a sitter to come help you today."

Brawley and his wife had four-month-old twin boys. They also had a three-year-old daughter, Jessica.

"No worries. We're doing very simple tonight. Hamburgers, homemade potato salad, green salad, and corn. I got ice cream for dessert. Just easy stuff. No candlelight gourmet meals tonight," she answered. "But we'll have plenty, so I hope she'll come and bring the kids."

Several minutes later, three other Team Guys arrived, each bringing more beer and a couple more salads. Fredo brought a rototiller and more garden tools in the back of his beater truck, including a flat scraper Tucker grabbed onto right away for stubbing out the tufts and roots in the future garden area. He also brought some scrap lumber for the firepit.

It was a typical SEAL work party. There was lots of attitude, some practical joking that had them chasing after each other, dousing themselves with water bottles or beer, and long silent minutes of solid work. Tucker laid out what had to be done, and without assigning anyone to any specific task, the men just filled in, working as one cohesive team.

That's how they worked overseas too. It was like they maintained a hive brain. One person's good idea would be supported and acted upon by others. It didn't take long before the entire front yard area was tilled, raked, and looked like powdered chocolate, instead of the abandoned weed fest it was when they first bought the home.

T.J. began to build a berm running parallel to the sidewalk, extending it along the side of the driveway. The rest of the men joined in, until it was complete.

"You gonna put in a fence on top? asked Fredo.

Tucker thought that was an excellent idea. "Maybe just a couple of feet high, tall enough to keep a toddler from escaping, yes! Gonna have to get the materials next paycheck, though."

"You got some extras left over from your new fence, T.J." Fredo nodded to the tall medic.

"I'll get Joe Benson. You remember? Frankie's dad? We'll come over and build that for you," said T.J.

"Dude, now you're making me feel obligated. Spoiling me." Tucker was a little embarrassed.

"Just say thank you, Tuck. I don't think you fully comprehend what it's going to be like here very soon. Life will never be the same," T.J. returned.

Fredo stepped up and pat his shoulder. The Mexican SEAL was more than a foot shorter. "We're helping you out now, 'cause no way you'll see us hanging around after the baby comes. I'll let Mia and the wives do all that shit."

Fredo's comments drew much agreement.

The men stacked Tucker's tools beside the front porch and returned the other tools and equipment to the bed of Fredo's truck. Tucker could hear soft music coming from the warm, orange insides of their little fixer as Brandy was beginning to set things out on two long folding tables. She brought a tray of hamburgers ready for the grill and turned the gas on to warm it up.

Her voice caught all of their attention. "You guys go on inside and wash up. You can text the girls to come over. I wanted to eat in about thirty minutes. That sound fine?"

"Yes, ma'am," was the resounding response.

As two of the men went inside, looking down at their cells, T.J. and Tucker moved several stumps next to the firepit, adding them to the large boulders to create makeshift stools for later enjoyment. An old wine half barrel was rolled over to join the circle.

T.J. dusted his hands together and wiped his forehead with the back of his shirt sleeve. He pointed to the palm trees, standing to attention, their long green fingers waving. "Those are real cool, Tucker. Where are you going to put these?"

"Haven't decided."

"I'd put them side by side up front along the berm. Sort of makes a statement, you know?"

Tucker examined the area where the berm turned to follow along the driveway. If he got a few more, he could make a palm tree entrance that would befit the Queen of Sheba.

He shook the vision off and nodded in the direction of the front. "I like putting them up front."

It would be the furthest from the house possible. But they'd be planted. And maybe they'd guard his little family like lions on a grand, gated entrance.

CHAPTER 2

B RANDY WAS RELEGATED to their large second-hand recliner and made to prop her feet up. Fredo's wife, Mia, had noticed her ankles were swollen from the heat and from being on them most the day. Dorie sat next to her with the twins fast asleep in a double stroller. Luci and Mia were cleaning up dishes in the kitchen and putting away leftovers.

Dorie's daughter, Jessica, had been running wild outside with several of the other kids, including Fredo and Mia's Ricardo and their twin toddlers. Danny and Luci Begay's two boys—Griffin and his adopted Iraqi boy, Ali—had been conducting sniper attacks on the adult population, and occasionally the other children.

At home, Griffin was Ali's favorite target. Here, the boys used cherry tomatoes plucked from Brandy's green salad. Every one of the children had red stains on their clothes and on their faces. Most of the SEALs did as well.

As Ali ran past Brandy, she grabbed him by the arm and firmly stopped his forward march.

"Ali, not inside the house!" She kept her grip on his upper arm until she saw a forlorn nod after several seconds of trying to wiggle free. She pulled him toward her. "I mean it, Ali. You're going to get one of the other ones hurt. They're smaller and can't keep up. And I've just painted the inside of this house, unless you want to come and spend all day repainting it. Right?"

His dark eyes grimaced as the group of younger children accordioned behind him, finally catching up. The little orphan was embarrassed, she could tell. Her heart softened.

She scanned the crowd of children and knew these were little eyes of future SEALs. At this age, Tucker would have been right in the middle of them.

Dorie inserted herself into the conversation. "Griffin, you know better. You have to show your brother. Don't let him get into trouble."

Griffin spouted off, "But he started it. It was all his idea. I told him!"

That caught the attention of Luci Begay from the kitchen. "You two!" she shouted, wiping her hands on a towel. "What am I going to do with you? Give me that," she demanded of Ali.

He pulled away defiantly, clutching the slingshot Danny had made for him out of an old inner tube and remnants of their burned-out soccer stadium.

"I won't do it inside. I promise. Honest." His expression was pure angel, and Brandy could see all the stories were true. He was so advanced for his age in physical ability, and, because of how he'd had to live in the war zone, he was stronger and faster than anyone else. He'd seen things none of the other children ever would, if they were lucky. Now in second grade, he was prone to getting into fights with much older boys.

And he usually won.

Luci sighed and told them to go outside and pick on the men sitting around the firepit. "And be careful that Jessica, Courtney, and the twins don't get hurt."

Ali and Griffin instantly showed expressions of horror. To make matters worse, Courtney Talbot scolded them in her pert, five-year-old voice. "Your mother's right. Don't you know you have to be nice to girls?" She gave the hands-on-her-hips pose just like a little mother.

In the background, Ricardo snickered, and Ali whirled around to face him but thought better of it before he could begin his defensive attack.

"What's this?" said Brawley, who suddenly appeared from the outside, holding Jessica.

"I started it," giggled Brandy. "This is a no tomato zone." She pointed to Ali's slingshot and his sticky red fingers.

"Oh, I get it now," Brawley said with a grin. He kneeled next to Brandy and motioned for the group to come closer as he set down the squirming Jessica. In hushed voice, he began creating a conspiracy the children were all too eager to participate in. "Let's plan a sneak attack on the insurgents out there. Not much fun attacking babies and mothers, is it?"

The children shook their heads in unison.

"Besides, they have ways of ruining your equipment." He was pointing to Ali's slingshot, but all four wives burst out laughing. Brawley himself was having difficulty keeping a straight face and kept his focus on the serious faces of his co-conspirators.

"You need more ammunition?" Brandy asked.

"Yes, ma'am. You got any?"

"There's another basket in the refrigerator. I guess this is for a good cause, but Brawley Hanks, if just one of those tomatoes lands anywhere in my house, you're gonna personally re-paint the whole place, inside and out!"

Brawley turned to the kids again after retrieving the red orbs from the refrigerator. "You see what I mean? You don't piss off the wife of a SEAL."

He winked at Dorie who beamed back at him. Brandy saw the love between them in full bloom again. It warmed her soul to see this. She hoped their hard days were finally behind them.

Brawley left with his merry band of outlaws in tow. They tip-toed out the kitchen door. Within seconds, their little bodies could be seen rounding the outside of the house, Brawley crouching in the lead. Jessica wandered back in, lethargic, seeking her mother's lap, rubbing her eyes.

Five minutes later, Brandy heard the pirate attack coming from the front yard with screams and shouts of tomato warfare piercing the peaceful night air.

SHE STOOD IN the doorway while Tucker helped their guests corral all the kids and see everyone safely off. He ran down the driveway toward her, barefoot, in his faded and ragged jeans, shirtless and happy, and it took her breath away. At forty-one years of age, he'd kept his massive shoulders and corded arms, and slim waist (at least compared to his upper torso) without an ounce of extra fat anywhere. He easily could have played professional football; he was so magnificently put together. She felt like the luckiest woman in the world.

As he approached, her hands went to her lower belly, rubbing their baby as she slept.

"Look at you, sweetheart! All ripe and ready to burst!" he whispered before he kissed her.

"Now I know why I feel so big," she answered, continuing to rub. Tucker's hand joined hers in the gentle baby massage.

"You *are* pretty big. Are you sure we got the dates right? You look ready to go, no more of this three-to-four-week stuff," he said.

"I was just wondering that until I watched your body move down the driveway like some huge, Greek god. Tucker, the baby is big, because of—well, look at *you*!"

"So what you're sayin' is that I'm going to have an Amazon daughter?" He cocked his head as if bracing for a slap.

"At least I'll be there to school her in the advantages of being a big girl. That way, perhaps she won't have to go through all the same things I did."

Tucker looked down at his toes. He was thinking about something, and Brandy could tell he was hesitant to speak it out loud.

"Go on. Spill it." She threw her arms around his neck, bellied up to him so he could feel the baby kicking, and said, "Whatever it is, I want to hear it."

He tenderly stroked her cheek with the back of his fingers then sifted through her hair, ending up with a long forefinger rubbing across her lips. "I think it was harder on you because you lost your mom just when a girl probably needs her mom the most. Does that make sense?"

"You were a woman in your past life, or is there something you're needing to tell me?" She was stifling a smile, but it was tough.

"Nah, I don't understand women much at all. But I know you, Brandy. And I know what's in your heart, I think. I think that's why you'll be a great mom, boy or girl. Because you know how it feels to not have one while you're still young, sweetheart. And you're going to make up for whatever you didn't get."

She was stunned. She'd never thought about it that way. The constant refrain of "Dad is the best dad a girl could ever want, and he's done the perfect job," was the only thing she allowed herself to consider. But viewing it now, Tucker was right.

"Did I mess up?" he asked, tipping back her chin with his thumb and two fingers. His eyebrows rose in a question.

"Not at all. You're more perceptive than I ever thought a man could be. You do know me. You know everything about me. And what I haven't told you, you've just learned on your own. I thought women were the only ones who were supposed to do that."

He leaned back on his heels, separating their chests as he

arched backward. "Ah, well, I think it's because I never met anyone quite like you. I never had this. And I'm not letting it go. Like you said, it was the perfect start. I'm up for keeping it that way, aren't you?"

"Absolutely, Tucker. We've both waited a long time to have our hearts fed the way they are now. I'm ready to spread the love to our baby."

She followed him to the fire pit, the embers glowing red but without flame. He brushed aside the coals and covered them with dirt then replaced the grate and stood with her, examining the stars above. A gentle breeze blew off the ocean, and the salty air was soothing. She knew she'd sleep better tonight. They'd both worked hard today and enjoyed sharing their project with their extended family.

The wind kicked up with more intensity, rustling the foliage at the neighbor's property line. It also caused the palm trees, still in their square wooden pots, to flutter, sounding more like a gentle waterfall.

He was turning to go inside, but she stopped him.

"Can we plant these tomorrow?" she asked, pointing to their gift.

"Okay. T.J. gave me a good idea today about putting them at the front of the property, like sentries."

"Sentries? I don't get it."

"Like two big guards at a gate. Like big lions on a gate."

"Guarding our fortress kind of thing?" She was still puzzled.

"Well, yes, and no. A statement of strength and grandeur, I think he meant. And power. Like they'll ward off evil spirits. Protect our family."

She shuddered. It never was a pleasant thought considering all the danger there was out there in the real world. Her warm and satisfying world was a bubble she never wanted to burst.

"It's a good thing, Brandy. That way, we can see these trees, as they grow, silhouetted against the orange sky, like it does here at sundown nearly every night. We'll see those trees, and we'll feel how strong our love is. How nothing can hurt us ever."

"Okay. Well, they don't look very majestic right now. Kind of stumpy but with lots of promise. Someday, like the man said, they'll be thirty feet or more." She was still slightly alarmed with where the conversation was going. "Are you thinking this way because of who gave them to us?"

"Maybe." He shrugged. "I don't know, probably a stupid thought." He chuckled before he continued. "It sounded better when T.J. said it, that's all."

She laughed at his return to being light-hearted.

"I think that sounds like a great idea, Tucker. We're creating a dynasty here. It's the start of a new adventure."

He wrapped his arm around her shoulder, and they headed to the door. Just before she stepped over the ledge, something made her turn and glance over her shoulder at the palm trees fluttering in the shadows. They were nearly invisible. She leaned back to study the sprinkling of stardust one more time before she said good night to the *outside* world.

She was going to dream tonight with great anticipation—all about her *inside* world and the young life waiting to be born.

CHAPTER 3

T UCKER GOT HIS orders two weeks later. The mission had been delayed another thirty days, which came as a great relief to him, since it meant he would not miss the birth of their child. But the bad news was that the deployment was indeterminate, which meant it might be longer than previously expected.

Their previous mission to the Canaries had been considered a fluke. They'd followed the trail of the missing American aid worker, Jenna Riley, who had been kidnapped and sold to the Dutch billionaire Jens VanValle in Nigeria and pirated away to his compound on Gran Canaria Island. In the firefight, the Dutchie was killed. Tucker didn't want to go anywhere near that place again and considered it a stroke of extremely good luck they'd made it out of there without Team casualties or sparking an international incident.

He was disappointed when he read that they'd be going back to the same island, this time to capture several kingpins the State Department had identified as being leaders of the organization in Nigeria. He knew human trafficking was spreading all over the world, but he was surprised it had spread to a mainly tourist location where the local police and militia would do just about anything to keep things quiet so as not to interfere with their primary industry.

He had lots of questions about going there. He also wondered about Colin Riley's involvement in this mission, since Riley practically bankrolled the last one. Their mission partner, a former FSK officer-turned aid worker, Sven Tolar, told him that the home of the trafficking cell was located near the Nigerian capital and operated with the full cooperation and protection of the local government. So why the Canaries?

He'd ask his questions when they called the Team meeting, which would be very soon. He'd been given a list of shots to make sure he was up-to-date on, and the usual reminder about getting his affairs in order, which pissed him off every time.

But he'd be home for the baby, and right now, that was where he was laser focused. He and T.J. scheduled the workday with Shannon's former father-in-law, so they could build that small fence and get the palm trees planted like he'd promised.

He hoped Brandy wouldn't go into labor before then.

Brandy seemed to perk up after the party. She turned the upstairs into a projects room where she set up her sewing workshop. He'd laid out sawhorses with full sheets of plywood on top, so she had room to cut and lay out curtains she was making, as well as a patchwork bedspread and other things for the baby's room. The Team wives bought them a new crib, and a beautiful rocking chair to match. These were the only pieces of furniture that weren't purchased at the second-hand furniture store or on eBay.

She was feeling so good that he brought her to the home improvement store to shop for the final things they needed in the bathroom.

"Now, remember, we can't buy the top of the line. Just enough to get by for now. We can always replace fixtures later on as we get more settled, okay?" he'd warned her.

"Gotcha. But, Tucker, I would like to see if we can find something that would fit on that refrigerator door. I'm breaking my nails trying to get it open all the time."

"We'll see. Might have to get that handle made. Those things change from year to year, and since it was a closeout, don't get your hopes up."

He could see she was going to object, so he interrupted her.

"We'll try, sweetheart. I promise."

That left her with a smile on her face.

They ran into another Team Guy and his wife from Team 5, Bryce and Geraldine Tanner. Tucker had served with Tanner during his first enlistment. The couple was around his own age and now had four kids in tow, all girls. The two older teenagers were fixated on their cell phones and didn't look up during introductions. Their father yanked the phones from their fingers and put them in his shirt pocket.

"There you go," said Bryce. "Problem solved." He gave a wide, confident smile.

"Daddy!" the taller one stomped and crossed her arms. She appeared to try to purse her lips, but her pink braces got in the way. Her fingernails were painted ten different colors.

Geraldine shook her head and nodded to Brandy's belly. "Kids. Hope you have boys. They're easier, I've been told!" she sighed.

Tucker noticed Brandy was eyeing the teens closely. Then she spoke up.

"Do you guys live on Coronado?"

"We sure do. But we're busting out at the seams, so we might be moving. You guys bought a neat place, I hear," answered Geraldine. "And call me Geri. That was nice of you, Tucker, but now I feel like I'm being scolded by my grandmother."

"Geri, then. How old are your girls?" Brandy asked.

"Fourteen and fifteen, going on thirty," answered Bryce.

"So they don't drive, then?"

"No. Are you asking if they babysit?" Geri asked.

"Well, I was thinking. I probably won't need anyone for a few months at least, but when the baby's maybe four months, yes, perhaps."

Geri leaned over, closer to Brandy, and whispered, "Most of us do trades. That way we don't have to pay for sitters, if you know what I mean. But they'd be delighted, I'm sure. Right, girls?"

"We'd love to," the shorter one said.

The older girl was still scowling from her father's confiscation.

Tucker put his arm around Brandy's waist. "We'll have to stoke up the BBQ and have you guys over."

"From the looks of things, perhaps you should let us do the honors," Bryce said.

Everyone laughed.

"I always hate to descend on someone else's home with our big family," said Geri. "Much easier for us to entertain you. Let's do it soon, if you can."

"Fair enough. Give me a call when you have a free evening," Tucker chuckled.

"GOOD THINKING," TUCKER said to his wife while they were walking away. "But don't you think they're kind of young?"

"Oh, I'd have them do it together. But just for your information, I started getting paid to babysit at twelve, or even a little younger. Not for late nights, of course, but I was in high demand."

"I'll just bet you were," he chuckled. "We'll talk to them a little more, and if you feel comfortable, I'll go along with it. Of course, your dad and Jillian will be jealous as hell. Don't forget that."

"I know. I'm just planning ahead."

That stopped him in his tracks. Brandy walked ahead several steps, pushing their cart, until she realized he had stayed behind. She turned and cocked her head. "Tucker?"

He slowly approached, reached out to hold her face in his

palms, and kissed her. "And just how many children were you planning on having, my dear? Or were you never going to tell me?"

Brandy blushed. But he loved that look that said her secret had been outed. She struggled to get away, but he held her close.

"Tell me, Brandy—"

"You never know, do you?" Her blush was still prominent, her chest blotchy red. She avoided eye contact, even though he was kissing her. They were blocking an aisle, but Tucker was driven.

"Two? Three? Four? More?" he called off to her between kisses, as softly as he could.

"Don't be silly. Let's start with one and see how that goes. And, Tucker, you're stopping traffic." She waived her arms, pointing behind him, so he let her go.

Brandy smoothed her hair, straightened her top, and let out a big sigh. She continued ahead of him again.

She was a miracle, this lovely woman who had agreed to be his wife. Had anyone else kept that kind of a secret from him, he'd have found it totally unattractive. But Brandy's schemes were like chocolate syrup and whipped cream. He was totally turned on by the fact that she wanted more babies.

And he'd love giving them to her.

CHAPTER 4

S TEVEN COOK AND his new wife, Jillian, offered to take them out to dinner. The timing of her dad's offer was great. Brandy began to feel tired the week after the party. She'd completed the room decorations, finished the quilt, and got it ready to be sent out to the topper to finish it off. None of her clothes seemed to fit right and she was finding it hard to sleep. She knew time was getting very close.

So the offer of a nice dinner that meant she didn't have to cook was pure luxury.

Jillian and her father were so much in love. Brandy was glad that it was something she and Tucker shared. Otherwise, it would have been unbearable to be with them. She didn't have to use too much imagination to understand why Jillian occasionally jumped and giggled nervously. Tucker had sometimes made little secret sexual advances to Brandy under the table in front of their friends as well. But it was not something she expected her *father* to do.

She knew Jillian was a little uncomfortable with such a public display of affection, so Brandy interrupted the conversation about gardens and gardening to lean forward and scold her father and her new stepmother.

"Dad? Jillian? I get it. But you're getting a little over the top. If you want to fool around, let's all leave so you can do that. But you don't have to show me how much you'd rather be doing something else than sitting here talking to Tucker and me."

Now she'd done it. She wished she could take back her words. No one was making a move, and her father and Jillian's mouths had dropped open. Tucker was squirming in his seat, tapping his foot against hers under the table, but his hands were safely folded on the tabletop.

Overwhelmed, all of a sudden, Brandy burst out in tears. Her sobs were long. Hot, gushing tears ran down her cheeks, her neck, and into the top of her blouse. Then a strange sensation began in her upper chest. She looked down, placed her palm against her right breast and saw there was moisture there. She was shocked, which temporarily slowed her heaving chest.

Jillian took quick notice, taking her other hand in hers. "It's all right, sweetie. That's normal. You're beginning to lactate. Perfectly natural."

Brandy didn't want to be talking to Jillian right now about her pregnancy. She wanted it to be her mother she was talking to. Her heart broke as she remembered her mother would never see her child, would not be there for her in the delivery room. She didn't want to take lactating advice from the woman her father was fondling and showing off like a high schooler. It was all wrong.

The tears burst forth again. She couldn't speak. It was like her eyes and her lungs were connected by something other than her brain, and it didn't have anything to do with her mouth, either. Her emotions rose to near panic levels. The sobbing resumed, and when Tucker put his arm around her, whispering something in her ear, she jumped at his touch. She knew it upset him because he tried to stifle his jump in reflex.

"Brandy, are you all right?" her father asked her.

It felt like he was clear across the room and his voice was muffled. For just a second, she couldn't recognize his face or remember his name. And then the wave of emotions washed over her again and she inhaled deep and let out a muffled scream.

Something warm and wet was happening between her legs. Her first thought was embarrassment, that she'd lost feeling and wet her pants. But as she concentrated on it, she discovered it had nothing to do with her bladder.

Tucker still had his arm around her. "What is it, Brandy?"

"My water's broken."

They cancelled dinner. Her father wanted to come with them to the hospital, but Brandy wouldn't have it. She knew it would make her more nervous. Tucker was the only one who could keep her calm and help her do this. After all the days she'd wondered how it would go, her new adventure had finally started.

Tucker called ahead, and the hospital staff was ready for her when they arrived. She was beginning to have sharp pains first in her lower back area then rolling up the sides of her stomach. The juncture between her legs was pulsing, and she could feel every muscle. As they were wheeling her up to the exam room, the baby kicked and nearly knocked her breath out.

"Wow, she's not happy, Tucker. She just kicked me."

"Not a thing to worry about. Glad she's strong. She's just letting you know she's damn good and ready. That's a good thing, sweetheart."

He had insisted on driving her wheelchair even though it was not hospital policy for him to do so. The admitting nurse jumped back nearly a foot after he glared back at her when she told him she'd take the chair.

By the time they got upstairs, she was already beginning to have small contractions. Tucker asked for some water, and the nurse quickly produced a small cup for her to take. The cool liquid tasted delicious. Their doctor hadn't arrived yet, so temporarily they admitted her to a room after the delivery nurse confirmed her water had broken, and she was in fact beginning to have contractions. They helped her change into a gown, and a monitor was placed on her belly.

Tucker stood idly by, his face long, as he watched everything the two nurses did. He made a couple of suggestions and a correction to the head nurse until he was ordered out of the room.

He refused.

"Come here and hold my hand, but you gotta let them do what they know how to do, Tucker. You need to trust them, or you'll start making me nervous too."

Tucker was by her side, squeezing her hand, just as a big contraction overtook her body, waking her up to the fact that she was indeed going to feel some major pain.

"They were right. Everyone was right!" she announced to the whole floor.

"Right about what, hon?" the nurse whispered calmly.

"It hurts. It's gonna hurt."

The older woman smiled. "Now, sir, you have a job. You're here to help her with the pain. Distract her and the time will go by much quicker. You're her coach, but you're also her support."

SIX HOURS LATER, Kimberly Lynne Hudson came into the world weighing just an ounce over nine pounds. She didn't seem to mind that her father cut the cord that had her tethered to her mom. Her first cries were robust, her arms and legs moved powerfully, objecting to the bright lights and the fact that the she was in a room with all kinds of new noises and strange people. Her body was covered in dark hair, even her chest and legs, just like her father. She was cleaned, weighed, and wrapped tightly in a blanket, and given back to her mother.

Earlier, when Tucker had been given the scissors to cut the cord, he just stood there, having to be prodded at first. But as

Kimberly was brought back to Brandy's side, he shook off the shock of what had just happened, and Brandy saw tears well up and then spill over his cheeks, dripping onto his light blue hospital gown.

The baby looked up at Brandy, blinking, trying to focus as she cooed and whispered back to her. "We're so happy you're here. What a beautiful baby you are, Kimberly. Look, this is daddy," she said as she angled the baby to face Tucker.

"See that big guy? He's not really as scary as he looks. He's your father, and he loves you."

She heard Tucker mumble, "I do. Er—he does!"

He lowered his face to give the baby a kiss on her forehead, and Brandy touched his cheek. "We did good, Tucker."

"It's a miracle, Brandy. I love her so much already. Thank you, sweetheart." He kissed her while she continued to stroke his cheek.

The baby took her first feeding ravenously.

"You little vampire," Tucker whispered to her.

"Shush. That's not nice. She's worked hard, and now she needs some sustenance."

When the baby fell asleep, she handed her to Tucker who sat in the corner of the dimly lit room while Brandy dozed off.

At last, they were a family.

The beginning of our dynasty.

CHAPTER 5

O F COURSE, THE mandatory pre-deployment Team meeting was called for the day Tucker brought Brandy and Kimberly home from the hospital. He'd spent the night before with them, resting off and on in the large armed chair in the corner of her hospital room. He held Kimberly to give Brandy frequent breaks so she could rest. Several times, the nurses tried to take the baby away when he'd fallen asleep, yet he refused to relinquish his prize. It was what the two of them had discussed prior to her admission. They both wanted as much time holding their daughter as they could.

Only once, he begrudgingly let the nurse take Kimberly away for an early morning clean up and vitals check. Brandy's doctor, who sported some serious tats on his muscled forearms, cleared them for the return home that morning. Tucker pegged him as a former Team Guy.

Just after the doctor left, Tucker broke the news to his wife.

"I'm so sorry, sweetheart. The worst timing." Tucker knew she understood, but still felt horrible about it. "It shouldn't be a long meeting, couple of hours at most."

The hospital refused to delay their departure, so he planned on taking her home and then heading back to base for the meeting.

"I'm good. If I need anything, I'll text you. Maybe you could call Dad before we go? They haven't seen the baby. Might be a nice time for them to come over."

"Good idea. I should have thought of that." He smacked his forehead with his palm.

Brandy giggled. "I think you're a little sleep deprived. You be careful on the road today, Tucker."

He returned a smirk. "There you go, still worrying about me. You're the one who needs tending to. I'm fine. Losing sleep is second nature, part of our training."

"Liar."

"Okay, I give up. You want them to bring anything, honey?"

"I'm good. How about something for you for dinner. That might be nice."

"Nah, I can stop on the way home. But if you think of anything, you let me know, sweetheart."

While the hospital staff gathered all of the baby's things, Tucker called Steven Cook, who was delighted they were invited to the house.

With Brandy's bag, the huge bag of diapers and supplies given them by the hospital, and the bouquet of roses he'd sent, Tucker let the young assistant wheel Brandy to the Hummer. He called T.J. to let him know there was a chance he'd be a few minutes late.

Walking inside their home for the first time, Tucker was moved by how incomplete everything was. He vowed to wrap up everything he could, including the front yard project, even if he had to use credit cards to get it all done. She'd delivered two weeks early, so he felt a little like he'd been caught with his pants down.

"I'd really like a shower, Tucker. I didn't get one at the hospital this morning."

Tucker checked his watch and nodded, holding a fussing Kimberly while Brandy stepped into the shower. He could tell the baby was hungry, the way she twisted her nose and that cute little mouth of hers, punching herself in the face with her fist. He was still amazed at the miracle they'd created as he talked to her, walking her around the living room. Though she was large, as babies went, she still looked like a doll, so delicate and pink, and totally reliant on his love. Initially, he'd been nervous to hold her, even though he'd delivered babies during deployment and medic training at Ft. Bragg.

We got this, sweetheart. You go ahead and scream your little head off, 'cause Mama has the cure.

They heard Brandy's father pull up just as he handed Kimberly back to her.

"I think your dad's here, and I gotta go."

"Ah, that felt great. Thank you, Tucker."

"She's more than ready for you," he said.

"I can see," Brandy answered.

It was amazing how the baby seemed to know her mother's voice already. Depending on whether or not she was hungry, it either made her fussier, as her little face and mouth moved to the side looking for Brandy or calmed her down if she was satisfied. He'd been careful to speak to her in soft tones, not wanting to scare her, but the little one's ears were already attuned to the voice of her mother and paid no attention to him at all.

Like everything else Brandy did, she held a certain confidence, even though she was a new mom. Tucker didn't think he'd seen anything so beautiful in his life as the sight of Kimberly at Brandy's breast.

He gave a hug and kiss to Steven and Jillian and then dashed out the door.

CONGRATULATIONS WERE IN order when he got to the Team 3 building. Someone was passing out cigars, which Tucker had forgotten. In a matter of minutes, the air was blue with thick pungent smoke, like one of their poker nights. Tucker actually began to get a buzz on. It had been so long since he'd had a cigar.

He neglected to mention to anyone how hairy his daughter was, knowing how he'd get razed for raising a baby gorilla, like his mother had been when he was born. That was going to have to be on a need-to-know basis.

"Listen up!" boomed Lt. Commander Andrew Gibson. "Babies are a fact of life. You should know that better than anyone, Tucker, with your training."

"Yes, sir." The room around him sat to attention.

"Your kid is going to be teased about being raised by her grandpa," Gibson continued with a twinkle in his eye.

"Guilty as charged. I can see you've been there, sir," Tucker barked back.

The room instantly reacted as Gibson sported a cheerful grin. "You're damned lucky I like you, Hudson."

When Lt. Commander Gibson straightened up, he scanned his audience with deadly focus, causing everyone else seated before him to sit tall. All chatter immediately stopped. They waited.

"Okay, what we got here is sort of a mess. This op was planned before the huge wildfires that have destroyed so many acres on Gran Canaria, causing the evacuation of thousands of residents. There are firefighting units and extra Civil Guard from the other islands, Madrid, as well as some from Portugal—even a little equipment help from Uncle Sam. The place is crawling with police, fire, and rescue workers. It's like an anthill."

Gibson showed several videos of flames reaching into the night sky and flotillas of evacuees, as well as roving police units helping with the evacuation and the damage.

"We delayed a bit when the fires broke out. But this extra activity has stepped up the urgency. We fear some of those being evacuated are part of the smuggling operation. Or, they could be operating under the guise of a humanitarian aid vessel, trying to pick up new contraband. State thinks they could be attempting to unload some of their human cargo within the refugee population landing in Portugal, Spain, or other countries in the Mediterranean. Because of the emergency operations there, it's getting very dicey and, well, unmanageable. They're just not prepared for this type of widespread tragedy all at once."

Tucker could see a whole range of potential problems. The mood in the room had suddenly become quite glum.

"State has received intel there are even perhaps American tourists caught up in the evacuation—either vacationers or long-term visitors to the island."

Lt. Commander Gibson turned off the video, and someone turned on the room lights.

"Gents, State is concerned about the possibility some U.S. citizens are caught up in all this and perhaps are being trafficked without their knowledge. That's why they've negotiated a short vacation to the Canaries, but only to retrieve our people. We can't touch or otherwise fuck with any islanders, anyone holding a Spanish passport, or a foreign aid worker who has diplomatic immunity."

Tucker knew before Gibson said anything further that they were on a tender leash.

"The problem for us is that while we're looking for our own, we'd like to rid the area of some of the bad guys with ties to Nigerian operators. We want to extract them quietly and hand them over to our Special Agent team for questioning and possible detention. We know some of them are there, because we've overheard conversations back and forth with one particular group we've been tracking in Nigeria."

He waited several seconds until the conversations before him stopped.

"We've got tourists, we got refugees from Africa who don't want to go back, we've got more arriving, and we've got people being evacuated. There's a list of names of certain individuals we are particularly interested in, and those are the only ones we want. Unless we walk into a hornet's nest. And with the history of this team, I'm not going to bullshit you to say it won't happen. We all know nothing happens like we planned, right?"

The general agreement on that point was loud and long.

"There's to be no fireworks. No blowing up buildings or causing any undue attention. And God forbid, no loss of life or even minor injury, especially to the Spanish or island population. If you don't know, you keep your hands off. Understood?"

Tucker nodded along with everyone else.

"There's a lot more coming, but I'm sure you have questions," Gibson barked.

"About how long will we be there, and when do we leave?" T.J. Talbot asked. He'd been mumbling, whispering things in Tucker's ear.

"Well," Gibson shrugged. "This is not a precise military operation, which sucks real bad. Never a good idea to not have a specific plan, but ours went up in smoke, so to speak, and now all hell's broken loose. We deploy in ten days."

Gibson was met with whistles as the group had been told it would be a month.

"Yeah, I know. Hurry up, then wait, then hurry up again. It took longer to get our permissions because the Spanish and island governments were consumed with the logistics of this fire, and our mission wasn't really a priority for them like it is for us. So let me sum it up this way. Don't pay attention to the worker bees; find the queen. And we also know the longer we stay, the more attention we'll cause. So, we get in and out before we step in it—I'd say maybe be there three weeks. I hope less. Get who we can, send back information for something in the future, and get ready for next time. You all know this human trafficking thing is on the rise and is not going to go away."

Several men nodded. Gibson was dead serious, but his audience didn't reflect any of the tension they probably were feeling. Tucker knew this was how they'd been trained. He raised his hand and was called on.

"Sir, are we going to use the two assets we used before, Jean Douchet or Sven Tolar? Sven, in particular really helped us out."

"Yes, Sven will be on the team. He's meeting you guys over there. We're not sure about Jean. He's gotten a little entangled in Paris, from what we understand. We haven't approached him yet until we know for sure he's free."

"Is our platoon the only one going, sir?" asked someone from the back.

"Yes, at this point. I'll be going along with you. We have Lt. Jack Gridley, a Little Creek transfer, who's flying home from his honeymoon in Hawaii as we speak. So, without Kyle, we'll be fourteen enlisted men." He rocked in his shoes, eyes darting around the crowd, including making contact with Tucker. "We're expecting big things from some of you seniors."

The meeting was adjourned. T.J. snagged Tucker's arm.

"I guess we better get that fence built, don't you think?"

"Well, it will take a few months before she's walking or even crawling, but yes, I'd like to get that yard finished. What's your availability now?"

"I'm going to need to talk to Joe, and I'll see if we can get by there in the next day or two, if we won't be in the way."

"No problem. Thanks, T.J."

"How's everyone doing?"

"So far, so good. Kinda sucks I'll be gone so soon."

"I hear you, but at least you were around for her birth. With these short ones, you never know. Everybody healthy?"

"I got a sweet little pink daughter weighing over nine pounds, and her mother with enough milk to feed the whole hospital nursery."

T.J. squeezed Tucker's shoulder. "Good for you, man. You deserve this. Then you can work on number two."

That left a smile on his face that lasted all the way until he got safely home.

CHAPTER 6

B RANDY GOT HERSELF up to make scones for T.J., Tucker, and Joe Benson, Shannon's father-in-law from her first marriage. Joe wore his carpenter's overalls and had brought two tool bags, with everything neatly organized, as if they were pieces of cherished antiques. So he holstered his hammer in the special loop created for it, took the pencil from behind his ear, and added it to the red and black crayon sticks lodged in his front pocket. His eyes were the size of basketballs as he lovingly accepted the hot scone Brandy presented to him on a paper towel.

"Why, thank you, dearie. You didn't have to go to all that trouble," he said and then took his first bite. "Oh man, this couldn't have come out of a box!"

She handed T.J. and Tucker each a scone. "It did. That's about all I can do when it comes to baking. Just my way of saying thanks."

Tucker gave her a kiss and a hug.

"She sleeping?"

"Of course, but probably not for long. With as much as she eats, she wakes up ravenous. But she goes right down when her belly gets full. She might be one of those who start sleeping through the night early," Brandy beamed.

"Larger babies are that way sometimes," added T.J. "Say, you don't happen to have any coffee in there, do you?"

"We have one of those one-shot machines. But I'm going to let everyone get their own. I gotta get back to check on Kimberly."

The men joined her and lined up behind Tucker, who prepared the coffee from freshly ground beans. He showed the coffee label to T.J.

"You get this stuff? These guys are former Team Guys. Their videos crack me up."

"I've seen them. Splitting beans with sniper fire. I've met them in Coronado too," said T.J. "Love the pirate on the front."

Brandy brought Kimberly into the kitchen, pulled up a chair, wrapped a small blanket over her shoulders, and showed Kimberly off to the men before she put the baby to her breast.

"Here she is!" gasped T.J.

"Now that's a pretty baby," said Joe Benson. "My wife, Gloria, would be right over if you ever need a sitter."

Brandy smiled and then focused on Kimberly's nursing, covering herself up discretely.

Tucker was telling Joe about his plans for the garden and what they wanted to do with the house, including Brandy's thought to perhaps make a second unit upstairs.

The older man inspected the ceiling while sipping on his hot coffee and then studied the narrow stairway. He addressed Tucker.

"I think you should make that stairway into a closet or maybe a half bath, and add the stairs outside. You could protect it with an awning or overhang. Not like we have monsoons here."

"Joe is an expert carpenter, Tucker," added T.J. "He still does little repair jobs for several of our friends and his neighbors. But he used to build houses, right?"

"We'd build one, move into it, then sell it, and build another one. I think Frankie lived in about ten, maybe eleven houses growing up."

Brandy noticed a silence had fallen on the group and deduced it was due to the subject of Frankie's passing. Tucker had told her the story, but he delicately began to explain part of it again.

"Frankie is Joe's son, and T.J. and Frankie became best friends during BUD/S." Tucker's voice was soft and careful.

"I think I remember that, Tucker. Thanks."

T.J. added, "I was best man at his wedding when he married Shannon. She wasn't very happy with me for getting Frankie so drunk he passed out during the ceremony." The tall medic shook his head.

"That's my boy," sighed Joe. "He followed you around everywhere, T.J. You got him in a lot of trouble, but you were like brothers."

"That's a fact," mumbled T.J. "Frankie told me to watch over Shannon, who was over six months pregnant when he got taken out." T.J. was staring at his coffee like a psychic reading tea leaves. "I always had a secret crush on her, but I was a good boy. Being friends with Frankie was more important. At the beginning, Shannon didn't want to have anything to do with me."

"I heard all about that." Tucker grinned and toasted his coffee mug.

"Old Joe here kind of helped me break the ice a little. It was a very unselfish act I will never forget and could never repay," T.J. said, his words dropping off to a whisper. He wrapped his arm around Joe Benson's neck, making him blush.

The older man wiggled loose. "It just fit in place like a miter joint on a fine cabinet. I lost my son. You lost your dad. I think we were made for each other, T.J." Joe Benson blinked and rubbed something from his left eye.

Brandy couldn't remember seeing Tucker or any of his friends being so forthcoming with cherished emotional details. It touched her. After a short pause, Tucker cleared his throat.

"Think it's about time to get back out there, unless you two want to sit around and have a little cry." Tucker put his mug in the sink.

"Shut the fuck up," barked T.J. "Sorry, Kimberly."

Brandy put the baby over her shoulder and patted her back gently. Kimberly responded with a loud burp, which echoed throughout the kitchen.

"The princess has spoken!" Joe left his mug behind and followed Tucker and T.J. to the front door. He turned and waved at Brandy. "Thanks again. Those were tasty."

"I have more."

"Maybe later. Thanks."

He disappeared into the front yard filled with late morning sun. Brandy took the baby and sat, watching them from the living room couch.

Joe was the general.

THEY'D GOTTEN THE fencing up and decided to expand the project to cover the berm with redwood chips. They planted the two palms in the front corners of the property, to the left of the long driveway. The three men made furrows following the path of the sun but left a large square section untouched. She watched as Tucker noted things in a small spiral book. They shook hands, and before they parted, T.J. and Joe waved to her and gave a thumbs-up.

She hadn't moved from the large window in the living room. As Tucker entered, she said, "Looks beautiful out there. I like where you put the palms."

"Yeah. T.J. was right. It's the perfect spot. And don't know if you want to come out to see, but we left you a nice space up front for flowers or whatever you want."

"I saw that. And you've got the rows all lined up."

"Yup. Think I'll get the redwood bark and the veggie starts.

You just tell me what you want to plant, and we'll get those puppies in."

Kimberly stirred, and Brandy adjusted her weight switching the baby to lie against her other side.

"Should I make you a sandwich?" she whispered.

"I'll do it. You're fine."

She followed him to the kitchen and sat at the table again. "You don't have to get those things today, do you?"

"No, but I'd like to finish." He stopped, his knife suspended in a jar of mayonnaise, his eyes dark and serious. "We don't have much time."

"I just want to spend as much time with you as possible before you go, Tucker."

"And I want to finish that garden, like I promised. You can look at it every day, water it, and think of me."

"How could I not think of you? I'd think of you if we lived in the desert in an old trailer. Everything makes me think of you."

Kimberly was getting fussy again.

"Think I'll go change her."

Tucker grabbed her arm before she could retreat to the back bedroom. "Hey, have I ever told you how much I love you?"

She kissed him. "Yes, all the time. But I'd love to hear more tonight after you've had a shower."

"Yes, ma'am." He picked up his keys, slipped his wallet into his back pocket, waved his goodbye with the hand not holding his sandwich, and was out the door.

She'd been waiting for their first sexual liaison to prepare a special meal, but tonight, she didn't want to wait anymore. This was the life she had, and it was special enough just being in his arms.

At first he wanted to be so careful with her, undulating inside, watching her face and asking over and over if it hurt. The third time he asked, she giggled, stopping him.

"I already told you, I'm fine. I don't want you to hold back. I want you to fuck me so hard I won't be able to think of anything else, understand?"

"You only have to tell me once, babe."

His enormous hands kneaded her flesh, his kisses turned her insides molten. He answered back her demand by changing positions frequently. His new question became, "You like that baby?" as he flipped her over and took her from behind. "What about this," he whispered into her ear.

She was left wet, gasping for air, wondering how in the world she'd ever be able to stand three weeks without him. Her last whisper to him was, "Mission accomplished."

HE LEFT ON a Tuesday, early in the morning. She noted he'd packed light this time, which she took as a good sign, meaning he wasn't taking any heavy firepower.

The sun was barely making it over the mountains to the east, and the area was bathed in a pink glow. The visions of their love-making last night was weakening her knees. They'd made love in the shadows, quietly whispering things she couldn't remember. It was more like an intense, goodbye kiss, a way to leave things on a positive note and wipe out the cobwebs of worry. It was something she'd learned how to do, to pretend that their life together would never end, while being realistic in the knowledge that he might not return.

She always expected a perfect outcome but prepared for the worst.

With Kimberly still fast asleep, she walked with him out to his Hummer in her nightgown, barefoot. The early mornings were her favorite in the garden. The plants had started to expand, and some of the seeds she'd planted in the flower garden had begun to send up shoots.

He hugged her from behind while they both looked at the Tucker's handiwork.

"Enjoy your days out here, Brandy. I'm going to be thinking about you taking care of this little piece of heaven."

She turned in his arms and placed her palms up to his neck, stood on tiptoes, and kissed him while he gave her a firm squeeze. "You pay attention and come home to me, Tucker. I know you will, but I still want you to promise."

He held her hand at his heart. "I promise, sweetheart. Nothing will keep me from coming back to you both. Nothing."

He climbed up into the cab, started the engine, and backed out of the driveway, giving her a quick wave and a smile. She watched him, waving back until he disappeared behind the neighbor's hedge. And then she waited until she could no longer hear the motor.

If she had to choose, she'd rather have him home with her. She'd sacrifice anything except Kimberly to have him stay. But watering and tending Tucker's garden was going to help her get through it.

Until they could do it together again.

CHAPTER 7

T UCKER WAS GLAD to find Sven Tolar waiting for him at the Gando Airport on Gran Canaria. The former Norwegian special forces guy greeted the Team as they entered the hangar serving as their temporary Team building.

The metal building would be a good staging area for a quick exit, should that be needed. It also enabled them to receive supplies, including required firepower and devices, which could be subtly unloaded in small shipping containers and stored for later pickup.

A small tourist hotel that had been evacuated was to serve as their eventual living quarters once they left the safety of the airport region.

"My friend, how are you? I hear your little girl is beautiful!" Sven boomed as he gave Tucker a big hug.

"That's on a strictly need-to-know basis. You didn't get out there this summer. You owe me a visit."

Sven nodded and greeted the rest of the platoon as they filed in.

"Lt. Commander Andrew Gibson. Nice to finally meet you, Sven," said Gibson as he extended his hand.

"Good to be here."

Tucker introduced him to Lieutenant Jack Gridley. "He's just joined us fresh off his honeymoon."

Sven shook the Lieutenant's hand vigorously and then commented, "Then you're a dangerous man, sir. You won't mind if I keep my distance?"

"Not at all," Gridley said with a wide smile.

Tucker liked their new officer and although it was his first deployment with their Team, thought he was a good decision-maker. He'd been a cop before he went to the Academy, and then became a SEAL, so he'd seen another form of combat that gave him some experience Tucker knew he could trust. They'd spent some time on the flight over getting acquainted. Normally, the two officers would be deferring to Chief Lansdowne, with his experience, though they outranked him. This time, part of that might fall to Tucker. Kyle was setting him up for a promotion and had told him so.

Light smoke still hung in the area, and the number of small-to-medium-sized planes had nearly quadrupled. Helicopters and light planes buzzed all around them. Sven noticed Tucker's focus.

"Way different than before, right?"

"I can see how easy it would be to have things slip by." Tucker knew the appearance of order was an illusion.

"They brought in more than three hundred extra controllers and airport personnel from Madrid just to handle the extra load. They already have one disaster on their hands. No sense creating another one—something like a mid-air collision or worse."

Tucker helped stack boxes of equipment they'd brought. The men were all assigned to a corner of the building where two dozen cots were set up, along with a makeshift mess and two bathrooms. A small trailer Tucker recognized as portable shower rooms had been brought in. Sven selected a cot next to Tucker's. T.J. was on the other side of him.

He stashed his duty bag under the cot, sat, and accepted the bottled water and sandwiches being passed out to all the men. His first bite signaled that he was long past due for a meal, and his stomach churned. But the hard roll containing a meat and cheese mixture was still delicious, and he'd devoured it in four bites.

"You stay in touch with Kelly?" Tucker asked Sven, cleaning his palate with water. Kelly Fielding was their State Department Special Agent liaison, as well as being the sister-in-law of the American nurse they'd rescued.

"She never returned any of my calls or emails. I'm giving her some time. You guys get together with Riley at all?"

Tucker imagined the two palm trees planted in his front yard. "At the hospital up in Redding, and then he sent us a housewarming gift. But no, we've not been in touch."

He decided not to say anything about Riley's offer to work with him again. He suspected perhaps the old man had made a similar offer to Sven. That left him with a question he was dying to ask.

"Is he a part of this one?"

Sven shook his head. "No, I don't think so. I mean, did you take a look at that bucket of bolts you flew in on? Even your naval transport planes are better than that thing. He'd have never sent you on a Spanish charter."

That confirmed what Tucker had been told by the two officers.

"Well, perhaps after this caper, you'd be due for a visit in Portland. I imagine Kelly'd like to see you."

Sven shrugged. "She'll reach out if and when she's ready. I don't chase women anymore."

Lt. Commander Gibson called a meeting, instructing them to stay comfortable. Most everyone stayed seated on their cots, readying themselves for an early turn in.

Gibson held a pile of papers in his left hand and started to pass them out.

"I need you to memorize all the faces and names on this sheet and take a picture of them on your cell phones, because we can't take these out of the building. I've got six targets identified who, as of two days ago, were still on the island. A number of them work at the Capri night club in Las Palmas. It's nothing special, a dance club and bar. It caters to foreign tourists. The rest of them are listed by last known address, or work affiliation, or neighborhood."

"Holy shit, we got a *General Two Fingers* here!" said Fredo.

Everyone looked down at the smooth-shaven black man with dreads, bearing a medal of some kind over his left breast pocket. All the other pictures except one looked like a rogue's gallery from some casting call in Nigeria, of mixed races and varying degrees of tooth possession.

One guy was crisply dressed in a white linen suit and had red hair and horn-rimmed glasses. Tucker read his name, Jens Vandershoot. His last known whereabouts was the Tradewinds Hotel in downtown Las Palmas.

Tucker and T.J. shared a look. T.J. rolled his eyes and mumbled *great.*

"There's also Red Arrow Employment, which they've been watching closely now for nearly a year. It's a domestic help employment service, specializing in placing nannies and domestic temporary workers with wealthy, mostly European families vacationing or with temporary residency here."

Calvin Cooper raised his hand. "Sir, operationally, how do you want us to do this?"

Gibson looked at Tucker. "I think you can split up into teams, just coordinate and share. No, we absolutely don't want the whole Team to descend on the dance bar or one location, if that's what you're thinking."

Everyone laughed.

"Are we allowed to dance?" asked Lucas.

"You can't dance, so the answer is no. And I sure as hell don't want to listen to you Karaoke, either," shouted Alex.

The Team erupted in laughter again.

Sven stood up. "Coop, most of you were here before. With everything going on, I don't think we'd attract too much attention if we stayed in groups of two or three. Is that what you mean, Commander?"

"More than likely, we'll find other areas to look for these guys once we start the visual," added Gibson.

Someone asked, "So are we limited to just these on the list? What if we find someone else we know's involved in the human trafficking?"

"That's a good point," answered Gibson. "For now, these are the only ones we're cleared to mess with, per our instructions from State. But you know what can happen. So let me be clear. You don't fuck with anyone else and then find out we've made a mistake, okay? We're on borrowed and very limited time. If everything blows up, we'll have completely destroyed our mission and the valuable intel assets State has in place. We play nice. Tough but nice."

Gibson went over other logistical items, and then the meeting was adjourned. As the group broke up, T.J. turned to Tucker.

"I've always been told I play nice, right, Tucker?" He followed it up with a smirk.

"My favorite way to be," he answered.

Fredo and Coop had joined their circle.

"Is it my imagination, or is every mission now more complicated than the last one? More rules, with just as much danger, but so many ways things could go all wrong," said T.J.

"The nature of the evil we fight is adapting and changing," added Coop.

Everyone nodded full agreement.

"When I was active, we always said we were working with the other units, but unless we were working with you Americans, we pretty much ran the show," said Sven.

Tucker didn't like the level of negativity being expressed. "Well, it's what we're trained for—to do the impossible so no one even knows we were there. War is changing, gents. The enemy is mobile and doesn't look like a soldier anymore. He could be a business-man, a truck driver, a clerk, or storekeeper. He speaks more languages than we'll ever know, and he moves in and out of multiple countries. He doesn't play by the rules, but we have to."

"Well said, Tucker," Coop whispered. "We use our experience and instincts, and we keep the information close."

"Roger that," several others responded.

TUCKER APPROACHED LT. Commander Gibson. "I forgot to ask in the group if we could call home. I'm assuming there's enough static out there that it would be okay. But can we get through?"

"You'd be right. Not sure about the connection, but I do have a sat phone, if you need it. But not outside this building, and I'm not sure if the metal will interfere, but go ahead and try and then let me know. I'll announce it."

"Thanks."

Tucker dialed Brandy and did get her voicemail so left a brief message that they'd arrived and he was headed for bed. He warned her about what she already knew—that his calls would be infre-quent and not to worry. And of course, he told her he missed her and the baby more than he wanted to think about.

He waited for a shower, got all the traveling sweat off his body so he could concentrate on some restorative sleep, turned on his small book light, and added to his journal.

Wondering what the hell I'm doing here with a beautiful wife and baby at home who need me. Not complaining, but boy is it different now coming here as a father. One saving grace is that I know somebody's kids are being trafficked, and if I can do anything to help stop it, I'm going to. We have a tight window and parameters, but the mission is clear, and we're not here to fight or blow shit up. Not saying it couldn't happen.

The island is crawling with ants from every country. At least from the air, that's the way it looks. I'll know more tomorrow.

Like any long travel, I'm anxious to get out and move my body around. I can't run or swim in the ocean to get rid of the jitters, so I'm hoping we get to do a lot of walking, trying to be invisible.

Glad I brought my good sunglasses.

I'm kissing you right now, honey. It's kinda tight, but you're gonna share my cot tonight and help remind me of my real purpose in life until we can do the real thing.

You never answered my question about how many. Was it two, three, or four? From where I sit, any one of those answers would be good. Hell, even ten would be fine. As long as some day they help me in and out of my wheelchair!

Tucker thought of Mr. Riley in his squeaky machine. He was rich, and he was disabled. And probably cut off from most of the world except for people or experiences he could buy. But he still lost his son and nearly lost his daughter.

That wasn't going to happen to the Hudson family. It had nothing to do with money, either. He wondered if Riley felt he controlled his empire or if it was the other way around.

A part of him felt sorry for the man.

CHAPTER 8

B RANDY GOT TUCKER'S message when she came home from her first outing with Kimberly. It had been a simple store run, but she brought way too many things for the baby. In the end, she realized she'd get much better streamlining and preparing in advance for these trips.

It warmed her heart to know he'd gotten to the Canary Island destination.

Christy Lansdowne, Kyle's wife, called to tell her the ladies on the Team had arranged to bring her hot dishes, or salads. Someone would be stopping by each day until she called a halt to it.

"The way I hear it goes, people get their refrigerators so full a lot of it goes out in the trash, but at least you don't have to do anything."

"Thanks, Christy. I ventured out myself this morning. I have to get much better at this before I'll do it again."

"Wise decision. Let us take care of you a little."

Brandy was grateful for the help.

She'd gotten into the routine of watering the garden with Kimberly strapped to her tummy, if she was awake. The two of them had meaningful one-way conversations. She explained what they'd planted and what she was doing, every single step.

Tucker had left the name and phone number of his former

Teammate who had the teenage daughters. Although they'd failed to get together with the family before he left, she decided she'd initiate a meeting. At her last checkup, her pediatrician told both of them it would be safe to bring Kimberly out in public.

She set up a visit, stressing it would be a very short visit and not a dinner, the next day, in the afternoon, when the girls would be home from school.

THE TANNER'S HOME was in a newer area but farther from the beach and downtown traffic. Geri was at the front door before she could ring the bell.

"Oh, look at her! She's such a beautiful baby, Brandy. And she's huge."

Brandy wondered how she managed to keep her trim figure after having four kids, but Geri was nearly model skinny. Inside, the girls were seated on the living room couch, all in a row. She nodded to each of them.

"Bryce isn't home—got something he had to do at the base, so I'm not sure he'll make it, unless I can convince you to stay for dinner."

"I better not, Geri. Thanks, though."

Brandy nestled down on the couch between the four girls. The youngest one moved in front and kept to her knees, peeling back the blanket to inspect Kimberly' fingers and toes.

"You want to hold her?"

"Yes."

"Keira, go wash your hands first," commanded her mother.

The six-year-old ran to the kitchen and scrubbed her hands and arms to her elbow. That prompted one of her sisters to do the same. The two oldest girls snickered.

"Make room for your sister," Brandy softly requested. The girls parted and the little one sat beside her, while Brandy handed

Kimberly over. "There you go."

The youngster's eyes became wide as she looked at her mother. "This is so cool," she whispered.

Geri laughed, clasping her hands together. "I've got to take a picture of this!" She ran out of the room in search of her cell.

The oldest girl produced a phone she'd been sitting on and snapped a picture. Geri returned and took pictures of the whole group of them together.

Brandy fielded questions for several minutes, but when the baby began to wiggle and then cry, little Keira immediately passed her off.

"She's just hungry, that's all," Brandy explained.

Geri added, "And she probably knows the difference between someone else and her mother. Babies are very smart."

"I want to hold her," said Shelby.

Brandy bounced Kimberly gingerly, hoping she'd calm down, but lay her in Shelby's arms anyway. "She's not going to last long, so don't feel bad. She's really waking up now."

And that's exactly what happened. Brandy took her back and placed her on her breast to feed.

A gasp emanated from the two youngest girls. Brandy smiled at their mother. "They're adorable, Geri. What a nice family you have."

Mrs. Tanner was near tears, her face beaming. "Tori, Lynn, you remember when we brought Keira home from the hospital? You remember all this?"

Lynn was checking her phone again. Geri tried to grab it from her hands, but her daughter sat on it.

"I've turned it off," Lynn said defensively.

"Honestly, your dad is going to be more than displeased when I tell him. I don't understand all this texting."

"Just kids from school, Mom. No biggie."

"But this isn't what we do when we have company. Your friends can wait." Geri's agitation was escalating.

"Tori, go take Shelby and let's serve Brandy with some ice water, okay? And bring some for me and everyone else."

"Roger that," Tori said as she extricated herself from the couch, pulled Shelby up, and left the room.

Geri gave Brandy a puzzled look. "I'm just glad they don't pick up on any of his other lingo. And he has some choice ones."

"I'll bet. So does Tucker." Brandy turned to Lynn. "Do you babysit?"

"Sometimes." She shrugged and stared down at Kimberly with her chin balanced on her open palm. "Does she use a bottle?"

"Not yet. I'm pretty much it for now."

"You have a pump?" Geri added.

Brandy didn't quite know how to respond. "Not ready yet. I'll wait until Tucker gets back. Just one of those things I didn't think about."

"Well, that's good you haven't needed it. I did with my first one."

"I'm right here, Mom. Lynn, remember?"

Brandy was shocked at the attitude of the teen and started to cross her off the babysitter list, when Lynn added, "Just kidding. I have to give you a hard time, you know that. It's what you do to me all the time."

Geri and Brandy exchanged a look. Brandy didn't say a word.

Later, the girls watched her change Kimberly's very messy diaper, examining the yellow-green contents and scrunching up their noses.

"She's got hair like boys," remarked Keira.

Brandy chuckled as she put the sleeper back on, wrapped the baby loosely and placed her over her shoulder for another burp.

"You should see her daddy. She takes after him."

The girls laughed while their mother delightedly looked on.

Brandy decided to bring up the subject of babysitting, explaining it would be some months, but asked Lynn if she and Tori would like to watch Kimberly together some time. They were both enthusiastic about the possibility.

Brandy didn't want to stay too long so began to gather her things to leave.

"Can I bring anything for you? How are you doing with cooking?"

"The ladies on Team 3 have been overdoing it."

"Yup, that's what we do all right. You let me know, though."

"Will do." The two hugged again.

"Here, Keira, take this for Brandy," Geri said as she handed the diaper bag to her daughter.

They said their final goodbyes, the girls waving to Kimberly's unfocused face over the top of her shoulder, all the way to the doorway. Keira walked with her down the steps and back to the car, watching Brandy strap the baby safely inside.

She handed back the diaper bag.

"Thanks, sweetie. That was fun. Do you like babies?" Brandy asked.

"Yes, but my dolls are teen dolls now. No babies." Keira was shy and so blurted out, "She smells nice."

"Yes, she does, doesn't she?"

A cloud came over her face as she spoke, "Lynn has a boyfriend. She doesn't want Mom and Dad to know. She texts him all the time. They would be super pissed if they found out."

Brandy was surprised with the reveal. "Really? Maybe you should tell them. What do you think?"

"Oh no. My sister would kill me. I can't do that."

"Well, think about it. If you think it's wrong, you should—"

"I don't like the picture he sent," she interrupted.

"What picture?"

Keira looked at the front door and saw the coast was clear. "He sent her a picture of his pee pee!"

Brandy arched up and made a mental note that somehow she was going to have to meddle, and she didn't like being in that situation. She didn't want to do this without talking to Tucker first, since it was a relationship he valued. This was going way beyond her babysitting needs. And that already short list had just gotten much smaller.

She leaned over and spoke softly close to Keira's cherubic face. "Keira, you know that's wrong. It's always wrong. You should tell her so the next time you see or hear about it. And you really should tell your Mom or Dad."

Keira's eyes grew wide and filled with tears. "I shouldn't have told you. Now you'll tell my parents. I'm going to get in a lot of trouble."

She turned and quickly ran back into the house, slamming the front door behind her.

Brandy's heart ached as she watched Keira disappear. She wanted to go back inside and let Geri know about the conversation, but the anger and concern had clouded her judgment, and she needed Tucker's opinion before she opened up that box of horrors. There would be no good way this could work. Geri and Bryce needed to know. Keeping everyone "happy" was the least of her concerns.

If the situation were reversed, she'd hope that someone would tell her the truth about what her kids were doing on their cell phone. She knew it was not only the right thing to do, but it might keep Lynn out of harm's way.

She drove home, pondering her decision, hoping that Tucker would agree with her. She missed him more than she ever had.

CHAPTER 9

T WO DELIVERY VANS showed up at dawn to pick up the team. They were to be transported to their new lodging, now set up and ready to go, where they could unpack. Then they'd divide up into smaller groups for their forays into town. State had hired a small team to help with their meals and logistics. A portable surveillance tower was installed, and they'd have direct communication with Washington for updates.

Gibson had received word that several cell phones were being tracked with the CIA "hairnet" device, giving them the opportunity to identify and monitor phone traffic, as well as pinpoint specific locations. Three additional hand carry devices were given to the team; one went to Tucker, Gibson kept one, and the last was given to Fredo.

Even at daybreak, the road into Las Palmas, located north of the island, was jammed with other delivery trucks, lorries, and buses. They passed emergency trailers, and staging areas loaded with pallets of supplies, and tents of varying sizes, including temporary hospitals and housing for displaced citizens, tourists, and workers. Tucker doubted their vans would wind up on anyone's radar.

They also passed several international relief organization mobile units, fire and rescue vehicles, and a fair number of media trailers. Seaside resorts were overrun with troops, transport trucks, and relief workers. It appeared even tourist buses were pressed into service. In the distance were spires from a dozen or more cathedrals.

Several large ships, including a cruise ship, were docked in the main shipping and industrial zone. In addition, hundreds of smaller vessels moved in and around some of the littler ports. The scale of the operation was massive, and with the proximity to the other seven islands making up the Canaries, as well as the eastern coast of Africa, the whole place resembled a large space station. It was the hub of a wheel involving dozens of countries and cultural differences, many of whom were closer in distance than Spain, the country they were part of.

The two vans snaked their way through the back streets of the city just as shopkeepers were readying for the day. Several school buses and black SUVs also fought for space. Once they cleared the capital, they turned sharply and began to climb into the hills, closer to the remnants of the fire, which had consumed thousands of acres and a huge national wildlife preserve. As the smoke got thicker, the buildings became less frequent and the temperature cooled. Several villages along the road appeared abandoned but were blocked by barriers, guarded by the local Civil Guardia in blue uniforms armed with semi-automatic weapons. Gibson had told them looting had been a problem in certain evacuated areas, and the Guard took their jobs seriously, being tasked with keeping order.

The view east, down toward the Atlantic Ocean, was spectacular as bright blue glimpses of it popped up through the dark smoky clouds. Rain was threatening, which actually would improve conditions on an archipelago known for a lack of annual rainfall. But with forty thousand acres smoldering from the raging wildfire, even mudslides would be welcomed.

When the smoke cleared, they were protected by winds coming off the bright blue ocean. At a distance, it looked like a colorful free-form patchwork quilt. Colorfully painted houses with flat roofs dotted the coastline and crept into the hills, shoved up against large boulders and outcroppings of jungle foliage.

At last, they came to a set of massive gates and stone columns protecting the approach to their lodging. A crudely made wooden sign attached to the façade indicated the property was closed. The first driver exited the car and entered a code into the communication box at the left of the gate, and several seconds later, the lumbering structure swung to the side, allowing them entry. The grounds beyond were lush, landscaped with flowering trees and tall grasses, bordering both sides of the crushed stone driveway leading downhill. In various locations along the way, tips of tall trees appeared to have been damaged by fire, green leaves turned into curled pieces of brown scrolls. Most of the landscaping and road-way was covered in light grey ash, as flakes swirled all around them, reminding Tucker of the first snow in the Sierras.

The stone and plaster hotel was tucked into the hillside with a spectacular view of the ocean and nearly all the coastline down to the airport. Tucker wondered if it had been a grand home at one time because it looked several hundred years old. The tall, ornate façade extending up three stories in the middle, like a crown. From here, they could see just about every ship or airplane coming on or off the island.

This area, thankfully, was completely free from smoke.

Sven paused on the patio outside the lobby, taking a quiet moment, his pack slung over his right shoulder. "I stayed here a long time ago."

"Oh yeah? When?"

"Gosh, nineties—late nineties. Overstayed my visa and nearly got married, too." He scratched the back of his head and re-hitched up his pack.

"She was a Spanish lass, then?"

"Oh yes, very Spanish." Sven sighed. "Knocked me right off my feet. Her parents were very wealthy, lived in Madrid. She was going to school here, studying art."

Tucker didn't want to pry, so he walked slowly beside his Norwegian friend as they climbed the painted tile grand stairway and kept his mouth shut. His background hadn't been anything as dramatic, or as romantic, until he met Brandy. He wanted to know more but knew Sven might enlighten him on his own.

"I'm never going to tell my new bride about this," started Lieutenant Gridley. "She'll think I did it on purpose."

"Yeah, but you were in Paradise, man," said Trace. "No fires, no bad guys, and it was your honeymoon."

"I think Trace is right," said his brother-in-law, Tyler. "This is nice, but I'd still choose Hawaii any day."

"You know they got a volcano on the other island?" added T.J.

"And snow," said Fredo.

"How the Hell did State find such a place, Gibson?" asked Cooper. "You must've pulled some mighty big strings."

Lt. Commander Gibson disagreed and barked back, "Not on your life. Just the luck of the draw. That's all it is." He stood his ground on the lobby floor as he studied the men climbing the stairs, examining the old wooden beams and unique carvings. Then he added, "Figure out your roommates. When you're done, come on down here for a chat in about an hour. That's when the food arrives."

"You taking one of the rooms up here, Commander?" Tucker asked.

"Already picked out. It's the one with all the crates in it."

Tucker knew Sven wanted to bunk with him, and he didn't mind. He'd picked out one at the end of the hall, next to the fire escape.

The rooms were huge, covered in crude paver tiles bordered with colorful hand-painted tiles used as baseboard and door trim. He didn't like the fact that he and Sven had to share a bed, albeit a king bed.

"Shit," he whispered.

"I was thinking the same thing," mumbled Sven. "I was so anxious to get the best view I didn't check out the sleeping arrangements."

"Let's see if there isn't a spare after everyone's situated."

Sven disappeared and returned with his report. "All taken. We got by far the biggest room, and even better, we got a desk and a bigger bathroom with a tub."

"Damn, and here I didn't bring my back scrubber and the salts." Tucker punched him in the arm. "You really think we'll have time for a bath, man?"

"Soaking in steaming water is a national pastime where I come from."

"Yeah and rolling around in the snow afterwards."

"Do you see any snow?"

"Good point. So if you're taking too long in the tub and I gotta use the john, I'm not waiting, but I won't look," said Tucker.

"Fair enough," answered Sven. "And I won't tell anyone we spent our days here in the honeymoon suite."

Tucker stiffened. "Say what?"

Sven pointed to the heart-shaped pillow on the bed Tucker had failed to see. Sven was starting to unpack. Tucker just threw his bag in the corner, his irritation burning a hole in his stomach.

"You tell anyone about this, you're dead."

"Got no one to tell." Sven's smile was evil, and when he wiggled his eyebrows up and down, he looked like an old Viking bastard straight out of the movies.

Tucker normally would have moved his journal under his pillow but now didn't want to risk its discovery, so he left it in his bag. He considered calling Brandy.

"Did the Commander say anything about using our cells?" he asked.

"I think he said we could, just not in town, unless it's work."

"I'm going to try to contact Brandy, if you don't mind. She should be getting up about now."

"Tell her I said hi." Sven pointed to the bathroom. "Taking a shower."

Brandy picked up before the third ring. He could hear Kimberly fussing in her arms. "Hello, sweetheart. How're my girls?"

"Oh Tucker, I was hoping you'd call. We're good. Staying busy. Let me get her situated, and then I can talk." She lowered her voice as he heard fabric and movement. "I'll have to whisper. She's already starting to figure out there's a whole world out there."

He waited until she came back on the line.

"There, all better. How is it over there?"

"Can't say much. I'm going to write it all down, like I did before. But I have to say the accommodations we've been scoring are first class. Am I making you jealous?"

"A little. So you're in another villa or something?"

"Sort of like that. Anyway, long trip. Same old, same old. I'm rooming with Sven, and he says to tell you hi."

"Give him my best. Does he know about the baby?"

"Yup, knew before I could tell him."

"You guys. Nothing gets by any of you. He going to go back to Africa?"

"I don't know. We didn't get that far. So what have you been doing? Can't stay long, but just a quick update, okay?"

"Actually, I have to talk to you about something. I was over at your former Team Guy's house. You know, the Tanners?"

"Oh, good. Sleuthing for sitters?"

"Started out that way. But I need your advice. I think I know what you're going to say, but I need to hear it from you."

"Is there a problem?"

"How well do you know them, Tucker?"

"They only had two when I served with him. I didn't see the family at all. Is she okay? Something going on?"

"Not Geri. It's her oldest daughter, Tucker. She's fifteen. And she's texting guys on her cell phone."

"Hardly a national tragedy. Happens all the time, Brandy."

"No, I get that. But her little sister said the boy was sending her pictures of his junk."

Tucker wasn't sure he'd heard Brandy correctly.

"Did you see it?"

"Oh Hell no. What do you think I am?"

"Well, you going to take the word of a little girl of, what, five?"

"She's six."

"Well then—that makes all the difference."

"Stop it, Tucker. I believe her. I feel like I should tell Bryce and Geri about it. Now, this could be like you implied, just a sister fight, or maybe she likes to tell stories. But think about it. What if Kimberly came home and told you this story? Would you believe her? Would you want to tell the parents of that child?"

Brandy was right, but it was damned hard to relinquish control over the situation. If he were home, he'd just jump in his truck and drive over there and get to the bottom of it. He thought Bryce would probably want to know, just like he would.

He remembered seeing the older girl transfixed with all the messages she was getting, and Bryce's reaction to it. He was going to have to trust Brandy to make that call to his friends. And if need be, he'd clean it up afterwards. It saddened him that they hadn't exercised more control over their daughter.

But Brandy was right. It was not okay to let it slide until he got home.

"Wow, you've got a tough one there. I think your instincts are correct. You need to tell Bryce and Geri. If he's got a problem with any of that, have him call me, okay?"

"I'm going to tell him we talked about it first. Can I say it was your idea, to protect their daughter?"

"Yes. Do that." He didn't hear a response and wondered if the phone call had been cut off. "Brandy? You there?"

"I'm here. I'm going to call them this morning."

"Please don't mention it to anybody else. That's their family thing, and he's not even on my Team anymore. They'll want to keep it quiet."

"Oh, absolutely. I wouldn't dream of it."

"So you let me know." He tried to think of something light-hearted to say to her, but his insides hurt. It underscored how vulnerable children and women were all over the world. And here he was all the way over across the Atlantic. Too far away to protect his own little family.

He thought about Colin Riley. He thought about how that man had suffered when his daughter had been trafficked. How he missed all the signs by his own admission. He saw himself reading that damned card and dreading to find a spot for those trees to root and become a permanent part of his little kingdom.

It would be impossible to ever really get away from all that. Everything was connected in a strange thread of human existence. He could tell himself differently, but it would be a lie. Then he thought of something.

"How are those palm trees, Brandy? You keeping them happy?"

"They're loving it here. You were right. They do feel like guardians. They keep watch over my garden. My sunflowers are already six inches tall. The cabbage and the broccoli are doing great. Not so much the lettuce. Too late for tomatoes, I think. But we'll have flowers all through the holidays. I love it so much, Tucker. Thank you."

"I'm glad. That makes me happy."

Sven exited the bathroom followed by a cloud of steam.

"I gotta go get cleaned up for dinner. Leave me a message on that other thing, and I'll try to call back tomorrow. No promises, though."

"I understand. Good night, Tucker."

"Night, Brandy. Kiss my angel for me."

"She kisses your back."

Tucker shut off his phone and placed it in his bag.

"Everything okay?" Sven asked.

"Nothing big. Just a tough call she's got to make this morning. I wish I was there to do it for her."

Sven left him alone, turning his back and getting dressed. Tucker dashed to the bathroom, tore off his clothes, and stood under the lukewarm shower, letting it wash off his worry.

Trying to make himself feel better, he mused that he was only about fourteen hours away. A couple of plane rides.

But he felt like he was on the dark side of the moon.

CHAPTER 10

B RANDY LAID KIMBERLY down while she showered. She made coffee and a little oatmeal, staring down at the slip of paper Tucker had written Bryce Tanner's cell phone number on. She knew she had to do it first thing, or she'd get caught up in the day. She wanted to make that call while Kimberly was asleep, and she'd not have any interruptions.

It was going to be one of the most difficult things she'd ever done. Could she trust herself with the truth? Did she hear it wrong from little Keira? Was there just a sisterly spat going on she was about to step right into? Would they say it was none of her business?

But the risk on the other side just wasn't worth it. What the younger sister had told her was wrong. It wasn't the sort of thing a six-year-old would just say out of the blue, which is why she believed her. And what was her reward for being honest? She'd feel like everyone was out to get her, that there wasn't anyone there to protect her.

She'd studied sexual assault in college. What she could remember from her studies was that it always started out innocently. And the unlucky ones lived in families where things either went unnoticed or unsaid. The lucky ones were when someone spoke up, questioned something that didn't sound appropriate.

And this was one of those.

She rinsed her dishes and placed them in the new dishwasher. She poured herself another cup of coffee, checked on the baby, and found her still sleeping soundly. She closed the bedroom door, sat down in the living room with her coffee mug, and dialed Bryce's number.

It went directly to voicemail.

She disconnected. For a second, she felt relieved, until she realized she'd have to keep trying, because that was just the right thing to do.

So she dialed again. This time, she left a message.

"Hey there, Bryce. This is Brandy Hudson. Say, I have something I need to talk to you about and I'd really like to talk to you sooner rather than later." She left her cell number and hung up.

Her hands were shaking, so she took an apple to help satisfy the churning in her stomach. She vowed not to have another coffee this morning, picked up a magazine, and waited.

She'd dozed off on the couch when her phone rang.

"Hey, Brandy. This is Bryce. How are you?"

"I'm good."

"You talk to Tucker yet?"

She panicked, thinking perhaps Tucker had called him instead of waiting for her to do it.

"Yes, they got over there. All fun and games, and you know I can't say more than that."

Bryce chuckled. "I deserved that. So what's up?"

"Well, this is a very difficult call for me to make. If it wasn't for the fact that I have Kimberly here, I really should talk to you in person, but I didn't want to wait."

"This sounds serious. Is there some problem with Tucker?"

"Oh God, no." Her nervous laughter sounded ridiculous. She was rethinking all her motives, her perceptions, and trying to blank out that she promised Tucker she'd make the call.

He had paused and was waiting, and she knew she'd feel horrible about sticking the knife into his gut.

"I'm afraid I have something I need to talk to you about that disturbs me. I—I wasn't sure, so I want you to know I talked to Tucker first. It was his suggestion I call you," she lied.

"You're scaring me, Brandy."

"Okay, here goes." She took a deep breath and began. "The other day when I was over at your house, Keira helped me put my things in the car. Geri had scolded your oldest about using the cell phone, er—getting text messages she was answering while I was there."

"God dammit all to Hell. I'm going to take that damned phone away."

"Well, I agree with you, Bryce. And here's why. Keira told me that Lynn was getting messages and pictures from a boy. Her boyfriend, she said."

"Boyfriend? She doesn't have a boyfriend."

"I think she does—or, at least, Keira thinks she does. And maybe Lynn doesn't. Maybe Keira made it all up. But here's the thing. Keira said she somehow saw pictures of the boy's *thing* that he'd sent to Lynn."

Bryce was breathing hard into the phone. Brandy knew how hard her words must be to hear. "Go on. What else?" His words were terse, and she could feel rage beginning to boil underneath.

"Keira's very worried you and Geri will find out about it. And she's worried her sister will hate her for telling me. Heck, I think they'll all hate me now. I can't say why, but I believe her, Bryce. I don't know her or your family, but I just get the impression she's not lying. She didn't say it like a joke. She trusted me with that reveal and then quickly tried to backpedal it. I guess that's what makes me believe her. Do you understand?"

"I don't want to. I wish you'd said anything else but that. I wish you'd told me my kids did something to you or the baby or said something mean. Any of those things I could take. But this—" His voice trailed off, and Brandy's heart plummeted to the floor.

"Like I said in the beginning, I didn't want to make this call, but I thought I had to. Both Tucker and I thought you should know so you could check it out on your own. I pray it's all wrong, and it's just been a horrible misunderstanding."

"Keira never lies," Bryce whispered.

"Oh Bryce. I'm so sorry."

"No, you did the right thing. As much as a part of me hates you for this, it was the right thing. I don't think I'll ever be able to look you or Tucker in the eyes again."

"But maybe it's not—"

"I had a funny feeling when all these text messages kept coming in, but I thought it was girls at school. Some of those girls can be a little wild. She wants to fit in. God, I hope she didn't feel pressured or—"

"Is there anything I can do? Please tell Geri she can call me. I'll see her anytime she wants."

"No, I've got to get hold of Geri, and then we'll get that damned phone and see for ourselves."

"If you feel it's appropriate, if you discover it's the truth, please tell Keira, if you want to—from me—that she's very brave. If you think it's appropriate."

"Thanks, Brandy. This is the last thing I wanted to do today, but Geri and I will talk, and I'll let you know, if you want."

"Oh, please. I hope I'm just having a good old-fashioned postpartum emotional meltdown. Honest."

"I'll bet. But you did the right thing. Tell Tucker you did the right thing. We'll investigate and probably get the police involved."

Brandy felt drained after the phone call. She sat in stunned silence, not even wanting to go outside to water the garden. Her heart ached. Her arms and legs felt heavy. She hated to trouble Tucker while on his mission and wished she'd been strong enough to make the call without his advice. But they always shared everything with each other. That was just the way they did things. She hoped that Geri and Bryce discovered it was some prank played by one of Lynn's girlfriends at school, but even that wasn't right.

She took several deep breaths and closed her eyes. She tried to feel Tucker's arms around her.

And then the baby cried and washed away all the pain.

CHAPTER 11

T HE TEAM HAD been issued used packs so they wouldn't draw attention. Just about every one of them was different, and some even looked like used children's school bookbags. Fredo's was more like a full tool bag, since he was tasked with bringing some small flash bombs, which he had strict instructions *not* to use, Invisios so each group could communicate with one another, and some tiny tracking devices with super glue sticky backs. These would be issued as needed. He also had wire cutters, both copper and aluminum wire and a tiny chain link bolt cutter Fredo and Coop were enamored with.

"Where the hell did you get these?"

Stuart Bonilla, one of the team who met them first at the house, answered, "I bought that in the Ukraine last summer. Very handy. Even works in freezing temperatures."

"I've seen those. Very useful," Sven Tolar offered.

State had hired twenty-five-year-old Bonilla, a crack radio guy, from smack dab in the middle of Ohio, borrowing him from one of their intelligence contractors. Stuart had spent quite a bit of time in eastern Africa growing up doing mission projects sponsored by his church. He had relatives who ran a mission school for girls in Benin, so he was familiar with many of the eastern dialects from Benin and Nigeria, and he spoke fluent Spanish and Portuguese.

Stuart showed them how to work the hairnet device, to track and capture cell phone signals so he and some of their brothers in Virginia could trace not only where the cell phone was traveling but what numbers it called. It was no bigger than a pack of cigarettes or a cell phone battery. He demonstrated how it worked with his own cleared cell, showing how it tracked a call he made in front of them to Gibson's cell.

"Now it will tell us who Gibson calls and so forth."

"Is there a way of masking this so the cell can't be picked up?" Tucker asked, examining the little black box.

"Not unless it uses something other than WiFi or Satellite. If it sends or receives a signal, it will pick it up."

"Short wave?"

Stuart wiggled his outstretched fingers to show that it was wonky. "Problem with that is that we know the signal is sent, but the bandwidth of anyone who receives it is too broad. Kind of useless. We want portal-to-portal signals. That's what we track."

"You must get a lot of data to cull through," remarked Gibson.

"We have computers upstairs that filter what we want. Yes, at the end of an hour or two, the screen looks like a spider's web. We look for patterns and movement, not actual conversations. That's not to say Fredo here won't be helping us out with some listening devices. Most of the smaller ones I've given him won't detect all the way up here, but we couldn't chance all this clunky equipment getting discovered. Plus, it's not very portable, so you'll only listen in when we have to. Great for hostage negotiations."

Tucker didn't like the sounds of that.

"You have to be worried about accidentally detonating a bomb?" asked Cooper.

"Yes, we do. Therefore, we don't *send out* a signal unless the bad guy is carrying something we want to detonate before he gets it placed. In that event, it can be kind of a weapon too. You want to make sure you don't do that, okay? It also makes you visible if other guys have some form of cell tracking."

"And what are the odds of that?" asked Tucker.

"In the states, with high-level drug dealers, they're very wise. They use burners and switch out SIM cards all the time, so you lose the trail. Mob crews in Europe and Asia do too. We're thinking we have a leg up here. They might know about them, but they haven't grown in their business acumen, so to speak. We got a tech advantage, gents."

It was obvious to Tucker that Stuart was rather proud of his equipment.

"You three carry these very close to your body, and only take them out when you use them. And you better bring them back."

Gibson asked that each man put a shirt and water into their pack, *not* their wallet. "Take something to jot down notes and a pen. Some sunscreen and whatever personal items you need. Make it look legit. No firepower. Sorry. Your weapons stay here."

Several of the Team grumbled, mouthing words like feeling naked without their favorite sidearm. Gibson wasn't making any exceptions.

"We're going in a little cold. You get caught and have a piece, you're probably going to be out for the rest of the mission, maybe longer. Just not worth it."

"I'm taking my slingshot."

Gibson didn't know Danny's story and gave a whimsical look. "Whatever."

Tucker was going to bring his NV binoculars.

After lunch, everyone readied themselves for the daytrip.

"Keys are in the vehicles, boys," one of Stuart's men blurted out. "Have fun and be careful out there."

TUCKER RAN FOR the Jeep before anyone else could claim it. The house had come with five other older-model cars and two pickups, all designed to help the men blend into the local population. The cover they'd designed is that they were firefighters from different jurisdictions in California, all friends, who decided to take vacation days to assist the island's population in the cleanup and recovery efforts. They were helping a friend tear down an apartment building. It was meant to look like an impulsive, self-funded operation to steer away from the concern they were connected to any government entity or had military background.

That would also leave things open for a little barhopping and making inquiries. And as firefighters, they wouldn't be expected to get too heavily involved in drinking and doing drugs but might get introduced to some things on a limited scale, recreationally.

In other words, they were going to pose as heroes with somewhat tarnished halos, who didn't want to cause trouble and lose their livelihoods back home. And they wouldn't be expected to know everything about the island like a frequent tourist or local would.

Calvin Cooper eyed the Jeep longingly. "Only for today, Tucker. Then you can have this old thing tomorrow."

Coop's mode of transportation was going to be a wine-colored 4-door pickup import that was missing the front bumper and had one tire that had been spray-painted green, for some reason. The front bench seat was ripped and could give anyone in shorts a nasty cut.

Tucker gave him the finger. "I rather think that suits you."

Two squads were to stay back at the motel, which included Lt. Commander Gibson, so he handed Coop another portable "hairnet" with the admonition, "Don't you lose it, Coop or you'll be walking."

"And that would be worse. Come on, Coop, let's beat them

down the hill," said Armando as he jumped in the front passenger's side.

DeWayne Huggles did an adequate job of nearly filling the entire second seat. Through the open window, he banged on the roof with the palm of his hand. "We go!"

Off they went, in a cloud of smoke.

Tucker swore that he'd let them get ahead of him and, with Sven and T.J., sped out the driveway, spewing flakes of ash in their wake.

Fredo and Danny took another older dark blue semi-compact with a large rubbed-out circle on the hood where someone had unsuccessfully tried to wax the vehicle with the wrong product. As they turned around, Jameson jumped in behind them, along with Jack Gridley.

Tucker was working like Hell to catch up to Coop's truck, but when he spun out on one of the gradual turns with a downward slope, he lost traction, which caused him to fan the brakes carefully until he slowed. He squeezed and let go his grip on the steering wheel until he felt more comfortable with the vehicle. He could feel T.J.'s eyes on him, but no one said a word.

"You see who got the sat phone?" T.J. asked him.

"That would be Jack," answered Sven.

The others stayed behind.

Coop got out first to punch in the code, and as the gate opened, Tucker's Jeep was able to slip by him and take over the lead.

Sven put his hand on Tucker's shoulder. "They have horses here, sometimes in the brush. Be careful, my friend."

"Good to know," Tucker said, as he slipped his sunglasses down from his scalp. "T.J., see if you can find some country music, will ya?"

Sven fell back into the seat, laughing.

NEARLY TWENTY MINUTES later, at the bottom of the hill switch-backs, they ran into the edge of the capital proper. He pulled over, parking behind a hardware and auto parts store.

"I'm noticing something different right away," whispered T.J. as he watched the other two vehicles join them.

"Different? Different than what?" asked Tucker.

"I'm not seeing as many dogs and chickens as on the mainland. But man, there are tons of cathedrals here."

"Big Spanish influence," said Sven. "You should see the ones closer to the city center. Really does remind me of Madrid. Wide streets, lots of churches. Bells ringing all the time."

"Not as many children here, either," T.J. added.

Tucker had noticed the same thing. A few children dressed in their school uniforms moved in and around the long lines of traffic, sometimes holding hands in a line. But not nearly the ones they'd seen in Benin and Nigeria. "Maybe because of all the rescue operations."

"Maybe they've already been sent elsewhere," said Sven.

Tucker knelt in the shade. It was hot already, and although he had a sleeveless shirt under his short-sleeved wrinkle-free golf shirt, it was one layer too many.

He turned on his cell phone and scrolled over the pictures of the six men they were to find.

"Anybody got a preference what position to take? We got the Red Arrow, the Tradewinds, and the Capri."

"I think I could use a little umbrella drink, so I vote we go to the Capri, Tuck."

"That sit well with you guys? Who wants to take the employ-ment agency or the Tradewinds?"

"We'll take the Tradewinds," requested Danny. "We got four, so it would be easier to hang out in the lobby or whatever they have.

"Okay, that leaves the Red Arrow for you guys," he said to Co-op.

DeWayne Huggles had a question. "Tucker, how the hell is this black man gonna go into the Red Arrow employment agency and go looking for a maid? Did anyone think about that?"

"Maybe you're looking for a temporary job, Huggins," said Cooper.

"Oh, you mean, like being a chauffeur. You see any big black limos hanging around taking rich folk out to dinner? You mean that kind of employment? No, sir. I don't think so. That's a bad idea."

Tucker needed to calm Huggles down. "Maybe today you just watch, record who comes and goes. Look for something you think should be investigated. Look for bad guys or guys who look like they don't belong."

"That's the problem, Tucker. *We* don't belong. How the hell am I going to figure out who else doesn't?"

"Did you take your meds, Huggles?" Coop interrupted.

Tucker was going to laugh until he saw Coop being entirely serious.

Their sharpshooter from Mississippi closed his eyes, "Dammit." A few seconds later, he whispered, "Forgot."

Tucker looked at Lt. Gridley. "Your call, sir. This is a call you get to make."

Gridley stared down at his sandals. Anyone with any kind of military background would spot him for an officer. Even while dressed down and casual, he still was the best-pressed and cleanest of the bunch.

Time to show what you got, Gridley. You've got to earn their trust.

"He goes back and gets his meds. We don't put the rest of the team in jeopardy because you forgot your meds."

"Good call, L-T." Tucker saw Gridley stand up straight and throw his chest out.

"Coop, you'll take them back. And I'll tell you what…you get to have the Jeep on the way home tonight, fair?" said Tucker.

"That's a good trade."

Tucker watched the three of them blend in with the slow-moving traffic north. He approached his Jeep as T.J. and Sven hopped in. He gave Jack a thumbs-up, and the foursome broke off, heading into downtown in the little blue import.

"What are the odds they got some George Strait at the Capri?" he asked T.J.

"Who's George Strait?" asked Sven.

T.J. spoke to the side of Tucker's face. "I'm not even going to dignify that question."

CHAPTER 12

JUST AFTER LUNCHTIME, Geri Tanner called Brandy and asked for a call back. Brandy was outside walking the garden when the call came in. Luckily, the phone didn't wake the baby.

"Hey, Geri, what's up?"

Geri's voice was scratchy over the phone. It sounded like she'd been crying.

"This has been a heck of a day. The kids were all in school when you talked to Bryce—and—"

Brandy interrupted. "I'm so sorry, Geri, about all this. I hope you don't think—"

"No, I understand. That was a tough call to make. I wouldn't have wanted to do it. But I have to thank you. We went through Lynn's things in her room, and she's got some pretty disgusting pictures."

"Pictures? Keira didn't say anything about that."

"I'll bet not. Keira would have told us immediately. I have no doubt about that."

"What kind of pictures, Geri?"

"It didn't look like some of her friends, but I don't know. Some were tied up; some in their underwear. It was hard to recognize anybody. One girl had a gag around her mouth. Stuff like that."

"Oh my God." Brandy didn't know what to say.

"Bryce has a friend on the San Diego police force, and he says we definitely have to make a report and get that cell phone to find out who did this. They don't want to spook whoever it is there at the school, so we can't just show up and make her tell us and get some kid arrested, but we're definitely going to bring in the police. I just don't want to cause a big scene for her. It will hurt all the girls. But this boy is a real creep with some serious problems, and we've got to get her away from him."

"I agree. But I'm relieved to hear that you're getting the police involved. That's what should be done. You have any idea who this kid is?"

"Nope. Not one picture of his face. Just pictures of girls. And they're young, too."

"Younger than Lynn?"

"I think so. One of them didn't have a shirt on, and she was prepubescent. I'm guessing about twelve. Bryce's friend was disturbed with all of it."

"I can imagine. So what's the next step?"

"Well, I wanted to ask you for a favor. I pick up Keira in a little bit. Shelby and Tori have a full day, like Lynn. But I was wondering if Keira could come over and stay with you for a little bit, maybe a couple of hours, until we get Lynn interviewed. I'm having my two other girls go home with one of their friends' mother. They have no idea what's going on. We're not going to interview Keira just yet. Hoping we can get information and cooperation from Lynn, first."

"You know, Libby Brownlee is a part-time marriage and family counselor. She's Coop's wife?"

"I don't know her."

"She'd be someone really good to be with Lynn when she's interviewed."

"They use a special social worker, child's advocate here. But maybe for something in the future. Right now, I feel like I need some counseling. I just never—"

Geri broke off, crying.

"No problem, Geri. Oh, I'll do anything to help out. Can you drop her by? Only wrinkle is I know she's going to be mad."

"She doesn't know we know yet. I'd just play it like that. Say Bryce and I had an appointment and we had to rush her over to your house. We thought she'd like to play with the baby. That sound okay?"

"Anything you want, Geri. Oh, I'm so sorry about all of this."

"Me too. Just what we get to do. On top of all this, Bryce is supposed to do a temporary deployment in about two weeks. Timing sucks."

Brandy was heartbroken Geri would be alone with the four girls, having to deal with possible police action and interviews.

"You know, you can have any or all of them come stay with me any time. Or maybe you want to take some time together, just the three of you, before he goes. I'll happily take the three girls for a few days. It will give me something to do, and I think they'd be a big help."

"Really? Well, I'll talk to Bryce. I couldn't ask you to do all that, Brandy."

"Think about it."

"I will. So I'll be over in about a half hour. Remember, you don't know anything."

"I got it, but do you think Keira has told her about the conversation I had with her in your driveway?"

"I don't think so, but I'm not sure. Keira's been very quiet. Lynn took her cell phone with her to school, which she wasn't supposed to do. We looked for it in her room and couldn't find it."

Brandy knew that little Keira, once she found out that her mother knew about her secret, would have one more reason not to trust her.

Right after she hung up, Joe Benson called to say that he had two retired friends he wanted to bring over, and if she was okay with it, there were a couple of things he wanted to work on in her yard. He also wanted one of his friends to look at the roof and the stairwell and help figure out if putting stairs on the outside would be feasible. His friend was a retired engineer.

"Well, Joe, I'm babysitting a six-year-old this afternoon. Her dad served with Tucker, so I'm doing them a favor. But I think it would be okay. I've got tons of food here."

"I'll have my wife get some sandwiches, and she can drop them by later on, so you don't have to cook. Anything else you need?"

"Oh, gosh no. You'd be doing me a favor helping me to get rid of some of these casseroles."

"Do you want her to bring Shannon over and perhaps Courtney? She's five, you know. The two girls are about the same age."

"That's a terrific idea, Joe! Go ahead and ask her."

"Okay, well, I'll see you within the hour."

It was going to be a full afternoon. But it would help keep her mind off how much she missed Tucker.

GERI WALKED DOWN the driveway, holding Keira's hand. She'd brought a small suitcase with a change of clothes and nightgown, in case they were late getting back.

Brandy knelt down to greet the child.

"I've been looking forward to seeing you again, Keira. Kimberly is about to wake up. You want to help me change her or maybe give her a bath?"

Keira wouldn't make eye contact. She buried her head in her mother's skirt. Geri's eyes were puffy and red, and she hadn't put on any makeup.

"Come on, sweetie. Mommy and daddy will be back before you

know it. Come be a big help with Kimberly," Brandy tried again.

"I don't want to go," Keira said meekly.

Brandy stood, gently brushing hair from her face, and then tapped the top of Keira's head. "We'll have fun, you'll see. Do you have any favorite movies I can put on the TV?"

Keira turned around, still leaning against Geri's legs, but delivering her answer like it was an order.

"Frozen."

WHEN JOE AND his buddies arrived, they carried a large crated box that appeared heavy enough to need a 4th man. Struggling down the driveway, Joe asked for directions to the back of the house.

"What do you have there?" Brandy asked.

"You'll see. Now, can I get to the back through a side gate, or do I have to come through the house?" he asked again, out of breath.

"You have to come through the house. The side yard doesn't have a gate."

"Well then, that's another thing we'll have to fix. You have to have a gate there," he said, shaking his head. She cleared a path at the front door and allowed them to walk in front of Keira, through the living room, and then through the kitchen and out the back-sliding glass door to the overgrown yard there. Keira didn't take her eyes off the movie or even seem to notice the men and their cargo.

Joe and his buddies set the large box against the backside of the house. With his hands on his hips, Joe surveyed the space.

"Honey, you don't have a rear-fenced yard."

"I know."

"Why the devil did they build a fence with no gate but not have a fence to protect the backyard?"

"The neighbor told us that someone behind us used to use this property as a cut-off and used to drive through."

"What? That's completely ridiculous."

"Apparently, he'd done it for many years. The owners had the fence built to stop him."

"That's not very neighborly," said one of Joe's friends.

"Oh, Brandy, this is Sy Woods. And Tom Nettles."

As she was greeting them, she heard the baby crying. "Duty calls."

Kimberly had hiked her shirt up over her shoulder and was waving her free arm back and forth, unhappy being uncovered. She was probably hungry too.

Brandy decided against interrupting Keira, so changed the baby and then brought her into the living room, taking up a seat next to her temporary charge.

Keira moved to the side, giving her more room on the couch, without removing her eyes from the big screen. The baby began to feed as Brandy watched the movie.

She knew it was going to be a long day.

She was only halfway there.

CHAPTER 13

THE CAPRI WAS the type of bar that could have existed in nearly any country in the world. The first thing that hit Tucker when he walked through the beaded entrance was the smell of alcohol, which meant they didn't wash the floors very often.

Coming from the bright mid-afternoon light into the dark and dank hole that was the bar hurt his eyes. The name, painted on corrugated metal, with a pink flamingo wearing a necktie, was a total misnomer. There wasn't much that reminded Tucker of Capri, of the Caribbean, or Florida, where flamingos lived in the wild and weren't tended in multi-million-dollar landscaped gardens.

It was just a bar, and a dirty one at that.

The floor was sticky as he made his way to a table in the corner covered with dirty glasses. Sven and T.J. pulled up two chairs around the table and stared back at him.

Tucker grinned. "I'm thinking no country music."

"You'd be one hundred percent correct," T.J. agreed.

"Doesn't look much like the Capri I remember," mumbled Sven, looking over his shoulder at the multicultural array of bodies hugging up to the bar like baby piglets getting suckled.

A tiny dance floor with blinking colored lights was empty, but Tucker spotted several scantily clad ladies hanging on customers in the periphery and figured they were probably the only ones who danced.

A woman washing down the next table asked, "You want some-ting?" in a heavily accented African dialect Tucker didn't recognize.

"You have beer?" asked T.J.

"Yes. Bottles."

Before they could ask what their choices were, she left, returned a few seconds later, and placed three unlabeled brown bottles on the table, opening them one at a time. They were not chilled.

T.J. examined it before he placed it to his mouth. "Beer?"

"Yes. Boss beer. Only kind." Her dark coffee-colored skin was covered in a fine sweaty mist. She had red nail polish, chipped, and deep purple lipstick on her full lips. "That's nine Euros."

Tucker gave her a ten-dollar U.S. bill and another five on top of it. Her eyes flickered slightly as she grabbed it off the table.

"Tanks."

They watched her head for the bar and whisper something to a rather rotund man with a thin moustache and an earring in his left ear. He wore several ornate rings and gold chains. His light-colored silk or rayon shirt stuck to his sweaty body. The waitress disappeared behind a doorway.

Sven examined his bottle like it contained ant poison. He looked to T.J. to get some encouragement. "How bad is it?"

T.J. had drained half of the bottle and set it before them. "I'm trying to figure out what they fermented here. It definitely wasn't hops or barley."

Tucker didn't want to taste his now.

"Oh, I think there's enough alcohol to kill whatever it has, but it's got a taste that's hard to place. Go ahead, Tuck. I think it's harmless, but probably very high in alcohol."

Tucker timidly sipped the bottle, after wiping the top off with his shirt. It wasn't sweet but had a honey-like aftertaste. He could feel the first few swallows travel down his parched insides, and it reminded him he'd better get something in his belly.

As his eyes became more accustomed to the darkness, he noticed a dusty collection of what looked like Voodoo dolls displayed above the lighted mirror behind the bartender. He counted over thirty, and there were no two alike. Some were made from straw, some from rags and yarn. Some had painted faces, and nearly all of them had hair. Upon closer inspection, the hair didn't look like yarn, but human or animal hair.

A chill slipped down his spine.

"Sven, you know anything about Voodoo?"

"Only what you told me when we were on the mainland." He turned to face the bar, following Tucker's gaze.

"Well, that's kind of creepy," whispered T.J. "Looks like some kind of admonition or something. Not very welcoming."

"Did you see the hair?" Tucker asked.

T.J. took a second look. "Like I said, creepy. I really didn't need to see that."

Tucker was aware they had attracted the attention of the bartender, who now waddled over to their table.

"Ah, the Americans have landed. We are all now saved! Praise be to God!" His English was good, and he appeared comfortable speaking it. "You wish that I bring you another beer?"

"Boss beer?" Tucker asked.

"Yes. Yes. Boss beer. Very, very good beer." He placed his palm to the middle of his chest. "I am Diego, the boss, and I make it. All natural. No preservatives."

Tucker didn't think there would be any. But he foraged his question. "What's it made from?"

"Maize, corn, you know, corn on the cob?"

"You make beer from corn. I didn't know that could be done," said T.J.

"You like it?" the bartender asked. "Corn is very, very good for you. It has a sweet taste, no?" When no one answered him, he shrugged. He looked behind him, scanning the room quickly. "You are here for work? Vacation?"

"We're here to help out a buddy. We're firefighters. He's had some damage we're helping him with. Clean up," answered Tucker.

"Ah, I see. Very good. Well, if it is your first visit to our little island, let me introduce myself and make some suggestions, okay?"

Tucker decided to play along.

"First, may I suggest you be careful about the food? And watch for bandits. Your wallet, understand?"

They nodded.

"Only eat food in reputable establishments. No carts on the street, understand? It will make you sick. Watch out for the little children who pickpocket. And the gypsies. And also stay away from the police, you know, the Civil Guard. No not get into a traffic accident, at all costs."

T.J. interrupted him. "Is there anything here we *can* do for fun?"

Diego's face widened, his smile showing off several gold-rimmed teeth. "We are known for many things, but at the top of our list is our lovely ladies. I can arrange some introductions, if you like."

Again, Tucker agreed to go along with Diego's line of thinking.

"We might be interested. But we're both, except Sven here, we're married men."

"The girls are very discrete. Very, very nice. We are a melting pot of Spain, Portugal, and Africa. Ladies from every country with very different tastes and talents." His eyes were glowing, his fingers itching with anticipation for the money he was thinking he would make.

"Well, we probably need to finish our work for today. When should we check back with you?" Tucker asked.

"Tonight would be good. The ladies come later in the evening, when we have more customer, you understand?"

They nodded.

"And you are single, yes?" Diego asked Sven.

"I am."

"So you can really play the field. You like experienced ladies?"

Sven, in spite of all his worldliness, was seriously embarrassed. He stumbled with his answer. "I like them pretty. But not too old." He took a quick glance at Tucker, and it registered what Sven was doing.

"Oh, yes. Young. Perhaps you like them young, then?"

Tucker's stomach lurched. Noticing the cell phone hitched to Diego's belt, he reached into his inside shirt pocket and slid the hairnet switch to on. Diego was intent on listening to Sven's answer and didn't notice.

Sven acted like this was news to Tucker and T.J. "Sorry, fellas. But, yes, I like them on the young side. Not children, of course." He scowled.

"No, no, never. But I understand completely. You like them fresh and untouched," he enunciated like he was reading off a delicacy from a menu. "This is always more expensive, but not impossible. I can also arrange that she come cook for you, keep house? She can be your wife while you are here—working."

Tucker could feel T.J.'s tension explode, noticing the veins in his neck protrude. He was also grinding his teeth.

Sven answered, "No. I don't need a wife. I just want to have fun."

Diego laughed, causing a couple of the bar patrons to turn around.

"Then fun you shall have, my friend. Your new friend, Diego, will see to it personally."

Two men darkened the doorway, and Diego immediately disconnected to give the newcomers his complete attention. Both were dressed in slacks and long-sleeved shirts rolled up to their forearms due to the heat. One wore a loosened tie, as if he worked in a bank or was in business locally. They were lighter in skin tone than Diego, with a mixture of Creole and Indian features. Neither took their shades off as Diego brought them to the opposite side of the room where no one was sitting. While the three discussed something private, T.J. retrieved his cell and snapped photos of the group.

"You still on?" he asked of Tucker.

"I hope so."

"I recognize one of those men from the photos," said T.J. "I think we just widened the net."

CHAPTER 14

THE MOVIE ENDED, and Keira wanted to go outside to watch the workmen, who were causing noise with their drilling and sawing. Brandy wrapped the baby tight and escorted the six-year-old out the sliding glass door and onto the patio. All of a sudden, she discovered what they were doing.

Bits of packing material and remnants of the original box lay on the ground off to the side. In the middle were several large pieces of painted plywood, bracing and a scattering of Joe's tools, including a skill saw. Joe was studying a sheet of directions he'd laid out at his feet just beyond where Brandy and Keira stood.

He looked up. "Surprise. Bet you never would have guessed."

To Brandy's amazement, Joe and his friends were assembling a playhouse kit. As the walls were raised onto the flooring material, Keira turned to her, suddenly more excited than she'd been all afternoon.

"It's a playhouse for Kimberly. Oh, you're such a lucky!" she said, bouncing up and down to look at the sleeping baby.

Brandy sat on one of the patio chairs so Keira could watch the baby sleep.

"Joe, I can't believe it. Where did you get all this?" she asked.

"Bought it from a friend I know who sold his toy store. I used to put them together for him, and he said he had a couple left over still in the box."

"It's pink," shouted Keira.

"It sure is, little lady," answered Joe. "We're going to have it up here in about a half hour. You want to be the first one to play in it?"

Keira was bouncing, cheering, running back and forth on the patio. Brandy asked her to stay away from the tools and equipment.

The doorbell rang, so Brandy walked back to answer it.

"Oh hi, Brandy. I'm Gloria Benson. I don't think you remember me, but I'm Joe's wife. Courtney's grandmother." The attractive woman held a shopping bag.

"Nice to see you again. Come on in."

"I brought some sandwiches and iced tea for the boys. Joe was so excited to come over today, Brandy." She wrinkled her nose and whispered, "It gives him something to do."

Brandy took the bag offered, placing it on the kitchen counter. Mrs. Benson followed right behind her, focused on the baby.

"Well, hello there," she greeted Kimberly, who had just opened her eyes. "She's a perfectly beautiful baby."

"Here," Brandy said as she allowed Mrs. Benson to hold her.

"Oh, it was such a short time ago Courtney was this small. I miss those days," she said as she made faces with the stoic Kimberly.

"Did you bring her over? I'm watching Bryce and Geri Tanner's youngest, Keira."

"I'm afraid not today. My husband thinks he can arrange the world in a matter of seconds. They already had plans." She looked back down at Kimberly. "Tucker must be over the moon with delight."

"I don't think he ever thought he'd have a child."

"Oh, nonsense, men can have children at any age. We're the ones with the expiration date."

Brandy saw that Gloria Benson was someone she could trust and was easy to befriend.

"You have to go for more," Gloria added.

"This is about all I can handle at the moment." A shadow passed over her as she thought about Geri and her four daughters. Mrs. Benson returned the baby.

Keira opened the slider and announced, "Look, Kimberly, your house is almost finished!"

The men finished putting on the window shutters and the front door. They tightened the screws with Joe's screw gun, while they cut extra trim pieces for the door frame and outside windows. They also created a ledge so that the kitchen window had a pass-through on either side. Joe held the door open, and Keira ran inside without fear, screaming in delight.

The work crew sat as Mrs. Benson brought them their iced tea and sandwiches. She knew them and their dietary likes and dislikes well, flirting slightly with each one. She also brought out a peanut butter and jelly sandwich, but hesitated.

"Can she have this?" Gloria asked.

"I think so." Brandy asked Keira, "Honey, can you have peanut butter and jelly? Does your mommy let you eat those?"

"Only strawberry. I only like it with strawberry jam."

"Well, what do you know. I got it right!" Gloria chuckled and handed it over. "Can I get you something, Brandy?"

"Water. I'd like a glass of water. The glasses are in the cabinet over the dishwasher."

Kimberly was wiggling, so she propped her up to sitting position on her knee and burped her. Keira was fascinated with trying to catch the baby's attention.

Minutes later, the men gathered up their tools and Joe took the leftover box remnants to his truck. Gloria said her good-byes, while Joe and his friends began discussing what should be done with the stairs to the upper great room. They measured, drew small sketches in a notebook, and looked for locations of studs in the walls bordering the stairwell. They went outside and measured the side of the house, called numbers to each other on sizes of windows both downstairs and upstairs, and measured the length of the side fence.

Keira was beginning to get in the way, running up and down the steps and weaving around the men. Brandy managed to get her attention, reading some of the books her mother had packed in the suitcase. She fell asleep on the couch.

Brandy put the baby down and then checked her phone for messages but found none. It had been nearly three hours, and she was hoping for an update. Then the phone rang.

"Geri, is that you?"

"Yes. Listen, it's not going well here."

"What's happened?" Brandy whispered, moving into the kitchen.

"They took her phone away at school. She was caught texting."

"Oh, dear."

"She got it back when school was over, but then she dumped the phone in the drain, Brandy, before we could reach her."

"Oh no. So now what?"

"Bryce's friend says they want to interview Keira. Lynn argued that this boy is in love with her and wanted to meet her. That's what she told us. She told us she didn't want him to get in trouble, so she threw the phone away."

"Wait a minute. You said he was one of her friends from school." Brandy's heart was racing.

"That's the thing. Now she says she's never met him. She says she found the pictures at her school and denies he ever sent them to her. Begged us to just throw them out. I know she's lying, Brandy."

"Of course she is. She's protecting him. Boy, this guy must be good."

"Well, Bryce's friend says we don't even know if it's a guy or who he is. But she's convinced he loves her."

"I can't imagine how you feel."

"Have you ever heard anything so insane? My daughter—" Geri's tears took hold.

Brandy let her cry. When Geri blew her nose and seemed ready to listen, she asked, "So what can I do?"

"They want to bring someone over to your house to question Keira, since she's the only one who saw the cell phone pictures. They think it would be better to do it at your place, rather than our home. Keira might feel less self-conscious."

"Whatever you want, Geri. I'm here for you guys."

Okay, let me get back, and I'll give you a call if we're coming over. In the meantime, can you give her some dinner? Maybe get her ready for bed in case we're late?"

"No problem. She had a sandwich late this afternoon, so I don't think she'll be hungry. I have chicken noodle soup. I have mac and cheese, tons of other things in the refrigerator."

"Perfect. Thank you so much."

"What about Lynn?" Brandy asked.

"I'm dropping her off at my mom's. They've asked that I keep the girls separated for now until we can get them interviewed."

Brandy dialed Tucker and got his message line. Her heart was banging so loud in her chest that she thought she might get sick.

"Tucker, I'm having one of those good and bad days all rolled up into one. Kimberly and I are fine. We have a new pink playhouse in the backyard, but the whole world around us is going crazy. God, I need to hear your voice, Tucker. I'm trying my best, but my world just isn't the same without you. I realize that more and more every day. You should be here with me and the baby.

Forgive me, because I know how selfish that sounds. I shouldn't be telling you this, but I just have to get it off my chest. And I'm scared. I don't feel safe."

She watched the sleeping form of little Keira and realized how vulnerable they all were.

What would Tucker do?

"He'd stick it out, make it work," she whispered to herself.

Of course. It was the obvious solution to a problem that couldn't be solved, except with the passage of time, because it was impossible to control. He'd watch and look and wait for the opportunity to be a hero. He'd stay focused and alert to all the forces. He'd never give up.

He'd protect them all.

She decided to just focus on that.

CHAPTER 15

TUCKER WISHED HE'D asked more questions of Stuart Bonilla when he was getting the hairnet demonstration. He didn't want to pick up meaningless information. There was no telling how many cell phones were located in the bar. He counted thirteen sitting on stools and bet every one of them had a device of some kind.

So he reached back inside his shirt and turned the switch off. If he caught either of the two newcomers answering their phone or making a call, well, he could reverse that.

"I think you need to get closer to them," Sven whispered.

Tucker looked at the back part of the dance floor and located a men's restroom. He again activated the device and announced, "Gotta take a leak."

He grabbed his unfinished beer bottle by the neck and sauntered past the three gentlemen. Just before he reached their table, he stumbled, dropping the bottle and following its roll until it hit Diego's shoe.

He didn't have to work hard to feign being tipsy. He'd shared most of Sven's beer with T.J.

"Gawd, I'm so sorry." He pressed too familiarly into Diego's side and didn't make eye contact with the newcomers, who both stood up and backed away, moving like powerful cats. Tucker immediately assessed they'd had some serious martial arts training. Their stares were hostile.

"Hey, don't touch me, friend," Diego said, pushing Tucker hard. "You can't just walk up to me in a meeting."

"I'm sorry, man. I thought you could get us more beers, that's all. I'm on my way to the head."

"Sonja!" Diego barked, while his two other associates quietly slipped their hands into their pockets where Tucker was sure they carried some sort of weapon.

The waitress appeared from around the curtain and scurried over to take Sven and T.J.'s order. Tucker raised his hands with a wavering "don't shoot" stance and sidestepped his way to the restroom.

The cracked mirror revealed what a hot mess he was. His nerves were on edge, and he had two days of stubble, which itched like crazy.

What the fuck am I doing here?

In case he was being watched, he used the John, leaning his elbows on his thighs and trying to calm himself. He rubbed his scalp vigorously, sighed, stood, and washed his hands. He swung the door open and nearly collided with one of the Creole gentlemen, who again backed up two steps to avoid having any contact with Tucker.

The man's smooth skin was nearly feminine, and Tucker noticed he wore just a touch of eyeliner and blush, which was something he never expected to see here. His dark hair was plastered down flat on his head, every hair in place. His cold black eyes emanated pure evil.

He was grateful for the gap between them so there would be no chance the device would be detected, yet he moved slowly so there would be a better chance for a signal to be captured at such a close proximity. Tucker eyed the ground, mumbled a, "Pardon," and then returned to the bar.

Sven and T.J. were ready to leave. T.J. suggested they head over to the Tradewinds and try to rendezvous with Lt. Gridley and the other three men. Tucker was going to jump behind the steering wheel when Sven slapped him on the upper arm and pointed across the alley.

The Tradewinds was less than two blocks away. It had been a nice hotel at one time with ornate balconies in wrought iron like Tucker had seen in the French Quarter in NOLA. It looked to have been built in the late eighteen hundreds and was plaster over wood construction with stone retaining walls and fireplaces. It didn't take much to envision Europeans from all over sitting on their balconies, sipping cool drinks and looking out at the blue Atlantic while the rest of the world went by. He felt the ghosts of escaped pirates and fugitives from government—perhaps several governments, as well as the dangerous liaisons and secret political meetings. This place was made for clandestine operations.

It always would be.

There was a quiet order to this place, he thought. Control was an illusion. He knew if he had to spend any time here, he'd wind up going native, which would mean one thing—he was back to a solitary life again where he didn't have to worry about anyone but himself. And his Team buddies.

"Tucker, want me to call Fredo?" asked T.J.

"Sure, go ahead. Tell them where we are."

A pile of crates was stacked just across the entrance to the hotel, nearly obstructing a narrow alley with clotheslines hanging from windows on the second and third floors facing the other stone and brick buildings across the small space. He imagined this was a natural form of air conditioning because very little light managed to carve out a spot.

He sat, swearing because he'd forgotten to turn off his device, and did so. T.J. had just hung up.

"They're still in the lobby. Not much happening. Most the rooms are being used by rescue workers and some foreign press," he said.

Sven checked his watch. "Should we gather up everyone and go back?"

"Let me find out if Coop's men are on their way."

His call was answered on the first ring. "Thought you'd be shooting me a message, Tuck," said Stuart. "Good job. We've got a ton of stringers out already and logged in nearly a dozen connections to phones on our target list."

"Good. I was wondering if I was too far away."

"You were just right. I've got some solid tracks going on now. We'll be busy tonight."

"Are Coop and the guys on their way down?"

"Gibson nixed that. You seven are on your own."

"Okay, we'll text when we leave. Just wanted to check."

"You did good."

Tucker was going to suggest they head into the lobby and pick up the other squad when, all of a sudden, their two visitors from the Capri walked past, forcing them to duck into the shadows of the alleyway. The men stopped at a sedan parked on the opposite side of the street, opened up the trunk and took out a large suitcase. After searching both ways on the street, they entered the hotel, wheeling the suitcase behind them.

"Call him back and tell him to get the net on," he said to T.J.

He didn't want to risk being detected so waited against the cool bricks. The noise from the edge of the busy city echoed off the walls, exaggerating the sounds of trucks, bulldozers, heavy equipment, scooters, and the sounds of horns blasting at the harbor. There was nothing familiar to him. He breathed in and out slowly and waited for his body to calm down—so his head could think despite all the noise. He closed his eyes and pretended he was watering Brandy's garden. Or nuzzling the baby in bed.

He'd made a miracle, and yet he'd chosen to put his ass all the way over here. But he was doing it to help protect someone else's innocent women and children. He hoped that, if the situation were reversed, someone would do the same—protect his wife and baby.

T.J. leaned over, "You okay?"

"I was just thinking—don't get me wrong now."

"Uh oh. Not one of those conversations." T.J. picked up a rock and threw it.

"Kyle told me you held him. Held Frankie."

"T.J. sorted the rubble at his feet, looking for another rock, and then picked up several.

"Yeah, I did."

"And he made you promise."

T.J. nodded.

"You're a good man. And now you're raising Frankie's daughter."

"Yup, I got a little piece of Frankie with me always. And she's my daughter now, Tucker."

"You're right. That's the way it should be, too."

"Yup."

"It must have been hard."

"Frankie wasn't going to make it. I would have promised him anything just to keep him alive. It wasn't going to happen."

Tucker was hesitant to continue. They sat in silence. Then Tucker had to speak. "Would you do the same for me?"

"Hell no."

"Why?" Tucker felt the tiny flame of anger growing inside.

"'Cause I'd go to jail, and I'd never do that to Shannon."

Tucker grinned. He hadn't even thought about Shannon. Of course, he wouldn't take on another wife.

"It's not funny, Tucker. That's a damn serious thing."

Sven was listening, his arms crossed, stifling a smile.

"I didn't mean *marry* her. What do you take me for? I meant help get her set up. With another Team Guy. Somebody good."

"Listen to you, Tuck. I never expected to hear those words come out of your mouth."

"But would you do it?"

"Well, let me ask you, would you?"

Tucker nodded again. "Yes. Yes, I would."

"Well then, there you have your answer."

The two men clasped hands to the sounds of Sven chuckling in the background.

CHAPTER 16

ERI AND BRYCE arrived an hour later. Keira was thrilled to see them, yanking on Geri's arm to show her the playhouse. She ran inside and out, opened the windows and doors and got Geri to bend down and join her.

Bryce was stiff and, as he'd said over the phone, was not making eye contact with Brandy. But he did look at the baby in her arms and finally said, "She's a cutie. God, I remember those days. Some of the best of my life."

Brandy smiled, but inside, she felt the pain this man was feeling. "They grow up quick, don't they?"

He did return her gaze this time. He had that same look about him as Tucker did, not shying from going to the heart of the problem. He showed no weakness, not even a little weepy-eyed tear. He was on a mission. His handsome face a total mask of what must be churning inside.

"Make the most of every day. None of us know what can happen in the future. And don't assume anything." He cleared his throat and watched his wife and child outside.

"I'm sure there's no way you—"

He interrupted her. "I'm not going there until we find this guy. There's always something we can do." He put his huge hand on top of Kimberly's head with a tenderness that made her knees weak.

"Goes to show how one little lapse in attention can cause things to derail." He smiled at Kimberly and then raised his eyes to Brandy. "I had a hunch, and I didn't act on it. That's on me."

Brandy knew better than to argue with him. She felt he was being far too hard on himself. But Tucker would feel the same.

"It's a good lesson for all of us." She saw the police car pull up to the front of the house. "I think your friend is here."

Bryce greeted the uniformed officer at Brandy's front door, as well as the social worker sent from the Department.

"Brandy, this is Kent Porter. He and I go way back to when he tried out for the Teams."

The handsome dark-haired officer extended his hand. "Brandy, just so you know, we don't talk about that much, and if Bryce is lucky, he won't bring it up again."

She liked him and felt reassured by his firm handshake.

"This is Mary Weck. She's one of our social workers we contract when we're interviewing kids. One of the best."

"Nice to meet you, Brandy. Thank you for reporting the incident right away. That gives us some ammunition to go on."

"You're welcome. So how does this work?"

The social worker began. "We'll interview her here, and I think I'll have her mom with her. Bryce, perhaps not you. I think you and Kent should go outside for a bit, go get a coffee or something, but be on hand in case we need you."

"Fine," he said. "Got my cell."

"Brandy, I think it would be good for you to be here as well, because she felt it was safe to tell you about it in the first place. And she will know what she told you, instead of trying to cover it up or deny it. But she may do that anyway."

"Okay. I may have to get up and down with the baby."

"I think that's good. Normal life here. We're in a friend's house. Her parents are here. Less scary than going downtown or in my strange office." She smiled. "Although I do have some pretty nice toys."

Brandy chuckled. "I have some books in the little chest over there, if you need anything like that. I read a couple of them to her earlier today."

"Perfect. Shall we get started, Bryce?"

The two men left in the patrol car.

Brandy went to the back door and motioned for Geri to come inside. Holding hands, they both walked inside. Keira's eyes got wide when she saw the woman sitting on Brandy's couch.

"Keira, this is Mrs. Weck. She's a nice lady who wants to talk to you for a few minutes, okay?"

Keira clutched Geri's skirt like she'd first done when she arrived earlier.

"Here, Mommy will sit next to you, right here, okay?"

The six-year-old climbed into her mother's lap and buried her face in Geri's neck and chest. Her eyes fixated on Brandy, standing to the side, as if she had some idea what this was all about.

"I understand your sister has a boyfriend," Mary began.

Keira's face wrinkled in pain as she shot Brandy a harsh look.

"Can you answer Mrs. Weck?" murmured Geri to the top of her head.

Keira kept her face turned away from the social worker and didn't move.

Mary Weck started again, "Keira, you're not in any trouble, but we wanted to ask you about your sister's boyfriend. What can you tell me about him?"

"I don't know anything," she said into her mother's chest. Brandy could see she'd begun to cry. Geri continued to rub her daughter's back in soothing, long motions.

Mary's voice was patient and slow, but she continued to pry for information. "How do you know she has a boyfriend? Have you seen him?"

"No," she mumbled.

"Keira, we understand you may have seen a picture of him on your sister's cell phone. Is that correct?"

That got her to sit up and face the room. "I didn't see his face, just his pee pee."

Geri's eyes closed, a single tear tracing down her right cheek.

"Thank you for that, Keira. That's very good," said Mary. She refrained from touching the child. "When did you see his picture?"

"I forgot."

"Was it yesterday or the day before?"

"I don't remember."

"How did you see it?"

"He sends her text messages. And he sent her the picture. I saw it before she put the phone away. She asked me if I saw it, and I told her no."

"What else?"

"She made me promise not to tell Mommy and Daddy. Made me keep it our secret." She looked up at her mother. "I didn't want to keep a secret."

"I know, sweetheart," Geri said as she hugged her.

"Don't tell Dad. He'll be really mad."

Mary looked between Geri and her daughter, then said, "Honey, he already knows. And he's not mad at you at all. Your mother's spoken to him."

Keira stared back into Geri's face. "Really?"

"Yes, honey. Nobody's mad."

"Well, Lynn will be. She's going to smash up all my dolls. I know she will."

Mary paused, waiting for her to finish and then spoke softly. "We're here to help Lynn, because we need to find that boyfriend quickly before he sends any more pictures to her, or to anybody else. Do you understand?"

Keira nodded.

"You wouldn't want to get pictures like that, would you?"

"No. They're yucky."

"Yes, they are. And have you ever seen any other pictures? Or has Lynn told you she received others?"

"She didn't tell me. I just saw one."

"Okay, so is this boyfriend someone she's known a long time or just a short time?"

Keira shrugged.

"Someone from school?"

She shrugged again. "He wants to meet her, so I think he goes to another school."

"So, she hasn't met him yet?"

Keira shook her head.

"Now Keira, I'm going to ask you a very important question, and it might be difficult to answer, okay?"

Keira nodded.

"Can you tell me, how did you know it was a picture of his pee pee?"

She frowned, puzzled. "I know what a boy looks like. I've seen my Daddy naked before—by accident."

"How by accident?"

"I've seen him getting dressed, on accident. I didn't mean to!" She stared up at her mother. "I'm sorry."

"It's okay, Keira," said Geri.

"So tell me more about what it looked like," Mary pressed.

"It was pink and fuzzy with hair all over it. It looked disgusting."

Geri gasped for air, and then softened, hugging Keira tightly, but she could not stifle the tears. Mary Weck sat straight and nodded to herself.

"Okay, I think we're done," she said.

CHAPTER 17

TUCKER'S CELL RANG.

"Fredo and the gang are done. You ready to head back?" barked Gibson.

"They picked up the target?"

"They did. We got a lot of information to digest. We'll see you back up here in a few."

"Roger that."

"We done here?" asked T.J.

Tucker spotted his four Teammates exiting the building. "Sven, go tell Fredo to put a mark on that car. I'll meet you back at the Jeep, okay?"

"I'm on it," Sven said as he emerged from the shadows to meet the other squad.

Tucker and T.J. waited until the tracker was placed, counted another five minutes to make sure no one had seen them place the mark, and then carefully emerged from the shadows. Sven was waiting for them at the Jeep.

The sun hung lower in the horizon as a golden bronze covered everything, softening some of the harshness of the bright colors they'd seen earlier on. It also smoothed over the contrast between the lush gardens that popped up on the shore side, behind guarded gates, and the highway and villages where most the population lived. It was like the population was divided into two groups, and it had nothing to do with nationality. There were the working people, families and children, shopkeepers and the rescuers and civil servants trying to help them function in all the chaos. Then there were the other people who worked very hard to separate themselves from that general population.

So what group do I belong to?

He decided he didn't belong in any group. Not above or below, but separate, operating in the shadows and free from the routine of everyday life. At least that's what it was like here. At home, well, in a way, he lived in the shadows too, since so much of what he did for a living was a total secret. They had their own world, and in that world, there was security, family, love, and a future.

"So those two are staying at the hotel, then?" Tucker asked Sven.

"Yes. The guys took some pictures of them checking in and heading upstairs."

"Did they meet up with anyone?" T.J. asked.

"They didn't say."

"So we kinda made Diego think we were coming back tonight, Tuck. We going to do that?"

"Let's wait to see what Gibson says. Maybe we should give one of the other squads a chance."

"I'm game for whatever," added Sven.

The crush of traffic grew more intense until they got through to the other side of Las Palmas, and then a steady stream of gravel trucks and bulldozers on trailers filed past them coming down the hill from the site of the fires. They turned up to finish the stretch to their motel.

A roadblock had been set up where a bus had overturned in front of them. Flares and lights flashed everywhere. It was difficult to see who was directing traffic, so everything just stopped. An ambulance passed them going up the oncoming lane and then a fire truck. Several groups of locals had gathered, watching the mess.

"Geez, hope Fredo got through," said T.J.

"No kidding." Tucker called the house and got Gibson. "We're stuck behind an overturned bus. Should we offer to help?"

"That's a negative, Tucker. We're not to get involved."

So they waited. He turned off the Jeep.

At last, as darkness approached, they were directed to skirt the accident. Tucker had to dodge curious onlookers—even a boy on horseback and half a dozen food carts. Faces of all colors shouted in languages he couldn't understand. Women wrapped in colorful drapes with baskets and children in tow were illuminated by the red and blue flashing lights. The whole scene looked like one of the many carnival parades he'd seen.

Compared to the snarled traffic jam, the rest of the drive home was uneventful.

The house was eating dinner when they arrived. Tucker wanted to get the grit and grime of the day off him but was too starved to wait. An enormous spread had been laid out for them with several local dishes, fresh fruits, and some barbeque chicken, which was heavenly. He stuffed himself.

They were to have an evening briefing, so he ran upstairs to make a quick call to Brandy and perhaps get a quick shower in. He found Sven just getting out.

"I feel human again," he said.

"That's right where I'm headed." As he slipped off his shoes, he asked his Norwegian friend a question. "How much time did you say you spent here? And when was that, Sven?"

"Oh God, twenty, yeah, twenty years ago. Just before I joined the forces."

Tucker had stripped off everything except his shorts. "What

brought you here?"

"I did a lot of traveling. We do a lot of that in Europe. Kids used to travel all over the place, all over the world in their teens."

"I've heard that."

"I'd never been to the Canaries. Someone said it had nice beaches."

"We never saw any of that before, did we? Haven't seen any this time, either."

"Nope. Not what we're here for. We've been in the seedier parts, the old harbor. Downtown has wide streets and cathedrals, very different than here. All the islands are different. But, yes, I had a good time."

"So she was an art student. How'd you live? Were you working?"

"Tended a little bar. That's how I met her. And then we had a place on Tenerife. Came here for a weekend. It was a lovely hotel."

"What happened?" Tucker asked.

"Life happened. Her parents demanded she return home. Said they didn't want to finance her Norwegian fling any longer." He laughed. "I think I made her drop out of school."

"I'd have thought you would have inspired her art."

Sven shrugged. "It was what it was."

The shower was heavenly. With fresh clothes, he flew downstairs and sat just as their meeting was beginning. Then he remembered he'd not called Brandy.

Lt. Commander Gibson began their briefing with, "We're off to a good start, gents. The hairnets are giving Stuart and his team fits. They've got so much information. Stuart told me we're going to have some very specific locations to kick some serious butt coming up here."

Tucker was relieved.

"Fredo's got a trace on a car we hope will help locate some of the players who aren't quite so public. We've identified one of the six names on our list, Javier Rodriguez, who we believe is staying at the Tradewinds. I think Tucker and T.J. and Sven have started something at the Capri, but we've definitely got a tight fix on Rodriguez, and that's huge for our first day out."

"Do we have to worry they'll find the tracking device," asked Coop. "I mean, should we try to mark them in more than one place?"

"That's up to Stuart and the guys back home. Our job is to find all six and bring them in, hopefully at the same time, and get them somewhere we can interrogate them." He paced the floor just as he commonly did back in Coronado. "What else we're following is some ferry activity down at Gondolia Harbor. Not sure if any of you noticed that large cruise ship that someone pressed into service. It's Italian registry?"

Several men acknowledged seeing it.

"We think there are ferries operating out of port, using this ship to offload or make exchanges. Jens Vandershoot's family is in shipping, and Jens was a known associate of VanValle, the guy you got last mission. This time, we want to capture the asshole and find out about all his locations, all his illegal businesses. We want to put him away so that someone else doesn't crop up later on and take over, like he did."

Gibson described several of the other characters on their list of most wanted. And he stressed that someone was going to have to make it onto that cruise ship somehow.

"Do we have equipment for that? Rebreathers?" asked T.J.

"We do. It's about a five-mile swim from where we can launch a team. We need some eyes on that ship from the inside. We've watched containers being off-loaded, but they're putting some back on, too. We need to verify what they've got."

Gibson brainstormed some of the intelligence theories and

asked for four men to show up at Diego's night club pretending to look for girls. Tucker was relieved when he chose Lucas, Alex, Jake, and Ryan, who were all long-time friends, for that mission.

"The rest of you, hang out a bit and turn in early. Tomorrow will be a long day. And I'll need one squad awake in case Lucas and the others get into trouble. We'll have our targets, as well as the required permissions, in the morning."

Tucker ran upstairs to try to get a call in to Brandy. He replayed her message back first and was alarmed to hear she was having difficulty. Checking the time, he figured she'd be awake and placed the call but didn't get an answer.

"Hey, Brandy. Just trying to reach you. Got me a little concerned. Call me when you get this. Don't worry about what time it is here. Wanna talk to you."

He straightened his things, located his journal, and began to write like he'd promised.

I'm kind of glad I'm not seeing the best part of the island. Sven told me he'd spent some time here with a Spanish girl twenty years ago. Talked about the beaches and the great hangouts on one of the other islands. Maybe someday we could do a "just vacation" trip over here, although avoiding anywhere I've been this time.

The buildings are like little pill boxes piled up on top of each other, colors of red, light blue, white, and bright yellow. They like their colors, similar to the Caribbean. It's a little more prosperous than Africa. More Spanish influence, which is why there are cathedrals everywhere.

We're over in a more remote portion of the island than we were before. More industrial. And, with all the international aid going on right now, it's so congested and noisy I can't hear myself think. That and the heat. Good news is, no bugs so far! And I haven't seen a snake yet, either.

Got to taste some Boss Beer, which is like it sounds—beer made by the "boss." Using corn, not wheat, barley, or hops. Can't say I'm a fan yet. But bottled beer and water are safest when you don't know where it's coming from.

Hope those palm trees are doing well. I miss everything about home, but mostly, I miss you, Brandy.

He folded up his notebook and lay back on the bed.

THE PHONE RANG and pulled him out of a deep sleep. Sven was snoring and apparently didn't hear a thing.

"Brandy?" Tucker checked his watch, and it was not quite 0300.

"So glad I could talk to you. I really needed to hear your voice."

"Your message—"

"I shouldn't have bothered you with it. That was me at a weak moment. Last thing you want to do is worry about things over here."

"So what's up?" he whispered. Sven stirred in his bed but didn't awake.

"This situation with Lynn Tanner. Today we had an interview with her little sister, and it looks like there's an older guy, perhaps a man, involved."

"Lynn's involved with an older man?" Tucker walked downstairs so he could speak without being overheard. "What are they doing?"

"So much has happened, and I don't want to bother you with it."

"Tell me. I'll stay up all night if I have to, Brandy."

"They interviewed Keira last night, at the house. They confirmed what Keira had told me and discovered that this person sending Lynn messages is probably an older man. Or, at least, not a child. Now they're looking for a sexual predator, that it wasn't just a kid's type of prank. Somehow this guy has gotten hold of her cell phone and convinced her he's a teenager."

"Bryce must be beside himself." Tucker's guts were in knots. He knew the waiting was the worst part of any emergency. His mind was filling with worry. "Brandy, listen to me. Maybe you should go over to Dorie's house or have someone come there to be with you. Get your dad to come or take Kimberly there."

"That's a good idea. But Kimberly is too young to take to someone else's place. Joe Benson and his friends were here all afternoon building Kimberly a beautiful little pink playhouse. You should see it, Tucker. Keira was so excited for her."

"Call Joe, Brandy. Call Joe and Gloria. You don't have to tell them everything, but it's important that you don't stay home by yourself. You'll be peeking out every window and making up things you might see. Will you do that, honey?"

"I should have thought about that. I feel so stupid. I hardly slept last night."

"You have to learn to reach out. I can't be there all the time, sweetie. I just can't. This is part of why it's hard, being a SEAL wife is hard. But you don't have to be alone and afraid. Being strong is asking for help."

"You're right, Tucker. I'm beating myself up now for not being tougher."

"And that's wrong too. This is all new for you. It's new to me, too."

He wasn't going to mention it was why SEAL marriages often failed. There was such a disconnect when they were away. Not everyone was cut out to handle it. He blamed some of that on the failure of his first marriage. Being scared to be alone made finding someone else an attractive option. It was the option Shayla took. Still, he knew Brandy would never do that. He'd have to pay more attention to things when he got home.

"Brandy, I'm going to say something that might sound harsh. Please just listen, okay?"

"Okay."

"You have to separate yourself from the rest of the crazy world. You have to build a wall around every awful thing that could happen when I'm away. You can't fix everything, help everybody. Terrible things happen within our own community. It's just life. And, as awful as this sounds, it has nothing to do with us. You've got to understand that. Let other people handle it the way they need to. You need to detach and try not to get involved."

"But that feels so cruel."

"You'll go crazy, Brandy. And I can't come home and fix everything all the time." He didn't want to go further, but it was time she understood some of the stakes.

"You have to ask yourself what you'd do if I didn't come home. What if it was like Frankie?"

"Don't say that, Tucker!"

"Sweetheart, I'm telling you this because that's always a possibility. It isn't all roses and glitter all the time. You have to be real."

"I don't want to think about that. Ever."

"You have to, Brandy. Your job is to take care of Kimberly. That's your only job. Everything else in the world can just go flush itself, for all I care. You have to be there for her."

He knew he'd made her cry. He was beginning to get angry with himself. He should have tempered his tone.

Dammit.

This is so fuckin' hard.

"Are you still there, sweetheart?"

He heard her sigh. "Yes."

"I get trained to do these crazy things. We learn how to tap down our emotions, even when they're raging inside us. Do you know why they teach us that?"

"So you stay alert."

"That's right. Because why we're worrying about one thing, something else pops up. The only difference between what I do and what you do is that you're a team of one when I'm gone. You are Kimberly's whole world. Am I making any sense, 'cause I'll keep talking until I do. I've got all the time in the world."

"But you won't get any sleep."

"Hell, I know what going without sleep is all about. That's not a problem." His heart lurched, and he dug his fingers into his palm, making a fist until it hurt and began to bleed. She was more of a rock to him than she realized. He wasn't sure he'd gotten through.

And then a miracle happened.

"Thank you, Tucker."

Her voice got soft. The tightness in her throat was gone from holding back tears.

"I think I understand now. I needed to hear that. You're exactly right. I was taking my eye off the ball for a while. I was over-whelmed."

"It's okay."

"But that part about you not coming back. I'll never forgive you if you do that."

They both laughed. He was laughing through his tears but con-trolled his breath so she wouldn't know.

"That's my girl. You see, the one part I didn't tell you was that I depend on you as much as you depend on me. I understand what you're going through because I *want* to understand you. You're my rock, baby. Yours is the face I come home to, see every night. Everything I see that's good in the world reminds me of you. All I need is for you to be strong for me. Just a few more days. And I'll be home, and we can celebrate."

She sniffled, and he knew she was a snotty mess, which gave him a chuckle inside.

"That will be a great day, Tucker. Can't wait."

"The whole world can go to Hell, and we're still gonna be here. It's you and me, Brandy. I see stuff every day in these places that's just fucked up. It just shouldn't be that way. Women and kids abused, innocents caught up in something they didn't create. They just want to have the kind of life we can have. I learned long ago that I can't fix everything. I can only do my part."

"You come home, Tucker. I want you to teach me how to be brave. Neither one of us knows what's in store for either of us. I want you to teach me to prepare for anything."

"You got it, babe. It will be my pleasure."

After they signed off, Tucker waited until the vibration he felt all over his body stopped. That familiar engine that was running inside, all the rage he felt at all the things that were wrong with the world would never leave him. It was part of who he was.

And it always would be his job to do whatever he could. He just couldn't live any other way. He would never quit. Not while there was work to be done.

It was what coming home was all about—to see his family live in the safety he'd helped to create. To enjoy the twinkle in their eyes and the freedom in their hearts.

CHAPTER 18

S TEVEN COOK CAME right over with his new wife, Jillian. He
brought several bags of fresh produce with them, and after
taking turns with Kimberly, the two of them took up their stations
in the kitchen peeling, chopping, and making heavenly smells.
Brandy was so happy she'd called him.

She asked if they could have Joe and Gloria Benson over for
dinner as well, and so, the five of them sat down upstairs on the
plywood tabletop, decorated with votive candles, drinking wine
and serving up the feast.

"Joe's still talking about all the projects he wants to do here,"
beamed Gloria.

"Steven, you're welcome to come on over, if you're handy. We
just need the okay from the boss, here," Joe Benson said, pointing
to Brandy.

"We're on a rather precarious budget at the time, Joe. But—"

"Hogwash," said Joe.

"Not a problem," said her father.

The two older women rolled their eyes and helped themselves
to more wine.

"Whatever do you mean, Dad?" Brandy asked him.

"Well, whatever he needs, I can buy. He's donating the labor. I
guess I could donate the cost of construction."

"You don't have to do that," she answered him.

"Of course he does." Jillian toasted her.

Joe retrieved some plans he'd started to draw up. "These are only preliminary, of course. And, before we dig in here, first priority is to get that backyard fenced and gated. Agreed?"

"I agree," she said.

"So here we are." He rolled out drawings done on tracing paper. "You can see how we can add this second bathroom downstairs, move the walls a bit and create a nice master bedroom closet?"

"Looks like we'd have two bedrooms and two baths then. Is that right?"

"You got it." Joe continued to demonstrate the changes to the downstairs while Jillian and Gloria cleared off the table and took everything into the kitchen.

Brandy leaned in on her elbows and studied the plans. "So you'd have the entrance for the upstairs here," she pointed out. "That would be right about there, by that big window."

"No, that would be the doorway. We take the window out and make it a doorframe instead. We also make a deck just big enough for a small table and chairs. Great place to watch sunsets." Joe angled for agreement from Steven Cook.

"I like it. But boy, I'd have a hard time deciding which unit to live in. Pretty nice up here," Cook said.

Brandy agreed. "I know. I love sewing and laying out projects here. The light is wonderful. Makes me want to start painting again."

"You should. Joe, she's really talented."

"Well, this could be your studio. Maybe find a couple other artists to share the space with. Who knows, maybe you could rent it out that way."

"It's a thought. Not sure the zoning would allow a commercial space. But we know for sure we can do a second unit. The city is trying to encourage more housing. I know we could use the extra income."

She hesitated to bring up the subject again.

"Just how much is this going to cost? I mean, I don't want you guys to do all of this for free."

"If I don't have to pay for materials, I absolutely don't mind doing the labor. You will have to get a plumber and electrician, and I know the permits will cost you something. A few thousand dollars." Joe shrugged, "But we'll know more after my friend Sy does the structural engineering. You're going to need all that to put in for your permit. I'll get an idea what Sy will charge, but we're all retired. We actually look for projects like this we can do together just to stay active. We built a big play structure over at the church a month ago."

"You like the ideas, Brandy?" her dad asked.

She thought about the conversation she'd had with Tucker earlier this morning. "I can't wait. I think Tucker would be pleased. I'm going to tell him first chance we get to talk."

The men sat back in their chairs.

"How's he doing?" Joe asked.

"I guess he and T.J. went on a little trip yesterday. He said it was very chaotic, with all the cleanup and evacuations happening."

"What's he doing, exactly?" her dad wanted to know.

"Beat's me," she shrugged. "Like all of them, it's just a mission. Something to do with bad guys doing evil things. Same old, same old."

Joe chuckled. "Frankie's mother went nuts every time he went over, before he got married. Of course, he didn't call us, like he probably does now, but he never would tell us anything. Said he was on the beach, chasing girls. His mom would get so frustrated with him."

Brandy's dad gave Joe a warm smile. "You've got a grand-daughter, right?"

"Love of my life!" said Joe.

"Who's the love of your life?" shouted Gloria Benson. She had a pie in one hand and a carafe of coffee in the other.

"I was talking about our Courtney."

"Look who's up," said Jillian, holding Kimberly. "I changed her for you. Hope that was okay."

"Oh my, thank you."

Kimberly's eyes were trying to focus on the candlelight. Her little head jerked from side to side as she tried to hold herself up.

"Look how strong she is already. That's amazing," said Gloria.

As the baby nursed, Brandy was suddenly grateful for the older people in her life, sharing her young joy with their years of experi-ence. Her father had found love again after the passing of her mother. Joe and Gloria lived through Courtney, their son's child.

She did feel safe. Tucker had been right. Her job was to make sure she wasn't alone, to make sure to stay plugged in and connect-ed with her family and her community.

After Joe and Gloria Benson left, Brandy's dad and Jillian were preparing for bed.

"You never did tell me why you wanted us to come over," her dad said. He was always the one who observed her many moods growing up.

"I told you. It was about time we spent more time together. I don't want to take her out too much until she's older." She checked his expression to see if he was buying the lie. "I was getting lonely, I guess. Stir crazy."

"Has something happened? Did you see something on the news?"

"I don't watch the news much. I don't want to see something about a conflict in Africa or someplace where Tucker might be."

She pulled the baby up on her shoulder and burped her. She considered whether or not she should tell her father about Keira and Lynn and decided to wait until she knew more what the outcome was. She remembered what Tucker had said, *Let the experts handle it. Nothing you can do.* "Thanks for being concerned. I'm fine now. Seeing all you guys tonight was exactly what I needed."

"Well, I'm off to bed. We'll make breakfast in the morning. Then we can discuss how long you want us to stay."

"Thanks, Dad," she said as she stood. They walked down the hallway to the bedrooms. Steven Cook kissed his granddaughter and then kissed his daughter.

"Love you, Brandy. Your mom would be so happy to see you and the baby. I'm glad you're so happy."

If he only knew.

CHAPTER 19

L T. COMMANDER GIBSON shook Tucker awake. At first, he couldn't remember where he was, but then Sven's familiar snoring brought him right back.

"We got a problem. One of the boys got arrested," Gibson said.

"Shit." He was putting on his jeans and a shirt. "Who is it?"

"Lucas Shipley."

"Stupid fuck. How did that happen?"

"Alex thinks it's a shakedown. They're staying down there at the police station until we can figure something out."

"You call State?"

Gibson hesitated. "They want to see if we can get him out first. Try paying them off, and that's what they think has to happen. But they'll contact the folks in Madrid if that doesn't work."

"I'd like to take T.J. then unless—"

"I'm good with that. You know where the station is?"

"No, but I'll find out. I need Alex's cell. I'll wanna talk to him on the way down."

Gibson shared the contact. "I'll go get T.J."

"I understand my presence is requested," he said, carrying all his clothes.

They checked in with Stuart Bonilla, who was fast asleep on a mattress in the corner of the communications room. One of his men sat at the console, removing his headset.

"Hola!"

"We've got to go get a man at the police station. Anything I should know about?"

Stuart jumped up off the mattress. "Sorry, I've been up for nearly twenty-four hours. I was seeing things."

"We're going back into Las Palmas to pick up Lucas, who's gotten arrested. Anything big going on that you know of?"

"No. I got no clusters. Nothing's moving. Right, Ray?" he asked the young agent at the desk.

"I got nothing. Lots of things I'm looking for in the morning, but all's quiet now."

"Tucker, check in so we know you got successfully home."

"Will do. You want me to take the net?"

"Let's leave that home, just in case you get searched. Say, Gibson," Stuart addressed the Lt. Commander, "who had the device?"

"I gave it to Jake. I know it wasn't Lucas."

"Okay, good. Those fuckers are expensive."

"Stuart," said the young agent. "They turned it off over an hour ago. I got nothing on it, just the bartender's signal and he wasn't making calls."

"Okay, we're on our way."

Tucker and T.J. started up the Jeep and used the glow from a nearly full moon to navigate the winding road down the hill.

He called Alex.

"We're on our way. Can you tell me what happened?"

"It was just a crazy bar scene. A couple of locals found out we were Americans and started messing with us. The bartender tried to make them leave, but they started a fight."

"How come they nabbed Lucas? How did that happen?"

The dead space on the other end of the line said volumes. "Lucas punched them back."

"That was smart."

"One of them has a brother who is a Civil Guard. Real mean dude. There wasn't anything we could say. I don't think they're going to hurt him, just keep him there overnight."

"And you think this how?"

"That's what the bartender told us. He told us to go home and not to worry about him."

"You think the bartender knows these guards?"

"I think everyone knows everyone. He just didn't want to have trouble. He'd brought some ladies for us to dance with, you know. We weren't going to do anything, just buy them some drinks and such. Then these guys got jealous. Had a chip on their shoulder about Americans."

"How close to the Capri is the station?"

"About five, six blocks. I'll drive to the Capri, and you can follow us over."

"Good. See you in a few."

They didn't pass a single vehicle until they got to the bottom and hit the outskirts of the city. The harbor was fully lit up, and as they passed by, they saw forklifts stacking small containers while a crane was loading a shipping car into the large cargo opening on the cruise ship. A platform had been attached to the outside to facilitate the transfer of goods. Men with lighted hard hats guided the container until it was swallowed in the belly of the ship.

"They're working late," Tucker commented.

"I was just noticing that. Wonder what they're loading."

"I guess we'll find out soon."

The temporary buildings were well lit, but it appeared most everyone was asleep. Several fenced off areas were patrolled by Civil Guards with dogs.

The Capri was closed, but Tucker found Jake, Alex, and Ryan in the shadows, along the side that lead to the Tradewinds. Tucker noticed the car that Fredo had tagged was still there.

Tucker rolled down his window. "Anyone notice you?"

"We haven't attracted anyone's attention that we know of."

"Where are the guys who picked a fight?"

"Gone. They were gone by the time the police showed up."

"Okay, lead the way, then."

He followed the dirty sedan with the rubbed-out paint, noticing that it also smoked like hell. They turned several times and then came to a small plaza with a fountain in the middle. The streets were paved in cobblestone, so the ride made Tucker's teeth chatter. On one end of the plaza stood a two-story building with a flat, tiled roof, and small windows. Tucker knew it was the local jail.

Two blue and white compact patrol cars and one scooter were parked outside. He asked Alex and T.J to come with him, and the three of them mounted the steps, finding themselves inside a tiled foyer. A blue-uniformed Civil Guard stood and immediately approached them with a stick of some kind. Tucker thought he was going to be struck.

The official said something in Spanish, and Tucker put his hands out to the side. "Americans. We're Americans. You have our friend inside," He pointed to somewhere beyond the wall.

"I scan," the guard said and waved a wand down Tucker's front and back sides, repeating it with all three.

"No weapons. No problem," T.J. said.

Tucker gave a scowl but then turned to discuss Lucas' situation. "You speak English, senior?"

"Little."

"We come to pay his fine," Tucker said.

"Fine? What is fine?"

"Money. We are sorry, my friend. He's my brother. He marry my sister. My sister be very angry if I don't bring him home."

"He marry your sister?"

"Yes, tomorrow. Ceremony tomorrow."

"No, Senior. Not possible."

"My sister, she loves this man. She will be very, very angry. She knows many rich people."

Tucker wasn't sure the guard was very interested in helping them. There was no way they should break Lucas out, although he knew they could pull it off. It was exactly the thing that they'd been told not to do. Then he had an idea.

"You can call my sister's boss, Jens Vandershoot. Call him. He will vouch for my friend."

The guard eliminated his slouch and practically stood to attention. "You know Jens Vandershoot?"

Tucker could see panic in the man's face.

"Old family friend. Go ahead, call him. But it's very early. Perhaps we pay the fine and take him home now, so he doesn't miss the wedding, okay?"

Tucker reached into his jacket pocket and brought out a stack of one hundred U.S. dollar bills, with its red sticker still attached. He held the stack up to the guard's face. "Brand new. Virgin bills. For my friend."

The guard indicated he'd be right back and left, without taking the money.

"Well, I've either fucked all of us up or made a dent in the problem."

T.J. chuckled. "We should have brought DeWayne. He could have talked to this guy no problem."

"Well, I was going for authenticity."

"You were that, Tucker," added Alex.

The door the guard exited into opened, and Lucas was pushed out in front of them. He had a swollen eye and dried blood from a cut lip. The guard unlocked his handcuffs and applied a damp towel to Lucas' face.

"Tomorrow, he will be perfect, see?" He dabbed the blood and pressed lightly on Lucas' eye. Lucas grabbed the towel and growled.

"Thank you, my friend," Tucker said bowing, presenting the stack of bills. When the guard took it, Tucker added, "And I will be sure to tell Mr. Vandershoot how cooperative you were."

The guard's eyes got wide. He started to push the money back. "No, no. There is no problem. It is my pleasure."

Lucas took the money back and started to stuff it back in his jacket but stopped. "Ah, hell, you earned it. Thank you, and I won't say anything to Mr. Vandershoot."

The guard held the bills with both hands, like they were a bouquet of flowers.

"You are most kind."

As they were leaving the lobby, Lucas asked. "Where did you get the cash?"

"Gibson gave it to me. But, Lucas, why did you think it was a good idea to punch the guy?'

"He said the Cubs sucked."

CHAPTER 20

B RANDY'S DAD INSISTED that either he or Jillian would spend the nights with Brandy until Tucker came home. She'd get more sleep, and they could help with the housework and the cooking. Jillian coordinated with some of the wives and tapered off the fried chicken and heavy foods. Each time, Kimberly was paraded out for all to see. Everyone offered support. Brandy saw that she'd not been taking full advantage of the help offered before, while she had it.

She also knew that this wouldn't last forever.

Geri gave her updates over the next few days. Despite the questioning Lynn had undergone, the person who had stalked her and her cell phone had completely vanished. The pictures were turned over to the police, but it was determined that not much else could be done. No one was sure how this person had obtained Lynn's phone number in the first place, but they suspected it was someone local when she'd ordered fast food or put her name down for a newsletter at a shop of some kind. The police continued to think it was a random occurrence and wasn't likely to reoccur.

Lynn's high school presented a program on human smuggling and sex trafficking for parents, as the result of what her family had gone through. But Lynn's anonymity was kept intact, and, except for her family and the school staff, what she'd gone through wasn't common knowledge. The social worker, police, and her counselor at school all told her how lucky she had been, and Lynn seemed to accept it and agree with them.

Steve enjoyed working in the garden, sometimes with Brandy, and kept the rows neatly tended. He helped Joe Benson and his two buddies work on the side gate and rear fence until it was completed. Sy had turned plans into the City to be approved for the addition, with Brandy's dad paying the permit fees, which amounted to nearly a thousand dollars. They were given a two-month window for everything to be processed. Of course, nothing would start until Tucker came home to approve everything. But it was all ready to go, just in case.

Dorie stopped by with her three. The twins were nearly walking. Jessica was very curious of the baby, but once she saw the playhouse in back, she refused to come inside and stayed until dark. She spent the whole afternoon presenting the men with imaginary tea and sandwiches from her playhouse.

"I think Joe's going to have a steady stream of orders for those," said Dorie. "You think he's ready for that?"

"Hope so. I'm so happy they've still got a home with all of us. It must be terrible to lose a son like he did."

"Brawley said one of the instructors told him about a man they lost a few years ago, who left behind a wife and two kids. The team nearly came to fistfights over the widow."

"No!"

"Oh, they're serious about that, Brandy. I mean, I know Brawley would want another Team guy to raise our brood if something happened to him. That's just how it's done."

"I know. Tucker tried to talk to me about that one time. I didn't like hearing it then, and I don't like it now."

"We just live for today and trust that tomorrow will be there too. I always keep a part of me in check, though."

"I've had the same thought, Dorie." Brandy put her arm around her friend's shoulder. "You guys seem happy now."

"We are. I didn't know I married such an asshole!"

Brandy laughed.

"He loves giving those BUD/S guys hell. I think it satisfies something inside him. Besides, he says, he's making them stronger for what they have to endure coming up. Not all his instructors saw combat when he was training. Now, all these guys have seen it multiple times. We're preparing a better team for the future."

"I didn't realize that would make a difference, but I can see it does."

"I've heard some of the older SEALs, who never really saw combat, talk about it. They look up to the younger ones. Have a whole lot of respect for what they had to do over in the Middle East."

"I never knew that."

"So when do they come home?" Dorie asked.

"I'm not sure. This one is very different."

"*All* of Kyle's missions are. Man, have they had some unusual assignments. You know they had a cruise ship taken over by terrorists some years back? It was supposed to be a vacation!"

"That was before Tucker re-upped."

"Yeah, Brawley missed it too. But it was something. Christy got a piece of luggage returned from that cruise a couple of weeks ago. That was, what, seven or more years ago? They finally found her luggage."

They both laughed.

"With Kyle gone this time, I'll bet Tucker is taking a leadership role."

"Yes, I think so." She sighed. "I'll just be glad when they return. We'll have to get together."

"We need to do that. Just think, Kimberly and my twins will be so close in age. I can't wait to plan those parties!"

Brandy was curious about something. "Dorie, I know I talked to you before about being a SEAL wife, but did it change once Jessica was born? I mean, you were engaged when he was going over, but after you had the baby, did you feel—"

"More alone?"

"Is that what I'm saying?" Brandy scratched her head. "Yeah, I guess that's it."

"You're taking care of someone nearly 24/7, and there's no end to the job. Plus, you worry all the time. My mom isn't especially the motherly type, with all her social stuff and her boyfriends, and Brawley's parents live way up on Oregon—well, I didn't have them either. I had you, though, and that was a Godsend."

She hugged Brandy.

"I am lucky with my dad and Joe and everyone. I really am."

"I'm glad you appreciate it. Some couples just don't have that support system. You have to create your own, when it's not there. Not to bring up the past, but I think that's what happened to Tucker's ex. She was afraid of being alone. It wasn't fair, because he was doing all he could. But she couldn't handle it."

Talk of Shayla still stuck like a thorn in her side.

Brandy shook her head. "Nope. I think she was just flawed. Man, she missed out on one of the best men in the whole world. You remember when we had that little encounter. I thanked her for releasing him."

"Oh gosh, I forgot. That was so funny."

Brandy unloaded the dishwasher while they continued.

"I don't miss the not worrying, Brandy. I won't lie to you. That was going to make me very old very quickly. Brawley had all that trouble; I just didn't know who was going to be the man who came home to me. Do you understand?"

"I do."

Dorie gazed out the window at the men who had started to pick up their tools. "It's good for your dad too, Brandy. He needs friends. Lived all those years without your mom, now with a new wife. A man needs man friends. Just something about them wanting to put things together or solve problems or go do crazy stuff. They have to go out and be men. Brawley is so much happier working with those other instructors, being looked up to by the tadpoles."

"And he'll get his twenty."

"Yes, ma'am. We've got a year to figure out what he does next. It's going to be hard finding something that satisfies outside this group."

Brandy could see Dorie was more worried about it than she let on.

What would Tucker do some day?

CHAPTER 21

THE PLATOON WAITED an extra day to track and locate as many of their intended targets as they could find. So far, there had been no trace of Jens Vandershoot, but their intel picked up chatter that he was planning to deliver a large shipment of guns—running them down the western coast of Africa, probably to Nigeria. Vandershoot was known to have extensive ties to government entities there that provided cover for his operations. The Special Agents in charge were betting he'd be using the cruise ship. It was said he never liked to be far from his cargo, so, although they'd not located him electronically, they were certain he'd be on the ship.

They hired a deep-sea fishing charter and used it for staging the three-mile dive Coop, Trace, and Tyler would make. The charter's size and weight put them in a class where they could operate at night without a pilot, which would have created too many questions and dashed the element of surprise.

Tucker, Sven, T.J., and Ryan were to drive down to the harbor and board the ship from land. This time, they were armed with their choice of firepower. Tucker chose the SIG Sauer with two extra magazines.

The rest of the team would split to search targets Stuart had identified. All five of the other targets were located within the past twelve hours on land, near the area of the Capri and Tradewinds.

Several were staying in residences nearby.

The squads used the cover of darkness, leaving the compound just after midnight. They only had one chance to make the raid, grabbing as many of the six targets as they could. Vandershoot was the prime target.

As their caravan approached the outskirts of Las Palmas, Tucker's and Fredo's groups headed south along the coast. Coop and the divers drove straight through the city to rendezvous with the fishing charter to get closer to the cruise ship via sea.

Tucker parked his Jeep in an alley across the main commercial harbor drive, leaving Ryan with the vehicle to coordinate with Stuart and Gibson at the hotel. Fredo, Armando and others had split off and headed back to the Tradewinds Hotel where two of their targets had been located. They would also explore the neighborhoods nearby for the remainder.

As planned, Sven cut the chain link fencing to gain entry, avoiding the guard station, and snuck along the dimly lit pier. Although some forklift operators were stacking pallets nearby, they were focused on their work. Tucker figured they'd wait for morning to start loading. The cargo bays had been left open, however, and the gangway was chained off, but not guarded.

Inside the ship, they spotted two armed guards sitting behind a desk.

With no one guarding the gangway's lower entrance, it was easy to climb the crisscross structure and wait just under the cargo hold opening.

"We're ready to board," Tucker whispered into his Invisio.

"Copy that," Ryan answered. A few seconds later, Tucker heard, "That's a go, Tucker. God speed."

Sven tapped on the side of the opening with his KA-BAR, which provoked the desired inquiry from one of the guards. As he peered over, Sven pulled him out, twisted his neck, yanked his upper back, and dropped him into the bay. At the same time, Tucker climbed up the other side of the gangway and tackled the distracted second guard, disabling him quickly but leaving him for Sven and T.J. to immobilize. He scampered into the crew hallway, searching both directions and found the area completely clear.

He signaled for Sven and T.J. to join him.

Staying to the outside stairwells, they climbed three floors until they reached the galley doors, which were chained shut. Sven's compact bolt cutters made fast work severing the lock, which gained them access to the kitchen. The entire galley was completely empty. Even the washers and garbage incinerators were idle.

They moved between stainless steel rows of food preparation stations and ovens then through a small crew lounge and out into one of the main restaurants and beyond to the lobby area. The fancy décor and the piped-in music was surreal. But instead of scores of housekeeping staff polishing the floors and wiping down the surfaces, the floors were littered with dirt, paper, half-filled crates, and broken bottles. Leftover trays of food and empty wine glasses were thrown on the floors.

They'd been given a diagram of the ship but also found one posted on the wall by the elevators. They were looking for the Penthouse Suite area, mid ship, floor 11. Amazingly, the elevators had not been disabled.

"We're on deck 11," Tucker informed Stuart.

"Roger that, Tucker. Still a go. Let us know when you identify the Dutchman."

There were four Penthouse suites on this level, two on each side. They agreed to do two at a time on each side, and if their target wasn't on this floor, they would continue going down each floor until they found him.

On the count of three, he and Sven used their small breaching charge, which was relatively quiet. Both rooms they opened were vacant. Down the hall, a door opened, and two young girls poked their heads out, clutching their nightgowns. Tucker put his finger to his lips, and they disappeared quietly.

Running to the other side, they did the same to the next two Penthouse doors, popping the locks simultaneously. This time, they hit gold.

The African warlord, General Two Fingers, sat up, staring into the barrel of Tucker's SIG. Two young girls with him scrambled to the other side of the bed and covered themselves, whimpering.

"You are so awesomely dead, my man," the General growled.

Tucker knew he was staring into the face of pure evil. "And you're going to jail, my man, for a long, long time."

Vandershoot, on the other hand, wore a flannel sleeping gown and socks and had been sleeping alone. He stared back at Sven in disbelief. T.J. secured both men in zip ties behind their backs while Sven gagged and hooded them.

"We have the General and the Dutchman," reported Tucker.

"Roger that. Great work."

They were escorted down the hallway like the scumbags they were. Doors popped open, young girls of several nationalities stepped outside to watch. As Vandershoot passed by one of them, she spat on him.

T.J. followed behind to watch for an armed attempt to foil the capture, but with the end of the barrel pointed to the General's temple, the few guards—who appeared to be private security and not regular Civil Guard—did nothing and dropped their weapons.

As the foursome left, using the gangway, a small crowd of dockworkers had gathered, without any armed militia. Just before they reached the Jeep, they heard the sound of several hull breaches being detonated.

Cooper's team had managed to make sure that ship and all its cargo would not be sailing for parts unknown without spending some considerable time in dry dock. It would remain in the shallow water until inventory and investigation could be completed.

Fredo and the boys who went into town had secured three of the four remaining targets, all without incident. Within an hour, all five men were delivered to the fishing charter. The dive team was loaded, and they all watched as the charter set out in the early morning fog to their rendezvous with the Stennis carrier group, for questioning. Seconds later, the four vehicles were back on the narrow road to the complex.

Other than the two guards on the cruise ship, no one was seriously injured. On the SEAL Team, only Lucas would be returning with a black eye.

It wasn't even daybreak when they returned to the hotel, where congratulations were in order. Lt. Commander Gibson was coordinating with a Spanish Civil Guard patrol to search the ship and seize the contraband. Their arrangement with the Spanish government had been kept to the letter. Now it would be up to the Spanish courts and their jurisdictional departments to bring charges for the corruption and bribery of the local police and to dispose of the contraband.

For now, they'd put a dent into Vandershoot's operation. It was hoped that with the interrogations, more arrests would follow and the smuggling operation would be seriously hampered.

Tucker knew better than to think they'd done anything permanent to the ring. But it was a start, and with the evidence they'd amassed both in person and with surveillance, it was unlikely that any of the men they captured would ever see their way outside of a jail cell.

He also knew that with enough money and power, anyone could ultimately get away. But they'd made it harder for the ring to function and perhaps given some of the families impacted time to take a breath and heal from the violence.

There was no celebration at the end of most their operations. Everyone just wanted to get home, so Gibson ordered them to retire and get some sleep in preparation for the long days of travel ahead.

WHEN TUCKER AWOKE, it was too early for him to let Brandy know they'd be coming home. They'd be stopping over in Virginia for debriefing, expected to take a day plus, and then, possibly be home in San Diego the day after, depending on the transport situation, he'd been told. Anxious to hear her voice, he dialed her anyway.

Her grogginess was such a welcomed sound.

"Tucker, what time is it?"

"Too early but wanted to let you know I'll be home in about three days. We're just wrapping up here."

"Wonderful."

"Now go back to sleep."

"No, I want to talk to you. I can sleep anytime."

He began to unthaw, just hearing her voice. He felt like he was home already.

"How are my two princesses?"

"Your daughter eats like a horse!"

"I would expect nothing less. Is she walking and talking yet?"

Brandy laughed. "Practically. All those nice twelve-month sleepers and tee shirts we got as gifts at the shower, she's nearly grown out of all of them. We're talking eighteen-month, Tucker. She's only a month old!"

"What can I say?"

"I've been spending a lot of time with Dad and Jillian. Thank you for that suggestion. And Joe's been over nearly every day. We have a new back fence and gate at the side of the house. And you should see the garden. You'll be impressed."

"Can't wait. How are you, sweetheart?"

"I haven't lost any weight. The ladies on your team have been forcing food on me. I'm going to have to stop it or I'll look the same as I did pregnant. Jillian has made some wonderful salads. Oh, and I have a surprise for you!"

"Tell me."

"Then it won't be a surprise."

He loved teasing her. He planned to do a lot more of that in the coming weeks.

"Give me a hint, Brandy."

"Nope. You'll have to just keep guessing until I can show you. It has to do with the house, but that's all I can say. I hope you like it."

"We didn't go out and spend a bunch of money, I hope. Did we, Brandy? Remember, our finances are spotty, at best."

"No. Not that."

"You found more palm trees."

"Of course not."

"I give up. Tell me."

"Joe and his buddies have drawn up plans for an addition to our place. Making the second floor another unit. We could Airbnb it or rent it out or make it a studio. We just need your approval to go forward, Tucker."

He was instantly concerned about where the money was going to come from to complete this major project. But he didn't want to dash her hopes. It was just fun to hear the laughter in her voice, the way she enjoyed being a mother.

He couldn't wait to get home.

CHAPTER 22

B RANDY WAS THRILLED to report to her father that Tucker was
coming home. She and Jillian cleaned the house while her dad
did some last-minute gardening. Some of the furrows needed to be
deepened, and since they'd been spending so much time in the rear
yard, weeds had cropped up.

The two palm trees were standing as tall as they could, although less than four feet tall. Her dad let her know that the shallow
roots had taken hold and were expanding outward, a sure sign they
were healthy.

Brandy loved to watch her dad tend to her garden. "You should
get one out at the ocean, Dad."

"I think I'd grow some killer artichokes, but I'd have to remove
the firepit and the patio. I just couldn't do that to Jillian."

"I get you."

"That's one of the favorite things we do these days, sit back
with a nice glass of wine and watch the sunset."

She hugged him from behind. "Happy for you both, Dad."

"I tell you what, though, just this little patch of yard is quite a
bit to take care of. You've seen how much work it is."

She nodded. "It's more beautiful than I ever thought possible."

"Wait until the flowers bloom. You'll have mums until Christmas. Then next year, we'll get an early start and get you some real

flowers. We'll get a climbing rose for your little fence here—maybe set up a trellis in front of the front door."

"That sounds lovely. I can't wait."

"The snaps we've started will be huge, so you'll have an outstanding spring. I plan on planting some bulbs, if you approve."

"Daffodils. Tucker's favorite flower."

"Ah, that was your mother's as well." He leaned on his shovel. "I know I say it too much, but she'd have been so pleased. I wish she'd have met Tucker."

"I knew she was with me that day we got married, Dad. I heard her talk to me. I really did."

Steve went back to working his hoe. Brandy knew she'd triggered a tear or two and realized he didn't want to show it.

"Where exactly did you two get these again?" he asked, pointing to the palm trees.

"It was from their last mission. They rescued a young aid worker, who'd been kidnapped and trafficked in Nigeria. Her father lives in the Portland area and sent these as a thank you."

"They're beautiful trees. You know they get tall, don't you? And they're not cheap."

"Oh yes. Tucker said he wanted to put them here in front like sentries, a good omen, protecting our family home."

"With your addition and all these gardens, you're building quite an oasis. Kind of reminds me of some of the places your mom and I visited in Italy or Southern France."

"I'd like to travel someday, see all those places. Tucker's been all over the world."

"Well, when he finishes his years with the Navy, he should have a nice retirement. Then you can travel."

"My thought exactly. Nine more years. Unless he decides to stay in longer."

Steven stopped his hoeing again. "You think he will?"

"I don't know. Now that we have Kimberly, I want him home more. But that decision is his to make and mine to support. That's how it goes on the Teams."

JOE STOPPED BY to check on the irrigation in the back yard. He'd heard the team was coming home.

"Do you know what day?"

"Shannon's expecting T.J. tomorrow."

"O-M-G. Are they back in the states?" Brandy had forgotten to check her cell phone when she woke up.

"I think so."

Brandy searched for her phone and finally found it tucked into Kimberly's diaper bag. The instant she plugged it into the charger, the messages lit up. There had been three from Tucker. "Oh crap."

She dialed and it went straight to voicemail. "I'm so sorry, Tucker. I just found out you guys will be home tomorrow. So excited here. Stuck my phone last night into Kimberly's bag and forgot all about it. Can't wait to see you! Let me know what time, and we'll be there."

Brandy did more laundry, mostly the baby's, and while Kimberly was sleeping, she washed her hair. She changed the sheets on the bed, using the freshly laundered cotton ones with the expensive softener. She prepared a special meal plan for the whole day, so she'd be ready no matter when he came home and made Tucker's favorite peanut butter brownies. Then she added a bottle of champagne to chill and checked on the beer bottle inventory, deciding it was adequate.

Now all she needed was Tucker.

Just after noon, she got the call she'd been waiting for.

"We're all done in Virginia, got a flight home tomorrow," he said. "Miss me?"

"Such a silly question! I've thought of nothing else these past couple of days."

"How about Kimberly?"

"You know how that goes. As long as she's fed and clean, she's happy. But I think she's waiting to be held by her big, strong daddy."

"You want me to bring anything back for you?"

"Nope. Just you. What time do I meet the plane?"

"We got the red-eye, leaving like 0100, so nine or ten we're estimating. Unless we get delayed."

"Perfect. We'll be there."

BRANDY HAD CALLS from several other of the wives, making sure she knew about the men getting home. It was agreed that there would be a beach get together with the kids on Friday night. She called Christy and asked her if Kyle was back in town.

"Oh, he'll be there. He doesn't like missing rotations, but it was important training."

She put the phone down to monitor kids she was babysitting. "Sorry. I'm sorry I didn't get over there to visit, Brandy. It will be great to see the baby."

"She'll be snuggled up."

"I heard you had some help from your dad."

"Yes, and Joe Benson came over and built our backyard fencing. He also built this beautiful pink playhouse, too. You'll have to bring the kids over to play in it."

"Yup, we'll plan that too. So how did Tucker do? Did he say?"

"You know Tucker. I'm afraid he had to spend more time calming me down than being able to share much of what it was like over there, but he did fine, I guess."

"So you were okay, then?"

Brandy realized too late that she'd perhaps alluded to the problems Geri and Bryce had had with their oldest. She didn't feel comfortable going there. She hadn't mentioned it to anyone but Tucker. Not even her father.

"Well, this being the first time I was alone with the baby got tough a couple of days, but I called in my chips. He told me to surround myself with the other wives and family. My fault for not thinking of that first. No worries."

"Okay, but you know you can call me if anything comes up, right? Anything."

Brandy felt slightly guilty not being completely forthcoming but didn't want to burden her.

THEN SHE GOT a call from Geri. The family was going through counseling. Lynn had gotten behind in school, but Brandy was happy to hear there had been no further contact with the creep who'd made the text messages.

"I guess your guy will be coming home any day now, so just wanted to say thanks for the support."

"Any time, Geri. I'm relieved to know things have begun to return to normal for you guys. It could have been much worse."

"You're right about that. Bryce and I talk about that all the time. You know, they had a bomb scare last year in the high school. The administration has to deal with so many issues these days, it seems."

"A bomb scare? I didn't know about that."

"Nothing was found. They evacuated the school. All a big hoax. Bryce's friend said they suspected a student, but the police couldn't prove anything."

"You don't think the two are related?"

"No. That's a completely separate thing. It was probably someone who was trying to get out of taking a test. I sure wouldn't want to be a high school principal these days."

"And here we thought our guys had the dangerous jobs."

"Well, they still do. But, honestly, all this social media stuff, like they said in the program the task force put on at St. Alma's, it's getting out of hand. Hard to protect our kids."

Worry dampened Brandy's good mood.

"We have to teach them, Brandy. I'm talking to other parents. Bryce and I felt like we really dropped the ball. We should have clamped down on her texting a long time ago. You never think anything about it, figure it's just kid stuff, but then something like what happened to Lynn occurs. They all want to be liked. They get pressured, I think."

"You're right, Geri. I see these kids dressing the way they do. Of course, I would look horrible putting on those tight shorts and tops they wear, you know. But I look at some of these girls, and they just look embarrassed to be wearing those clothes. Why do kids feel they have to do that?"

"I don't know, but you're right. And Lynn is mortified at how easy she fell for the attention. The counselor explained it was natural to feel that way and to understand she had no experience to know any better. It wasn't her fault. That it was the predator who found her, not the other way around."

Brandy made a mental note for the future. Although tragic, she was glad she was now fully aware of what could happen. She asked a question that had been worrying her. "Geri, where did those photos come from? I never heard about that?"

"They were left in her locker. He slipped them under the door."

So that meant the guy had come onto campus. It wasn't random, after all. She shuddered and vowed to discuss it with Tucker.

"How's Keira?" she asked, trying to keep it light.

"She hasn't stopped talking about that pink playhouse. I've got a call in to Joe."

"That would be nice for her."

"Well, enjoy your homecoming. I just wanted to thank you for having the guts to give us a heads-up on all of this. Without your call, it could have gotten much worse."

"You're welcome. I hope someone would do the same if it were reversed."

"When you guys want to, we'd like to take the two of you out to dinner. Until then, have fun!"

The two ladies giggled and hung up.

KIMBERLY HAD A fussy night and didn't go back to sleep, so Brandy wound up bringing her to bed with her, hoping she wouldn't now expect this new routine. As the bright sun crept into the cervices of her blackout shades, she awoke and felt she'd hardly slept at all. Of course, Kimberly was out cold. And she'd wet the bed.

Brandy decided to let her sleep until the last minute then bathed and fed her. She put the sheets in the washer and put the old ones on. So much for a lovely, scented homecoming.

At the base, she drove Tucker's Hummer, lining it up next to all the other wives. Kimberly was the magnet of attention until they all heard the drone of the lumbering transport plane.

Her heart raced every time she heard the darned thing. The ground shook. Her stomach churned in knots. Kimberly must have heard it as well, because her expression was puzzled. With her pink rabbit ears cap, her ears were protected from most the outside noise, but Brandy knew she could still feel the rumble of the big plane until just before the thing landed and began to taxi closer to their hangar.

As the men filed out, wives and children were clutching the chain link fence for that first glimpse of their husband or father, brother or son. Unlike the time before, there wasn't a flag-draped coffin returning with the group to greet a grieving mother.

Danny and a couple other guys ran toward the gate, greeting the kids first and then wrapping their arms around the whole family. Most took their time. Brandy saw one member with a swollen eye looking very nasty. One of the women whispered, "Oh my God." The lanky SEAL shrugged and hung his head down as he approached his wife and three school-age children.

At last she noticed Tucker's swagger, that distinctive way a large man moved. Brawley had called him the steamroller SEAL. He cracked a wide smile, giving just a hint of a wave, and threaded his way through the narrow opening jammed with reuniting families. Brandy held back so she could behold him sauntering toward her.

"Well, hello there," he said, staring down at her mouth and giving her that signal he was completely hers.

She kissed him hard, careful not to squeeze Kimberly too tightly between them. He stepped back and looked the two of them up and then down again.

"Am I lucky, or am I lucky?" he said with his hands on his hips.

"You're definitely gonna get lucky."

That earned her another quick kiss, and then he pulled Kimberly from her mother's arms. "Look at you, little pink bunny princess. I'll bet you're gonna steal hearts away from tough men, just like your mamma does."

Kimberly drooled, and Brandy thought she was trying hard to focus. He nuzzled her with his nose, and kissed her cheeks, making her pull her fingers up against her face. And then she sneezed.

"It's the stubble," he whispered. "I'm not as soft and delicious as your mamma."

He handed her back. Searching behind him, nodding to men and wives here and there, he hoisted his duty bag over his shoulder.

"Let's get the hell outta here."

CHAPTER 23

T HE HOUSE TUCKER had left behind was not the same house he came back to. With the garden laying out the thick, ruffled carpeting of mature vegetable plants in neat rows, the painted fencing that accentuated the border with the driveway and the two palms waving their welcome back, the transformation was astonishing.

Over the old wood floors, she had thrown bright red and brown area rugs, filled in the sparse living room furniture with an antique rocking chair and added a hand-stenciled storage chest. She had truly made their house a home.

"I can't believe what you've done," he whispered. The house was still uncluttered but fresh-looking and modern.

Brandy beamed over her shoulder, bouncing Kimberly in front against her chest. "Look at the back yard."

The pink playhouse was featured in the middle of the yard, just past the concrete patio. Redwood fencing with a lattice top design completely enclosed the space. She'd picked up a used outdoor table and chairs and had started adding plants around the perimeter.

Tucker opened the sliding glass door and walked out to examine Joe's handiwork, moving the door and window shutters back and forth on hinges. The swept and clean wooden floor made a heavenly place for his little girl to spend hours and hours of free play. Joe had even stenciled Kimberly's name over the doorway in red.

"You can't see it now, but they put a gate in on the side, so now we don't have to carry stuff through the house."

"Magnificent, honey. What a transformation. You guys were busy."

Brandy leaned against him, and he wrapped his arm around her waist. Then he began to worry.

"H-How much did all this cost?" he asked.

"Well, Dad paid for all the material, and Joe and two of his friends did the construction. Jillian gave me several things she didn't need anymore, like the furniture in the living room, an old dresser I repainted and a set of side tables you'll see in the master. So nothing, really."

"Nothing?"

"Well, I did buy some bigger clothes for Kimberly. I kind of splurged on that, but all this was done without costing us a penny."

"This is too good to be true. I'm amazed. I hadn't realized the rear fencing would make such a difference."

"I thought we could either put in bricks or do a lawn, if it wouldn't be too much work. Maybe some fruit trees?"

"Anything you want, sweetheart. Might have to wait a month or two, but I think a lawn would be nice."

Brandy led him back inside. On the dining table were a set of plans rolled up. "Here's the surprise I was talking about." She rolled out the paper, securing it from curling back with the salt and pepper shaker and a couple of magazines. "Joe has a friend who was a Civil and Structural Engineer, and he drew these up. Dad paid for the permit fees, and we turned everything in to the City for approval. Even if they approve them, we don't have to pull the permit until we're ready. In the meantime, we can still make changes. If you don't like any of it, we'll wait until we get something you do like."

His hand smoothed over the bright white surface, noting the design of a front door trellis.

"Roses, Tucker. I'd like white roses there covering the whole trellis."

The side stairway to the second floor had an observation deck. He looked over the drawings for the conversion of the downstairs stairwell into a second bath and storage.

"We need another bathroom. We have no closets!" she explained.

The engineer had also drawn ideas for adding more cabinets and countertop space in the kitchen and an addition of a flat-roofed garage on the right side of the walkway. The garage managed to hide the bottom stairs leading to up top and created a small, private yard around the back, as well as a lower floor deck area for the upper unit.

"He's thought of everything, Brandy. Don't know how we'll pay for it, but it really transforms the use of the property." Tucker hadn't seen any of this in his mind.

"Dad's been very up front about helping to pay for all this."

"But he already helped with the down payment."

"And he loves being part of this project, Tucker. Both him and Joe are excited about it, maybe even more so than I am."

His duty bag was still hung over his shoulder, and now he felt the weight of it and dropped it to the ground. It finally dawned on him that he was *home*. She was making this their home.

That this is our house.

It was time to forget all the chaos in the rest of the world and just enjoy this lovely new space with his family.

"I'm amazed. You guys were busy," he said as he wrapped his

arms around her and the baby. The softness of her lips kickstarted his libido and, like a lumbering and rusty machine, began revving up and coming back to life. All the familiar smells and tastes of her wet kiss flooded his senses.

He was finally home.

HE'D STRIPPED OFF his traveling clothes and jumped into the steaming shower she'd prepared for him. As he dried off, Brandy put the baby down and waited for him on the edge of the bed. She hadn't bothered putting on anything to cover herself up. She knew it was going to stay on her body for mere seconds.

The look of her regal form, the way she held her head, waiting for him, her deep breathing, showing all the signs of her arousal, and her understanding they were back together again, and that she wanted it to be special.

He'd make sure it was special. That's what he fully intended to do. He'd thought about not much else all the way home, even as he was joking, signing reports and debriefing staff, he thought of her sitting here, for him. Waiting to bring him back to life again. This was what he was really here for, not that other stuff.

This was man's work, real man's work. His job was to make her feel more loved than she ever had in her whole life.

He approached his queen, sat and looked into her eyes, their bodies barely touching.

"Every time I think I know what it feels like to come back to you, the real thing just kicks that memory to the curb."

"Me too. But I still love the dreams," she whispered.

"Oh yes, I do too. The real thing is better. So much better."

He started slow, kissing her neck and chest. She acted almost shy, protecting herself in her tender places with her palms as he gently kissed her, removing barriers to his touch, his tongue, to the glorious sight of her quivering body. He'd forgotten how strong she was, and also how delicate she felt beneath his hands as they lay back naked, feeling the timbre of her soul.

She arched to his touch and, as his intensity grew, she accepted him, her hands guiding and showing him she too didn't want to wait a moment longer before he could be inside her. His hand found hers, and together they explored the miracle of the space they formed as one. Then he spread her right arm first, and then the left out to the side on the bed, squeezing her fingers before releasing. He slid his fingers beneath her buttocks, raising her pelvis to accept him. His shaft entered her, drawing out that first stroke as long as he could. He watched her hitch her breath, close her eyes and then open them again with a smile. She flug her arms up, wrapping around his back with her legs around his hips so he could go deep.

She gave back all the goodness of her fierce love.

The rhythm of their bodies re-told the ancient stories men and women have shared for centuries—all about loyalty and devotion, honor and forgiveness. And the healing power of love—the most powerful emotion in the universe. That power increased the more it was shared, amplified by the constant beats of their hearts as relentless as any surf on any shore.

Brandy stayed right with him, matched his movements in her soft and gentle way, opening herself up and loving with abandon.

Her deep sigh and soft moan at their climax broke Tucker's heart, wishing the sunny morning would never end. His thumbs pressed her forehead, wiping the little beads of sweat into her hair. He devoured her hot breath and later held her like a fragile doll while she shattered beneath him.

The miracle of Brandy's body and the joining they shared filled him with gratitude. Their urgent lovemaking shed twenty years off him, washed away all the memories of where he had been and what he'd seen. The problems of that far away land subsided like memories of a movie watched years ago. He kissed her until her heart stopped racing and her breathing returned to normal. At last, he became whole and alive, healed.

Looking down on her soft face and long hair splayed over the pillows, he reveled in the magic she spun all around him. He wanted to pleasure her all over again, because he simply could never get enough.

Tucker kept vigil until she fell asleep, kissing her hair and whispering secrets she'd not remember. He loved the feel of their entwined bodies entangled in the sheets. She was his reward for coming home, and worth the price of being so far away.

In risking it all, it made having her in his arms again that much sweeter.

THE FIRST FEW days back were always dreamy afternoons and evenings filled with sex. He loved that she never denied any and all his advances, even encouraging him further. He demanded she not get dressed, so she took to walking around the house barefoot in her opened silk robe, bending over to pick up things she'd "accidentally" drop so he could look at her ass again. It drove him crazy, in a good way. No one would ever understand how magical those first days back would be—had to be—for him. Even working around the baby's nap times and feedings, was fun, adding a sense of urgency to their lovemaking.

He could have never imagined that life could be so perfect.

THE PLANNED TEAM beach party came three days later, starting in the afternoon and ending in a big bonfire under the stars after dark. It continued to be the tradition Kyle Lansdowne, their Team leader, had set right from the start. It was something they practiced both before and after their missions. The kids, offspring of these men he shared his brotherhood bond with, played together as one big family.

Brawley was whole again and enjoying his instructor stint. Several others were considering retirement. Some of his brothers were getting re-married, and some were in the early throes of separation. It all added to the patchwork of their Team and the resiliency of their bond. No matter what, they would always be brothers, even if the families sometimes drifted down a different path.

Tucker knew that would never be the case with him and Brandy.

The next week he got a phone call from Bryce Tanner, asking for a meeting. They met at a local coffee shop.

"Heard you had some success over in the Canaries. Good job," said Bryce.

Tucker shrugged. "Sometimes it works out. Sometimes we come home empty-handed. Still so much more to do over there. We just do our little piece. You know."

"I do know. I know, indeed. We ship out in three days."

"South America?"

"Yup. Got some Americans stranded down there and some friends of the U.S."

"God speed."

Tucker squirmed in his seat, took another sip of his latte, and waited for Bryce to get to the point. The man was studying him, like he was going to be asked for advice. He hated giving advice to another long-time Team guy. But he'd do what he could. It was clearly not a social call.

"Tucker, I'm sure Brandy filled you in on all this stuff that happened with Lynn."

He nodded agreement and waited for Bryce's next question.

"I have a buddy on the San Diego P.D. who says they arrested a child pornographer recently—this is strictly off the record."

"I got it. Brandy said you trust him. Go on."

"Probably wouldn't surprise you to learn there are thousands of these creeps all over the U.S. And they link hands with those that traffic in selling women and children for sex, which sometimes, if a person has means, is the next step in the chain of evil."

"Good way to put it. Happens over there as well."

"Yes, and from what I understand, over sixty percent of those children and ladies kidnapped—the ones that survive, that is—are sold to willing buyers in the U.S."

"Whoa. I didn't know that one."

"Google it. You'll see the trends."

"So this has to do with Lynn somehow? God, I pray it does not."

"Not directly, no. She fully understands what happened and that she never should have encouraged the conversation with someone she didn't know—even someone she knew who sent those texts and those disgusting pictures. Like most kids, Tucker, she knew she'd done something wrong by inviting him into our lives, and she didn't want to get in trouble, so she covered it up. I think a lot of kids behave that way."

"Understandable."

"This internet thing, the way kids are on social media—we can't protect them. We can't wait for the government to protect them. The police have their hands tied. I sometimes wonder, if we put a few SEAL teams on it, what they would do locating these rings and putting them out of business."

"In a perfect world. But we're not allowed. You know that."

"So we spread the news, wait, and hope it doesn't happen." Bryce leaned forward and drilled a look that told Tucker he was dead serious. "How well does that work overseas? Waiting, I mean?"

"That's what we're there for."

"Right. Invited by governments, provided by our government. Meanwhile, some of our kids are getting abused back at home. And do you think it will get any better on its own? I gotta hand it to the police, but they're outmatched, Tucker. You know that."

Tucker's adrenaline switch had flipped. He'd had the same thought many times over.

"What are you saying, Bryce?"

"I go over in three days. I stay perhaps two, three weeks, whatever. But when I come back, I'm thinking I'd like to do something about all this."

"How?"

Bryce checked the surrounding area to make sure he wasn't being heard. "I don't know. Perhaps find someone who could help us out? Give us an inside line on the bad guys, help support our efforts?"

"You're talking about *posse comitatus.*"

"I am. Except I'm not sure it can be a government entity. Might have to be private."

"And that would be illegal, Bryce."

His friend nodded again and stared off into the distance. "I can't wait, Tucker. That's the hardest thing I could do. I'm one of the old guys now. Probably time for me to hang it up before I get injured or get someone else hurt. I need a new hip, and my knees are shot from all those jumps."

"Same here. I'll be needing new knees before I'm fifty."

"We've done good work, protecting those we love from foreign evil coming here. But we're losing the way, Tucker. It's coming anyway. We got terrorist plots and training camps, and some of us have seen them, too."

Tucker had heard the stories. It was common knowledge.

"We have to take a back seat to guys—I'm talking police and social workers—who are terrific but just don't have the same training we have. They're like janitors in our inner cities. The cleanup crew."

Bryce leaned forward again.

"We need someone to go in and take them out. As many of them as we can find."

Tucker waited before responding. "I hear what you're saying, Bryce. How are you going to know the difference? What if the wrong person gets taken out? That's why we have the courts. It's slow, and yes, some of these dudes get off, but we can't have citizens taking the law into their own hands, Bryce."

"*Most* citizens. Tell me, Tucker. Would you be able to tell the difference? If you got right up into the face of pure evil? You've seen them before, as have I. If you had the opportunity to make sure one of these creeps would never hurt another innocent child or woman, if you could bring them in to face justice, what would you do?"

It was the same thing they did overseas all the time. They weren't assassination squads, yet, things were done. Some enemies would fight to the death.

Tucker thought about the offer Colin Riley had made. He personally wasn't in a place where he could consider going to work for the man. Not yet.

But maybe he could make an introduction.

CHAPTER 24

Three months later....

T UCKER AND BRYCE flew into Portland where a black town car waited for them. The two had not spoken much since Bryce's return from his mission. Tucker had hoped Bryce had reconsidered the ideas he'd shared. But that wasn't the case. He was even more determined than before.

Bryce told him his San Diego P.D. buddy let him know that they'd solved a bomb threat case at Lynn's school last year. It had been arranged through a chat on a gaming site. A sophomore at the school paid an anonymous person five hundred dollars to hack in and email the threat to the school administration.

The student was questioned extensively, but the money transaction happened outside the banking system with crypto currency and therefore was untraceable. It was a case of a kid who wanted a few days off from school to visit his girlfriend in the Bay Area. The girlfriend casually mentioned it to her parents months later, and they called the police. Otherwise, no one ever would have known.

Just knowing this type of thing could happen set off red flags in Bryce. He felt more compelled than ever to somehow make a difference, make himself the barrier between evil and innocents.

Though the story wasn't about sex work or human trafficking, it very easily could have been.

Tucker told his buddy about Mr. Riley and agreed to accompany him to meet the gentleman. He wasn't going to join up, just make the introductions.

"Did he say his daughter is recovering?" Bryce asked.

"I didn't ask about her, and he didn't bring it up. Sven keeps in loose touch with her."

"You trust the man?"

"That's going to be up to you, Bryce. It's an awfully big step, doing this. I presume you've said nothing to Geri."

"Nope. We're just fishin'."

"You gotta think very hard before you jump into this. You could be sent to prison if caught. What would Geri and the kids do without you?"

"We gotta talk first. Hell, he might not like me. He might only want you," said Bryce.

"Well, he's not getting me. I'm not ready to take that leap, and don't pressure me. It won't work. I'm doing this for you because I don't want you mixed up in something that's underfunded. This guy has billions. That part is real. The rest is up to you."

Colin Riley sat in his specialized wheelchair in the middle of his wood-paneled office overlooking the Columbia River. He briefly scanned Bryce but moved his chair forward to shake Tucker's hand first and then turned his attention to Bryce, as Tucker introduced him.

"Nice to hear from you, Tucker. Someone sent me a picture of the palm trees in your front yard. I like what you've done with the place."

Of course Riley would have done this. He'd be checking up on Tucker for the rest of his life.

"So you probably know about my daughter, then."

"I heard about that too. I think we have a little token for you, something you can stash away for her college fund."

"I didn't come here for money, sir. I'm just here to make an introduction." Irritation made a familiar appearance in Tucker's gut.

"I do understand." Riley angled his head, pointing to the large leather couch placed beneath an enormous photograph of a bald eagle hanging on the wall above. "Please be seated." Mr. Riley asked Tucker to begin.

"Sir, I told Bryce some of what we discussed in the hospital some months back. I told you then I wasn't interested, but Bryce here is."

Riley studied Tucker for several long seconds then turned his gaze to Bryce. "And what were you told Mr. Tanner?"

"You asked Tucker if he ever wanted to do something else, take care of bad guys here at home, that you might be interested in supporting him."

"Not supporting him, Bryce. May I call you that?"

"Yes, sir. You may."

"I said I'd make him rich beyond his wildest dreams."

Bryce leaned back into the back of the couch and exhaled. "Okay. Wow." Then he placed his elbows on his thighs, coming closer to the billionaire. "Tucker isn't interested. But I am."

"Your reason?"

"My daughter was recently targeted by a predator. Everyone knows the facts. The police, the FBI, everyone agrees that it would be nearly impossible to find this creep. He'll probably get caught in some raid at some future date. Or not. But day after day, there are these rings of people who traffic young girls, women. And there are thousands of them. The number is growing, not getting smaller. Tucker and I both have seen some of these human smuggling rings in action—like the one who nabbed your daughter."

"And you would consider what I asked Tucker to do?"

"I'd have to think about it. But that's what I came here to talk to you about."

Riley's eyes sparkled as he turned to Tucker. "Why did you come? Were you curious?"

"I wanted to help him, as a brother, not make a wrong decision. I don't want to see him going to jail, even if he's trying to do good here. What we're talking about is not legal. Not sanctioned by any government entity."

"Do you know others who you might be able to recruit, to set up a team, Mr. Tanner?"

"I think I do."

"Former SEALs?"

"SEALs, law enforcement, and patriots who just don't want to wait around to let someone else clean up the trash. I know men who have the skills and knowhow to make a difference."

"Like Robin Hood and his merry band, eh?" Riley chuckled.

Tucker dug his fingers into the soft leather and nearly punched four holes in it.

"With all due respect—" he began.

"I meant no insult. I meant it in the most respectful of ways. If I was healthy, it's what I'd do. I have the money, and I have the connections. But I cannot be the weapon. That part of my life is over. I don't know how much longer I have—even a simple cold is life-threatening for me. But I don't want to wither away in a rest home when I can make a difference. I want to spend my money creating good, stamping out evil, and supporting those warriors who can help me accomplish that."

Riley's eyes were unwavering. Tucker knew the man meant every word he'd just uttered. A part of him wanted to seize the chalice and grab the golden sword to take on the challenge. But the loyal husband and father and decorated Navy SEAL wasn't there yet and would not be taking that step.

"What would it take for you to join him, Tucker?" Riley pondered.

It was not a difficult decision. It wasn't even his decision to make. There was only one answer to that question.

"Time. *Lots* of time, sir."

THAT AFTERNOON RILEY and Bryce Tanner agreed to have several meetings to iron out the details before anything would be said to anyone else, including his wife. Tucker was sworn to secrecy.

On the flight home, Tucker admitted, "You're either a crazier man or a braver man than I am, Bryce. Part of me wants to go do this with you. But I just can't yet."

Bryce was thoughtful. "I'm not going to lie. I feel as excited as the day I was told I had a chance to go to BUD/S. Maybe you're the braver man, Tucker. Only time will tell."

"Roger that, my friend. You make sure you look at everything before you commit. And I'm going to have to work on my conscience if anything happens to you. But damn, wouldn't it be great if it would work?"

"And then you can join me."

"Not promising. Don't say that." He chuckled. "Now you have to come up with some awesome name like *Posse International.*"

"*Fuck You Society.*"

"*Elimination Inc.*"

"I got a better one. How about Bone Frog Protection?"

Tucker smiled to himself.

Yeah, that would work.

CHAPTER 25

B RANDY HAD TRIED for days to find out about his fishing trip with Bryce. Tucker came back from it like he'd just spent two weeks at a Man Camp or Olympic Training Camp, she told him. He was light on his feet, happy, and fully engaged in life. It was as though he'd finally had an epiphany and had settled into his own skin.

She watched him closer that day, Tucker holding Kimberly on his belly, her arms and legs moving as he played horseshoes with Bryce, who was now a frequent visitor. Bryce was like one of the Team 3 guys.

Geri had told her that Tucker had given Bryce some really good advice. When she asked about it, Geri said she had no idea, just that they'd had a long talk and both of them got clear about what their life's purpose was going forward.

He knew he was going to have to tell her something. She wouldn't let up. She'd gotten a bead on this thing between he and Bryce, and she wouldn't let go.

Re-enlistments, if it happened when they were overseas, netted them extra bonuses at signing. But when that opportunity came and went, Bryce had made the decision not to renew his hitch and started his disassociation paperwork. A small ripple had been caused in the community, wondering what he was going to do.

Tucker didn't care about it. He actually felt settled, good about his decision to watch Bryce do something he wanted to do. Tucker wasn't there yet, and he'd been honest with Riley, and with his Team buddy.

"There's one thing I've been wondering about, Tucker," she said as he stepped out of the shower.

Here it comes. She was asking very sweetly, so naked and rubbing herself all over him. It was a twisted way of getting information out of him, but Hell, he was game for making love to his stubborn wife however she got to that point.

"What's that?" He was looking at her standing behind him in the mirror.

She began to dry off his back, kissed him in several places along his spine, at the same time letting him feel the bare skin of her thighs rubbing against the backs of his. She pressed her breasts into his back, allowed the towel to travel from his chest, down his hip, and then drop. She squeezed him which was one of his favorite things. He flipped around to face her.

"What is it, Brandy?" He begged her to tease him, say something either dirty or inappropriate.

"What happened on that fishing trip?"

His quick intake of air almost let the cat out of the bag. He didn't want to reveal their conversation, or decision.

She gave him a wicked smile. "Should I be jealous?"

"Hell no." He abruptly moved away, grabbed a glass, and poured himself a drink of water. "Why do you ask?"

"You've just had this cat-that-ate-the-canary look to you ever since. And now Bryce is leaving the teams. Are you thinking about doing that too?"

"Why would I do that?" He knew she was beginning to suspect something. She'd pushed too far, and now he was getting annoyed.

"Come here, Brandy. Let's talk."

He took her by the hand, bringing her into the bedroom, sat down, and had her sit on his bare legs. Her silk shortie robe opened down the front. He licked his lips as he focused on the way her nipples knotted between his thumb and fingers.

"I love everything about you, Brandy. Some days, when I see you lying asleep or watch you nursing Kimberly, I think to myself that perhaps I don't deserve this."

"Nonsense," she said, moving against him, pushing him back on the bed, placing her knees on either sides of his hips and delicately riding him, teasing to get him snagged. He tried to angle his hips to facilitate this.

"You're silly," she whispered, watching him play with her.

"I mean it," he said, his fingers now squeezing her tits.

She rose up and then deliciously settled back down on him, touching and squeezing the base of his shaft as he plunged in slowly. She leaned forward, tilting her rear up. He bent his knees, forced his hips upward, thrusting so deep she caught her breath. Her internal muscles took hold and she leaned back and sighed.

"Oh God, Tucker. I never want this to end. I want us to fuck like this forever."

The conversation was gone. The only thing he could focus on was making Brandy explode. He stepped up his pace, grabbing her hips, grinding them down on him, then rose her up so he could pump in and out until his speed caused her to scream, "Yes!"

"Absolutely, sweetheart. You want more?'

"Always."

"Always what?"

"Always more." She was going to object as he kept up his furious pace, but she corrected him. "Always fuck me more."

"That's my girl." He could feel she was going to come again for the second time. He was having a hard time holding back.

"Tucker?"

"Yes, Brandy?" He was losing it. He felt her muscles in that delicious spasm of hers. She forced herself harder against him with each stroke.

"I want to fuck all night long. Can we please—"

Finally! She'd lost her train of thought. He started to spill.

"Would you fuck me all night long?"

"If I'm physically able, you bet."

"And Tucker?" He was coming inside her, his hot sperm coating her everywhere.

"No more questions, Brandy. Sweetheart, I just want to do this."

God, she was stubborn!

BUT OF COURSE, Brandy never forgot a thing. As soon has he'd nearly passed out, she was at it again.

"That happiness in you. Tell me what it is," she asked.

Her body was still sweaty. He knew he wouldn't have much more time until she'd have to get up and feed the baby again.

He drew his arm up over his forehead, thinking all while his shaft was growing again.

"Bryce has decided to follow a different path, one that I cannot take. At least not yet."

"Go on."

"That's it, really. You are more precious to me than my own life. I've got everything I need here."

"And Bryce?"

"He's going to chase some demons. He wants revenge. He wants to balance the scales of good and evil. All I want to do is complete my job and come home to you, Brandy. I would never do anything to get in the way of that."

She would tell him later that his kisses were sweeter that night.

He'd walked through some kind of a threshold recently and it didn't really have anything to do with her. He didn't have the demons Bryce did.

He'd told her that he thought she was stronger than he was. She told him he was so wrong. That he'd taught her how to love him.

And it was the easiest thing in the world to do.

He vowed he'd keep teaching her, because without her, his life would become hard and small. He wanted the pink miracle that was their family.

He didn't care who thought that was funny. It was the damned truth!

Have you enjoyed Brandy and Tucker's story? Stay tuned for more episodes, including some of the other men who might find themselves part of the Bone Frog Protection team. One by one, they'll decide where their higher calling comes from. They'll rise to the challenge.

If you are new to my books, you might want to start with the very first SEAL Brotherhood book, **Accidental SEAL**. Or, with the **Ultimate SEAL Collection**, which has the first four books in the series, with two bonus novellas.

Or, you can read any of the other popular series:

Bad Boys of SEAL Team 3

Band of Bachelors

ABOUT THE AUTHOR

 NYT and USA/Today Bestselling Author Sharon Hamilton's SEAL Brotherhood series have earned her author rankings of #1 in Romantic Suspense, Military Romance and Contemporary Romance. Her other *Brotherhood* stand-alone series are: Bad Boys of SEAL Team 3, Band of Bachelors, True Blue SEALs, Nashville SEALs, Bone Frog Brotherhood, Sunset SEALs, Bone Frog Bachelor Series and SEAL Brotherhood Legacy Series. She is a contributing author to the very popular Shadow SEALs multi-author series.

Her SEALs and former SEALs have invested in two wineries, a lavender farm and a brewery in Sonoma County, which have become part of the new stories. They also have expanded to include Veteran-benefit projects on the Florida Gulf Coast, as well as projects in Africa and the Maldives. One of the SEAL wives has even launched her own women's fiction series. But old characters, as well as children of these SEAL heroes keep returning to all the newer books.

Sharon also writes sexy paranormals in two series: Golden Vampires of Tuscany and The Guardians.

A lifelong organic vegetable and flower gardener, Sharon and her husband lived for fifty years in the Wine Country of Northern California, where many of her stories take place. Recently, they have moved to the beautiful Gulf Coast of Florida, with stories of shipwrecks, the white sugar-sand beaches of Sunset, Treasure Island and Indian Rocks Beaches.

She loves hearing from fans through her website: authorsharonhamilton.com

Find out more about Sharon, her upcoming releases, appearances and news when you sign up for Sharon's newsletter.

Facebook:
facebook.com/SharonHamiltonAuthor

Twitter:
twitter.com/sharonlhamilton

Pinterest:
pinterest.com/AuthorSharonH

Amazon:
amazon.com/Sharon-Hamilton/e/B004FQQMAC

BookBub:
bookbub.com/authors/sharon-hamilton

Youtube:
youtube.com/channel/UCDInkxXFpXp_4Vnq08ZxMBQ

Soundcloud:
soundcloud.com/sharon-hamilton-1

Sharon Hamilton's Rockin' Romance Readers:
facebook.com/groups/sealteamromance

Sharon Hamilton's Goodreads Group:
goodreads.com/group/show/199125-sharon-hamilton-readers-group

Visit Sharon's Online Store:
sharon-hamilton-author.myshopify.com

Join Sharon's Review Teams:

eBook Reviews:
sharonhamiltonassistant@gmail.com

Audio Reviews:
sharonhamiltonassistant@gmail.com

Life is one fool thing after another.
Love is two fool things after each other.

REVIEWS

PRAISE FOR THE
GOLDEN VAMPIRES OF TUSCANY SERIES

"Well to say the least I was thoroughly surprise. I have read many Vampire books, from Ann Rice to Kym Grosso and few other Authors, so yes I do like Vampires, not the super scary ones from the old days, but the new ones are far more interesting far more human than one can remember. I found Honeymoon Bite a totally engrossing book, I was not able to put it down, page after page I found delight, love, understanding, well that is until the bad bad Vamp started being really bad. But seeing someone love another person so much that they would do anything to protect them, well that had me going, then well there was more and for a while I thought it was the end of a beautiful love story that spanned not only time but, spanned Italy and California. Won't divulge how it ended, but I did shed a few tears after screaming but Sharon Hamilton did not let me down, she took me on amazing trip that I loved, look forward to reading another Vampire book of hers."

"An excellent paranormal romance that was exciting, romantic, entertaining and very satisfying to read. It had me anticipating what would happen next many times over, so much so I could not put it down and even finished it up in a day. The vampires in this book were different from your average vampire, but I enjoy different variations and changes to the same old stuff. It made for a more unpredictable read and more adventurous to explore! Vampire lovers, any paranormal readers and even those who love the romance genre will enjoy Honeymoon Bite."

"This is the first non-Seal book of this author's I have read and I loved it. There is a cast-like hierarchy in this vampire community with humans at the very bottom and Golden vampires at the top. Lionel is a dark vampire who are servants of the Goldens. Phoebe is a Golden who has not decided if she will remain human or accept the turning to become a vampire. Either way she and Lionel can never be together since it is forbidden.

I enjoyed this story and I am looking forward to the next installment."

"A hauntingly romantic read. Old love lost and new love found. Family, heart, intrigue and vampires. Grabbed my attention and couldn't put down. Would definitely recommend."

PRAISE FOR THE
SEAL BROTHERHOOD SERIES

"Fans of Navy SEAL romance, I found a new author to feed your addiction. Finely written and loaded delicious with moments, Sharon Hamilton's storytelling satisfies like a thick bar of chocolate." —Marliss Melton, bestselling author of the *Team Twelve* Navy SEALs series

"Sharon Hamilton does an EXCELLENT job of fitting all the characters into a brotherhood of SEALS that may not be real but sure makes you feel that you have entered the circle and security of their world. The stories intertwine with each book before...and each book after and THAT is what makes Sharon Hamilton's SEAL Brotherhood Series so very interesting. You won't want to put down ANY of her books and they will keep you reading into the night when you should be sleeping. Start with this book...and you will not want to stop until you've read the whole series and then...you will be waiting for Sharon to write the next one." (5 Star Review)

"Kyle and Christy explode all over the pages in this first book, *[Accidental SEAL]*, in a whole new series of SEALs. If the twist and turns don't get your heart jumping, then maybe the suspense will. This is a must read for those that are looking for love and adventure with a little sloppy love thrown in for good measure." (5 Star Review)

PRAISE FOR THE
BAD BOYS OF SEAL TEAM 3 SERIES

"I love reading this series! Once you start these books, you can hardly put them down. The mix of romance and suspense keeps you turning the pages one right after another! Can't wait until the next book!" (5 Star Review)

"I love all of Sharon's Seal books, but *[SEAL's Code]* may just be her best to date. Danny and Luci's journey is filled with a wonderful insight into the Native American life. It is a love story that will fill you with warmth and contentment. You will enjoy Danny's journey to become a SEAL and his reasons for it. Good job Sharon!" (5 Star Review)

PRAISE FOR THE
BAND OF BACHELORS SERIES

"*[Lucas]* was the first book in the Band of Bachelors series and it was a phenomenal start. I loved how we got to see the other SEALs we all love and we got a look at Lucas and Marcy. They had an instant attraction, and their love was very intense. This book had it all, suspense, steamy romance, humor, everything you want in a riveting, outstanding read. I can't wait to read the next book in this series." (5 Star Review)

PRAISE FOR THE
TRUE BLUE SEALS SERIES

"Keep the tissues box nearby as you read *True Blue SEALs: Zak* by Sharon Hamilton. I imagine more than I wish to that the circumstances surrounding Zak and Amy are all too real for returning military personnel and their families. Ms. Hamilton has put us right in the middle of struggles and successes that these two high school sweethearts endure. I have read several of Sharon Hamilton's military romances but will say this is the most emotionally intense of the ones that I have read. This is a well-written, realistic story with authentic characters that will have you rooting for them and proud of those who serve to keep us safe. This is an author who writes amazing stories that you love and cry with the characters. Fans of Jessica Scott and Marliss Melton will want to add Sharon Hamilton to their list of realistic military romance writers." (5 Star Review)

"Dear FATHER IN HEAVEN,

If I may respectfully say so sometimes you are a strange God. Though you love all mankind,

It seems you have special predilections too.

You seem to love those men who can stand up alone who face impossible odds, Who challenge every bully and every tyrant ~

Those men who know the heat and loneliness of Calvary. Possibly you cherish men of this stamp because you recognize the mark of your only son in them.

Since this unique group of men known as the SEALs know Calvary and suffering, teach them now the mystery of the resurrection ~ that they are indestructible, that they will live forever because of their deep faith in you.

And when they do come to heaven, may I respectfully warn you, Dear Father, they also know how to celebrate. So please be ready for them when they insert under your pearly gates.

Bless them, their devoted Families and their Country on this glorious occasion.

We ask this through the merits of your Son, Christ Jesus the Lord, Amen."

By Reverend E.J. McMalhon S.J. LCDR, CHC, USN
Awards Ceremony SEAL Team One
1975 At NAB, Coronado